Tsunami's Scars

Tsunami's Scars

HANNAH J. KUO

To Eunice, Katelyn, and Sarah, for being the best sisters in the world. :)

Tsunami's Scars

Prologue

On a dark, moonless night, a ship sailed across an opaque sea. There were two lanterns lit, but the black midnight swallowed the light if you tried to see it from a distance. Most of the crew were asleep in their cabins, with the exception of the captain, some of the staff, and....

The clicking of heels against the floorboards sounded ominous. The woman was dressed in full black, wearing a tight business suit, even though the ocean air was biting.

"How long until we reach our destination, Captain?" Aura Ivoria asked coolly.

The captain puffed on a pipe and shrugged. "Dunno, ma'am. I've a'ready told'ye, such places ain't in existence no more."

Ivoria didn't say anything. Just smirked. "Yes, I suppose you're right. Such places should not exist."

The captain cast her a quizzical look, but Ivoria took no notice. She turned on her heels and walked out the small room. She waved over her shoulder, "See you tomorrow, Captain." She didn't turn around as she said, "Your cooperation and dedication is expected. I've spent the past half-year preparing for this trip. Don't sabotage it." She continued walking again. "I'm heading to prepare my machine. Nothing had better happen to it."

The captain kept his eyes on her until she disappeared into her cabin. Then he turned back to the sea, shivering. It wasn't from the chilly night, nor the sea air.

"That woman's hidin' somethin'...."

Chapter 1

I fingered the light blue half-face, glad to have the leaves as a cover. The mob hunting for me couldn't spot me here.

"Hey, whatcha hidin' from?" My best friend Galen Maelstrom's head swung down, upside-down, right in front of my face.

I yelled, startled. Instinctively, I scooted backward a few paces, accidentally rustled the leaves, and essentially gave away my position.

"There she is!" The herd of students charged down the path, holding up their phones to snap pictures.

"Flames," I muttered. "GALEN!"

He swung down from his branch and peeked at the crowd. "Oh, I see." He snickered. "Why'd you come to my tree, then? I hid here first!"

"GALEN!" I looked around frantically,

searching for another place to hide.

"Fine. You do know that you can just vanish, right?" He waggled his fingers. "Why don't you just do it now?"

I growled. "Because, evaporation is for invisibility. If I evaporated now, everyone would see me do it!"

"But then no one would see you afterwards! Oops - too late. They're here now." Galen flashed me a grin before fading away.

I waved my arms angrily in the space where he had been.

"Rina! There you are!" someone called. "Can you come here, please? We're with the school newspaper, and-"

"No! Come talk with me! I want to hear the story from your point of view on how you saved the Islands!"

"Can you perform your Talent again? It was so cool when you carried everyone up at the Queen's assembly like that."

"No! Come be my friend! I just got this really awesome thing I want to show you!"

Alright. In case you don't know what's going on, let me back up a little.

Half a year ago, the queen had organized a Mainlander kidnapping, but we didn't know she had planned everything at that time. Two hundred kids were taken, including my twin sister, Mira. My friends, Elece, Derrik, Galen, and I were sent to rescue them. Long story short, we found the captured kids, picked up the queen's successor along the way, and formed bonds with pixies!

So where did that lead to afterwards? Fame. Popularity. Recognition. Things I never had before. I should be glad and so-very-proud of myself, but now, I realized that I liked being unnoticed more than being known. Everyone only wanted to be my friend because I was a "hero", or because I was one of the future queen's closest friends.

I slid down the tree and brushed off my hands. Immediately, all the students crowded around me, yammering requests into my ear. I pressed my finger against a ringing eardrum, hoping that my half-face would hide the fact that I was overwhelmed.

I'm going to kill you, Galen!

Only if you can find me! he taunted.

The mob was squeezing in tighter, their hands reaching out desperately to me. I brushed away the hands and walked away. Of course, they followed me, so I flew up high into the air and watched.

Half of the students gave up. The other half followed my trail. I led them in a wide circle around the school and evaporated myself the second the building blocked me from their view. I crouched on the school's domed roof, watching. Waiting.

The students flew by and stopped when they couldn't see me anymore. "Where'd she go?" one asked. Another shrugged.

"You made us lose her!" yelled a girl who looked older than me. "You guys were so slow!"

As they bickered in front of me, I slipped past them and flew toward a grove of trees. I knew this small forest like the back of my hand now. I glanced cautiously behind me, and when I decided that the coast was clear, I materialized and pulled down my half-face. I landed on the leaf-covered ground and ran straight. I kept running until I reached a tree so big, many people looked right past it, like I did when I first arrived. I'd named this tree, "Beast" in my mind.

I walked toward the roots of the tree and pushed back the curtain of ivy hiding a hole. I crawled through and climbed the trunk's interior, grabbing at the knobs of wood like a rock wall.

Once I reached the part of the tree where the

6

trunk split off into branches, I crawled off the trunk and rolled onto the flat platform. There were many tunnels where the branches branched off the trunk, but I laid there, panting and resting.

I heard footsteps coming from the second branch and sat up slowly.

"Rina?"

"Wow, you look beat. What were you doing?"

I looked up and my heart warmed at the sight of my friends, Callan Cragmire and Kodiak Torrent. Callan's dark eyes were tinged with curiosity while Kodiak's blue ones were filled with worry. These boys were like my older brothers.

I sat up fully and scratched my neck. "The usual chase," I replied. "It's getting tiring."

They stared at me for a few seconds, exchanged glances, and burst out into laughter. "Boy, Rina. If you look this beat now, you're getting out of shape!"

I scowled at them. "And what were you doing?"

They smiled mischievously. "Same as you. Only not as fat."

I roared and lunged at them. They laughed and staggered backward as I scratched at them like a wild animal.

"Hey, hey, just kidding," Kodiak said.

Callan pulled me back to my feet, brushed his hair out of his eyes, gave me a small smile. He'd recently dyed his hair a lighter brown, which I was still struggling to be familiar with. I'd always been used to seeing his darker brown hair. "I don't think it's ever going to get better." He frowned, looking over me with a scrutinizing glance. "Hey, where's Zinnia?"

My pixie flew out of my pouch with a twirl. The pouch was always strapped around my waist, but nobody really took notice of it. She crossed her arms, "Here!"

Zinnia Allegra had bright pink hair with a blue music-note clip. She had piercing yellow eyes and always seemed to find fashionable clothes for herself. Today, she was wearing dark skinny-jeans and a pale shirt. I don't know where she gets them. Altogether, she was as tall as my palm. Maybe a bit taller.

Hunter and Blizzard popped up from behind Callan and Kodiak. When they saw Zin, they grinned. "Hey, Zinnia!"

Zin smiled. "Hey, guys! How's it going for you?"

Hunter and Callan exchanged glances. Hunter shrugged. "Okay, I guess. All the giants are still

8

pestering Callan about what it was like to get captured, and if he was grateful, and if he has a crush on -"

"Okay, that's enough," Callan swatted at his blue-haired pixie, glancing quickly away from me.

Blizzard nodded. "Yeah, that's what Kodiak's been hiding from, too," he said, with a strange smirk at Hunter.

I frowned. "So, what are you guys doing here right now?"

Callan looked confused. "You don't know?"

I looked at the boys suspiciously. "Don't know about what?"

"Emily and Universa called for us. They told us to meet them after school at the Royal Island immediately."

Chapter 2

I blinked. "Really?"

"Yeah." Callan leaned forward. "You didn't get the letter?"

I frowned. "Letter?"

"It came in the mail," Kodiak explained.

"Oh." I shook my head. "No." I paused, then sighed. "My mom and dad probably hid it before I could see it. Or, maybe they gave it to Mira instead."

Callan's eyes darkened and he growled. "Why?"

I sighed again and leaned against the wood. "Reasons. They want Mira to have a high position in the Fire Army. They'll do anything to get her to win the queen's favor."

"Only her? Why not you?"

Zin flew down and settled on my hands. I

gave her a small smile and touched her soft pink hair. "Reasons," I said again.

Kodiak frowned. "Well, that's not cool." He stretched. "Anyways, Elece sent us to pick you and Galen up." He walked over to the trunk and looked down. "Where's he?"

"BOO!"

Kodiak yelped, slipped, and tumbled down the trunk. Callan and I shouted, but for different reasons.

"KODIAK!" Callan cried.

"GAAAALEEEEN!" I roared furiously. I lunged for my friend, who had materialized behind Kodiak.

Galen howled with laughter, falling down to the floor and rolled around, kicking his legs and holding his middle. "You guys are hilarious!"

I dragged him to his feet and pummeled his shoulder. "You blockhead!" I yelled. "Kodiak dropped down the trunk!"

Galen snorted. "Don't worry. He's fine. He can take care of himself. "Besides," Galen spread out his arms. "Elece let us use this place as a safe house, base, or whatever you want to call it. She probably wouldn't let us in here if it was dangerous."

I growled. "I'm very surprised you think that.

Didn't you used to say she was ninety-eight percent beast or something like that?"

Galen paused, thinking, then nodded. "You're right. She is. But now, that number has been reduced to ninety-five. She's one percent girl, one percent nothing, and three percent protective sister." He flashed me a grin. "See, we get along! We've improved now!"

I rolled your eyes. "So has your math," I muttered.

Callan was pulling Kodiak up from the trunk. Kodiak looked winded, shocked.

"Are you okay?" I asked.

He shook his head roughly before smiling. "Yeah, I'm alright. I caught myself in time. Then it turned out I didn't have to because there was already wind there to catch me." He looked over at Galen. "So, I'm mad, but not mad, you know?"

Callan, on the other hand, was furious. "You could have injured him!" he roared, advancing on Galen. "Why are you like this all the time?"

Galen rolled his eyes and stuck out his tongue before vanishing. "It's the way I am, mush brain!"

"Blockhead!"

"Rock face!"

I groaned. "Guys...."

Callan stopped and sulked instead. In case you haven't figured it out, Callan and Galen were mortal enemies, which stuck me in a hard position.

"So are the others waiting?" Zin asked.

Callan nodded. "We're granted permission already, so we can get in anytime."

I brushed myself off and headed for the trunk. "Let's go!"

The Royal Island was just as beautiful as I'd remembered. The lush green grass bent gracefully in the wind. The sea splashed gently on its sandy shores. The castle in the distance looked just as intimidating as ever.

Emily Carters, the next queen, was there, waving. The rest of our group waved along with her. "Guys! Over here!"

I dashed over, grinning. "Hi!"

Zin flew by my head, laughing. "I can't wait to see the others! You guys really need to get together more often."

I laughed too. "Yeah, we do. It's hard to see them at school since we're at different levels."

Zin gave me an evil smile. "You are in a

different level than Callan and Kodiak are, but you see them very often."

I glared at her. "They come find me, that's why!"

"Mm-hm." Zin rolled her eyes.

"ZIN!" I cried.

"I'm just kidding!" But her smirk said otherwise.

Emily ran over and met us halfway. "Hey, guys!" she said loudly. Suddenly, her voice dipped into a whisper. "Hide your pixies! Quick!"

"Why?" we asked.

Emily gestured silently to the group. "Rina's sister is here!"

Zin zoomed into my hair. Hunter and Blizzard disappeared behind their Links.

"She got an invitation too?" I asked.

Emily nodded as we made our way over to the rest. "Yeah, I sent two to your house. One for you, one for your sister."

I nodded. "Ah, okay." Now I know for sure that Mom and Dad probably hid my invitation.

"So what's this about?" Callan asked curiously.

Emily winked. "I'll show you."

When we reached the group, we all gave

14

happy greetings. I hugged Sirocca Sandings, then high-fived Derrik Jayson. Elece and Thora Cracklen gave me twin nods, except Thora's was decorated with a bright smile. Everyone looked happy to see each other, except Mira. My sister kept staring at Callan, and I quickly turned away. I gagged with Galen.

When everybody was settled, Emily, Universa, and Andy Carters stepped forward. Emily clapped her hands. "Guess what? During my Queen training, I learned how to do this really cool thing the other day. I combined it with my own designs, and created something new!" Emily grinned. "Wanna see?"

We all nodded, and she walked over to me. She stuck out her hand. "Can you hand me all your Crests?"

I frowned and dug in my pocket. I had every connection possible: Tie, Bond, even a Link! I dropped my two Crests and my Tie bracelet into Emily's hands.

"Alright. Now, watch and see!" Emily pressed her other hand on top of the Crests, and closed her eyes. A bright, amber light shone out from between her fingers, and when she opened her eyes, she removed her hands, and there was a white, jeweled wristband lying on her palm.

"Ta-da!" she crowed. She slipped it onto my wrist and smiled with satisfaction. "Look!"

I did. My wristband was decorated with all of my Crests: Tsunami, Snapdragon, Tie, and.... I squinted at the last image. "Are those....fairy wings?"

Emily nodded. "I searched up the Link image. Apparently, it's a pair of fairy wings."

"Whoa. Cool!" In the center of the wristband, there were two, small, rectangular jewels. An amber, and a lapis lazuli. "What are these for?"

"You press on those to call us whenever you need us," Emily explained. "Me and Andy. It also grants you permission to use the Royal Tunnel anytime."

I grinned. "Wow, this is really cool, Emily!"

Andy laughed. "Of course it is!"

Everyone started to crowd around Emily, so she continued to make more wristbands. After she was done, we all had similar white wristbands.

"This is interesting," Mira mused. "But I have one question. What are Links?"

Everyone jolted, then fidgeted. "Um.. er..."

"It's a connection with the queen," Emily blurted.

Mira looked up. "Really?" She stared at her

wristband, then at everyone else's. "I don't have a Link?"

Emily forced out a laugh. "Sorry. I think I forgot to add it on when I made yours. Was getting kind of winded after doing it ten times, you know? Don't worry, though. You still have full access to the Royal Tunnel like everyone else!"

Mira narrowed her eyes, but nodded, not saying anything.

Universa clapped her hands. "Well. Now that this is finished, you may go home! See you soon!"

That's it? Oh, okay. We all waved goodbye to the Carters and walked back toward the Tunnels. I chatted with Sirocca as we walked to see how she was doing.

"Pretty well, actually," she said. "Except for all the mobs." She shook her head tiredly. "You'd think that after a year, the popularity would decrease. I think it increased instead."

"Yeah," I said glumly. "I'm still not used to it. What should we do?"

Sirocca shrugged. "Live with it, I guess. I'm sure this would blow over soon enough."

I doubted, but nodded. "Okay." I lowered my voice. "How's Scorch?"

Sirocca kept walking and suddenly flipped

17

her hair. Scorch flashed me a radiant smile and wave from her position behind Sirocca's neck before Sirocca's honey-colored hair fell back into place. Sirocca gave me a small nod and wink.

I snickered. "Great!"

We reached the Tunnels. I headed toward the Fire Tunnel after Mira and called over my shoulder, "See you tomorrow!"

I stepped inside, heading home.

When we entered the house, Mom and Dad were there to greet us. "Welcome home, girls!"

I walked over into the kitchen where Mom was making dinner. "Mom, did you get an invitation for me to see the queen?"

Mom nodded, then looked at me quizzically. "You didn't see it?" She looked over my shoulder at Mira. "Mira, didn't you give it to your sister?"

"I forgot," she said apologetically. "But Rina showed up anyway."

Was that a dark tone she was using? Mira gave me a quick glance, a small glint in her eyes, then headed upstairs.

I shrugged then turned back to Mom. "I'm going to my room."

"Oh, right, honey. I cleaned your room today. It was a mess!"

I froze, halfway up the stairs. "You did?" I started to panic. Did she see anything?

"Yeah! I was kind of surprised at that small, soft, square, plushie-pillow-thing. You know, the one that's been dented in the middle? Where'd you get that?"

Zin's bed. I took a second before answering, "Oh, I found it at Thingamabobs. I thought it was really cute so I just bought it."

"For what?" Mom asked. She walked over to the stairs, peering at me curiously. "You're not using it for anything."

"Ahahaha…. Nah, I just thought it looked nice. Call me when dinner's ready!" I pelted toward my room and slammed the door.

"Nice going, Rina." Zin flew out of my hair and bounced onto her blue bed. "Slamming doors. So not suspicious."

"Sorry," I snapped. "I was panicking."

Zin sighed then flopped backward. "Your life is pretty tiring, you know that?" She sat back up. "Your mom's actually pretty nice."

I cringed. "Yeah, I guess so. I'm not used to all that 'honey' and 'sweetie' stuff."

Mom and Dad always liked Mira better because she was more perfect than I was. In fact, they kicked me out of the house because I had cultivated the Water Talent! I think I still would be living at the school if Universa hadn't sent us on that mission. I had a suspicion that Mom and Dad are taking care of me now because I'm a friend of the queen. Wouldn't want to displease or mistreat her close friend, now, right?

The door opened and Mira peeked inside. "I need to talk to - Oh!" Mira flew inside, crouching by my nightstand. "A fairy?!"

Zin and I exchanged horrified glances.

Oh. No.

Chapter 3

"Uh...." I said intelligently.

Zin backed up slowly, crawling off her bed. Mira picked her up by the back of her shirt and studied her. Zin squealed angrily.

"Let me go!" she roared.

"Hey!" I shouted at Mira. "You can't hold her like that!"

Mira paid no attention to me. "Where'd you get one?"

"Excuse me! I wasn't bought!" Zin snarled and writhed.

"Let her down!" I shouted. "Mira! Stop!" I snatched Zin away, cupping my hands around her protectively. "What do you want?"

Mira's eyes were fixed hungrily on my hands. "Why do you always get everything nice?" she asked quietly. She blinked and turned to me.

"Where'd you get that fairy?"

I decided not to tell her that it was a pixie. Fairies were more common, so the less she knew, the better. "I found her," I said vaguely.

Zin bit the inside of my hand, so I added, "It was more like she found me. You better not tell Mom and Dad."

Mira frowned. I could see a billion more questions in her eyes, but she said, "Okay. What do you think of Callan?"

I blinked. "What?" That's a totally different topic.

Mira stared hard at me. "Tell me."

I sighed. "Didn't we have this conversation last year at the assembly? He doesn't like me like that! He's like my older brother. Why do you keep asking?"

Mira doesn't respond. She walked over to my window and stared. "What about Kodiak Torrent?"

"Same. They're like Galen, but older, okay?" I said, irritated. I wanted her to leave. "Is that all?"

"What do they think about me?"

I'm not a monster. I didn't want to tell her that they didn't really appreciate what she did back when they were cellmates. "I don't know. You should ask them."

Mira didn't budge. She turned to me. "How'd you enchant people?"

I sputtered into a laugh. "Enchant? Who?"

"Them!" Mira said, as if it should have been obvious. "The other four!"

I curled one hand into an almost-fist and pretended to scratch my head. Zin rolled off and clutched at my hair.

I pulled my hand back. "What? My friends?"

Mira snorted. "You still call them friends? They're from different tribes! They're going to be your enemies!"

I blinked. "So?"

"'So'? That's all you can say?" Mira took a step forward. "You were always a little slow, Rina. Most of them will probably join their military. What are you going to do if you have to fight them one day. Huh?"

That worry had been bugging me for the past year. Callan, Kodiak, Elece, and Sirocca were old enough to join their tribes' military forces. Mira was already registered, due to her perfect grades at school, and she was advancing up the ranks quickly, even though she was home most of the time.

"I'm not in the Fire Navy," I told her. "I never will be."

Mira scoffed. "Really? You really think so?"

I nodded. "My Talent won't allow it. Besides, I have other things to do."

Mira rolled her eyes. "Like what? Frolic in the meadows with your 'friends'? Let me tell you something, Rina. A word of advice." She leaned in close. "Make friends where you are safe. Don't make friends that make you feel weird about yourself. Do it like me. Claim friends in your own tribe! Not the ones in other tribes!"

I became enraged, but I made my voice smooth as I replied, "Your word of advice is right, sister. But it doesn't really apply to me. I make friends where I can find them. I choose wisely and don't associate myself with the ones that would make me do strange things. My friends now fit perfectly into my criteria. So I think we can both agree when I say you stick with your friends and I'll stick with mine."

Mira's gaze was hard as she stared at me for a moment longer. I stared at her right back. She couldn't push me around in fear anymore.

She gave a soft chuckle. "Rina. That's so you." She turned and walked toward the door. "Keep my words in mind, though, sister," she called. "You might need it someday."

"Maybe, but my method is good enough,

thanks!" I called back. "You should tell your friends that! It'll make you look wise!"

Mira's stride didn't break as she walked across the hall to her room.

I closed my door and breathed. Zin flitted out. "Good going, Rina!" she cried. "Now your sister knows about me! What do we do?!"

"Calm down, Zin," I soothed, even though I was rattled myself. "She doesn't know everything. Just stay close. You'll be fine."

Zin glared at me, but slipped into her pouch. I placed a protective hand on it before a knock sounded at my door.

"Dinner's ready!" Mom sang. She peeked inside my room, looking at me curiously. "Who were you talking to?"

"Nobody," I said smoothly. "Just myself."

Mom didn't look convinced. "Mira's downstairs already. She's acting strange Did something happen between the two of you?"

I shrugged. "I don't know. You can ask Mira." I walked past her and headed for the dining room.

Dinner was awkward. Mira was strangely silent, and Mom and Dad chatted softly with each other. I slid some of my food into a napkin, wrapped it up, and placed it under the table next to me. Mira watched my every move.

"What?" I hissed at her.

She shrugged and looked away. "Nothing."

I scowled and continued to eat my food.

"So, girls," Mom said. "Queen Universa called another assembly. It's all-day tomorrow, but the most important part is tomorrow night, so I want you to look your best. The invitations are coming in the morning, but the queen let the council know ahead of time."

"So does that mean we have no school tomorrow?" I asked, mouth full of rice.

Dad grimaced. "Don't talk with your mouth full. And, yes. School is canceled for tomorrow."

My fork clattered against my plate and I raised my hands victoriously. "Yes!"

Mira pouted. "Aw. I was going to go study with Alina and the rest of them in the library." She sighed. "Guess I'll have to go the day after."

I made a face. "Study? I've watched your study session before. You hardly ever study!"

"Do too!" Mira snapped. "It's just that there are so many people that come and join us, so we always have to stop and explain where we are."

I frowned. "Really?"

Mira nodded furiously. "Yeah. But now that you've taken all that attention from us, I can actually study for once!"

I glared at her. "Isn't that a good thing? And do you think I *enjoy* being the center of attention?"

Mira had raised her voice by now. "It sure looks like it! You get everything you want! Everyone pays attention to you now!"

"Girls!" Dad shouted. "Break it up! Please!"

I gripped my fork and started shoveling food angrily into my mouth. So I was right. Mira was jealous.

"Honestly, girls," Mom sighed. "When did you guys turn against each other? You've never fought before."

"That's 'cause she was always too shy to talk," Mira sneered.

I refused to retaliate. "You were the one always filling in the silence, anyways," I muttered. "There was *no room* for me to talk."

Mom sighed before we can say anything else. "You guys are tired. I get it. Finish your homework, then you can go to sleep early."

I took the napkin-full of food in my lap and picked up my plate. "Done. Thanks for the food." I brought the plate over to the sink, blocking the napkin from my parents' view with my body. I jumped up the stairs and rushed into my room.

"Here, Zin." I placed the napkin beside her bed and she grinned. I sat down on my bed and watched her.

"Yes! Salmon!" She started to stuff her face joyfully. "I love it!"

"Even though you're a pixie?" I teased. "I thought you had a close connection with everything in nature!"

Zin frowned. "Yeah, I guess we do. But I'm a plant pixie. Not an animal one." She took another bite. "Your mom's a good cook!"

I smiled. "Yeah, I guess she is."

I leaned back, staring at my ceiling. Emily had already told me what the assembly was going to be about. I didn't really have to worry about what I would wear - I'll just put on the same dress as last year's assembly. Zin would probably do my hair.

I sat up and looked out my window. The moon shone brightly, a big pie in the sky. It gave each tree and its leaves a decorative sheen of pale light. Summertime. The hottest time of the year on the Fire Island. I put my chin on my arms and stared, losing myself in my thoughts.

Mira barged into my room and ran straight for my nightstand. Zin squeaked and tried to fly away, but Mira clapped her hands around the pixie before she could get very far.

"Ah. I knew it. You snuck food to feed your fairy," Mira cried triumphantly.

"Shh!" I hissed. "Let her go! Why do you always trap her like that?"

"What? It's not like she's a human. She's part of nature, right? So she's pretty much like a pet."

Mira gave a sudden yelp and her hands opened. Zin zipped toward me and hid behind my neck, baring her teeth at my twin sister.

"Ow. She's a biter." Mira scowled at Zin and shook her fingers. "Anyways. How long do you plan on keeping her? Are you going to release her back 'into the wild' or whatever?"

"How long do you think you can barge into my room?" I retorted. I leaped from my bed and pushed her roughly toward the door. "Have some manners, will you?"

Mira glared at me. "I'm telling Mom."

"And I'm telling her you're invading my privacy. Seriously, Mira. When did you become so disagreeable, moody, and difficult?"

"Since you came back," Mira snarled before I slammed my bedroom door. "You made everything worse!" she screamed. "Why'd you come home?"

"In case you forgot, Mom and Dad asked me

to!" I yelled back at her. "And I recall you passing on the message!"

"That doesn't mean I want you here!"

"I'm sorry, but we're twins! No matter how many times you try to separate us, the fact that we're related doesn't change!"

"ARGH!" I heard her stomp and slam her bedroom door.

I heaved a heavy sigh and slid down the wall beside my door. I rested my forehead on my knees and Zin flew over.

"Why do you think she hates me?" I asked her.

Zin shrugged. "She's probably just jealous of you. And she's snobby and spoiled, so that's a factor too. She's used to being pampered, by the looks of it."

I scoffed. "Yeah. She is." I sighed, then changed the subject as I stood up and walked over to my bed. "Can you help me prepare for Emily's coronation tomorrow?"

Zin smiled. "Of course!"

I thumped backwards on my bed, my head hitting the pillow. I sighed once more, then fell asleep without changing into my pajamas.

Chapter 4

My family spent the next day rushing, trying to primp and polish until they were picture perfect. The invitation had come that morning, mentioning an important assembly, startling my parents, even though they already knew about it. Me, I locked myself in my room and refused anyone's help.

"I'm fine!" I yelled for the hundredth time when Mom knocked on my door.

"Are you sure?" she called. "You've never prepared yourself for an assembly before. You're helping to represent our family, remember? You need to be perfect."

"I know!" I hollered. "You told me the same thing last time! And the time before that! Don't worry, Mom! I prepared myself last year, didn't I?"

"But that was last year!" Mom fretted.

"I'm fine!" I said again. "I'll surprise you later. Bye!"

I could hear Mom murmur nervously before she left my door alone.

Zin was frowning at me. "Yourself?"

I smiled apologetically. "Sorry. I couldn't exactly say that someone helped me, you know?"

"You could've just named one of your friends," Zin pouted. "I'd be satisfied with that."

"Okay. I'll do that next time." I rifled through my closet and pulled out the soft blue dress I'd worn to the assembly last year. "Do you think this is too small?"

Zin squinted at it, then shook her head. "It should be fine," she said. "You didn't grow that much over the past year, maybe an inch or two, but it should fit."

I grinned. "Okay!"

This dress was my favorite. Even though I wouldn't wear it more often, Zin helped me take care of it. It was a beautiful dress, light blue and soft. It even had a hidden pocket where Zin could hide.

Zin flew up and yanked on my hair. "Want the same braid?"

"Sure," I told her.

Zin smiled. "It's going to look a bit different now that your hair's a lot longer."

I shrugged. "Whatever you think looks good," I told her. "You're the expert."

Zin seemed to straighten up at that, and she began to analyze my hair. I stepped into my closet to change clothes.

"Alright," I told her when I stepped out. "Go ahead!"

"Actually," she mused. "I'm going to do something a bit different. Don't worry, it'll still be a braid," she added hastily, "but the design's going to be altered a little bit."

I smiled. "That's fine."

I sat down on the bed and Zin began. "Wet your hair first," she commanded. "Like, completely soak."

I reached a hand up to my hair and drenched it without ruining my dress. The benefits of the Water Talent.

I read a book for the remaining hour as Zin twisted my hair.

"Done!" she cried, flitting in front of my face. "You look awesome!"

I stepped in front of the mirror, grinning. My hair had been twisted on one side, merging into a complicated braid later on. Everything else was a mix of twining hair that somehow didn't look messy, but like a work of art.

"Awesome," I agreed. "Good job, Zin!"

Zin folded her arms and smirked. She flew into my pocket and I unlocked my door.

Unfortunately, I opened my door to find Mira opening hers at the same time.

She looked up, saw me, and stared enviously. "When'd you get the time to do that?"

I blinked, about to say my default response when Zin poked me. "A friend," I said instead.

"Who? What do you mean?" Mira kept walking until we were standing face to face. She had just taken a shower, her head wrapped up in a towel, and was standing in her fuzzy pajamas.

"Sirocca," I told her. "She did it for me last time,"

"What about this time?" she challenged.

"Uh, I did it myself, but she directed me over the phone," I lied.

"Thanks," Zin whispered cheerfully.

Mira studied me through narrow eyes before nodding slowly. "Sure." She stepped away to let me pass.

I was walking down the stairs when she said, "By the way, don't you think that you look a bit plain?" She turned to face me. "I mean, you're wearing the exact same thing as last time. Don't you think that's strange?"

"No, why?"

Mira shook her head pityingly. "Nothing." She headed for the bathroom and locked the door.

I scrunched my eyebrows in the direction she left. "She's weird," I muttered.

Zin giggled. "Yeah! Why would she care if you're wearing the same thing? You look great, so you deserve to wear it twice!"

I patted my pocket gently. "You're laying on it a bit thick," I teased.

I stepped into the kitchen, where Mom was busy cooking and Dad was asking her for fashion advice.

"Hi," I said.

They looked up. Mom dropped her spatula and Dad's tie slid onto the ground. "Rina?"

"What?" I asked casually.

They both came onto me at once. "Aren't you wearing the same thing?" Dad asked. "Don't you have anything different?"

"What are you talking about? She's amazing! Where'd you do your hair?" Mom asked.

I plugged my ears. "Stop! I'm ready. Can I go outside now? I'll meet you guys at the island.

Bye!"

I picked up my flats, slid my feet into my sneakers, and ran outside. I dove through the Royal Tunnel, grateful for the wristband.

I breathed a sigh of relief when I saw the green meadow. Zin flew out of my pocket, sighing.

"Wow, Rina. You really need to get out more often. You're always having close calls!" Zin snapped.

"Well, excuse me!" I snipped in reply. "My family is a bit nosy, okay? It's not easy."

Zin's eyes flared, but she plopped onto my head. "Right. So where're you going?"

I shrugged then walked toward the castle. "Let's just stay here until the party starts."

The castle doors flew open and Emily stepped outside, scanning the island. When she saw me, she squealed and waved.

"Come inside!" she called.

I flew over until we were close enough to talk without shouting. "Are you sure?" I asked. "Are you busy?"

Emily shook her head. "I'm pretty much finished," she told me. "Tawny helped me prepare, and all that's left are the coronation preparations, which I've already mastered."

Emily winked, cleared her throat, and said professionally, "I do."

I snickered. "Is that really all you have to say?"

Emily shrugged. "I mean, if I want to be less diplomatic, I can nod and say 'Yeah, sure. Why not?'"

We laughed until Zin said, "Rina's a big blockhead."

"Zin!" I snarled.

"What? It's true! You let your sister find me, didn't she? And here you are, having fun."

"She what?" Emily's eyes widened in horror.

I groaned. "Yeah. Mira suddenly took a liking to barging into my room without knocking."

"So what happened?" Emily asked anxiously.

I made a face. "She thinks that Zin is a fairy, so I think we're in a yellow zone right now. She caught me sneaking food to feed Zin, then became really suspicious of me when she saw my hair. I told her Sirocca helped me, but I don't think she bought it."

Emily glanced at my hair, then smiled. "Nah. If you tell Sirocca, I'm sure she can replicate it."

"Hey!" Zin shouted. "Pixie-styled hair can never be copied!"

"Sorry," Emily said. "I'll rephrase that. Sirocca

will do her best to replicate it enough so that it's convincing."

"Better," Zin said.

"Well, I see that Tawny's been hard at work, too!" I gestured at Emily's hair. "So queenly!"

Emily grimaced. "Maybe."

Different locks of her hair had been pulled and pinned in similar places so that it gave her a very professional look, but kept her youthful shine at the same time.

Zin flew over and picked up a strand of Emily's blond hair. "Wow! This is a really good design! It really compliments everything on your face!"

Uh…. That was a weird comment.

Zin started to tug on Emily's t-shirt. "Hey! Can we go inside now? I want to see Tawny!"

"Zin…." I groaned.

Emily took no notice. "Of course! You guys are always welcome inside this castle!"

She led us inside the humongous building. I gaped at the towering ceiling and marble floors. There were many hallways leading from the greeting room, but Emily walked down one with confidence.

"Memorize this way," Emily suggested. "In case you'll have to live here."

"Live here?" I echoed.

"Yeah!" Emily turned to me. "Come to me anytime you need something. I mean, this castle is too big for three people. I'd invite everyone to come stay, but some of their parents might not like it."

"You should suggest it, though." I told her. "I think it's a great idea!"

Emily nodded with a bright grin. "Okay. I will today."

"Are you nervous?" I asked curiously.

Emily shuddered. "Of course I am. Who wouldn't be?" She flashed me a strained smile. "What if the people don't accept me?"

I pumped a fist. "Don't worry about that. We got it covered."

Emily grimaced. "Eh… don't do that. They wouldn't like me even more."

I patted her back. "Don't stress over it. You can't please everyone; just do whatever feels natural. Try to be as honest with the people as possible. They might appreciate it."

"You should be queen instead of me," Emily said.

I barked a short laugh. "No. What would I rule for?"

Emily shrugged. "I don't have anything

motivating me either."

I blinked. "You don't? Then why are you doing this?"

Emily frowned. "Or, maybe I do. I just can't determine what it is yet."

She led me into a large section of the castle where it was pretty much like a house-city kind of place. There were pantries full of every kind of food, and an enormous kitchen. Behind that were two large bedrooms, each with rows and rows of bunk beds, large and pixie-sized.

"Whoa." My jaw dropped. "I never knew the Terrene Castle had this kind of place."

"It didn't," Emily said, smug. "I added it. In case any of you are going to stay over."

I grinned, running into the pink room. "THIS IS SO COOL!" I leaped up and bounced on a bed. "Seriously?!"

Zin bounced on the bed below me. "Can I have a human-sized bed?"

Emily laughed. "Of course! I've already told you that everyone is welcome! I needed to prepare a cozy place for you guys to stay." She motioned for me to come over. "Can I ask you something?"

I bounced off the bed and walked over. "Of course!"

"I mean, I know I asked you this before, but are you sure?" Emily looked up at me anxiously. "Being part of the Queen's Guard?"

A few months ago, Emily had pulled my friends and I aside, offering us a position to be her personal bodyguards in case more Mainlanders came back. Of course, we all agreed immediately, but Emily still didn't look too happy about it. She was worried she was forcing us into an obligation.

"Emily," I said. "We all agreed. We're willing to protect you! You're not forcing us into anything."

Emily managed a weak smile. "Are you sure?"

Zin flew up in her face. "Yeah! Rina's real glad you asked her, you know? It gives her a secret to keep from her sister, and something else to do than join the Fire Army."

"Zin!" I said, panicking. "Don't say so much!"

Emily giggled, then her eyes darkened. "Rina, about your sister...."

"Yeah?" I looked her in the eye. "Just say it. You consider her as a threat, don't you?"

Emily blushed. "I'm sorry. It's just that she knows so much, but knows so little, you know? What if she starts rumors that the pixies are back?

41

It's going to be so dangerous!"

I frowned. "You're the queen, right? If you feel like someone's a threat, it's your job to subdue them. It's okay with me if you decide to keep Mira on a short leash. She hates me anyways."

I tried to say it lightly, but Emily looked at me worriedly. "Are you sure? What about your parents?"

I brushed it off. "You're the queen, right? I'm sure you can figure it out."

Emily sagged. "Sometimes, being queen is not that fun."

I patted her back. "Don't worry. We'll be here to help you in any way possible."

Emily's smile was a little brighter as she said, "Hey! When you train, are you going to live here or at home?"

Universa had mentioned training to be a member of the Queen's Guard. Apparently, it was going to be intense since the queen needed protection 24/7. We were given the choice to wake up super early and come home late, or just stay in the castle every day during our training period.

"I'll probably stay at home for now," I told her regretfully. "My parents are getting better,

42

and I kind of like how I'm more important to them now. Even if it's because you're one of my best friends, and I'm a national hero and stuff."

Emily gave me a sad smile. "Okay. Feel free to come anytime, though."

I nodded. "Anytime."

A small yellow pixie flew in. "I heard Rina's voice, Emily! She's here!" Tawny flew in circles around Emily's head, completely unaware of my presence. "Come on! Let's go say hi!"

"Hi, Tawny!" I laughed.

Tawny jumped back in surprise, then blushed. "Oh. Sorry. I thought you were still outside."

"Tawny!" Zin zipped over and barreled into her friend. "Nice to see you!"

"Nice to see you too!" Tawny giggled and pushed Zin off of her. "And it looks like I'm going to be seeing you a lot more often!"

Emily's pixie had a sunny personality. Her blond hair had a faint glow and her smile shone. She and Emily were perfect matches.

Andy walked in afterwards, rubbing his eyes. "Em, can you go check the decorations? The butler guy asked me to - hey!" He pointed at me in surprise. "When'd you get here?"

"Hey, Andy!" I smiled. "You look drained."

He sagged. "I am. The butler guy keeps

driving me on full force. It's tiring. I barely have enough time to breathe!"

"That's 'cause you're not taking your jobs seriously!" Cyan smacked Andy's forehead from his perch on Andy's head. "You're too busy goofing off."

"Hey! I thought you're supposed to be on my side!" Andy complained.

Cyan made a noise of indifference and looked up. He nodded greetings. "Hi."

Cyan and Andy were kind of polar opposites. Whereas Andy was cheerful and playful, Cyan was serious and… serious. In fact, I've never seen him smile, but his ombre blue hair and small figure were so cute! All the pixies were!

Emily had to go check the decorations and Cyan hustled Andy back to work, so Zin and I roamed around the guest wing. We counted ten bathrooms, ten hot tubs, ten pools, ten desks, one big kitchen, and more!

"It looks like she built a mini-house for each of us," I commented. "All smashed together into one mansion kind of thing, you know?"

Zin whooped with glee and zipped toward the beds. "I love these beds! They're so soft!" Zin giggled and rolled on the soft material. "Can I take this bed?"

"Are you crazy? No!"

Zin stopped rolling and glared at me. "Why?"

"Because! *Those* beds are yours!" I pointed at the long row of multicolored cushions each the size of a pillow. "They are big enough, aren't they?"

Zin's eyes shone and in a flash, was jumping on a pale pink pillow. "They're not as bouncy, but they're way softer! Rina! I want this one!"

I sighed hopelessly and carried the pillow to one of the beds in the corner. I chose a bottom bunk, smiling at the window next to it. There were two windows beside every bunk bed - one high, one low. Emily really outdid herself!

I decided to claim this bed for whenever I chose to sleep over. Zin was curled up, dozing lazily. I snorted at her sleeping figure.

I laid the pillow gently at the head of the bed and sat down. "You look like you could get used to being pampered," I told her.

"Mm-hm...." Zin murmured sleepily. "I'm tired. Good night."

I snickered. "I'll wake you up when it's time."

Zin was already snoring softly.

Chapter 5

Emily stuck her head inside, motioning for me quietly.

"Is it time?" I asked, standing up. I brushed off my dress and walked over to the door.

Emily fidgeted nervously. "Almost. Do I look okay? You look fabulous, of course. But I don't know if I should trust Tawny's sense of fashion. Zin's style is perfect on you, so...."

I laughed softly. "Stop. You're babbling. Where's Tawny?"

Tawny peeked over the head of Emily's tiara. "Right here! Emily's being kind of mean to me."

I laughed again and shook my head. "No, you look beautiful, Em!"

Emily's body shuddered with relief. "Good. Thanks, Tawny!"

Tawny had chosen a yellow gown for Emily.

It was formal, but simple at the same time; there weren't so many jewels. Her silver tiara gleamed, resting on her head.

Altogether, Emily looked like a bright light. Tawny had chosen well.

"Are the others here?" I asked her.

Emily nodded. As if on cue, the rest of the group in formal attire bustled inside, marveling at the guest wing.

"Wow, Emily. You really did all this?" Sirocca's jaw dropped as she counted the number of bathrooms.

Emily blushed. "Well, since I asked for it, I had to build it as part of my training. It took me months to perfect it."

"IT'S AWESOME!" Derrik hollered. Even though he was twelve now, he still had a childish demeanor about him. He ran into the blue room, bouncing on a bed. "I CALL THIS ONE!"

His pixie, Maple, face-planted on a dark-green pillow that contrasted with his pale hair. "I CALL THIS ONE!"

The other pixies began to call their pillows, and the boys began to fight for beds. The girls, however, were much more calm as we shuffled around, talking.

Mira hadn't arrived yet, so I quickly told

47

Sirocca my predicament. She winked and said, "No problem! I've done something similar before, but not so exquisite. I'm sure it'll pass."

"Thank you!" I breathed, a rush of relief filling my soul. Sirocca was like the older sister I've always dreamed of.

"Anyways, where is she?" Elece mused. "Is she coming with her hotshot parents?"

I growled. "Hey. Watch it. They're my parents too, remember?"

Elece winced. "Sorry. Emily told us what happened, so I'm being cautious."

The atmosphere suddenly chilled. The girl pixies stopped their game of trying to wake up Zin to glance fearfully at us.

I sighed, rubbing the back of my head. I felt my braid swish down my back. Before, it was only able to reach past my shoulders. "I don't know," I said finally. "What should we do if she asks?"

Thora spoke up, "We can't tell her the truth?"

I grimaced and shook my head. "She kept staring at Zinnia and called her a pet. Zin doesn't like my sister at all."

"No, I don't!" Zin muttered. She opened her eyes blearily and sat up. "We're talking about Mira, right?"

"You're awake!" The other pixies immediately began to tease Zin about what a cat she was. "You were all plopped down like a dead thing!"

"Hey, stop!" Zin snapped. "You hear some devastating news about a pixie but can't cut her some slack, huh?"

"Your Majesty?" A maid stuck her head inside, dipping her head at Emily. "Ms. Flameton... er, requests your presence."

"Lily?" Emily walked over. "What do you mean request?"

The young maid flushed. She couldn't have been more than one year younger than me. "I mean, she came in and asked if you were here. I told her I'd get you."

Emily nodded. "Alright. Lead her here."

Lily dipped her head and hurried out of the wing. All our pixies immediately hid by their Links. Emily alerted the boys, then led us all into a common room. I didn't even know it was there!

We all sat silently, tense, until Mira came in, all smiles. She was wearing the signature Fire-Tribe red, and her hair was up in a sophisticated bun pinned with a rose. If I didn't know any better, I'd say she was wearing makeup, but she wasn't. Talk about stunning!

"Hi, everyone!" She rushed in and sat down

49

on a couch. "How did you guys get here so fast?"

"My parents decided to come early," Kodiak said politely. "The butler gathered all of us and ushered us inside."

Mira nodded understandingly. "Oh. I see. I would have come earlier, but my mom and dad wanted everything to be just right, so," she shrugged, "here I am."

Nobody really said anything afterwards. Emily cleared her throat awkwardly and rose. "I need to go and check the preparations. Feel free to talk until the walls glow. That'll mean the assembly is about to start, so you can find your seats in the VIP section." She rushed out of the room without another word.

Assembly? Galen asked questioningly.

No one knows it's a coronation, I explained. *Except us, I think. Then there's the Queen's Guard position announcement.*

Oh. I see.

"Okay, what's going on here," Callan interrupted. "I saw that secret conversation you guys were having."

Mira's eyes flickered into a glare for the briefest second, I wasn't sure if I even saw it.

"I was just explaining a few things," I told him vaguely. "Why? Do you need something?"

50

Callan scowled. "No."

I rolled my eyes at Kodiak and we exchanged amused glances. Sirocca came over and sat down by my side. "Can I check to see if you pinned your hair up correctly?" She gestured at my hair.

"Yeah, go ahead!"

She leaned in close, whispering, "So what do we say if she asks?"

"I don't know," I whispered back. "Just try not to give away anything. Evade the question or something, I guess."

"Hey, Sirocca!" Mira called.

Sirocca jumped, then turned toward her with a smile. "Yes?"

"Rina told me you did her hair. Can you teach me how?" Mira asked expectantly. "It looked really nice when Rina did it, but I'm sure I can do better."

Everyone's eyes frosted for a second before turning away. I stormed but kept my expression oblivious. Thora cleared her throat awkwardly.

"How arrogant!" Zin whispered indignantly. "I think she thinks it's ugly because you're wearing it. If it were Thora or Elece, she'd flatter them."

"Doesn't matter," I told her. "She doesn't realize how she speaks. She's been talking like

51

that about me my whole life. I'm used to it."

"Oh! Rina, did you bring your fairy?" Mira asked pointedly. She gestured toward my dress. "You keep whispering into your pocket."

I gave a jolt. "What?"

Everyone looked to me, horrified. Mira seemed to think they were interested, because then she rambled on about how she found Zin in my room.

"You should show them!" she encouraged eagerly. "Show them your new pet!"

Everyone stiffened, and I growled, "She's not my pet."

"Well, you're not planning on releasing her back into the wild anytime soon, right? So she's yours for the time being." Mira opened her bag and pulled out a dark-blue book. "I've been reading on fairies. They have wings, but yours doesn't. How come?"

Zin flew out of my pocket and in front of her face. My blood chilled. No! What if she revealed she was a pixie?

"My wings were lost because of giants like you!" Zin snarled. "They were messing with me when I was doing my own business, so I lost my wings! It takes a lot of magic to just fly, you know?"

52

Mira didn't look at all sorry. Instead, she looked even more interested. "You lost your wings? How? This book says that if fairies lose their wings, they die."

Zin scoffed, but I could see her eyes flitting around nervously. "Obviously, that book is wrong. Was it written by a fairy? No! Of course it's inaccurate!" She stuck her tongue out at Mira, then made a show of flying back to me for safety. She even hovered behind my shoulder like it was her shield!

She hates shoulders!

Everyone was silent for a moment. I pretended to duck my head in embarrassment. "Sorry for not telling," I mumbled. Did I mention I couldn't act very well?

Luckily, the others were way better than I was. They immediately scrambled to say apologies or how cool my "fairy" was.

"Aw, I hope you feel better soon, little fairy," Thora held up a hand invitingly. "You want to go home soon, don't you?"

Zin's eyes glassed for a bit. "Yes, I do. I miss my parents sometimes," she murmured softly. I couldn't tell if she was really homesick.

Callan, Kodiak, and Galen just slapped my back. "Hey, dude, next time, tell us if you find a fairy. You don't have to hide it from us!"

"Yeah!" Derrik piped. "We're not going to hurt you, fairy. I'm sorry about your wings."

Zin started to sniffle. I could tell she enjoyed being the center of attention. "Thank you, kind giants," she sobbed. "You are much nicer than the ones that took my wings as a prize." She cast a hateful glare at Mira.

Mira looked taken aback by all the attention we were getting, so she tried to make it up. "Sorry. I didn't take your wings, though," Mira said loudly.

"Maybe not, but your aura says otherwise," Zin snapped. "It looks exactly like those evil giants'." She huffed, but didn't say anything else.

Everyone started to look cautiously at Mira. "Really?"

Mira looked flustered. "She's just a fairy! It's not like she's telling the truth! Can fairies even do that kind of stuff?" She began flipping through her book.

"Can I?" Zin asked ominously. She glanced toward me, her yellow eyes sparkling joyfully before returning to her villainous act.

"Uh, okay, okay." I said, holding up my hands. This went on long enough. "Thanks, guys, for trusting me. But we need to get outside. Don't you think the walls are starting to glow?"

Everyone looked at the stone walls. Luckily for me, they really were starting to light up.

"Yeah. We should go," Sirocca said decisively. She stood up. "Hide your fairy, Rina. Somewhere where she'll be safe."

I saluted her. "Will do, Ms. Sandings." I stood up and tucked Zin gently into my pocket. "Well done," I whispered to her.

Zin flashed me a wink before disappearing into the fabric. You know, however sassy she may be, it came in handy sometimes.

Mira tucked the book back in her bag and stood up. "I wonder what the assembly's going to be about this time."

No one replied. Instead, everyone started to chat among themselves, some purposely discussing the "fairy's" origins.

"Maybe she's from the Earth Island," Derrik suggested loudly.

"No way. How would Rina find her there?" Callan asked. "The Fire Island is more reasonable."

"That was close," Galen muttered to me. "Did you plan that out with Zinnia?"

I shook my head. "No. She's an awesome actor."

Galen snickered. "Yeah, she was! I actually believed for a second that she was a crippled fairy!"

I laughed and Mira glanced over at me. Why does she keep looking at me like that? "You know," I murmured softly to Galen, not looking at my sister. "I might be wrong, but that seemed like a deliberate attempt to get you guys to turn against me."

Galen nodded. "Yeah, I was thinking that too. I'm sure everyone was thinking that. You heard how many awkward silences there were. Or unheard!" He started to snort with laughter. "Get it?! Ah, I crack myself up sometimes."

"Dude. That was a terrible joke." I said seriously. "You need to make it sound more clever."

Galen glared at me. "Gee, thanks for bursting my bubble."

In response, I encased him in a real bubble, then popped it. He flinched and blinked. "You're welcome," I said smugly.

I flicked all the water out of his clothes before he could complain.

We reached the castle doors. The doorman-butler opened it, letting us out. We dipped grateful nods to him as we passed.

Just like last time, everything was decorated spectacularly. Since it was summer, twinkling lights like fireflies drifted around, lighting up the night. Every tree was decorated with glowing flowers, each a different color of the rainbow. The green grass had been sprayed with luminescent paint, giving it a faint glow as well. The waters were so clear, it reflected off any light that hit it. Basically, everything was glowing with life. It was beautiful!

Many people have already been gathered in the meadow, crowding around the food tables and laughing with their friends. Children pretended they had activated Talents and played with the lights. Parents milled around, discussing business stuff. I felt a hand on my shoulder and looked up to see Universa gazing at the crowd.

"It's time," she murmured softly. She led us down the grand stairs that led us to the meadow. People caught sight of us and began to clap, cheer, and whistle.

We took our seats at the front of the meadow, inside a roped off area just for VIPs. I sat between Galen and Sirocca, watching. Listening.

"Good evening, ladies, gentlemen, children," Universa began. "As you already know, on my invitation, I had said that the purpose of this

57

assembly would be a surprise. Now, that surprise is going to be revealed. Emily Carters, please step forward."

Murmurs of surprise and understanding flooded through the crowd as Emily stepped through the castle doors. She stood regally with no sign of nervousness. Go, EMILY!

"From this day forward, this queen-in-training will co-lead with me on the throne until I am unable. She will be known as Queen Aurora. Everyone is expected to call her by her new title. Emily." Universa turned to the fourteen-year-old girl. "Are you willing to rule this nation through everything? Are you willing to stick by your people when times are rough, or when it's smooth sailing? Are you willing to keep the nation's need in mind and do your best to protect them? Are you willing to make wise decisions and to not harm your soldiers unnecessarily? Are you willing to have patience to become the next principal of the Academy?"

After a few more "are you willing"s, Emily answered solemnly, "Yes, I am."

Universa smiled. "I proclaim this young lady the queen of the Terrene Islands. Stand up and greet your new queen.... Aurora!"

Everyone clapped and whooped in

acknowledgement. The children jumped and squealed, happy to have a young person on the throne. "Maybe she'll give out free candy and no homework!" a boy cried hopefully.

Emily dipped a graceful curtsy to the crowd. "Thank you for your support," she began. "Forgive me if I'm not diplomatic enough. I have a gift for everyone as a token of my gratitude and appreciation. I will do my best to take your interests to heart and to become a worthy ruler." She dipped another curtsy as the crowd roared with approval.

She called for her brother, then raised her hand into the air, eyes glowing. Andy copied her and twin ribbons of light exploded from their palms, twining around each other - amber and dark blue. When they reached around sixteen feet in the air, the colors merged into a brilliant white light before exploding out into the sky.

Everyone gasped in awe as individual lights began to dance in the air, leaving bright trails behind them. After two minutes, the lights stopped moving and everyone saw the bigger picture.

It was a map of the Terrene Islands, outlined with a wide circle. Along the bottom of the picture were the words: MANY ISLANDS, ONE

NATION.

Everyone cheered, full of enthusiasm for the new queen. They chanted, "*Au-ro-ra! Au-ro-ra!*" as Queen Aurora dipped one last graceful curtsy, waiting for the crowds to calm.

"Thank you," Aurora said warmly. "According to Terrenian tradition, my first act as queen is to appoint the members of my Guard." She glanced at me with a wink. "During my reign as queen, there will be at least four Guardians: Fierina Flameton, Derrik Jayson, Elece Cracklen, and Galen Maelstrom. Please step forward."

There was a round of polite applause. Callan, Sirocca, Thora, and Kodiak glanced at us in surprise. Mira gazed at me with (surprise!) envy.

My best friends and I stepped up to the platform and Emily took our wristbands. She pressed them in between her hands, and when she released them, I saw that there was a sword and a crown right in between the two jewels on the wristband. The sign of the Queen's Guard.

"I understand that you fear many things since your new leaders are all teenagers," Emily spoke to the crowd. "But I have already appointed Universa to be one of my advisors. She will continue to be my mentor until I am eighteen. She will also be in charge of my Guardians' training until she deems them ready." She dipped her head to the crowd respectively. "I hope you agree with my boundaries before reign. Let us grow into a great nation!"

Everyone cheered again, and I could tell the majority of it was sincere. I clapped along with everyone else as Emily dipped one last graceful curtsy before disappearing back into the castle with Andy and co-queen Universa. Everyone mingled happily afterward for a few minutes before dispersing. Parents called for their children as they walked toward the Tunnels.

I laughed and talked with my friends before Mom and Dad called for us. "It's time to go home!"

Aw, man! I wanted to congratulate Emily - I mean, *Aurora* - before I left. "Tell Aurora 'Great job!' for me, okay?" I asked my friends before waving goodbye. "See you tomorrow!"

I caught up with Mira just as she was about to enter the Fire Tunnel. "Hey. I need to talk to you."

We stepped inside and continued to walk along the street. "About what?" she asked innocently.

I gave her a hard stare. "Why'd you tell my friends about…. you know?"

Mira shrugged. "I thought they already knew."

"Does this mean you're going to rat me out to Mom and Dad?" I hissed. "You promised!"

"I heard my name!" Mom sang. She turned around. "Are you gossiping about me?"

"No, Mom!" I said cheerfully. "We're not talking about you."

Dad looked interested. "How about me?"

I waved a hand dismissively. "Nah, you must have heard it wrong. Don't worry. We're not spreading rumors or whatever."

Their eyes hardened for a second. "I hope not. You know how much danger we'd be in if anything false got out."

I nodded reassuringly. "I know. Don't worry."

Mom and Dad switched back into their cheerful attitude and the subject was dropped. "Good. Don't you think that assembly was just wonderful?" Mom smiled approvingly. "I see a lot of potential in young Queen Aurora."

I eyed her suspiciously. "Really? Are you sure? She's a Mainlander!"

Dad looked at me funny. "Aren't you her friend?"

I blinked, horrified. "No, that's not what I

meant! I mean, I'm surprised you guys would support her."

Dad chuckled. "Well, not a hundred percent, honestly. But it does help that she chose to stick with the traditions. It pleases me to see how hard she tries to adapt our culture."

I smiled proudly. "Of course!"

"And great job on agreeing to the Guardian position," Mom remarked. "It's really going to help you and our family!" Her eyes gleamed. "Maybe we'll get a promotion!"

I grimaced, and forced out a laugh. "Hahaha…. Yeah…." Why can't they be happy for just me? Why do some things still have to be used to uphold Mom and Dad's reputation as Council members?

Except for that, we talked jovially until we reached home. I entered my bedroom, sighing. "Whew. That was a good assembly, don't you think?"

Zin poked her head out and drifted toward her bed. "Yeah, I guess." She yawned. "I'm tired. I'm going to go to sleep."

"You've been really tired lately," I commented. "Are you feeling alright?"

Zin waved her arm airily. "Oh, yeah… I'm fiiiiiine."

She promptly fell asleep. I bit my lip, worried, before undressing and undoing my hair.

"You know?" she mumbled. "I think I do feel a bit homesick."

I gave a start. "I thought you fell asleep already!"

Zin started to mumble unintelligibly, so I concluded that she was sleep-talking. "I want to see home again. That fresh air….."

I gazed sadly at the little pink pixie when a brilliant idea suddenly struck me. I'm good friends with the queen, aren't I? I'm sure Aurora would let me into the Onyx Garden to visit the pixie city. I should surprise Zin!

Feeling all excited, I spent the next few minutes in bed, brainstorming. I decided to present this idea to my friends to see if their pixies would like to be surprised too! I fell asleep, dreaming of seeing Zin's sparkling smile again.

Chapter 6

"Rina, I'm feeling a little sick today," Zin moaned. She flopped limply onto my face. "Can I stay home for today?"

"Zin!" I cried. "Are you okay? You've never been sick before!"

Zin groaned and I picked her up gently. "I don't know why either," she mumbled. "I think it's the toxic gas you giants keep having around you."

"Hey…." I said, trying to make her laugh. "That's offending."

Zin's eyes stayed closed, but the corners of her mouth twitched. "I'm going to stay by that plant downstairs, okay?" One eye opened a crack. "Can you carry me downstairs?"

I bit my lip. "Okay, but try not to be seen, okay? You're vulnerable enough as it is."

Zin managed the tiniest nod and I placed her on my pillow as I got ready. When I was ready to go down, I picked her up from my pillow, and my heart twisted. Zin had stayed in the exact same position I'd left her.

I picked her up with one hand, my backpack in the other, and carried her gently downstairs.

Luckily for me, Mom was in the kitchen making breakfast, Dad and Mira haven't come down yet, so I was able to hide Zin behind the potted plant's stem. It sat by the window so it could get lots of sunlight. Unfortunately, the dining table was right in front, so I had to hope that my family wouldn't see.

Zin took a deep breath, sighed, and opened her eyes. Already, they were looking clearer and she gave me a weak, grateful smile. "Thanks, Rina. Don't worry. I'll be here when you get back from school." She stuck her tongue out at me. "Don't be a sloth slug!"

Hearing Zin's favorite insult didn't do much to ease my worries, though. "Stay put, okay? Don't leave the plant if anyone's home."

"Who're you talking to, Rina?" Mom walked out, carrying a bit plate of pancakes.

"Oh! Uh…." I shuffled my body to hide Zin. "The plant…. Mom."

"Why?" she asked curiously. "You've never really cared about that before."

"Eh heh...." I coughed. "Well, you know. I guess I felt kind of guilty that it's been neglected for so long. I'm happy to see that it's still really healthy! So, what's for breakfast?" I asked, quickly changing the subject.

Mom looked at me funny. "Are you okay?"

I kicked myself inside. Of course! SHE WAS CARRYING A HUGE PLATE OF PANCAKES!

I forced out a laugh. "Sorry. I guess I didn't get enough sleep."

Mom chuckled. "Obviously." She placed the pancakes in the middle of the table. "I hope they give you a small bit of time to nap in between your training."

"Training?" I squeaked, my heart thudding onto the floor.

"Yeah, remember?" Mom looked up. "You need to start sleeping earlier. Instructions for us came in the mail this morning. Today is a special case, since it's the first day, but starting tomorrow, you'll need to be at the Royal Island by five and come home at around eleven."

I groaned. "NO!"

Mom frowned. "Why not?"

"That's too late!" I whined. "That's only five

hours of sleep! Do I have to come home that late tonight?"

Mom nodded. "You just start later today, that's all. You need to wake up early so you can make it there on time."

I bit my lip, contemplating my situation. If I went to training today, I won't be able to check on Zin in the afternoon. She was already starting to look healthier, so at this rate, by the time I get home, Zin would be perfectly fine. If she managed to stay hidden for that long. But what if something happened while I was gone?

I chewed my lip, torn, until Mira and Dad came downstairs. I didn't need to make it worse than it already was.

"Fine," I said. "Okay."

Mom laughed. "I didn't know you needed your own permission to go!" Mom went back into the kitchen and brought out more utensils. "I prepared a special breakfast for you to celebrate!"

Mira stared at the pancakes, expressionless. I sat down, trying hard not to glance at the plant every now and then.

Since I had to hurry, I shoveled the pancakes into my mouth, grabbed my backpack, and raced for the door. Before I left, I gave a quick glance behind my shoulder to check the plant again. My parents waved; they thought I was saying goodbye to them.

I stepped out of the house and raced for the Royal Tunnel.

When I arrived, everyone else was already there. I plastered a smile on my face and waved. "Hi, guys!"

Derrik was bouncing excitedly on his toes. "I can't believe we're going to train for the Queen's Guard!"

Elece bopped his head. "Pipe it down, mister." But her eyes were shining with excitement also.

Galen smiled at me, then frowned. "Are you okay?"

"Yeah, why wouldn't I be?" I asked through the smile.

"You look real fake, you know that right?" Elece pointed.

I dropped my act and sighed. "Zin's sick."

Maple, Electra, and Stratus immediately flew out from behind their Links. "Zinnia? Really?"

I nodded. "She woke up feeling sick and asked to stay home, so I left her by the plant next to the dining table. She looked better after that, but…." I sighed again.

Maple exchanged glances with Stratus. Electra flicked her electric purple hair and fixed me with a look. "Sounds like she's homesick."

I looked at Elece's pixie, confused. "Zin did say she was homesick, but I didn't know it was an actual disease."

Electra shook her head. "No. For pixies, some emotions are stronger than others. Homesickness is one of the strongest emotions because it is a sense of longing. If Zin is homesick, she needs something to remind her of home."

I nodded with understanding. "I see. That's why she felt better by the plant."

Electra gave a single nod.

"I'm sure she'll be fine," Stratus reassured. Galen nodded to what his pixie said.

I groaned. "Okay. Thanks." Then something hit me and my eyes brightened. "Hey, I had a brilliant idea last night!"

When I told them about my plan, everyone's eyes lit up. "Great idea!" Galen said enthusiastically. "I'm sure Em - *Aurora* won't mind. Besides, it'd be great to see the pixie queen again!"

I smiled, happy that they liked it. "Great! Let's

ask Aurora later, and tell the others."

We headed for the castle, discussing. Aurora was waiting at the doors with her brother and Universa. She jumped and waved when she saw us coming.

"Hey, guys!" Aurora smiled. "Can't wait to watch you start training!"

Everyone smiled awkwardly. "Sure, Queen Aurora."

Aurora grimaced. "Can you guys not call me that? I don't want to be Queen Aurora around my friends. Just stick with Emily. Please?"

I breathed a sigh of relief. "YES! I didn't really want to call you that. It didn't feel right, you know?"

Emily grinned. "Yeah. I know what you mean."

Universa led us into the castle and into a large training room. It had hundreds of weapons and dummies; it intimidated me to think that I was expected to be an expert swords-girl and stuff like that.

Four young instructors in black jumpsuits were standing by the swords - two women, two men. Universa led us over and started to introduce them.

"Here are the current members of the Queen's

Guard. They will train you four in the skills of being a Guardian." Universa stepped up to the first trainer. "This is Glenn. Derrik, he'll be your trainer."

Glenn was a muscle-packed young man with a buzz-cut. He stepped forward, and one glance from him sent all of us cowering.

"M-My trainer?" Derrik peeped. He had come to hide behind me.

Universa smiled. "Don't worry. Glenn looks tough, but he can be really nice."

Glenn rolled his neck and cracked his knuckles.

Derrik trembled, but stepped forward. "O-Okay."

Glenn suddenly broke out into a wide smile. "Cool, boy!"

Derrik looked less peeved after that. He walked with Glenn toward the other end of the training room.

"This is Melody. Elece, she'll be your trainer."

A slight woman with a long brown ponytail stepped forward. She gave Elece a warm smile and beckoned her to study the swords. Hearing her name made me think of Zin. She was a Hybrid between plant and music pixies, which meant she could communicate with plants and control music. How was she doing right now?

"Galen, this is Skye. He's your trainer."

The young man stepped forward, flashing Galen a playful smile. "Ready to have some fun?"

Galen's eyes lit up. "Oh, yeah!"

The last young woman gave me a small smile and stepped forward. Universa introduced her as Jordan. She had tied up her hair like Melody's, but she gave off a serious air when she walked toward me.

"Good luck, guys!" Emily called.

"Let's have a talk before we start," Jordan said once Universa, Emily, and Andy stepped back to watch behind a glass wall. "Have you fought anyone before?"

I nodded. "Back at the Mainland."

Jordan gave me a steely look. "Alright. I suppose that counts. What'd you have to do?"

I thought back to those days years ago. "Well, we had to hide, fight -"

"With what?" Jordan interrupted, arms crossed.

I furrowed my eyebrows. "With our Talents, and our weapons."

"Weapons?" Jordan peered at me curiously. "What weapons?"

"Oh, it's….." I fumbled in my pocket for my

73

Snapdragon Crest when I remembered that I don't have it anymore. "Uh…."

"Well?" Jordan quirked an eyebrow.

"Uh, can I ask the queen something really quick?" I asked. "My weapon used to be part of my Bond Crest, but Emily put it into my wristband."

Jordan looked like she only understood half of what I said. "Fine. But when you come back, you have a lot of explaining to do."

"Thank you." I hurried out of the room to talk to Emily. "Hey, uh, does my Snapdragon Crest still have the sword in it?"

Emily's eyebrows furrowed. "I think so. I didn't take that into consideration when I made your wristband, so…"

I frowned at the wristband, thinking. I turned it over until my Snapdragon Crest was visible, then brushed my thumb over it. Instantly, my sword appeared in my hand.

Emily's eyes lit up in delight. "Yes! It still works!"

I smiled. "Great! Thanks, Emily!"

I rushed back to Jordan, quickly explaining what happened the past year before showing her Snapdragon.

Jordan's eyes widened and took the sword

with both hands. "Wow. I'm supposed to teach a girl who's a Bond, friends with the queen, and to top it all off, saved everyone?!" She sighed and handed me back the sword. "I see I have my work cut out for me."

I blinked nervously. Did this mean she didn't want to teach me?

She looked up and smiled. Really smiled. "Let's get started!"

I grinned. "Okay!"

"Whew. I'm beat." I plopped down on the bench and dropped my head on the table. "We're going to do this everyday?"

Galen sank down next to me. "Ugh.... I can't even go get lunch!"

Even Elece looked tired! She staggered into the gym-like cafeteria and collapsed against our table. "Mm...." she groaned.

Derrik bounced inside happily, shaking the table as he crashed into the bench. "Ow!"

I barely had energy to laugh. "Whoa. What's gotten into you?"

Derrik sat up, rubbing his head. "Training was so fun!" he hollered. He scrambled up to his seat and started chattering about how fun Glenn turned out to be. "He's like a pillow that's trying to become a rock!"

Butlers and maids came by, holding enormous platters of food. They set it down in front of us, opening the lids with flourishes. The dishes had really complicated names, but all I saw were battery chargers.

I gobbled down salmon, rice, asparagus, and some kind of salad that looked like pasta. When I was done, not even half of the food had been eaten yet!

I sighed contentedly and rested my head on the table again. A maid's voice - I recognized it as Lily - trilled at me with concern. "Do you have indigestion?"

I looked up and smiled at her reassuringly. "Don't worry. The food was delicious!"

She looked relieved. "My cousin will be happy to hear that."

"Oh! Your cousin is the chef?"

Lily nodded modestly. "She always wanted to be one. When she became the head chef for the queen's kitchen, she nearly fainted!"

I laughed. "She sounds like a nice person! You're lucky to have someone like her in your family!"

Lily blushed. "Thank you, ma'am."

I made a face. "You don't need to call me that. Just call me Rina."

"Mm hm!" Galen mumbled around a mouthful of ice cream. "Uff too!"

Elece gave her a small smile. "Anytime you need us!"

"Yeah!" Derrik said cheerfully. "You seemed to be good friends with Emily!"

As the rest of the gang chatted amiably with Lily, I felt a strange tug in my midsection. It almost made me vomit. I clutched at my stomach, squeezing my eyes shut.

"Rina?" Lily turned to me again, alarm lighting her face. "Are you okay?"

I gasped for air, gripping the table. "Yeah. I'm fine. It's just -" I clamped my mouth closed as another wave hit me. I convulsed slightly. "It's not the food," I told them. "I know it's not."

"Are you sure?" Galen's eyes never left me. He even stopped chewing. He eyed me suspiciously. "Were you the one who ate my chicken? Karma is taking its toll!"

"No!" I gasped. I gritted my teeth. "It's something else. Like... like I have a string connecting my gut to something and the other end is being pulled, like...."

Every muscle of my body froze. When the tug came again, I vomited into my bowl, wiped my mouth, and staggered toward the cafeteria doors.

"Wait!" Lily cried anxiously. She rushed after me, catching me by my arm. "You're not feeling well! Are you allergic to something? I'll tell my cousin to watch out for -"

"It's okay, Lily." I told her again. I took her hand off my arm. "I'm fine. I'm not allergic to anything."

"Then what is it?" Elece walked over to me, the boys following behind, sneaking extra bites along the way.

I shook my head, anxious to get going. "Just tell Jordan that I can't be there! Tell Emily that it's urgent! She'll understand!"

"But what about us?" Derrik hollered after me as I tore for the door again. "Are you going to come back?"

"Maybe!" I called over my shoulder. "I'll explain it later! Bye!"

I burst through the doors, raced for the Fire Tunnel, and dove through.

I'm coming, Zin!

Chapter 7

I didn't stop running until I slammed open the front door to my house. I stared straight ahead at the plant by the window and my heart sank. "NO!"

Mom had her hands clapped around something by the kitchen counter, and Mira was gazing eagerly at her hands. They both turned around, startled at my entrance. "Rina! Come look!" Mom jerked her head toward the kitchen excitedly. She seemed to have forgotten I was supposed to be training. "Look what I found!"

I was there in the blink of an eye. "What?" I demanded.

Mom's hands tightened a bit as she slid her fingers in between her palms to pick up whatever was inside. She held up Zin by the back of her shirt, not noticing how terrified Zin was. "A pixie!" Mom's eyes shone. "I, Fia 'Flare' Flameton, caught a pixie!"

Everything around me faded until it was just me, Mom, and Zin dangling from her fingers. No....

"A.... pixie...." I swallowed, my saliva doing nothing to soothe my dry throat. "Wha...."

"Mira asked me for a pixie out of the blue," Mom explained. "I was just in the middle of telling her that there were no such creatures anymore, when this one flew by my face!" Mom chuckled. "It's a lively one, this is. Took me a good half hour to catch her."

It was then I noticed the mess around the house. The furniture had been overturned, shoes were littered all over the floor, and the potted plant lay crushed between pieces of clay.

"Mira..." I whirled on my sister. "You told!"

Mira blinked at me innocently. "What do you mean? I like fairy tales, and wanted a pixie as a pet!"

"You monster!" I snarled. "You're way too old for fairy tales!" Before Mom could move, I lunged for Zin. "Give me back my pixie!"

Mom was a second too fast. She jerked backward, my fingers missing Zin's reaching hands by a hair's breadth. "Your pixie?" Mom shook her head. "No, I'm giving this to Mira. She asked for it first."

Mira smirked. I felt tears prick at my eyes. "How'd you know?" I demanded her.

"Know what?"

I couldn't take it anymore. I curled my fingers around her shoulders, staring her full in the face.

"Rina!" Mom shouted, astonished.

"Stop playing dumb!" I shouted at her. "How'd you know that she was a pixie?"

Mira's face was stone. She reached down and picked up a book by her feet. She waved it in front of my face. "Look familiar?"

My eyes locked on the dark blue cover.

"Did you really think it was a book on fairy care?" Mira sneered. "People don't keep fairies as pets." She shoved the book in my face. "It's a book all about pixies."

My body went numb and I released my sister. I stared at the book in disbelief. "No…."

Mom slapped the back of my head angrily. "What do you think you're doing, attacking your sister like that!"

I lunged for Zin again, my heart breaking as Mom pulled her out of my reach once again.

"Rina!" Zin wailed.

"Let her go!" I yelled. "She's mine! We're

81

Links!"

"What?" Mom stared at me in astonishment. "Links? Really? How come you never told us?"

"You can't figure it out?" I shouted again, my tears blurring my vision. "This is exactly why!"

Mom actually looked a bit hurt. Just the tiniest bit. "You couldn't trust us?"

"I was starting to! That's why I chose to live at home instead of at the castle!" I swiped a hand across my face. "You ruined it."

"Rina! -" Zin's voice was cut off by Mira's.

"Done!" my sister crowed. She held up her hands, which were closed around something. "Thanks, Mom!"

Mom's sad look disappeared with a look of delight. "So it's yours?"

Hers?! "What?! NO!" I shrieked.

Mira smirked. "Oh, yeah!" She released her hands, releasing a dark-blue pixie. "Hey, girl! What's your name?"

The pixie had blue hair so dark, it looked like black. It was tied up into a huge ponytail that flowed down past her feet. She wore a black dress with dark blue boots and gloves. Her dark blue eyes glittered strangely, her face void of any expression. She wore a hair clip with a strange black swirl. But the scariest thing was, she had the exact same face as Zin. "I'm Midnight," she said. "Nice to meet you."

Her voice was faint and shadowy, the complete opposite of Zin's light, flutey voice.

My eyes twitched. I took a tentative step forward. "That.... That's not Zin," I said finally. "That's not my pixie."

Mira laughed. "It is, and it isn't. I forced a connection with her. She's mine, now!"

I shook my head, unable to believe it. "No. Zinnia!"

Midnight turned her strange eyes on me. "Zinnia?" she sneered. "I'm sorry, but you've got the wrong girl. Do I need to repeat my name again?"

Her voice sent strange chills down my back.

Mira flipped her long ponytail behind her shoulder and spoke, "So, what can you do?"

Midnight held up her arm and flicked her wrist. Immediately, all the shadows in the room swam towards her, a huge fountain behind the tiny pixie. "This," she replied. "And this." She pointed at the tree outside the window, and immediately, it shriveled.

I backed up fearfully. "You -" I blinked. I opened my mouth and tried to speak, but nothing came out. It was as if my voice had been

83

sucked away.

"That too," Midnight said, her face still expressionless. "Silence is my best friend. You talk too much."

Mira's eyes shone. "You're just my ideal type of girl! Let's go! I can't wait to show you to him!" She raced for the door, Midnight hovering behind her.

I screamed, desperate, and my voice came back. "Wait! Where're you going?"

Mira glanced back, eyes glittering smugly. "Curious? I asked Callan to meet me after school by the campus park. I'm finally going to get him to like me better than you!" With that, she disappeared through the door.

I screamed again, this time, in pain and frustration. I whirled on my mom, who looked shocked. "That's it!" I screeched. "I'm going to live at the palace!"

I raced out the door after my sister.

I've never been more grateful to have Water as my Talent. It carried me through the air faster than I could ever run, so I was able to catch up with my sister until I was only a few pace behind her.

"Stop!" I yelled.

"Jealous?" she laughed in reply. "Don't be. Just go home!" She ran on, faster.

My lungs were already burning, and my legs were turning into jelly. I tore on anyway. I could rest later. Unfortunately, my body decided to slow down anyway.

We dove through the Fire Tunnel and reached the school campus. I spotted Callan checking his watch under the tree. Apple Tree. The one I'd stayed in after I was kicked out last year.

He glanced up at our approaching footsteps. He looked annoyed. "What is it, Mira? I have to go somewhere after this, and - Rina?"

Mira plopped herself right in front of Callan, blocking me from his view. I collapsed on the sandy path, wheezing and gasping for breath. My sweat and tears drew dark dots on the ground.

It was strange. I wasn't sobbing full on; my tears just seem to be flowing numbly, like a river on ice or something. My eyes felt dry, but I could feel wet drops rolling down my cheeks.

"Look, Callan! Look!" Mira was gasping too, but her excitement overrode it. She beckoned to the air above her and Midnight flew down. "I've got my own pixie!"

No. I can't let Callan think that she formed a Link naturally on her own. I staggered to my feet, tottering to the side, trying to get closer to Callan. I fell back onto the floor again, tears flowing. My legs hadn't recovered yet.

How can I tell him? I was too tired to speak, and even if I could, Midnight would probably take my voice again. All I could do now was watch.

Callan blinked in surprise, dropping his binder. He shrugged off his backpack and propped it against the tree, then picked up his binder and leaned it against his bag, eyes still on Midnight. "A... pixie?"

"Surprised, right?" Mira asked, smug. "Mom helped me catch her! I have my very own pixie!" She tossed her head. "I bet I'm the only one in the whole islands that has one, right?"

"Ah...." Callan paused. "Wait, caught her?" Mira nodded enthusiastically. I sighed, leaning on my arms before straightening back to my hands-and-knees resting position again. It would look like I was bowing to my sister.

"Yeah, she was flying around our house after school. It was perfect because I was thinking about finding one!"

"Your house? Wait, isn't this..." He pointed a

finger at Midnight before glancing over at me. "Isn't she - Rina!"

Callan stepped over to me and crouched down. "Wow, you look terrible. Did you really run that far?" In a quieter voice, he asked, "Is that...."

I tried to swallow and nodded, drying my tears on my sleeves. I gave him a pleading look. "Please," I whispered. "You gotta help me catch her! I need to take her back to Queen Amaryllis so she can fix her!"

Callan looked uncertain. "But what if I hurt her?"

I squeezed my eyes shut before opening them again. "I know you won't," I told him. "If you can knock her out for a little bit, that'll be good. Where's Hunter?"

Callan nodded down toward his pocket, his eyes flickering with understanding. He quickly whispered something to his pocket just as Mira called out, annoyed. "Oh, her? Rina looked a bit jealous, so I let her follow me. She seemed to really like this pixie." She tapped her foot impatiently. "Are you done yet?"

Callan stood up, and I could see the fury in his eyes. His voice stayed calm, though, when he said, "Did you think I would be impressed?"

Mira blinked. "Huh?"

Callan turned to look at her, and Mira took a small step backward. "You forced a Link with your sister's pixie! How could you?!"

Mira's eyes hardened. "She told you, didn't she?" she hissed. "You're always on her side! Why do you always believe her story and not mine?"

Callan took a threatening step toward her again. "Because I know that Rina's telling the truth. I knew Zinnia before you discovered her. Rina trusts us completely."

Mira's jaw dropped slightly. "You-you knew? But how?" She frowned at him. "Come to think of it, when I told you guys about Rina's 'fairy', you guys acted a little bit strange." She turned her suspicious glare on Callan. "Do the others know too? Was I the only one that didn't know?"

Callan glanced toward me inquiringly. By now, most of my strength had recovered, so I staggered slowly to my feet. Callan started forward to help, but Mira grabbed his arm and I held up my hand to stop him.

"She can do it herself," Mira said tersely. "You haven't answered my question."

I sat down gingerly on the bench next to me and started rubbing my cramped legs. I met

Callan's eyes and gave a shrug. "Might as well tell her," I rasped. I cleared my throat and continued, "She already knows about Zin, so we should just tell her everything."

Callan grimaced. "Are you sure?"

Mira's eyes flared angrily. "Of course you should!" she shouted. "Don't keep secrets from me!"

Callan sighed reluctantly. "Fine. Where's Midnight? I need her to help me explain."

Midnight flew out from behind Mira's hair and hovered in front of Callan's face. Mira stared at him expectantly.

Callan didn't move for a second. I thought he was trying to figure out where to start when he suddenly shouted, "NOW!"

Hunter zoomed up from Callan's pocket, catching Mira and Midnight off-guard. The male pixie tackled Midnight, dealing a blow to the back of her head and disappeared back into Callan's pocket before Mira could get a good glimpse of him. Midnight was immediately knocked out cold and plummeted from the air like a stone. Mira gave a shout and tried to catch her, but Callan was faster. He snatched Midnight from the air, ran to me, and grabbed my hand. "Let's go!" he said. He pulled my hand as he ran toward the Royal Tunnel. I was half-running, half-being-dragged as we made our way toward the Tunnel.

"Stop!" Mira screeched. I glanced backward, my breath catching in my throat when I saw that she was only a few feet away. Her eyes glinted murderously, fixed on me. "What do you think you're doing?"

"I'm taking my pixie back!" I shouted at her.

"Your pixie?" Mira screamed. She lunged for me. "She's mine! I found her!"

"She was mine to begin with!" I screamed back at her. Callan leaped through the Royal Tunnel just as Mira's fingers grabbed the back of my shirt. When we landed on the grass, she immediately began scratching furiously at me.

"You're always taking things away from me!" she snarled. "First, my position, then my crush, then my reputation, and now this! You're always getting in the way of what I want!"

I cried out as she raked at my arms and my cheek. I held up my hands, trying to defend myself. Callan charged at Mira, full of rage, but I shouted, "No! Stop! Don't waste time! Tell Emily what happened!"

"NO!" Mira stopped attacking me for a second to lunge at Callan. "Don't tell the queen!"

A rock rose out of the ground just in front of Mira. She slammed into the rock with a cry and crumpled to the ground. By the time she got to her feet again, Callan was far away, running toward the castle.

Mira glowered at me. "ARGH!" Pulling out her fist, she punched the air in front of me and a fireball the size of my head hurtled straight for me. I barely managed to shield myself with water just in time. "You're still in the way!" she shouted. "When are you just going to back off?"

"Back off?" I defended myself from another attack. "My whole life, I've been trying to become as good as you. As excellent as you. As loved as you. I've finally found my place in the world and now you want me to back off?!"

"YES!" Mira roared. I blinked at her in shock. This wasn't my sister. This couldn't be my sister. "I WANT TO BE THE ONLY ONE THAT STANDS OUT! NO ONE CAN TAKE MY PLACE!"

I screamed when the grass below me caught fire. I hurried to extinguish it, then focused my attention on my sister. A thick stream of water wrapped itself around her body, pinning her arms to her sides. I lifted her up in the air, watching her squirm.

"Sorry, Mira," I said. "This is the only way we can talk safely."

She just snarled at me, her face distorted with rage. "YOU USELESS BRAT! How could you activate such a useless Talent?"

I gazed at her sadly. "I finally managed to learn how to live with my Talent. How to use it. Now, I need it to protect myself from you."

Mira let out a horrendous scream of fury. "Why you? Why do you have to be the one that takes everything? That gets all the attention?"

I blinked at her, struggling to keep my own anger under control. "I took everything? I finally made nine friends, and you're trying to take them away from me, even though you have millions! You took my pixie," my voice cracked. "An endangered species - you took Zin! And for what? Just to impress a guy!"

Mira glared at me, full of hatred. "I was trying to take Callan back. You became the most loved, most adored, most popular person in the Terrene Islands. You and your pathetic circle of friends. You used to be anti-social. I bet you didn't even know who Callan was before you had to save him!"

"I didn't know him," I told her through clenched teeth. "But why does that matter now?"

"Because I knew him and you didn't!" she hollered. "I knew him longer than you did, but you're the one that got close to him! Him and Kodiak! The most popular guys at school! She twisted herself, trying to get free. "If Callan didn't like me, I would have tried for Kodiak. But you became friends with both! LET ME GO!"

I smirked. "Water quenches fire. You're stuck, sister."

"Sister?" Mira spat. "You're not my sister. Who would want to be related to you?"

That comment was a knife through my heart. I flinched and the water tube lost its hold. Mira landed on her feet and charged toward me, arms ablaze with fire. With a battle cry, she jumped, her arms slamming down towards me.

Chapter 8

"RINA!"

Sharp shards of ice the size of my fist smashed into Mira. She grunted and toppled to the side, her burning hand missing by inches. I jumped away from the flaming grass next to me, my sister already scrambling to stand up.

Someone spun me around and I found myself staring at Kodiak's face. "She didn't get you, did she?" he asked, frantically checking me for burns.

"N-no." I stared at him, stunned. "You were here?"

"We all are." Sirocca rushed forward, embracing me. "Are you okay?" She pulled back to study my face.

Thora ran up to me and tapped my arm. "We brought Zin to Queen Amaryllis already."

"You did? What did she say?" I asked

frantically.

Galen shook his head. "She wouldn't tell us. She said that everyone had to be there before she could say anything."

I bit my lip worriedly. Was Amaryllis mad at us? Was Zin's condition unchangeable?

Elece stalked over, staring over my shoulder in disgust. "It's a good thing we got here in time," she scoffed. "You were about to get roasted like Thanksgiving turkey! Why did you hesitate?"

I ducked my head. "She said I wasn't her sister," I mumbled, my eyes filling with traitorous tears. "She disowned me," I said softly.

Elece growled. "Don't worry about her," she barked. Pointing an intimidating finger at my face, she said, "She's not a sister, either. It's good that she did that, actually. It would be detrimental to your well-being if she went on like that. THE FUTURE LOOKS BRIGHT!"

I blinked. Why was Elece acting so weird? "What?"

Thora pulled me down to whisper in my ear. "Just go with it. Elece gets very prickly when people aren't being good siblings."

"Oh. Okay."

Kodiak patted my head. "Don't cry."

I glared at him. "I wasn't crying."

Sirocca laughed. "Leave her alone, Torrent."

Kodiak frowned, then drew his hand back. "Fine."

Callan walked up to us, brushing off his hands satisfactorily. "There. Done. What should we do with her?"

I spun around to see what he did. A big stone block answered my question. "You trapped her in a rock box?"

Callan nodded. "Stones don't burn, right? She's not strong enough to push those over, anyways. If she did, they'd topple right on top of her, so she's trapped. Good riddance! Don't worry, she has no light in there right now."

I scratched the back of my head, troubled. Callan turned, noticing me. "What's wrong?"

I tilted my head. "Nothing. I don't know."

"You know, she doesn't deserve the title of 'sister'," Callan said. He looked at the box like it was a piece of poop. "I DIDN'T KNOW YOU BEFORE I GOT CAUGHT EITHER, YOU KNOW?!" he hollered. "DON'T TALK ABOUT ME LIKE I'M YOUR BEST FRIEND!"

Callan turned back to the group, sighing. "There. Got that settled. Man, she's annoying!"

"WHERE IS SHE?!" a voice bellowed.

Everyone turned and our jaws dropped in shock as Emily thundered over to the stone block. With a single punch, the rocks disintegrate into dust finer than sand.

Callan turned white. "Whoa. Don't ever get on her bad side. Those rocks had quartz in them!"

Emily stared down at Mira, eyes burning with anger, body alight. Mira glanced up, her own body still flaming, but when she saw the queen, the fire disappeared and Mira turned white. She licked her lips and attempted to smile. "H-hey, Emily!"

"Did I give you permission to address me by my name?" Emily asked coldly. "I thought the rule was that everyone needs to address the queen by her given name unless told otherwise."

Mira swallowed. "Sorry."

Emily's eyes were chips of black ice. She held out a hand, and Mira stared at it before tentatively taking it. "Thank you."

"I'm not trying to help you," Emily said harshly. She dropped Mira's hand and held out her palm again. "Give me your wristband."
Mira looked on the verge of tears. "What?"

Emily's expression didn't change. She barely blinked. "Your wristband will be destroyed. You have lost the privilege of accessing the Royal Tunnel by will."

Mira swallowed again. "My parents will kill me," she whispered.

Emily was unrelenting. "You should have thought of that before you acted. Wristband."

Mira slowly slipped off the white wristband, placing it in Emily's hand. Emily curled her fingers around it, crushing it in bits of light. When she opened it again, Mira's Crest was in her hand.

Emily tossed the pin to Mira. "There will be a black mark on your record," Emily said. "You have violated the queen's trust and assaulted a person. A tribemate and a family member at that. Originally, this would have put you in jail for half of your life." Mira trembled, and Emily continued. "However, I choose to be merciful. You will be stripped of your position in the Fire Army and will not be able to return. You must find another occupation."

Whoa. Emily was hard-core. It made me feel uneasy.

"Wh-what about my parents?" Mira whispered, tears streaming down her face. "Would they be in trouble? It's not their fault, you know?"

"Did they assist you in poaching an endangered species?" Emily asked dangerously.

Mira started to shake really hard. She buried her face in her hands and started to sob. I felt a twinge in my heart. It hurt me to see my defiant, proud sister reduced to this. I started to walk towards Mira. As I got closer, she shot me the most hateful, murderous look I've ever seen in my entire life. It withered any sort of compassion I had for her, and I backed off.

"Your parents will be taken out of the Council. I already have two Fire Tribe replacements in mind."

"Queen, please…"

"I am already showing you mercy. You are free to live back in your tribe. Isn't that good enough? Do you wish to spend your entire life in prison?"

Mira shuddered. "No, no. I appreciate your grace. But, I have one more question."

"Speak."

"Will there be a way to… to redeem myself? To earn your trust again?" she added quietly.

Emily stared coldly down at Mira. "It depends. I can't guarantee it will happen, but nothing is impossible."

Mira looked up hopefully, but Emily had

already turned away. "Leave now. I will be sending a notice to your home later tonight."

Mira stood up on shaky legs, then ran as fast as she could toward the Fire Tunnel. With one last look behind her before she left, she gave me that dangerous glare again.

"I hate you," she hissed. "I'll never forgive you."

With that, she disappeared into the tunnel.

Chapter 9

Emily immediately turned around and stormed back to the palace. "COME ON GUYS!" she snarled. "WE NEED TO GO CHECK ON ZINNIA!"

The rest of us followed timidly behind her. I was feeling pretty shaken. Nobody wants to see their sister humiliated like that. I was having mixed emotions about the whole thing.

I hate you!

I'll never forgive you.

I shuddered. Ever since we were young, Mira and I have been taught to never use the word hate to describe something we don't like. It was too strong of a word, and was actually cursing something whenever it was used. It was even worse if we were talking about a person. So ever since we were able to speak, neither Mira nor I have ever used the word "hate".

Until now.

I rubbed my head hard. It was bothering me. I couldn't let it bother me now. I had to check to see if Zinnia was okay. If there was anything to fix her.

I sprinted to the head of the group where Emily was. I didn't say anything to her for a while.

"Are you okay?" Emily asked suddenly.

"Huh? Oh, yeah, why wouldn't I be?"

"You're not fooling anyone you know?" Emily said quietly. "I know how much you still love your sister, even if she doesn't. What I said back there, I'm sorry."

I scoffed. "For what? You did what you had to do. I don't blame you. Part of me is happy you did what you did."

Emily tensed. "Really? You're not mad?"

I shook my head. "Of course not. I'm just disappointed she acted the way she did. And what she said." I sighed, shook myself, brushing off the rest of the negative thoughts about my sister and asked, "Can we pick up the pace? I'm anxious to hear what Amaryllis is going to tell us!"

We ran the rest of the way to the castle and

didn't stop until we burst through the glass doors into the Onyx Garden. We hurried over to the beach by the Crystal Sea and almost crushed Pixie Town in our haste.

"Queen Amaryllis!" I cried, the churning feeling in my stomach making me want to vomit. "Did anything happen?"

"You guys are late!" The pixie queen's normally cheerful voice was sharper than a knife. It cut deeper, too. "Even if you are giants, you shouldn't have taken so long!"

"Sorry," I mumbled. "We got held back by my sister."

Amaryllis waved her hand. "Later. Come look at what has befallen your pixie."

Everyone turned to look at the little figure at the center of the square. A multitude of rainbow-colored pixies formed a circle around the little black figure lying on the ground.

I started to shake uncontrollably. I squeezed my eyes shut, blinked them open, and squeezed them again. The air was thinning; I had to get out of here.

Kodiak's hands gripped my shoulders. "Get a hold of yourself," he whispered firmly. "You'll get out of this. It's going to be okay."

He kept his hands on my shoulders and

rubbed my back until I stopped shaking and took deep breaths. "There you go," he murmured soothingly.

I forced my eyes open and turned to the queen. "Sorry, Your Highness. I just have a few questions."

Amaryllis shook her head. "It's not a problem at all. It's totally understandable to see you distressed over your Link. Fire away."

"Didn't you say Links were for life? Why would Zin suddenly become Mira's pixie? What exactly happened? Why is she the total opposite of what she was before?"

Amaryllis waited until all my questions were spilled before answering, "Links, indeed, are for life. But unlike your Bond, it can be broken, especially if the Link is weak for a certain period of time. If something interferes with your connection, then...." The queen let her gaze drift toward the unconscious Midnight. "Giants have a way of forcing a Link. There is a certain phrase they say that forces pixies into Linkhood. The phrase has been lost, but apparently, there are other methods. When a Link is forced, a pixie becomes the polar opposite of who they originally were.

"As for your Link, it must have frayed a little

bit. Beginning Links are usually very strong, so something must have thinned it."

I frowned. "Zin mentioned that she was homesick. The morning before Mira... um, she was looking very, very sick. Electra explained that it was because pixies sense emotions stronger than humans do."

Amaryllis nodded. "Yes. That must be it. Unfortunately, your sister chose the perfect time to pounce."

"Is... is there a way to undo it?" I was pretty sure my stare bore holes into Amaryllis's brain as I wished for her to say yes.

Amaryllis gave me a slow nod. "Yes, there is. It's very difficult, and you might not pass, but yes, there is a way to get Zinnia Allegra back."

Our whole group pushed forward. "Tell us!" we demanded.

Amaryllis bit her lip. "Hold on a second. I need to consult the councillor over in Silver Birch," she said and rushed off into her castle.

"Silver Birch?" Sirocca asked.

"It's one of the other pixie settlements," Scorch explained. "There are twenty six settlements in the Onyx Garden. Twenty six settlements of surviving pixies."

"Oh. I thought it was just Pixie Town here," I

said.

"'Pixie Town'?" Scorch let out an insulted snort. "No! We're the Arrowwood settlement. It's the capital town, you could say, since the queen lives here. She has twenty five councillors."

"Oh, that's cool! There are more of you!" Derrik leaned in, interested.

Sirocca's pixie grinned. "Of course. Did you really think that the pixies had been reduced to a handful?"

"From what I'd seen Mira do, I wouldn't be so doubtful," I said quietly. "It could happen pretty fast."

Everyone was silent after that. No one moved until Amaryllis came forward.

"Yes," she said, strained. "It's true. There is a way, even though it hasn't been used for hundreds of years."

We all leaned in. The pixies below leaned in also.

Amaryllis closed her eyes mournfully. When she spoke, her voice was shaky. "You must complete the Cinnabar Trial if you want Zinnia Allegra back."

"Cinnabar Trial?" I repeated. "Why do you look so terrified? Is it that bad?"

Maple flew up to the queen shakily. "The

106

Cinnabar Trial is a myth. I didn't know it was real."

Amaryllis gave Maple a small smile. "Every legend has an element of truth to it, you know?"

"What is the Cinnabar Trial?" I asked.

Stratus flew to me. "From what I was told, the Links are locked in a room and fight each other to the death." He looked at his queen.

"The.... death?" I gulped.

"DEATH?!" everyone else shouted.

The pixie queen sighed as if she was defeated. "Yes. In a nutshell, that's what happens. You're supposed to kill your turned pixie or your pixie kills you."

My hands started shaking. "But... if I kill Zin, or if Zin kills me.....there'd be no Link. What's the point?"

Amaryllis gazed sadly at me. "The point is to destroy the infected Link so there's a chance you may form a new one. Zinnia Allegra will be free if she kills you successfully."

The world tilted sideways. I felt Galen catching me as I struggled to breathe. "So... you're saying that there's no cure anyways, so just destroy the Link and forget about it?"

Amaryllis frowned. "It sounds inhumane if you put it that way."

107

I shut my eyes, trying to control my breathing. I had to choose. Kill Zin, or let her stay corrupted. I couldn't do that to her, but I couldn't kill her either. There had to be another way. A plan started to form in my mind.

"I'll do it," I said.

Chapter 10

"**W**HAT?!" My friends were immediately on top of me, scrabbling to have a say.

"ARE YOU OUT OF YOUR MIND?!"

"You're crazy!"

I didn't look at them when I said flatly, "It's my pixie. I decide what happens."

After that, everyone backed off, but they still looked worried.

I turned to Amaryllis. "When do I start?"

She looked at me with concerned eyes. "Are you sure you want to do this?"

I nodded, forcing my hands not to tremble. "I'll do anything. This happened because of me, so I need to fix it."

Amaryllis bit her lip. "I guess we could do it now. We need to move this pixie before she wakes up. It'll be harder then."

She started to fly toward the glass doors of the viewing room. "Follow me. Hunter, Blizzard, bring the pixie." Amaryllis turned to me. "What'd she call herself?"

"She said her name was Midnight."

Amaryllis nodded. "Of course. That's typical."

Everyone followed the queen out of the garden. Hunter and Blizzard picked up Midnight between them. The whole town of Arrowwood followed us.

"Why are we going there?" I asked when I noticed we were walking into the viewing room to the garden. "Are we... fighting... in there?"

Amaryllis shook her head. "No, but there are controls there that will enable me to create a safe room for you to duel. Emily, please call the queen and notify her of this event. The other twenty five settlements will be here shortly. I have already sent messengers."

I gulped. "Everyone is watching?"

Amaryllis nodded. "Of course. It's tradition. And also because we need many people in case something goes wrong."

In case something goes.... You know what? Whatever. I've worried myself way too much. The less I knew, the better.

The queen swept into the viewing room. "Emily alerted me," she said breathlessly. "What can I do?"

Amaryllis didn't look up from the controls. "I'm setting up the room. Can you make sure I'm doing it correctly?"

I sat by the wall and prepared myself. What I was planning to do was the riskiest thing I'll ever do in my life. There was a ninety-nine point nine percent chance it'll fail. To be honest, I'm going in with nothing but my life to lose. But if I lose it, at least I tried. At least with my death, Zin would be free and I wouldn't be there to put her in danger again.

Callan, Kodiak, Galen, Elece, Derrik, and Sirocca came to sit by me. "Hey. You okay?"

"Yeah. Just… need some time to think."

Callan frowned. "You shouldn't have gone with that."

I knew. Everyone's been telling me that for the past ten minutes. Galen turned a stink eye on him.

"Hey, if you don't mind, the three of us need to talk to Rina. Alone."

"Three?" Kodiak questioned.

Galen nodded. "Me, Elece, and Derrik. The closest team in the world."

"Gee, thanks." Kodiak stood up with Callan, but gave us a small smile to show that he understood. "See you later."

Callan left, muttering angrily under his breath about "that pebble-hearted bug" and "may his winds crush him in the end".

Wow.

"Thanks, Galen," I mumbled. In reality, I wanted to be completely alone. But knowing who Galen, Derrik, and Elece were, that was just wishful thinking. "How'd you know I wanted them to go?"

"Do you really have to ask?" Galen gave me a forced smile. "We're Bonds. We're Snapdragon, and we always will be."

I gave him a smile - a real smile. "Thanks, dude."

Elece stared at me. "You better make it out alive, Rina. Or else we're going to barge inside for you."

I laughed shortly. "Of course you will."

"Rina, please be safe," Derrik said anxiously. "We're all worried for you."

I smiled. "We're Ties," I said simply. "You're the best friends in the world."

After a short hug, Amaryllis and Universa came over. "It's ready," Amaryllis said. She pointed to the next wall, where a door had appeared. "There's another floor where we'll be watching," the pixie queen said. "You'll be safe there, and pixies would still be able to fly down quickly from the windows if needed."

"Do your best," Universa said gravely. "There's nothing more to say."

I nodded. "There isn't."

"We must hurry," Amaryllis said. "Before Midnight wakes up."

"We've already put her into the arena," Hunter said, flying up. "She's in a cage, still unconscious. Queen, should I go and explain the situation to her?"

Amaryllis nodded. "Please."

Hunter flew off. I curled my hands into fists. "Well, here goes nothing."

I stepped through the door, forcing myself not to look back. Everyone else walked up a hidden stairway as I stood in the center of the arena. It was a huge space, completely made of glossed wood. I looked up. The perimeter of the upper walls were all glass. I kept watching until familiar faces started to appear behind the windows. Everyone flashed me worried smiles. I didn't smile back.

"Well, well, well. It's you again."

I turned to the voice. Midnight.

She was trapped in a steel cage, glaring at me dangerously even though she had been unconscious just moments before. Her lips curled into a chilling smile. "Looks like it's just you and me."

I gave a single nod. "Looks like it is."

"Don't be too scared when I take you down," she taunted. "Giants always have been weak."

I swallowed; my throat was dry. "Same for you."

The pixie bared her teeth. "We'll see."

Amaryllis's voice echoed throughout the arena. "On the count of three, Midnight will be released, and you can start fighting. We wish luck to the both of you. There are no rules.

"One…."

I locked eyes with Midnight.

"Two…."

The dark pixie sneered at me, ready to spring out the second the cage door opened.

"Three!"

I stood there, unmoving while Midnight burst out of her cage.

The Cinnabar Trial had begun.

Chapter 11

I opened my mouth to speak. As I expected, nothing came out. I had been silenced.

The rest of the room turned dark. "Aw, afraid of the dark, girl?" I heard Midnight's jeering voice over to my right. I turned in that direction, even if I couldn't see anything.

"You must be thinking of my sister," I said coolly, my voice returned. "She's afraid of the dark, not me."

"Ah, ah, ah!" Midnight trilled. "She's not afraid of the dark. YOU are. Or are you too cowardly to admit it?"

"Cowardly?" I spat, spinning in a slow circle, trying to follow the sound of her voice. "Says the one who needs to hide behind darkness to fight."

Midnight snarled. "Don't challenge the darkness, girl. You should not be afraid of the dark, but you should to be terrified by what's in it."

With a strange roar, something barreled into my stomach. I gasped in surprise and pain. Turns out, Midnight head-butted me.

"Hey," I coughed. "If you're so great, why aren't you just killing me immediately? I saw what you did at my house. I saw what you did to the tree."

"Tsh. Everything your sister said was true. She's much brighter than you are.

"For your information, giants are too big. It's too much work to take their life force immediately like I can do with plants. Don't think that's a weakness. In fact, I'm prepared to make you suffer slowly instead of dying right away."

No, not yet. I needed light to see.

I lashed out blindly, pushing the water to find the pixie. When I heard a strangled gulp, I trapped her in a bubble. I hoped I had aimed correctly.

"Now, I can easily drown you right here. Coward," I spat. She was not my pixie. She was not Zinnia Allegra. She was not the pink-haired, sassy pixie that I knew.

She was a monster.

"Dismiss the shadows and fight me face-to-face," I commanded. I was going to say more, but Midnight silenced me.

We stood there like that for a long time. I couldn't do anything but wait. She couldn't do anything but choose. What would it be?

In a flash, all the lights came on, blinding me. I backed away, rubbing my eyes and blinking, barely remembering to keep my hold on the corrupted pixie. When my vision recovered, I found my voice had been given back to me as well.

"Fight face-to-face like you said," Midnight said venomously. "Or is your honor so low that you'll kill me here trapped like an animal in front of the world?"

The bubble was filled with so much darkness, I couldn't see anything inside. The shadows swirled and billowed, blocking any source of light.

"Do you even have any honor at all?" I said. I steeled myself for what I had planned next. Glancing up once, I saw the faces of my dearest friends. Callan. Kodiak. Thora. Sirocca. Queen Amaryllis. Universa. Emily. Andy, if he were here. Derrik. Elece.

Galen.

All of them were looking worriedly at me.

117

Their faces were pressed against the glass, their handprints smearing the windows.

I just gave them a sad smile. Then I popped the bubble.

In the same second, Midnight rushed at me with the speed of a thousand cheetahs. I made no move to stop her. I made no move to protect myself.

I focused on her flying form then caught her with my hands before she collided with me and held her tight.

"Hah! Dummy," I heard Midnight sneer. "You're so close, I can take your life force ten times faster. Your heart would be the ideal place, but no matter. Any last words?"

I shut my eyes tight, struggling to keep her in my hands. "Zinnia…" I whispered.

Midnight scoffed. "Weak giant. Zinnia Allegra is gone. Dead. I, Midnight, stand as a stronger being in her place."

A sudden jolt of pain shook me. I gasped and sank to my knees. I opened my eyes.

My hands were turning gray and wrinkled. I was withering away.

I struggled to breathe. "Z-Zin…."

"FIERINA TSUNAMI FLAMETON IS NO MORE!" Midnight let out a hysterical cackle.

"GOODBYE!"

I shivered violently. Apparently, death was cold. "Z-Zin-n-nia…." I kept my eyes closed.

I could faintly hear someone pounding on glass. There were footsteps all over the place, the noises thundering, threatening to break my eardrums. Oddly, I briefly wondered how decayed I looked.

The pulsing energy in my hands grew hotter and hotter as I grew colder and colder. I shivered, not realizing I had toppled over until my right side hit the floor. It got to the point where I was cold as ice, yet my hands were burning like the sun.

Faintly, somewhere, I heard my name being called, but I was sucked too far into the cold dark to be sure.

Then, finally, the pulsing in my hands stopped, freezing my heart.

Am I dead now? I wondered.

I felt something on the back of my neck, and I dared to open my eyes. Just the mere act of lifting my eyelids exhausted me.

My vision was too blurry for me to see, but I caught a glimpse of a dark-haired boy. "G-Galen?" I moaned hoarsely. "Or are you Kodiak? Callan?"

The voice was familiar, but didn't register in my ears. I closed my eyes. "At least I know you're one of my friends," I murmured.

All thoughts became jumbled in my brain. Memories of reality became fused with the illusions of dreams. I didn't know where I was anymore. I didn't know who I was anymore.

But one thought was clear. One image.

Zinnia Allegra. My pixie.

Was she okay? Was I still holding her? Was she back?

I felt my lips whisper her name, but no sound came out. I felt hot air blast me and inside, I reached for it.

But it never reached me.

Even half-dead, a frightening thought struck me.

Was I to be stuck here forever?

A faint whisper, a faint voice echoed through my brain. Slowly, I tried to grasp it, search for it. Nothing seemed clear.

Rina?

It was barely there, quieter than a mouse's whisper, but I heard it. I started to run desperately toward the voice.

Rina?

It was familiar, but I couldn't remember,

couldn't speak.

Rina, please! Answer!

The voice was growing louder. I started running harder. For my life. For my lost memories.

For Zin.

Rina!!

I found the voice. It was on the other side of a huge chasm. An abyss I couldn't cross. I searched around, feeling hopeless, but I couldn't do anything. Everything was dark. Everything was cold. I couldn't see. I tried to yell out, but my voice had been silenced. Murdered.

Still. I had to find a way across. I had to find the voice that would bring me back.

I ran along the edge of the precipice, struggling to find a way across. The voice on the other side was fading. Giving up.

NO!

The ground started to shake and split, creating yawning cracks in the earth.

NO! I was not going to give up this way. As long as the voice was still there, I had to keep going.

I found something. A thread. A spider web that stretched across the chasm and connected me to the other side. One wrong step and I die. One wrong step and I vanish from the face of the earth.

The voice across the chasm sounded sorrowful, fainter. No, I couldn't let it get away! I couldn't let it disappear!

I threw myself onto the thread. It almost snapped beneath my weight, but I didn't care. I had to get to the other side.

Slowly, slowly, I inched my way across. I had no choice but to look down, to look down at my conseequences if I didn't succeed. I listened to the voice; it was my anchor.

The crawl across the thread took five years. It may have been three seconds, but time is irrelevant in this place. I did not let myself rest. I ran toward the voice, energy slowly filling my being.

I found my sight. I found my voice. Best of all, I found myself.

The voice called out again, softly, as if for the last time. All the sorrow and tears were formed into my name.

Rina...

I'm here! I called, desperate. *I'm here! Don't leave!*

Rina?

I'm here! Joy flooded me as I realized I

recognized the voice. *Galen! I'm here!*

Rina! RINA!!

I found the voice floating in the air as a white, wispy thing above the ground. I grasped it between my hands, keeping it safe between my fingers. My light in my dark world.

The voice carried me up, up, up. It passed many layers in the sky until I dared to open my eyes again.

The light blinded me at first, and I had to blink a few times for my eyes to adjust. When I finally could see, it took me another moment for my mind to register what was happening.

Strong arms were around my neck, holding me tightly. A bright pink pixie stood eye to eye with me.

"Well, you've always had a knack for taking unnecessary danger," Zin smiled.

Chapter 12

I swallowed a few times, struggling to get the words out. "Z-Zin....? Is that really you?"

Zin snorted. "Of course it's me!" She gave me a sad smile, her face pale. "I'm sorry I've been gone for so long,"

I started to sob freely. "I'm so sorry, Zin," I blubbered over and over again. "I'm so sorry!"

Zin flew over. It broke my heart to see her flight pattern crooked and irregular.

My pixie touched my face with her tiny hand. "It's okay, Rina," she whispered. "I'm fine. You saved me."

I shuddered, swallowing my tears. "I'm sorry."

Feeling returned to my body, and I realized the arms around my neck hadn't let go, and that the back of my neck was wet. I glanced down and recognized those arms. "Hey... Galen. Thanks for pulling me back."

The arms didn't move.

"Galen?"

I felt the back of my neck.

It was wet with red.

"GALEN!" I screamed. Or tried to. "GALEN!!!!"

Zinnia shushed me. "It's okay, Rina. It's going to be fine."

I wailed and sobbed and wailed some more. "Zin, G-Galen's..."

"Galen's fine," Zin said; her voice had never been more gentle. "Galen's totally fine."

"Then what's this?" I shoved my fingers at her. "What's this blood?"

A cough sounded behind me. My body felt like a thousand weights were strapped on, so the most I could do was turn my head slightly. "Galen?"

A shudder passed through the body behind me. There was no answer.

"Galen?" I asked, all hope leaving. "Galen, please. Don't leave me after you brought me back."

I was too weak to speak to his mind. With great effort, I placed a hand on the arm around my neck. "You're my best friend."

I sat like that for a bit longer, remembering the friend that had always been there for me. His laugh. His smile. The way his eyes sparkled whenever I tripped over myself.

I thought back to when I first met him:

I was in first grade. Even then, I was an outsider. Mira had quickly made friends and played on the playground while I stayed on the benches, wishing I could play with her.

Suddenly, a ball rolled by me. A dodgeball. My favorite game in the world.

I picked it up from the ground and looked up. A boy ran over, gesturing at me. He had thick, black hair and twinkling dark eyes. "Thank you!" he smiled. The first real smile anyone had given me. "It was rolling really fast! Good thing you were sitting here!"

His smile caused me to smile too. "Yeah!"

He took the ball from me. His cheek showed the slightest indentation of a dimple. Barely there, but still visible. "Do you want to play?"

I blinked. "Dodgeball?"

"I'll show you how to play! It's really fun! It's my favorite game in the WHOLE WIDE WORLD!"

I grinned. "Me too!"

I ran with him to the dodgeball area, laughing….

Afterwards, he always invited me to play dodgeball with him. We ended up becoming good friends. Galen always had so much energy, always happily bouncing whenever we played.

Now, he was a motionless body. I was a limp human being.

But right now, on the floor of the arena, we were able to stay in a sitting position. We leaned on each other. Without the other, we would be sprawled on the floor with no hope of getting up.

He was the other half of the Snapdragon Bond.

"Galen?"

Another shudder. I gripped the arm. Zinnia leaned on my head. "What happened with Galen?" I whispered.

Zinnia patted my hair. "He used up all his energy, calling you back. He even used some of his own life force to make sure you heard him."

"His life force?"

Zinnia pointed at the blood on my hands. "He dripped some of his blood on you so the connection would be stronger. He kept you close so you would hear his voice with more clarity. He really wanted to bring you back."

Enough energy had returned to my body for me to turn my head fully around. Galen's arms were wrapped around my neck. He was sitting with his right side pressed against my back, his head cradled between my shoulder blades. His legs were sprawled out beneath him.

"He's always been a good friend," I told Zinnia. I touched the scar on my arm where the bullet wound had been. "He's always been there for me."

A violent shudder passed through Galen. I gripped his arm, forcing myself to turn around. I held him up, willing him to wake up, banishing any fear I felt. "He'll be alright, wouldn't he?"

Zinnia nodded. "He just needs a LOT of rest. Exerting himself to that extent would exhaust anybody."

"It's possible to die from exhaustion, isn't it?" I had to get the question out.

Zinnia gave a reluctant nod. "Yes."

One more shudder passed through Galen. This time was even worse than the last. I peeled off my jacket and put it around his shoulder. It was weird, I know, but I couldn't stop the logic that Galen was feeling cold.

The shudder lasted for a few seconds, then abruptly stopped.

"Galen?" I dared to whisper. I could barely see him breathing. "Hold on. I'll come get you."

With immense pain, I pushed my voice into his head. I only had enough strength to call once.

Galen!

I gasped with pain, but smiled anyway. I had felt him. Galen was still there.

I shook his shoulders gently and his eyelids twitched. With a soft groan, he opened his eyes. "R-Rina?" he whispered.

I smiled so big, my lips threatened to break my face. "Thanks, buddy."

Galen sighed, a relieved sound. "You're alive."

"Of course I'm alive!"

"I was beginning to think you were gone. That I was too late."

"Thanks for bringing me back before I fell deeper, Galen."

Galen nodded and closed his eyes. "Your welcome, Grandma."

Grandma?!

Thundering footsteps echoed around the arena. I looked up and saw the arena doors explode open. Kodiak and Callan flew towards me.

"RINA!" they shouted.

"You're alive!" Kodiak rejoiced.

I swallowed to wet my dry throat and nodded

once. "I am."

"I was worried you wouldn't make it," Callan said softly. He looked haunted. "Why didn't you tell us you were going to do... that?"

I licked my lips. "You guys wouldn't have let me."

"True," Kodiak said. He didn't laugh.

I stared at them for a moment longer before frowning, "What's wrong?"

"What? What do you mean?" they asked uncomfortably.

"Don't think I didn't notice you two looking at me weird ever since you entered the arena," I told them.

"Well, um," Kodiak stammered. A sheet of ice appeared in front of him and he angled it towards me. "Look."

If I had enough strength, I would have screamed. I was too drained to even gasp.

My hair was whiter than silk and my face was spotted with marks. A million wrinkles creased my face, and a few gray hairs decorated my chin.

I looked like a hundred years old.

I glanced down at my hands, which were also spotted and wrinkled. "Wow."

And then I fainted.

I woke up at the castle infirmary. Again. I was in the same room as the one I had been before when Mr. Leafstern treated my arm. I slowly turned my head to the right, my eyes still half-closed.

Galen slept on the next bed. His eyes were closed peacefully, but he was breathing normally. I smiled, then lifted my hand.

It had returned to normal. I realized I had never appreciated how young my hands looked. I touched my face and smiled again. No wrinkles! I tugged on my hair and chuckled. Dark brown.

I sat up slowly. I felt a lot more energized than I had back at the arena. I could definitely move effortlessly now, and I definitely unaged again.

All that was left was Galen.

I sat there, watching him sleep. Fifteen minutes later, his eyes blinked open. He stared at the ceiling for a few seconds before shooting straight up from the bed. "RINA!"

"I'm right here."

He whirled around and stared at me disbelievingly. "You - you're really okay! You even unaged!"

I smiled. "Yeah. Thanks to you, dude. You brought me back from a very dark place."

Galen grinned, a carbon copy of the smile he

had given me back in first grade. "Of course I did!"

We high-fived and laughed.

My friend is back!

Chapter 13

It took a few tries, but Galen and I managed to stumble out the infirmary. Yeah, I had said that moving was now effortless again, but apparently, my coordination was still a lost cause.

We also managed to make it all the way to the dorms in ten minutes. When we burst through the door, it was more like we fell through the door. Galen tripped over his own feet then and sprawled onto the floor. Everyone inside stood up in alarm, then joy.

"Rina! Galen! You're awake!"

We nodded. "Yeah."

After a few crushing hugs, they exclaimed, "Wow, you guys recovered fast!"

I exchanged a glance with Galen, who hadn't bothered getting up from the floor, and grinned.

"We're Bonds."

Sirocca came and opened her hands. Zinnia sat there, smiling.

"Zin!" I cried.

She was still pale and slouched, but she was there. She was alive. "Are you okay?" I asked. "How are you feeling?"

"Stop fussing!" Zin snapped, her smile turning into a frown. "I'm not that fragile."

Sirocca nodded. "Yup. She's back."

I grinned.

Suddenly, Emily swept into the room, breathless. "Guys! I need - RINA!" I was immediately hit by a bone-crushing hug that toppled me over. "You're awake!"

"Yeah," I gasped.

"But how?" Emily pulled away to stare at me. "The doctor said it would take a person months to recover, but it's only been, like half a day or something."

"Galen and I are Bonds," I said simply. I looked at him, who was still on the floor. "We help each other."

Emily gave me a small smile. She didn't understand what I said. "Oh, that's cool." Her eyes darted around nervously.

"Hey, is something wrong?" I asked her.

Emily jolted. "Huh - Oh, uh, I, uh…"

"Spill," Callan said. "You're stammering."

Emily pursed her lips. "Okay, look. I didn't want to bring this up since you've been dealing with a lot just now, but it's urgent." She glanced around nervously again, glanced down at Galen, then said, "I'll just bring it here since you two obviously need therapy." Then she rushed off.

"Excuse us?" Galen muttered. "I can walk just fine." Yet, he didn't move off the floor.

Emily rushed back inside with her personal maid, Lily, and something in her hand. It was rolled up and had yellowed edges.

"Honestly, I don't know why she used this parchment," Emily said. "It's so old. We have white paper, you know?"

"Who?" Galen said.

"Ivoria."

Everyone froze. A chill ran through my body.

"IVORIA?!" everyone hollered.

Emily nodded. "She sent a letter to me."

She rolled out the scroll and asked Lily to find something to hold it down. After Lily placed a few weights on the edges of the letter, everyone stepped closer and began to read:

Dearest Em,

Greetings, Your Highness. We must start with formalities after all. Congratulations on your coronation. I must say, those Terrenians are brainless to accept YOU as their rightful queen. But, that will be put to an end. As for us, we are actually doing fairly well. Your father and I have been making very important... how should I say it? Plans.

I'll get straight to the point. Soon, your adopted lands will be under siege. Yes, I will block your flow of supplies. Your economy flow will be controlled by my hands. Of course, I cannot expect you to understand. You are just a child. But I trust that even you would understand the gravity of your situation.

Send representatives to meet me at the third Stone if you will agree to my conditions. You may not send an army. Should you ignore my instructions, I will not give you time to fight and resist. The moment I see that you have disobeyed my orders, I will torch and send bombs your way the second I touch land. This would not be a happy thing for me to experience. I would like to see your "people" dwindle and suffer before being extinguished.

Your representatives are to be unarmed. We will meet

only to negotiate. Send a letter of notification to the seventh Stone in two days. If your response is not received by 11:59 P.M. on the second day, I will take that as resistance. Then there would be no hope for you saving your nation.

You cannot say that I am an evil person. As you can see, I am giving you a chance to save yourselves. A slim chance, but an opportunity, nonetheless.

Give Andy a big thank-you for me. His assistance was much appreciated.

Sincerely yours,

Aura Ivoria

There was a shocked silence for a few minutes. Then Emily said, "Well?"

"IT WAS THAT KID!!!" Callan exploded suddenly. "'His assistance was much appreciated.' I KNEW IT!!"

"Callan! Stop!" Emily scolded. "You are not to accuse my brother. I have already shown him the letter, and he claims innocence."

"Yes, he claims," Callan sneered. "But he didn't prove."

"Callan, can we focus on the more important

137

problem?" I asked, annoyed. "Emily, this is a threat letter. Are you going to go with it?"

Emily frowned. "It's a threat, alright."

"Why aren't you frightened?" Galen asked, eyes shining with awe. "You're not scared at all!"

Emily scoffed. "What do you mean? I freaked out the second I finished reading the letter the first time. Lily can tell you all about it. There was broken furniture involved and holes in the wall, and a few blinded maids. But anyways, I checked with my brother first. He's my advisor, after all. He said he didn't know anything about it. Cyan testified his innocence. Then I brought it to you."

"Us? Why not, like, the Queen's former Guard? They're much more experienced than us. Which reminds me, what about Universa? Did you show her?" I asked.

Emily shook her head. "Universa hasn't been feeling well. I think it has something to do with her very short reign. She said she had only ruled for fifteen years before the Ores started to fade. I didn't want to bother her."

I frowned. "So, what? You're going to send us?"

"I'm fine with it," Elece said, standing up. "But I can't go. Thora needs me to be here and my parents are starting to get clingy."

Emily nodded. "That's fine. I only need one representative for each tribe. I already had the team in mind: Callan, Kodiak, Rina, Galen, and Sirocca."

"What? You don't have a Cosmos representative!" Elece snarled.

Emily nodded. "Originally, Sirocca's position was yours. But since you cannot go, I'll have Sirocca be your replacement. Tell her all the information or opinions you want her to voice."

"What about me?" Derrik whined. "I was a part of the original team that saved you guys, so why aren't I part of this?"

Emily bit her lip. "Don't take this the hard way, but you're -"

"Too young, too small. Got it." Derrik stomped over to the other side of the room and started to rant angrily to a spider.

"But," Emily spoke up quickly. "Those of you who aren't going, I'll need your assistance back here at the castle. Elece, I wanted to ask you if you'd be able to help me organize and train the newly registered soldiers of the different armies of each tribe as soon as Melody deems you ready."

Elece's eyes lit up. "Awesome!"

"Thora, can you help me wire an upgraded

intercom? Derrik will help you with the technical stuff, and you just need to make sure the sound will flow better."

Thora smiled. "Derrik! Wanna help me?!"

Derrik frowned. "Fiiiine." He trudged over and Thora explained what their roles were. Derrik blinked. "I don't know how to build an intercom."

Emily patted his shoulder. "I'm sure you'll figure it out. You're pretty brainy for your age, aren't you? Your school records show that you're above all the other twelve-year-olds at the Academy. And you're also part of the Queen's Guard, so you have to keep up with training."

Derrik nodded. "That's true. I'll try."

"What about Mira?" I couldn't help asking. "Do you have a role for her?"

Emily's eyes darkened, and she shook her head. "No. Unless she insists, I currently don't have a role planned out for her."

"Oh."

"So what do you want us to do?" Galen asked, finally struggling to stand up. "Just talk?"

Emily's eyes took on a mischievous glint. "We're gonna break some rules."

Chapter 14

All of us stared at Emily blankly. "What?"

Emily rolled her eyes in a very unqueenly fashion. "Come on. You don't get it? We're going to disobey whatever Ivoria told us to do!"

Elece flared up in horror. "You can't! Didn't you just see in the letter? She's going to send bombs on us if we do!"

"We'll just have to take that risk," Emily said calmly. "Honestly, I thought that out of all people you would be the one who would agree most with what I had planned."

Elece snorted. "I agree with breaking unreasonable rules. I disagree with breaking unreasonable rules that would kill everyone."

Emily curled and uncurled her fingers. "I know. But when she gets here, she's going to torch our lands, anyways. Since we're meeting up with her, I want the Rep Team to find out what she has planned. Do you guys really think that Ivoria is going there just to talk?"

"Yes," Derrik squeaked. "I try not to think of anything that would cause me to lose sleep."

Emily sighed. "I don't want to force you guys, but this is what I want happening as a queen." She looked up. "Tell me your choice."

"Rep Team, let's talk about it," Callan said.

We all gathered in a circle.

"I think we should do it," I said automatically.

"Me too," Galen said.

"What? You're crazy!" Callan protested.

"Why?" Sirocca said. "I mean, we're going to be destroyed either way. Might as well just prevent it from happening in the first place, right?"

"Or," Callan said meaningfully. "Or we would just be speeding up our deaths."

Kodiak shrugged. "I'm personally curious to see what Ivoria has thought up of. What kind of gruesome plan has her devious mind come up with now?"

"That's kind of dark, you know?" I told him.

Kodiak shrugged.

"Why do you think we should do it, Rina?" Sirocca asked.

"Same reason as you," I said. "If Ivoria's going to lay siege to the Terrenian Islands and make us suffer for no reason at all, I'm going to do whatever it takes to stop it. There are kids younger than us here, and I don't want them to see what some people are capable of doing."

"Wow...." Galen applauded me. "You're one for thinking about the next generation."

"Alright, let's do it then!" Callan said.

"I thought you were against it," Kodiak nudged him. "Quick change of heart, I see."

Callan glared at him. "It's not... whatever you're implying. I was just providing the negative side to this argument so we have a solid reason for going. You need to take debate classes to understand what I mean, Akie."

"Okay, okay, I get it, Callie!"

We told Emily our decision. She smiled really brightly after that. "Yes! Awesome! I'll let my brother know, and he'll arrange all the supplies you might need for the trip."

"Can we talk to your brother really quick?" Sirocca asked. "I want to ask him something."

"Sure." Emily called for Lily. "Tell Andy to meet us here." Lily nodded and ran off.

"When are we leaving?" I asked.

Emily frowned, then shrugged. "Whenever

143

Ivoria commands us to, I guess. I don't want to risk this mission too early. For now, just keep living normally and doing your normal everyday things like training until I notify you."

"Oh, right! That reminds me: I'm going to be staying at the palace from now on," I told Emily. "After the whole Zinnia incident, I decided to stay here."

Emily nodded. "That's fine. How about you, Zinnia? Are you going to stay with Rina or Arrowwood?"

Zinnia scrunched up her eyes. "I want to stay here, but my queen told me to stay in Arrowwood for recuperation."

I nodded. "That's probably for the best. I'll drop you off, then go home to get some stuff."

Zinnia sighed sadly. "NO FAIR I WANTED TO GO!" she screamed right after, which ended in her having a coughing fit.

I flicked her head with a finger. "I'll bring you a souvenir."

Zinnia's eyes lit up. "Ooh! Bring me one of Ivoria's teeth!"

"Uh.... no."

Zinnia rolled her eyes. "I'm just kidding. Just bring me whatever looks cool."

I nodded. "I was planning to do that anyway,

you know?"

After I dropped Zin off at her home in the Arrowwood settlement, I headed home to get some things. It was already nighttime, and it was going to be an awkward exchange, but whatever.

I rang the doorbell instead of walking right in. Mom opened the door, and her eyes opened in surprise. "Rina?"

I nodded solemnly. "I am here to pick up a few things."

Mom kept staring at me in shock. "Where have you been today?"

Fighting for my life. Unconscious. It's hard to believe that all that happened in the span of 12 hours, give or take. "That's not something you need to worry about," I told her instead. "May I come in?"

"O-Of course. Why'd you have to ask?" Mom opened the door wider and gestured for me to enter. I walked in seriously and headed up the stairs toward my room.

"Mira's not home?" I asked, noticing that her room was empty.

"No, Mira said she had to do something."

"Do what?" I entered my room and started taking a few things.

"I don't know. She didn't say. Only that it was classified and none of my concern."

Ah, I guess she didn't hear about how Mira lost the favor of the queen.

Suddenly, Mom's voice turned sad. "It's strange. The older you two get, the more you're hiding from me. Even Mira."

That made me feel kind of bad. But Mom had helped capture Zin, which led me to fight my own pixie, which almost led me to death. I had to stay away for awhile.

"So, you're really moving out?" Mom's head peered through the doorway.

"Yup."

"What happened to Mira's pixie?"

I stiffened. "She was mine to begin with," I said harshly. "Thanks to you and Mira, she almost died."

I almost died. But I wasn't going to tell her that anytime soon.

Mom blinked. "Pixies don't die, do they?"

I slammed a stuffed animal into a backpack and ripped the zipper closed. "Of course they do. They're living things like you and me." I shouldered the backpack and headed out the bedroom door and down the stairs. "Now, if you'll excuse me, I'll be taking my leave. Have a good day, ma'am. Please pass my parting words to Dad for me."

Then I was outta there!

Sirocca helped me move my stuff into the bunk. We were just getting finished when Andy called out from the common room. We all shuffled out of the girls' wing and greeted Andy.

"You said you had something to ask me?" he said.

Sirocca nodded. "If it's okay with you, I wanted to test out a guess I had while Emily was telling us about the threat letter."

Andy blinked. "What, are you going to inspect me for a tracker or something?"

Sirocca nodded. "I had a hunch about the tracker, but it's going to need close examining. Can I do it?"

Andy shrugged and plopped onto a chair. "Go ahead."

Sirocca leaned in really close and started to carefully inspect Andy's face. We all waited with bated breath.

"I might need to use my Talent on you. It won't hurt, but do I have your permission?"

Andy shrugged. "Sure. Whatever."

147

Sirocca leaned forward again. When she reached his right cheek, she froze, then leaned closer.

"What? Are you going to pop my pimple?" Andy joked.

"It's no pimple," Sirocca said. "Get ready. I'm going to do something. It might hurt, but be strong. Here we go."

A small breeze trickled through the door and blew right at Andy's face. He squinted, trying his best not to move. Sirocca moved her hands over his cheek.

"Done."

She leaned back, holding out her hand. Everyone crowded to take a look.

A device the size of a small crumb.

"That was on his face?" Elece asked, disgusted. "How'd he not notice?"

"It was embedded into his skin. That's why it was flaring up over there," she told Andy.

"Huh," Andy said. He rubbed his cheek. "Well, I'm glad that's gone."

"How'd she put this tracker on you?" I asked. "I mean, she never touched your face, right?"

Andy's face scrunched up with disgust. "She touches my face all the time. I think it's supposed to be 'motherly', but it's not. Remember when she grabbed my face back at the garbage disposal at Provincia? Yeah, that was more painful than usual. She probably stuck it in my face then."

We all made repulsive noises. That's gross.

"At least the tracker's gone." Andy rubbed his face again and turned to Sirocca. "Good job."

Sirocca smiled. "No problem. That actually went by a lot quicker than I expected."

"By the way," Andy turned to me. "Emily told me about what happened this morning. Are you guys okay?"

Galen and I nodded. "We're good now. Thanks for asking."

Andy nodded back. "Anytime."

"So what do we do now?" Kodiak asked. "I mean, I have to get back home to do something important, but I meant what do we do since everything is not happening the way it was supposed to?"

Emily frowned. "Well, you guys keep doing what you're doing. Go to school and things like that. We'll have meetings; I'll contact you for those. But for Galen and Rina," she turned to us, "since this was your first day of training, and it didn't go well, I'm giving you guys a month of break. It was originally a week, but I decided to prolong it when both of you guys almost died at the same time. I know you guys look fine, but I'm going to stick with what the doctor said."

"What?" I said. "But I already told my mom I was going to live here."

Emily laughed. "Of course you can live here. What I meant was that you two will go back to the Academy for a month before you switch back to training. I'll let Skye and Jordan know."

Kodiak's eyes stayed glued to his watch. As soon as Emily stopped speaking, he nodded rapidly and bolted out the door.

"Wow," I said. "Looks like it's REALLY important."

Callan nodded. "Yeah. I wonder what it is."

"You don't know?" I asked, surprised.

"Nope. He didn't tell me," Callan said.

"What are our schedules?" Galen interrupted, shooting a glare at Callan. "Are we still in the school roster?"

Emily shook her head. "I pulled your names out yesterday. I'll put you guys back in the register. Starting tomorrow, stick with the same schedule you had before the coronation."

I shrugged. "Okay, then."

Emily nodded. "That should be about it. Galen and Rina, you two just rest for today. Everyone else, back to whatever you were doing before the Cinnabar Trial."

We all said goodbye then dispersed. I flopped onto my bed, glad that everything was finally settled, then fell asleep.

Chapter 15

I attended school the next day. Everyone stared at us with strange expressions, and I did my best to ignore them. Unfortunately, it wasn't too easy.

"What's up with them?" Galen muttered.

"They're probably wondering the same about us," I whispered back. "Remember, we're supposed to be training for the Queen's Guard right now."

"Yeah, but they don't have to stare at us like we're wearing some animal's waste," Galen frowned.

I glanced at him. "Are you in a bad mood?"

Galen's glare pretty much burned holes into the ground. "Maybe."

I nodded. "Not going to ask." His sister had a habit of barging into his room and kicking him off his bed to wake him up. That's probably the reason why he's grumpy.

Every time I entered the classroom, everyone stopped to stare. Even the teacher stopped teaching to stare!

"What's she doing?"

"Wasn't she part of the Queen's Guard?"

"Did she get kicked off?"

"Maybe, but Galen is back, too."

"What do you think happened?"

I ALMOST DIED, THAT'S WHAT HAPPENED!!

But it's not like I needed to announce it to the whole school. Everyone was just being annoying, that's all.

Still, can't they think of some other reason? Why did they all think we were kicked out? Correction: why I was kicked out. Everyone loves Galen.

At lunch, Galen looked equally as tired. "They think I was goofing off too much," he growled. "Since when do I goof off too much?!"

"Uh, all the time?"

"NOT HELPING!"

I sighed.

Just then, Callan, Kodiak, and Sirocca walked up to us and sat down.

"How're you guys faring?" Sirocca asked. She took one look at Galen's storming face and said, "Never mind."

I nodded. "Did you know everyone thinks we were kicked out of the Queen's Guard?"

Kodiak nodded. "We all heard it."

Callan rolled his eyes. "People are always like that."

Kodiak poked him. "You mean you are always like that."

Callan punched his arm. "What do you mean?"

Kodiak shook his head mischievously. "Nothing, nothing."

I dropped my head onto the table. "It's only the first day! Why does this seem so boring?"

Galen growled. "Can we just go to school at the castle? Why do we need to go back to studying at the Academy?"

"What are you talking about? The Academy is great!" Kodiak glanced up really quick. "Hey!"

We all turned to look. A beautiful girl with long, jet black hair and bangs was struggling to climb a tree.

Kodiak stood up and rushed over. "WHAT ARE YOU DOING? GET DOWN!"

I stared as Kodiak snatched the girl off the

tree and started to reprimand her. "Who's she?"

Callan looked up and squinted. "Can't tell. I forgot to wear my contacts last night. But that's probably his sister."

"Kodiak has a sister?" I glanced at the girl.

She looked about eight years old, but her features gave her an innocent look. She smiled brightly, even though her brother was steaming with rage.

"She's funny," Sirocca said. "I like her!"

"What's her name?" Galen asked.

"Alaska," Callan said, still squinting in the distance. "What's going on over there?

I glanced backward again, where Kodiak was apologizing to Alaska. Alaska was grinning hugely, obviously laughing at the older boy.

Kodiak walked back with his head bowed, eyes slightly confused.

"What happened?" I asked as he sat down.

Kodiak rubbed his head, then his eyes. "Nothing. Just a misunderstanding."

"Your sister is so pretty," I said.

Kodiak gave me a small smile. "Yeah. She is."

Galen sighed. "She seems a lot nicer than my sister. Do you know what Wendy did to me today? She barged into my room, stole my pillow, tossed my blanket out the window, then

155

KICKED ME OFF MY BED!! AND I HAVE HARDWOOD FLOORS!"

Yup. I was right.

Kodiak chuckled. "Yeah, that's definitely not my sister."

"Wanna switch?" Galen asked grumpily.

Kodiak scooted away. "Uh, no, I'm good. Thanks! Good luck with your wake-up calls!"

Galen's head dropped into his lunch bag. He muttered something unintelligible and probably not worth repeating.

"Well, anyways, school is boring," I said. "Why do we have to be stuck here when everyone else is at the palace training or helping Emily with some kind of job?! IT'S NOT FAIR!"

"I hear ya," Galen muttered through his lunch bag.

"Get up, you look really sad like that." Kodiak yanked the back of Galen's shirt, throwing his head back up out of the bag. In his mouth was an apple slice.

"Hey, you almost made me choke!" Galen complained. "This is such a convenient way of eating!" He dropped his head back in his bag.

"Ew, gross, dude," I said. "You look like an animal."

"Well, deal with it 'cause I don't feel like

using my hands today," Galen snapped, his head still in his lunch bag.

"Fine."

We all sat there, bored. There was nothing to talk about, nothing to do, except wait for Emily's messages about Ivoria. Who knew how long that was going to take?

About a month later, the intercom buzzed. I had been half-asleep in math class, so when I jolted awake, the spiral binding on my notebook stuck to my face for a second before my notebook fell off and landed on the floor.

"Good morning, students and staff, and please excuse this interruption," Emily's voice sounded as polite and formal as a cup of china. "Students Fierina Flameton, Galen Maelstrom, Callan Cragmire, Kodiak Torrent, and Sirocca Sandings must report to the Royal Palace now. I repeat, these students must report to my palace immediately. Thank you."

The intercom clicked off.

"Ooh...." a few students glanced my way. "Did something again, Rina?"

I scoffed at them. "You wish."

I packed up my stuff and headed out the door. I raced for the Tunnel and jumped in.

Yes! I was the first one!

I double-checked Zin's recovery first.

"She's recovering well," Amaryllis told me warmly, "but it's going to be a long time before she is able to leave Arrowwood."

"Aw, okay." I sighed. "Tell her that I'm sorry I won't be able to visit her for a long time. I'll try to bring the coolest thing I see there."

"Consider it done," the pixie queen said.

Afterwards, I burst into the guest wing. "EMILY!"

Emily rushed in. "Is everyone else here?"

"Yes!" Callan and the rest of the team dashed into the common room. "What happened?"

Emily held up a yellowed scroll. "Another message from Ivoria."

Chapter 16

"This is of utmost importance," Emily said seriously. "Whatever is in here is classified. I expect you all to know this already."

We nodded solemnly.

"But before we begin, there is an equally important question I must ask. It will affect the overall performance of this team. Rina, what class did you come from?"

I blinked. "Math."

"Obviously. You have an imprint of the notebook binding on your face with a few smears of graphite."

The team laughed as I furiously tried to scrub it off. "What's this got to do with 'overall performance'?"

Emily's tone was dead serious, but her eyes sparkled. "You need to be alert and ready at all times."

"Haha, very funny."

"Anyways, back to business."

Lily darted into the room with the paperweights as Emily sat down on one of the couches in the the center, spread the letter out on the wooden table and began to read:

To the Highness of the Terrenian Islands:

As expected, you would never have let your adopted country go to waste. You have made a wise choice, deciding to heed my suggestions. I hope the wait was worth it.

Meet me at the third Stone in one week. I'd like to take this time to remind you of your consequences. If you do not send representatives, your nation will be torched. If you decide to back out off this negotiation, your country will be bombed. Try anything funny, and your people's death will be sealed.

I look forward to your attendance.

~Ivoria

"This cruel lady...." Kodiak leaned back and shook his head in disbelief. "These are terrorist letters! I know I agreed to it, but I still can't believe we're actually doing this."

Callan growled. "No comment. I don't want to waste words on something like this."

Emily looked up. "Any other thoughts before I add mine?"

We shook our heads. It was worthless to say anything else.

"As soon as this letter arrived, I had your personal caretakers prepare all the essentials you'd need for this mission. Your wristbands will remain active so you'll have access to your weapons," Emily said, looking at Galen and I. "As for you three, the new and former Queen's Guard had been given the assignment of finding suitable weapons for you. I'll take you down there later.

"Your mission goal: find out whatever Ivoria is up to and stop it. Cliche, I know, but it's easier said than done. You have a twin goal to meet as well: complete the first without raising suspicion from Ivoria. This is also obvious. Do I need to explain anything else?"

I furrowed my brow in concentration. "Are we going to have any contact with you at all?"

Emily blinked. "No."

I chewed my lip. Galen exchanged glances with me. Sirocca, Kodiak, and Callan exploded,

"WHAT?! How are we supposed to know what to do?"

Emily watched them calmly. "Rina and Galen are there."

"Yeah, but we need suggestions from the commander of this mission!" Kodiak protested. "So we'll have no contact to home?"

Emily sighed. "I didn't say you'd have no contact with the Terrenian Islands, whatsoever. I said you won't have contact with me."

Kodiak blinked, then breathed a sigh of relief. "Oh."

"But I wouldn't recommend it," Emily said.

"Why?" Callan asked.

"Think about it," Sirocca said. "Last time they had connection with the queen, they got part of their brains ripped out."

I winced. "It sounds... disgusting and zombie-like when you say it that way."

"But it's true," Callan said. "In a way."

"But even we have to admit that it's going to be difficult without any connection to you, Emily," Galen said.

Emily frowned. "Yes, I know. I've lost sleep over this decision. But there are more pros than cons. One: like you said, it protects you. Two: it will protect me, which leads to three: it will protect the Terrenian Islands. If Ivoria figures out a way to trace the connection back here, things will go from bad to ruin. Ivoria will find out all these secrets from me - where the kids are, everyone's schedules, the weakest points in our army - I can't let that happen because of me."

We nodded. "You're right."

Emily nodded back and set her lips in a firm line. "So. No connection with me."

"How soon do you want us to leave? ASAP?" Sirocca asked.

Emily thought about it. "We have a week. It'll take you guys about three to five days to get to the third Stone. Rest for the remainder of today, then leave tomorrow."

The Representative Team all exchanged glances.

Here we go on another mission.

After Kodiak, Sirocca, and Callan visited the weapons room and chose their weapons, everyone spent the rest of their day contacting their parents. Of course, they didn't say where we're going or what we were going to do. Just that we were on a classified mission from the

163

queen.

Did I contact my parents?

Yes.

Of course I didn't want to. But part of me knew that they were still my family, so I had to treat them like one. I dialed my mom's phone number and waited for her to pick up.

The phone rang exactly four times before she answered. "Rina?"

"Uh, hi."

"What happened? Are you alright? Why are you calling?"

Was that real concern in her voice? I didn't know. Recently, Mom had constantly been confusing me. Did she really worry for me? Was she really scared for me?

Did she really treasure me?

I cleared my throat and closed myself off. "I'm leaving."

"Leaving? What do you mean? You've already left our house."

"I'm leave the Terrenian Islands. I don't know when I'll be back," I said through gritted teeth. It was so hard and so strange to talk to a mother who sounded like she cared.

"Did the queen send you?"

"Yes."

"Be safe," she said hesitatingly, as if she wasn't sure if she should had told me that. "Come back soon."

I pulled the phone away from my ear for a bit. I blinked my eyes and took deep breaths.

What was going on?

Why was I so emotional? This had to mean that Mom really does love me.

Right?

But why wouldn't she say so?

I picked up the phone again. "Sure. Make sure Mira keeps up in her studies. I'm sure she'll be ecstatic when you tell her I'm gone."

"Mira? Sure, I'll let her know as soon as she gets back."

I frowned, then looked at the clock. "What do you mean? School's over already."

"Mira went out saying that she had to do something at the park with her friend. Probably a project."

The park? A friend?

This normally wouldn't have sounded suspicious, but I saw right through Mira's lie. In the Fire Tribe, we don't have any parks. Sure, we have a few large spots of dry grass that is considered as a "park", but nobody goes there to do anything because it's so boring.

Second, Mira and her friends are too clean to want to do anything with dirt.

So what was my twin up to now?

"What time did she leave?" I asked Mom as casually as I could manage.

"Um, let's see. She messaged me as soon as school was over."

I bit my lip. So it had been about half an hour so far.

"Why are you so curious? Mira can take care of herself."

"Mhm, yeah," I said absentmindedly. "Hey, Mom? Can you do me a favor?"

There was a big sigh at the other end. "A favor? Like what?"

Ah, the old Mom. "Can you let me know when Mira comes home?"

"You guys are worried for each other?" There was a delighted laugh. "This is just like old times!"

No, this never happened in the "old times".

"Of course!"

"Just don't tell her, okay?" I added quickly. "Mira doesn't like it when I check up on her. Please?"

I could imagine Mom nodding like, "Yes, I know, your secret is safe with me. You don't need to explain further."

What she really said was, "Fine!"

That's all I wanted to say. "Okay-thanks-Mom-bye!"

I hung up.

There was a whistle behind me, and I spun around. Kodiak was on a beanbag chair, arms crossed, smirking at me.

"What?" I said, annoyed. "Were you there the whole time?"

He nodded. "Yup. And I have to say, you are not the lovey-dovey, warm fuzzy feelings type with your family."

I scowled. "You never knew before?"

Kodiak shrugged. "No, I knew. Just never seen you, you know, talk like that."

I frowned at him. "Are you close with your family?"

Kodiak's smiled slipped, just for a second. "Yeah. I am."

"Really?" I leaned in. "I smell a lie."

His eyes blazed immediately and he stood up. "You dare speak that about me?"

I leaned back, laughing. "Just kidding."

He stared at me for a few seconds, as if he couldn't take me seriously. "You shouldn't joke about family."

I stopped laughing. "I know."

"Family should be the closest, most precious thing you have," he said. Suddenly, I couldn't tell if he was talking to me or himself. "Treasure it. They'll always be by your side."

"Hey, you okay?" I asked tentatively.

Kodiak blinked. "What?"

I frowned at him. "Is something wrong? You lost yourself for a bit."

Kodiak nodded and gave me a tight smile. "Yeah. Why wouldn't I be?"

I looked closely at him. "I'm not buying it."

Kodiak sighed. "What do you want me say? 'No'?"

"No, just the truth. But if you don't want to tell me, that's fine. I'll just be here if you ever need to talk," I told him, smiling.

He looked at me intensely. "Do you really mean that?"

I nodded. "Of course! That's what friends are for!"

He looked away with hesitation, then looked back at me. "I know this is weird and awkward, but promise me."

I stared at him. "Uh, okay."

We linked our pinkies. Now it was a promise that couldn't be broken. It had been sealed.

Kodiak's face broke out into such a bright smile, I had to glance down. His eyes sparkled joyfully, like a child's. It made me fear: would I be the one to shatter this jewel?

I would never forgive myself if that happened. But then again, promises should be kept.

I'd never break this promise.

"Thanks, Rina! You promised," he said, before running off.

I stood there, pinkie still in the air. "Uh, no problem...."

Chapter 17

Early the next day, we were standing in the lobby of the Royal Palace. Emily handed us our bags and double checked our weapons. Her face was creased with worry.

"You guys better make it back alive," she commanded. "If not, I'm going to put your souls in prison for disobeying my orders and making me angry."

We smiled bitterly. "Yes, Queen."

Emily bit her lip and hugged us all. We stood there in a group hug for a while. Who knew when we would come home?

"If anything gets too dangerous for you, but there's still a slim chance that you can defeat Ivoria or save the Terrenian Islands, you better run for your life." Emily pulled away and looked at us sternly. "I don't want you risking your lives for a slim chance. Find an opportunity later."

I honestly don't know how many of us would actually follow that. We love our country too much, so none of us responded to Emily's order.

"Just make sure you make it back alive," she said softly. "I don't want anyone to die."

We looked at each other then back at Emily. All of us knew that this negotiation was going to be dangerous and there weren't any promises.

"Sure," I said eventually, trying to pretend that everything really was going to turn out right.

"We'll do our best," Sirocca said.

Emily walked us out as far as the ocean. Afterwards, she turned to us. "If I don't see you back within a month, I'll assume the worst."

I swallowed hard. A month.

"Alright."

This felt like last year all over again, except with more dire consequences.

Kodiak was fidgeting. I gave him a reassuring smile. He smiled thinly back.

"Okay, then. Good luck." Emily waved at us. We waved back and faced the ocean. For a long moment, none of us moved.

"Uh…. Any ideas on how to cross?" Callan said.

I frowned, trying to think. "I think Galen and

Sirocca can carry you and Kodiak while the rest of us fly."

"Excuse me? I don't need to be carried." Kodiak slammed one foot on the water, and the second his foot contacted the ocean, the water froze six inches around his foot. "'Bye, Callie!"

"Hey, no fair!" Callan whined. "I'll just follow wherever you step."

Kodiak shrugged. "Suit yourself." He pulled his foot back and the ice floated away. Callan gave his friend a dirty look.

"It's okay," Sirocca said. "Both of us will be carrying you, so you'll be fine. Plus, you won't need to work as hard as we do."

"True, but still!" Callan protested.

"I'm not carrying him. You can do it." Galen turned his back and walked up to me. "So how long are we going to stand here and chat?"

I sighed. "Let's go, Galen."

"Hey, wait -" Callan protested.

"Too bad, rockhead!" Galen jumped up and sat on his tornado. He became stronger after last year. His tornado had been showing up a lot in terms of transportation, but I've never seen it flare as strongly as it did back in Ivoria's facility.

Speaking of Ivoria...

"Let's go." I jumped into the ocean.

Last time, I used the water to help me fly. That took up way too much energy until I realized I had gills and could breathe underwater. If I let the current take me wherever I needed to go, that'd be easier for me.

For the record, no one would be happy to have gills.

The water muffled every sound. It was deafening yet serene at the same time. I took a small breath in and shifted an arm. A current appeared and channeled me quickly up ahead.

"Hey, Rina!" Galen's voice sounded gurgly from underwater.

I poked my head up. "Yeah?"

"Uh, are we heading in the right direction?"

I glanced around. The Royal Island was right behind us, with Emily still standing on its shores. The sun hadn't fully risen yet, so I squinted in the distance trying to find a silhouette of land. "I think so."

"Okay, just checking."

I glanced backwards. Kodiak was skating on the water while Callan was "sitting" in midair, grumbling and glaring at Kodiak. Sirocca seemed to struggle between keeping herself and Callan in the air.

"Hey, Galen! Help Sirocca with Callan!"

"What? Why?"

"Because! Sirocca can't carry him by herself!"

Galen sighed loudly and flew backwards. The burden on Sirocca's face immediately lightened. "Thanks!"

"Yeah, I'm just helping you because this guy ate too much."

Callan blinked. "What?"

"You're heavy," Galen said bluntly.

Callan stared at him for a second before leaning back, "Well, I am taller than you-" He flipped backwards and started to plummet. Galen caught him when his face was inches from the water. "HEY!"

"Sorry," Galen said, obviously not apologetic at all.

Callan growled. "You…."

I sank back into the ocean. I didn't need to hear them argue.

We kept travelling in the same direction for some time. I wasn't sure exactly how long since time's presence wasn't noticeable when you're in the middle of the sea, but by the time we reached the first Stone, the sun was already in the sky.

We collapsed onto the rocky beach. I recognized the rocks and the ring of trees before seeing the buildings in the distance as I flung the

174

excess water back into the ocean.

This was the place where our first team finally started to trust each other. I smiled when I recalled the warm feeling of finally knowing that Elece wouldn't abandon us.

"Hey," Galen grunted. The second he reached land, Callan crashed face-first onto the beach. Or, he would have if Callan didn't catch himself in time and hurl the rocks at Galen. Galen reacted fast and shot the rocks back at Callan with his tornado until it was practically a battle zone between them. Their eyes blazed pale gray and bright green.

They were only ten feet apart.

"HEY!" I hollered.

I've had enough of this.

I stomped right in between them, even though I was pelted by sharp rocks. Seeing that continuing could potentially kill me (I know, I'm laying on it a bit thick here), they ceased their rock fight.

"Why are you guys enemies?" I asked.

"Because he's a rockhead," Galen said the same time Callan said, "He's conceited and doesn't know anything."

Then they went right back to glaring at each other.

I sighed. I never know what to do to reconcile people. "Make up right now, or at least come to an agreement, or else I'm linking you two together for the rest of this mission."

Callan stood up. "That wouldn't be wise, you know, if we need to fight, which we probably will."

I stared at him. "Nice try. You can use your feet."

"WHAT?! You can't be serious!" Galen protested.

I turned around and started walking away. "Better make up quick. Or else you guys would be the first people who can use their Talent with their feet."

Twin groans resounded behind me, then a stuffy silence. I hid a smile.

Not bad for the first day!

Chapter 18

We camped out on the first Stone for the night. Since the Stones were the "stepping stones" of islands connecting the Terrenian Islands with the Mainland, we couldn't travel more than one Stone a day. The Stones were miles apart!

Sirocca's duffel bag had everything we need. Emily really was a person who actually knew what we needed. She packed two tents! (Ahem, *Universa*….)

After we finished setting up the tents, I stepped outside to take a look at the sky. It was a mixture of pink and purple - cotton candy sky. That's what we always called it when I was a kid. Mira made it up. I wonder how she came up with it….

Anyways, it stuck, and it spread to all the

kids, which usually happened whenever Mira did something. Now everyone calls pink and purple clouds a cotton candy sky.

Mira…. Mira…. What was she doing? Where was she going? My gut kept telling me that this wasn't an ordinary trip with her friend to the park. It was something more….

My thought was cut off when Kodiak emerged from the bushes looking worriedly at his phone.

"No reception?" I asked.

He jumped and shoved his phone in his back pocket. "Uh, I mean, yeah, reception is terrible here!" He glanced around and frowned at the trees. "Do the people here actually prefer mail over texts?!"

I narrowed my eyes. "Is something wrong?"

Kodiak jumped again and looked away guiltily. "…. No?"

"You're a terrible liar."

He cleared his throat. "I mean, it's nothing you should worry about. It's fine."

I stepped closer. His mouth was set in a firm line. His eyes kept darting about; he couldn't meet my eyes. His eyebrows had a worry crease between them, and his fingers kept twitching in the direction of his back pocket.

What was happening?

I sighed. "I won't ask if you don't want to tell me. But you've been like this for some time already. Are you sure you don't need help? I'll keep my promise." I held up my pinkie for him to see.

Kodiak stared at my finger for a moment before looking away. "It's nothing. I... I'll be fine." He forced a smile.

I frowned. I didn't like this. I didn't like knowing that my friend was hurting, but I couldn't know what or what to do to help.

I reluctantly lowered my hand. "Promise to come to me when you're really alright?"

Kodiak grinned. "Yeah."

I sighed, then rubbed my eyes. "Okay, then."

Just then, Galen came storming up to me. "RINA!"

I jumped back, then rushed forward. "WHAT?! WHAT HAPPENED?!"

"CALLAN PUSHED ME INTO THE OCEAN!"

It was then I realized that Galen was sopping wet. His thick hair hung flat against his head and dripped water all over his shoes. His eyes blazed underneath his flat bangs.

I growled. "And here I thought it was an

emergency."

"IT IS! How am I supposed to put up with this for the ENTIRE MISSION?!"

"Rrrr.... CALLAN GET OVER HERE!" I hollered angrily.

Galen's smile could have lit up the island. "Thanks, Rina!"

"You stay here," I snapped.

"Aw, why?"

"JUST SIT!"

Galen's butt hit the floor barely a second after. "Okay."

Callan appeared from behind a tree a few moments later. "Uh, Rina, you okay? 'Cause I heard you yell, and -"

"Come here."

"Oh. Okay, then." He cautiously made his way over to me. "So...."

"Sit. KODIAK!!"

Kodiak was at my side in less than a nanosecond. "I'm right here; you don't need to yell."

Oh. That's right.

"Tie these two together," I said.

Galen and Callan immediately sat straight up. "WHAT?!"

"You can't be serious," Galen looked at me in

disbelief.

"Kodiak, hey, come on," Callan pleaded.

Kodiak looked at me curiously, then shrugged. "Okay."

In a split second, an ice handcuff linked the boys together. Galen and Callan immediately stood up and tried to walk in opposite directions.

Of course, it didn't work.

"You guys are avoiding each other like the plague," I commented when they sat down as far as they could from each other, arms outstretched. "What, you need to be at least five hundred feet away from the other person?"

"Ideally," Galen said. "Rina, do you really have to do this to me? I'm your best friend!"

"Yeah, and it's because of that that she needs to do this." Sirocca appeared from behind the girls' tent. "While you guys were yammering away, I finished securing all the tents. You're welcome."

We all ducked our heads. "Sorry."

Sirocca rolled her eyes. "Anyways, Galen and Callan, you guys really do need to resolve your differences. How are we supposed to be a team with you guys acting like a mongoose and a cobra?"

"A what?" Callan said.

"Animals, genius!" Galen sneered. "I can't believe you don't know!"

Rocks the size of half my body appeared out of the ground. "It's because I didn't hear what she said, gas guy!"

"You're sitting closer to her than I am, cotton ears!"

"Cotton brain!"

"Rockhead!"

I rubbed my head. "Here we go again...."

Sirocca tapped one of the humongous boulders. "Uh, can we focus on the more immediate problem here?"

The rocks sank back into the ground without Callan or Galen breaking their glaring contest.

"Thank you. Problem: you guys are so loud, I'm pretty sure Ivoria has already been alerted of our presence."

That got everyone to be quiet and listen to reason.

"And they have an advantage because if they know we're here, they probably know that Callan and Galen do not get along." Sirocca crossed her arms and tilted her head meaningfully at the boys. "Just to let you know."

They both opened their mouths, but Sirocca held up a hand. "I don't care who started it. It

182

doesn't matter anymore. Just be quiet for the rest of the day, and I'll be satisfied."

They both closed their mouths and returned to glaring.

I sidled up to Sirocca. "Thanks. As you can see, I am not good at this stuff."

Sirocca shrugged. "Don't worry, you'll get it one day."

"I hope so. How early do you think we need to wake up tomorrow? Ivoria might want to chase us down and forcefully bring us to her in case we decide to bail or something."

Sirocca glanced at me with a gleam in her eye. "Don't take that seriously."

My jaw dropped. "Whoa. It's so believable though!"

Sirocca laughed. "I finished setting up tents a long time ago. I was up in the sky estimating the distance from this Stone to the next. But what I said could be partially true, though. Have you scouted to see if there was anybody in the buildings?"

My cheeks burned. "I got, uh, a little bit preoccupied…."

Sirocca smiled. "Don't sweat about it. Let's just quickly do it now."

"Can we go?" Callan tried to stand up.

"Huh. This seems to be working," Sirocca commented. "You're starting to say 'we'. And no, I'm sending Rina and Kodiak."

"What? Why?!" Galen whined. "I'm her best friend and her Bond!"

Sirocca shook her head. "If you show me you can behave, then I'll let you off the hook."

I couldn't stop laughing afterwards. I whispered to Kodiak, "She treats them as if they were six!"

Kodiak nodded, trying to hide a smile as well.

Galen grumbled and sat down. I was beginning to feel bad for him, though. He really didn't deserve this... ish....

But I really didn't want him to fight with Callan. They needed each other's backs for the journey ahead.

"We'll be back soon," I promised Sirocca.

She nodded. "Go on! I'll take these two boys out to gather some wood for a fire."

I dipped my head once in understanding then headed off toward the buildings with Kodiak.

"Show me the way," he said. "I'll just follow you."

I made a face. "I don't know where I'm going."

"You don't?" he exclaimed. "I thought you

guys got to the Mainland through these islands!"

"We did," I replied. I ducked under a low branch. "But when we got to this Stone, Elece wouldn't let us scout with her. She said one person was less conspicuous than four."

"That's a good point, though," Kodiak said thoughtfully. "Let's keep going and see if she's right."

We walked silently until we reached the peach-colored structures. They looked just like they did last time I was here: peeling paint, dusty walls, but not too old or run-down-looking.

Kodiak squinted, trying to see beyond the bushes we were crouched behind.

"Do you see anyone?" I whispered.

"No…. I don't think anyone's in there," he whispered back, neck still outstretched. "All the windows are dark. Do you still want to go inside and take a look?"

I thought about it. "Might as well be thorough."

"Alright."

"Besides, if we get into anything, we have your ice and my water to help you."

Kodiak smiled. "Yeah."

We crept out of the bushes and walked slowly towards the facility.

Chapter 19

We reached the tallest building in ten minutes. Both of us stuck close to the ground and to the shadows as if we were paranoid about light. We probably were, considering how this was an enemy base.

Large double doors marked the entrance to the biggest building. We stood there for some time, not moving.

"You really think we should go in?" Kodiak asked for the hundredth time.

I bit my lip. "I don't want to, but I feel like we have to."

"That's what I was afraid of. I feel the same way."

I took a small step forward and gripped the handle. After a sharp inhale, I pulled the door gently, hoping the door wouldn't open.

It was unlocked.

I squeezed myself inside, trying to let the least amount of light in. Kodiak followed me, and then we were plunged into darkness.

My heart thudded in my chest. My lungs squeezed. I groped around for something to hold. "K-Kodiak...?" I whispered, slightly panicking.

"Yeah?" he asked, somewhere to my left.

My hands twitched. "Where are you? I can't see anything." I was starting to see spots, and my vision swam. The last time I was in darkness, Midnight almost killed me.

I really despised not being able to see.

My hands found cloth, then the touch of human skin. "Here. Found you," Kodiak's voice said. He held my hand tight and asked, "You okay?"

I gulped. "Yeah, of course."

No. I wasn't.

But holding on to someone made me feel a lot better.

"You sure?"

"Yeah, why wouldn't I be?" I forced the lie out of my dry throat and slid my foot forward in an attempt to walk.

"Well, if you're sure. I figured you probably developed a fear of the dark after the Cinnabar

Trials. Maybe tight spaces, too, but definitely darkness."

"Shh...." I rasped. "Someone might hear us."

I really hoped nobody was watching us.

My heart was about to explode. My eyes kept blinking instinctively, trying to make out any shape in the dark, but it was useless. My breathing rhythm was increasing.

I had to get out of here.

I flung my other hand out, hoping to find a wall, but there was nothing. I took a few steps forward, but it got even darker.

"K-Kodiak! W-where's the door?" My voice cracked in ten thousand different places within those sentences.

"Hey, hey, it's okay," he soothed. "I'm right here."

I felt another hand grip my shoulder and turn me around. I let Kodiak take me closer to the door. It felt like hours before I felt the cool metal of the double doors. When I did, I threw my whole weight on it, tumbling out into the remaining light of the sun.

Then I just lay there, breathing.

Kodiak crouched beside my head. "Are you okay?" he asked, his voice thick with concern.

I picked myself off the floor. "That was

embarrassing. Sorry you had to see that." I brushed myself off and walked away, trying to be as nonchalant as possible. "I just hate the dark."

Kodiak shrugged. "No problem. My sister is the same. I'm used to it."

I was grateful that he didn't say anything else about it. "We really should investigate," I said. "They've probably cleared everything out, but it's still best to make sure."

Kodiak shook his head. "If everything is abandoned like this, then there's a high chance that this place really has been cleared out. I think Ivoria may have moved everything back to the Mainland."

I grimaced. "But why would she do that?"

Kodiak frowned. "I wouldn't know. But my guess is to leave no traces behind."

"But that makes no sense," I said. "If she wants to destroy the Terrenian Islands, she wouldn't move all her stuff back home then move them back here again. That's not very wise."

Kodiak scratched his head. "Well, it was just a speculation."

I set my teeth and clenched my hands into fists. I whirled around and started marching back toward the building. "I'm going to take a look."

189

"What?!" Kodiak scrambled to follow me. "But we just came from there! You can't take it!"

I forced myself not to turn around. "Kodiak, help me. We need to make sure there is nothing there. Something isn't right. If Ivoria is planning for war, or a battle, this place shouldn't feel so empty."

Kodiak didn't say anything for a while. Finally, he sighed and said, "You're so stubborn. Fine. But where are we going to get a light?"

I stopped right in front of the doors. "Kodiak, I'm going to rely on you in here. You're not afraid of the dark, right?"

"No."

I nodded. "Then just keep walking until you find something. I can't do much, but I don't want to wait outside. This place is starting to give me the creeps."

Kodiak stared at me then offered me his hand. "Would you rather hold my hand or have me hold your shoulders?"

I shrugged. "Whatever you think is best, I guess."

"That's weird. It should be whatever gives you the most comfort when you're scared."

I blinked, then grabbed his hand. "Don't say anything, please. This is just awkward."

Kodiak smiled. "Of course."

I stared hard at the dirt floor. "And..., don't tell the others that I'm suddenly afraid of the dark.... Okay? I can pretend I'm fine."

Kodiak looked at me for a moment, bit his lip, then nodded reluctantly. "If you're sure...."

I opened the door and led us in. Right when I entered, I slammed my eyes shut, even though it was impossibly dark already. Keeping my eyes closed gave me a strange sort of comfort, tricking my brain into thinking that it is dark only because I closed my eyes.

"Oh! Hey!" Kodiak's voice exclaimed.

I could see light through my eyelids. I opened my eyes and my jaw dropped.

"I found a light switch!" Kodiak said gleefully.

I slouched defeatedly. "Why...."

Kodiak laughed. "It's okay! I didn't see it the first time either."

I wanted to kick myself. "But the solution was so obvious!"

Kodiak laughed harder. "This is hilarious!"

I sighed and walked a bit faster. This was too humiliating. "Let's go."

Kodiak's footsteps resounded closely behind me. I wished he wasn't walking so close. "You don't need to stick that closely anymore," I told him. "I'm fine since there's light."

"I know," Kodiak said. "But I lost all feeling in my fingers since you're still holding my hand so tightly -"

I dropped his hand.

Kodiak's voice painted a grin in my mind. "Don't worry. Not going to say anything."

I made a noise of frustration. "Why didn't you tell me?"

"I thought you were going to stop after I turned on the light! But then -"

"Okay! Never mind! Forget I asked!" I stomped around the upcoming corner. "I need to wash my memory and forget everything that has happened in the last five minutes."

Kodiak laughed out loud then ran to catch up. "Why are you so embarrassed? It's natural to be scared and need something to hold on to."

I left him hanging. Partly because I didn't want to answer. I'd finally noticed (after I went back to school) what the older kids did when a boy and a girl were... attracted to each other. I didn't want all that awkwardness yet.

But it was mainly because I was staring at rows and rows of cannons.

Chapter 20

When Kodiak reached me, he froze in his tracks, just like I did. "What...."

I found my voice. "What'd I say, Kodiak? This is their weaponry Stone."

I took a few steps forward. The barrels were all tilted upward, but I was still cautious and crouched when I walked past. My heart stopped when I saw what was labeled on the first cannon:

FIRE

I don't get it. I ducked under the second cannon to read the label:

WATER

No. Nonononono!

EARTH

WIND

COSMOS

FIRE

And the pattern continued. The Cosmos cannon confirmed it. I dropped to my knees and stared. These were cannons specifically created to destroy everybody from a certain tribe.

This was genocide all over again.

Kodiak ran quickly to where I was sitting. "Rina, what's this? Is this what I..." His voice shook when he saw the label on the fifth cannon.

I nodded numbly. "At first I thought they were the labels on what types of cannons they were. I thought the "Fire" one shot fire, and the "Water" one shot water, but there isn't an earth cannon...."

"So.... That means...."

I turned to him. Our horrified eyes met.

"Ivoria really is planning to wipe us out."

Reality hit me and I scrambled to stand. "We've got to tell the others!"

Just then, I heard strange voices and footsteps.

My heart sank.

Kodiak grabbed my arm and dragged me behind the cannons. We laid on our sides, backs pressed against the wall, not breathing.

"Are you sure you locked this place up last night, Brian? The lights were on and the door was unlocked," a man's voice asked mockingly.

"Do you need to ask for the third time? YES I LOCKED IT UP LAST NIGHT!"

"Pfft. Whatever. I can't believe Boss wants us to check this place again! Didn't she tell us to do this yesterday?"

"Well, you know, Boss is boss," Brian said.

"That was the worst pun I've ever heard," the first man said.

There was a growl, then the first man spoke again, "Come on. Let's just do a quick walk around, then I'll lock up this time."

Kodiak and I exchanged fearful glances. We needed to leave this building before these men did.

"Connery, don't you think Boss is weak?" Brian asked suddenly.

I narrowed my eyes. Interesting....

"Be quiet! You'd be dead before you would hear an answer!" Connery said fearfully.

There was a pause, where I guessed that Brian

shrugged. "Fine. Not weak. She's… secretive."

"I don't know how you tied secretive with weak," Connery said disgustedly. "I can't believe you nearly got us killed! You don't know who might be in here!"

He has no idea….

"Well, she doesn't tell us what she's doing! She just says, 'Do this. Do that. Don't do this. If you don't, you die. And above all else, don't question me.' I mean, all we know about her is that she's a woman. We've never seen her face to face! We've never even heard her voice! There's a high chance she's not even a woman at all!"

My lips curled into a calculative smile. So Ivoria's people are doubting her…. I stretched my neck to peek out from between two cannons.

Both men were middle aged, but the man with blond hair and light eyes seemed younger than the brown-haired man. The blond guy looked about mid-thirties and wore a gray t-shirt and khaki shorts with running shoes. The other man looked about late-forties and had gelled, thinning hair. He was wearing a casual business shirt and pants. His face was creased with wrinkles of labor.

I could tell immediately; these people were ordinary. They haven't been injected with

Terrenian blood.

And judging by the disapproving way they spoke of Ivoria, they were newbies.

The blond guy swallowed, fear in his eyes. "Well, we know that if we speak ill of her, we'll die. Remember what happened to Jesse?"

Grief and horror passed over the older man's face. I shuddered, my brain coming up with horrible imaginations of what could have happened.

The blond guy nodded gravely. Though he was younger, he seemed much more experienced than the older man. This must be Connery. "All the cannons in this room have been accounted for. Let's move on to the next room."

They walked off somewhere to the left in silence.

Kodiak motioned for me to stay low as he raised his upper body to peek from behind the cannons. He quickly motioned for me to stand up.

We both crept out from behind the cannons. There was a turn at the far end of the room, where I could hear Brian counting more cannons, so Kodiak and I didn't waste any time. We bolted.

We didn't stop running until we reached our

camp. The sky had darkened by now, but I spotted a small speed boat docked farther down the beach. My first thought was to steal it. Then my second thought was that the five of us would never be able to fit. I sighed.

"Guys!" Kodiak panted.

Sirocca and the boys emerged out of their tents. Callan and Galen were still grumbling, but at least they weren't viciously fighting anymore. "You're back!" Sirocca exclaimed. "What's wrong?"

We told them the whole story.

Chapter 21

I could feel the boys eavesdropping from outside our tent. Sirocca sat in the corner, frowning.

"What do you think we should do?" I asked her.

Sirocca looked up. "You're the leader of this team. What do you think we should do?"

I was taken aback. I had forgotten I was the leader. "But you're a lot more sensible and reasonable than I am," I protested.

"But you're more experienced in this field," Sirocca told me. "I wouldn't know what would be best for our team right now. You've been in these kinds of situations before. You and Galen are the only ones who would know what to do."

Half of the tent suddenly caved in and we screamed. I scrambled out of the tent ready to drown whatever hit us in a bubble when I saw Galen lying on our tent.

"That's right, Sirocca!" he grinned. "We are the most experienced ones in this team!"

I growled in frustration. Callan's connection with Galen's arm forced him to bend over. "Couldn't you have come up with a different way to get their attention? And can you GET UP?"

Galen rolled his eyes. "You know, for P.E. at school, we've had to do much more extensive training than this. You can handle bending over for a few hours."

Callan's eyes darkened and he pulled back his leg.

"Kodiak!" I shouted.

"Got you," he said. He broke the link and I immediately lifted the boys up off the ground in separate bubbles.

Callan's foot followed through the swing and he fell backwards inside the bubble when he lost his balance. Both boys froze when they realized they weren't on the ground anymore.

"Come on, Rina!" Galen protested. "Not again!"

"We just told you some devastating news and you guys are still not fixing yourselves?" I scolded. "Shame...."

Galen and Callan ducked their heads. "Especially you, Callan!" Kodiak said. "You're older than Galen, and you let him drag you into a fight like that?"

"Excuse me?" Galen asked, hurt.

Callan glared at Kodiak. "Not helping, dude."

Sirocca brushed off her hands. "So. Take it away, Rina."

"I CAN'T BELIEVE YOU TWO!" I exploded. "Ivoria has really declared war on us. She's prepared millions and millions of cannons in that facility right over there," I pointed toward the buildings, "and you guys are still set on arguing with each other when we should be coming up with a plan to either blow up this place or at least destroy every cannon inside!

"AND DID I MENTION THAT THERE ARE PEOPLE INSIDE RIGHT NOW?!"

"Whoa...." Galen leaned forward. "I'm sorry, Rina. I didn't know you would get this upset."

"I'M NOT UPSET!" I roared. "I'm frustrated!"

Galen leaned back with a 'yup, she's upset' face. "Sorry, Rina."

I let them sit in there for a bit while I fumed. Kodiak appeared next to me, hesitatingly patting my shoulder. "You done?"

I roared in reply. I swung my arms upward. "KODIAK FREEZE THESE BUBBLES!"

"Wait, NO! RINA!" Galen's arms twitched as if he wanted to pound against the bubble walls, but since he was now ten feet in the air, that might not be the best idea, especially since there were trees. "PLEASE!"

Kodiak grabbed my shoulders. "You can't freeze your friends in a bubble."

I rolled my eyes. "I know that. I mean freeze it just enough so they'll be stuck in a tree until I calm down!"

Kodiak stepped back. "Well, I can't argue with that right now." He waved his hands.

The tops and bottoms of my bubbles iced over until they froze to the tree branches. The rest of bubbles frosted until they were thick enough to be unpoppable.

"They won't freeze," Kodiak promised.

I sniffed. "Let them freeze." I stomped away toward the ocean.

I sat down hard on the rocks. Why were they so *annoying?!* What are they even fighting about anyways?!

I picked up a rock and hurled it into the ocean. This didn't do anything to calm my temper, so I ran and dove straight in. I swam farther out to sea and sat on the ocean floor, breathing in, and out. In and out. In. Out.

This was a lot more relaxing than sleeping.

After I felt better, I climbed out completely dry and sat down. I started to think about many things: why I had to do this sort of thing again, why this team couldn't cooperate, and what was going to happen in the end.

I suddenly felt an overwhelming sadness. I missed Elece and Derrik. We were the perfect team. I had to talk to them.

I pulled out my phone and dialed Elece's number.

No response. I glanced at the sky. It was dark; she was still training.

I slowly turned off my phone and tucked it back in my pocket. I rested my chin on my knees and stared out into the dark horizon. This darkness felt more calming, especially since I could still see.

Footsteps behind me revealed that I wasn't alone. I turned around.

Galen stood there, staring at the ground and shuffling his foot. "Hey."

I stared at him. "How'd you get out?"

Galen swallowed. "I, uh, convinced Kodiak to let me out."

I arched an eyebrow. "Really?"

Galen bit his lip. "Well, it went both ways. I tried to convince him, and in the end, he decided to let me out so I could talk to you."

I blinked at him. I didn't answer.

Galen walked over and sat down next to me. "I'm sorry," he said again. "I wasn't thinking straight."

I snorted. "You sure weren't. Why do you fight with Callan all the time? I mean, there really isn't much for you two to fight over. You guys aren't that different."

Galen scoffed. "Sure."

I shrugged. "But still, why?"

Galen looked out to sea. "It's... it's nothing you need to worry about."

"You do know that when you say that it makes me worry?"

Galen blew out a breath. "Just... just know that I'm on your side no matter what. Callan and I have some conflicting ideas we need to work out, that's all."

I kept looking at him. "And I'm guessing I will never know what it is."

Galen flashed me a small smile. "Depends."

I sighed. "Okay, then. I'm trusting you on this."

Galen grinned. It was a smile that always made me feel better. It told me that I would have someone there to help me whenever and whatever.

"So.... Does this mean you'll choose me next time you go scouting?" Galen leaned in expectantly.

I laughed. "I don't know. Maybe."

"Aw, come on, Rina! How many times do I need to say this? I'm -"

"My best friend, I know!"

"Yeah! See? You already know! I'll take this as a yes. Let's go back." Galen stood up and ran. "YOU CAN'T CANCEL IT!"

I rolled my eyes and ran after him. It was then I realized that my nostalgia had disappeared just a little bit.

Chapter 22

When we got back to camp, Callan was already freed too. When he saw me coming with Galen, his eyes darkened, but he stepped towards me. "Rina, sorry about earlier."

I waved a hand. "It's fine. We're all tired. Let's figure out something quick tomorrow. Galen, can you take first watch?"

"Sure."

"Thanks." I ducked into the tent I shared with Sirocca. "Good night."

The next day, we headed off toward the second Stone the same way we travelled yesterday. For some reason, the distance between this Stone and the first Stone wasn't as great as the distance between the Islands and the first Stone. Maybe we were stronger and traveled faster? It doesn't matter. It saved a lot of time for us.

Galen came with me to investigate the second Stone's buildings this time. It was just as dark as before, but it was better since Galen could hold the door open with his wind as I found the light switch. I peeked around the corner before walking in case Brian and Connery were here as well.

I felt sick.

Galen gagged.

This room was filled with millions of vials and lab equipment. The vials all contained one of six colors: fiery red-orange, electric yellow, rich brown, pale gray, transparent clear, or deep red. I leaned in and almost threw up when I realized the red one was blood.

"These are the liquified elements we learned about last year," Galen commented, his face a bit green when he came across a pale gray vial. It was in a complex lab thing with blood. "What is this?"

"I think Ivoria is still trying to recreate the Talents for herself," I told him, disgusted. "This is probably her lab for studies."

"But, this...."

"Probably from the kids abducted last year," I said grimly. "We've collected some vital information. Let's go back now, before she sends people here to check on it again."

Galen and I flew out of the building and back to the others who were setting up camp again.

"We erased all our tracks at the first Stone, right?" Sirocca was saying to Callan.

"Yeah, I covered it all," he said, picking up a bundle of sticks.

"Guys!" I called.

Kodiak, Callan, and Sirocca dropped whatever they were doing and rushed over. Galen and I landed and sat down under a tree. We summarized our findings.

The others looked green by the time I finished speaking. Sirocca especially. "I'm sorry," she said. "I can't deal with blood."

I looked at her sadly. "Then last year was torture for you, wasn't it?"

Sirocca grimaced. "I can deal with miniscule injuries like cuts and scrapes. When a needle is stuck into you and it draws out two teeth of blood...." She shuddered.

Galen made a face. "So. Conclusion. She keeps her weapons closest to us, then her lab experiments. The third Stone is probably her new headquarters."

I nodded. "Now, I'll let you guys choose. Do you want to leave tonight or tomorrow morning?"

Kodiak and Callan exchanged glances. Sirocca tugged on a lock of honey-blond hair thoughtfully.

"Well, it's already dusk, and if we want to be there early tomorrow, then the obvious choice would be later tonight," Sirocca said slowly. "But if we want to be there ready, then I would choose tomorrow."

Kodiak rolled a ball of ice between his fingers. "I think tomorrow is best. We might have to go through a test or a fight or do something Ivoria throws at us. If we leave tonight, we won't be able to do well."

Callan nodded. "I mean, I personally want to get there tonight, but yeah, tomorrow is probably the best answer."

I nodded. "It's unanimous. We leave tomorrow before dawn."

Callan took the first watch this time. I lay in bed thinking. How long would this take? Why did Ivoria hate the Terrenian Islands so much? I mean, yeah, I knew that she was bitter that she didn't inherit a Talent, but did that hate run this deep? To the extent of willingness to commit genocide? I sighed and turned over.

Sirocca blinked at me. "Something wrong?"

I sighed again and sat up. "The sky is still bright. I can't sleep."

Sirocca nodded and sat up too. "I know what you mean."

I groaned and fell backwards. "Sirocca, can I ask you something?"

"Go for it."

"Why'd you decide to go on this mission?" Sirocca was quiet for a moment. "Well, the obvious answer would be because I want to protect my nation. And it's true."

I sat up again. "But...."

Sirocca smiled, a bit ashamed. "None of us are perfect. I've been thinking that same question for the past two days. I think.... I think I decided to go because part of me, deep down, wants revenge for the hurt that happened to me last year."

I stared at her. Sirocca wants revenge?

"You're the last person in my mind who would want something like that," I told her. "You seem too kind to want something as dangerous as revenge."

Sirocca laughed softly. "Well, I wish I really were that kind to forgive someone who wanted to take my Talent away. And abduct two hundred kids in the process. And torture them."

I nodded. "You have a point."

Sirocca looked up at me. "Anyways, why were you wondering?"

I looked away. "I'm not sure. All I know so far is that I really want to protect the Islands from Ivoria, but the fact that I'm the one leading this mission, and I'm the one that everyone relies on...." I exhaled. "I don't know."

Sirocca leaned in. "You know what? You're putting too much pressure on yourself. Hello? Do you notice the rest of us?"

I blushed. "I didn't mean it that way."

Sirocca leaned back. "I know. But what I'm trying to say is, you're not alone in this. There's me, Kodiak, Callan, and Galen, of course. Emily is cheering you on from the Islands. Elece and Derrik are probably worried for you as well. Your parents miss you."

I stared at her. "My parents won't miss me."

Sirocca gave me a sad smile. "They do." She didn't say anything for a while, but she suddenly spoke, "My father passed away a few years ago."

I looked down. I didn't know what to say.

"I'm sorry."

Sirocca played with her fingers. "My grandparents didn't have a good relationship with my dad. From what I've heard, he was very rebellious when he was a teen, and the rift between them still hadn't healed." She looked up at me. "When my dad died, I was angry at my grandparents. It was irrational, I know. But other than my dad, there wouldn't be anybody to take care of me. I thought my grandparents wouldn't want me since they didn't seem to like their own son.

"But at the funeral," Sirocca swallowed back tears. "At the funeral, I saw my grandparents for the first time in ten years. They were weeping their eyes out. They were sobbing out sorrowful words about...," Sirocca cleared her throat and didn't speak for a while.

I scooted closer and wrapped an arm around her.

It's strange. From the first look, Sirocca seemed to be the perfect child. The person who had it all. Her confidence and beauty displayed that her life was the one that everyone envied.

But deep down, she concealed a lot of hurt and scars. She was able to keep smiling despite the fact that they were there.

212

I admired her so much.

When Sirocca found her voice, she continued, "I heard some of what they said. They kept crying about how sorry they were. They blamed themselves for not showing how much they loved my dad sooner. That they prevented him from doing certain things because they knew it would come back to hurt him in the end. That they never got to express how they loved him so, so much."

Sirocca looked up at me. "That hit me the most. The grandparents that I thought were never capable of having any emotion towards my dad actually held a love that ran deep for him. When they came up to me, they said they would now take the responsibility of being my parents. They were going to do for me what they couldn't do for my dad."

I was in a different place. A different time. Sirocca suddenly looked at me with a fierce expression.

"I know your family isn't the best right now either," she said. "Your sister fights with you. You were kicked out for not turning out to be who your parents wanted you to be. But guess what? You better tell them right now how you feel before you regret it later."

I ducked my head. Tell my parents? Tell them that how much I've always yearned for their love and affection?

How?

Sirocca smiled at me. "Trust me, it would go two ways. Your relationship with your family would heal, or, you would see how they feel towards you. It's a win-win, actually, even if you don't like their answer. But I don't think it's going to go there."

I looked away. How did this conversation go here?

Sirocca laid her hands on my shoulders. "Have you ever told your parents 'I love you'?"

I froze. "No…." This was really awkward and personal….

"Try it. That might be the thing that they've been wanting to hear for a long time."

I didn't say anything for a moment. "Right now?"

Sirocca shrugged. "If you want to. But postponing it for too long won't be good."

I sighed. "I'll wait until later then. I don't like them right now. They stole Zin, gave it to Mira, and they're always thinking about their position on the Council rather than just being happy for what I've actually accomplished in my life."

Sirocca smiled sadly. "At least try. I'm sorry if this made you uncomfortable. I'm just really passionate about this."

"No, no! It's fine!" I said hastily. "It's just... I'm just used to the space between us. Actually, my parents have been... nicer to me after I came back...." I exhaled. "I think it's just because I was gone for so long."

"Or," Sirocca said. "It's because they realized how much you mean to them."

I made a face. "I don't think so."

Sirocca shrugged. "You'll never know unless you talk to them. But enough deep stuff for today. I think I ruined your sleep for tonight. Sorry about that."

"Nah, it's okay!" I waved a hand.

"But, don't be afraid to come to me if you want to talk about anything." Sirocca smiled gently.

I grinned. "Okay, thanks!"

I lay down, expecting to ponder more about life. What happened instead was I fell into the best sleep I've ever had ever since this mission started.

Chapter 23

Emily walked slowly to the training rooms. It had been only been two days since the Rep Team left the Islands, but it already felt like two months. Every second that ticked by tied another bag of anxiety to her heart, threatening to be the straw that broke the camel's back. She wanted to call her team, to command them back home where they'd be safe, and magically destroy Ivoria forever.

Reality was cruel, sometimes.

Emily watched the tile floor. Her feet had subconsciously started to step in each tile, avoiding the cracks. Cracks... so many cracks in this nation ever since she became queen....

When will it fall apart?

A small tickle behind her neck told her to stop for a bit. Tawny flew out from her hair and hovered in front of her face. "Emily…?"

Emily watched her pixie. "Yes?"

"Are you okay? You haven't been yourself since the coronation."

Emily smiled tiredly. "Being a queen is starting to take a toll on me." She continued to walk.

Tawny flitted nervously.

"How is Zinnia doing?" Emily asked suddenly. Perhaps this small task would allow Zinnia to cease worrying about her. "Rina would want to see her completely healed by the time she returns."

Tawny smiled. "I'll check up on her." She flew off.

Emily breathed a sigh of relief just as she approached the entryway to the training room. She passed by the arch and glanced to her right, through the glass windows that overlooked the gym-like facility.

"STOP!" Melody was shouting. "ELECE!"

Elece sat hunched on the floor, gripping her forearm. Streams of red trickled from between her fingers. Emily's breath caught.

"What?" Elece demanded harshly. She glared at her trainer. "I'm a warrior. A small injury like this isn't supposed to stop me."

217

"A warrior knows when the battle is not worth fighting," Melody retorted. "Your arm was right in front of your chest. If it had been from another angle, it would've killed you."

Elece glowered at the gash in her arm. "This is training. I'm fine."

Melody rolled her eyes. "I'll believe it when I see it. It won't be a simulated battle in real life."

"I'm training to be part of the Queen's Guard," Elece said hotly. "Injuries are expected."

"Yet, you're trying to be trained so you can emerge out of battle unscathed," Melody responded coolly. "But if you rather fight with gashes in your body, be my guest."

Elece let out a frustrated growl. "Fine."

"Wrap it up nicely like I taught you and be back here in ten minutes," Melody said. "Your time starts now."

Elece stomped off, muttering to herself and glaring at her wound.

Emily bit her lip. Elece's temper was getting shorter.

Emily glanced at the wooden door up ahead. She walked through and leaned on the glass windows that lay after it. A huge control room was spread out on the other side, wires and computers littered everywhere in a strangely neat pattern.

In the center of the room, Derrik sat hunched over a large screen, fingers flying over the keyboard, eyes drilling holes into the code that was struggling to keep up with his typing.

"FASTER!" Glenn roared behind him. One hand gripped the back of Derrik's seat, leaving dents where his fingers pressed too hard into the plastic.

"I'm trying!" Derrik said through gritted teeth. "My fingers are cramping!"

"You can't have that happening when your companions are depending on you to hack through the security system before their guts are splattered across the field," Glenn said sternly. "We're going to use the training room after Melody and Elece are done. We need to sharpen those sword skills of yours in case someone breaks through."

"But I use a crossbow," Derrik protested, pausing in his hacking.

"DON'T STOP!" Glenn roared. "I'm one of your teammates, fighting to keep you protected as your work. Do you want me to die in vain?"

Derrik started to type faster. "And... done! I'm through!"

Glenn let out a loud laugh then smacked

Derrik on the back, causing the younger boy to nearly smash his face into his keyboard. "Nice job! Getting there."

Emily watched them celebrate a second longer before turning and walking back outside. They're so young... yet they're being forced to train so hard....

It is under my command they're training so hard, Emily thought. They want to train this hard. Especially since Rina and Galen left. They needed to double the workload they take to make up for their absence.

As if on cue, an alarm sounded, the room blaring with red light. Emily froze, terrified for a second before rushing down the stairs and into the training room. "What -?"

She froze. In the time it had taken her to fly down the stairs, Elece and Derrik had already suited up, weapons drawn, facing their trainers. All four people stopped to stare in surprise as Emily flew down in a panic.

"Emily?" Elece said. "What are you doing here?"

Emily stood, muscles still tensed. "There was an alarm. Is everything alright?"

Melody and Glenn burst out laughing. Jordan appeared from the alcove in the back, grinning.

"Relax. The trainers and I agreed that having random alarms throughout the day would prepare them to be ready for any kind of threat instinctively. Since Rina is gone for the time being, I've taken it upon myself to sound the alarms."

Emily relaxed. "Oh. Okay. That startled me for a second."

Skye emerged from the alcove as well. "Any news from Galen and Rina?" he asked, rubbing his wrist.

Emily stared at the ground regretfully. "I've ordered no contact with them whatsoever during the duration of their mission to ensure the safety of our people. Their progress is unknown."

Derrik and Elece exchanged glances. "Emily, you doing okay?"

Emily furrowed her brow. "Yeah, I am perfectly fine. The stress and worry for the team is... harder to deal with than I had initially expected."

"Okay. Just checking. You're using bigger words now," Derrik said. "You're speaking more... formally now."

Emily glanced at him in surprise, then snickered. "I am training myself to speak this way. A queen needs to be eloquent in her words, am I right?"

Elece laughed. "If you're going for formal, say, 'correct?' instead of 'am I right?'"

Emily groaned. "Whatever. Back to the point. Galen and Rina aren't here, and I don't know how long the negotiation will take."

Elece grimaced, touching her bandage. "We can cover for them for now."

"Slow down, speedy," Melody said teasingly. "You two aren't ready until Glenn and I deem you ready. You still haven't been able to take down Skye and Jordan yet. You won't last ten minutes against one of her soldiers."

Elece and Derrik frowned at her from behind their ninja masks.

Melody held up her hands. "Right. I forgot. Single-handedly took down twenty men or something. My bad."

Emily dipped her head at the four trainers. "I'll leave you guys to it, then. I'll see you later."

The six warriors said their goodbyes to the queen as she strode out of the training room.

Just that moment, Tawny flew up to her. "Zin is slowly recovering," she reported with a pretentious military pose. "Would you like me to assign a permanent guard over the recuperating pixie?"

222

"Yes," Emily said, playing along. "Assign all our pixies to watch her and keep her company. I will have your head if she is not well by the time the team returns."

Tawny's eyes sparkled with mock fear. "Roger that, Your Highness." And she flew off.

Emily allowed herself a small chuckle before she thought back to the conversation back in the training room. She made her way to her chambers as she thought about it.

You wouldn't last ten minutes against one of her soldiers.

Emily pursed her lips and kept walking.

Chapter 24

We all woke up early (again) the next day. This time, we got to the third Stone a lot faster than usual. I'm not sure if it was because we all naturally flew faster due to nerves, or if the island was closer. It was probably because of the former.

When we washed up on the beach, everyone stood very close to the water's edge. The waves licked the heels of our shoes as everyone stood there, staring at the trees.

"So. What do we do now? We're at the third Stone before a week has passed, just like Ivoria instructed," Kodiak said.

I squinted off into the distance. "This place has changed a lot since the last time we were here, Galen."

"You're right about that. Look at that

mansion!" Galen pointed through the trees.

A huge building loomed through the trees. The strange thing was, it was beautiful. The walls were white, vines of beautiful purple flowers grew artistically on the plaster. The trees had been cut into shapes of different animals: an owl, a swan, a peacock, a falcon, and an eagle.

Huh. Ivoria must have a thing about birds....

"So, uh, are we just going to stand here, or are we going to actually do something?" Callan asked.

I kept staring at the mansion. "I don't know. It's up to you."

I took a step forward. Then another. I counted my steps in a steady rhythm until I reached the trees.

Twenty-six steps.

I looked to my left. Galen looked up, matching my pace exactly. He grinned, and I smiled back.

Knowing that Galen was there gave me a new surge of confidence.

You ready?, he asked.

Nope. Let's go.

The other three followed closely behind. We walked up a stone path decorated with potted plants.

How could such an evil person live with such beauty?

We approached the huge pearl-white doors. Thin strips of gold were set in an artful curl around the border of the doors. I took a deep breath. I raised my fist.

I knocked on the door.

Immediately, someone answered. I almost wet my pants when I saw who it was.

Enzo. The burn scar was still on my left arm.

"What?" he asked gruffly.

I kept my expression calm. "Ivoria has requested our presence."

Enzo blinked. "Speak English."

That was English. "Ivoria wants to see us."

Enzo peered closely at me. "Hey, wait a minute...."

"Just let us in, Beefster!" Galen shouted. "You don't need to know who we are. Lead us to Ivoria."

Enzo glared at Galen. "You don't want to mess with me, youngster." He held up his hand and a ball of flame danced between his fingers. "I bet you've never seen this before, huh? That's right. Back off."

I exchanged glances with Galen. Enzo was pretty dim.

226

"So. Are you going to let us in or not?" Galen asked, eyes intense.

Enzo growled. He shoved the door open. "Try to keep up," he barked. "Ivoria does not like to be kept waiting."

"Well, he was the one holding us up in the first place," Callan muttered.

"Shh!" Kodiak hissed. "Let Rina talk."

I followed Enzo inside. The interior was very similar to the Royal Palace back at home. I focused on every detail. Did it really only take a year for them to build this place?

I had no idea where Enzo was taking us. There were many hallways, many windows, many stairs. After ten minutes, Kodiak said, "Hey, uh, so, where is Ivoria exactly?"

Enzo rubbed his nose. "I don't know."

"WHAT?!" We all exploded.

I struggled to control my temper. "So. What's the point of this?"

Enzo turned to look at me, a gleam in his eye. "You're supposed to know. You've been here for some time already."

I blinked. "I just got here. I'm afraid I haven't seen you before," I lied.

Enzo shook his head. "You pretty little liar…." he said menacingly.

Just then, the click of heels on marble floors froze everyone in place.

Finally.

A lean woman in a tight business suit walked into the large ballroom-like hallway. "Enzo."

Enzo quickly ducked his head. "Boss."

Ah. So Enzo was one of the few people who actually knew who the Boss was. THEN WHY DID HE LEAD US ON A WILD GOOSE CHASE?!

"I'll take it from here," Ivoria said coldly. "What you see is not what it seems."

Enzo's face actually turned red. "Yes, ma'am." He hurried off.

Ivoria turned to us, a strange smile on her face. "You came."

I stood tall. Ivoria wasn't that much taller than me. I shouldn't feel so intimidated. "We came to negotiate," I said coldly.

"As instructed," she said smoothly.

"As suggested," I shot back calmly.

"My, how much you've grown," Ivoria said with a casual chuckle. Her gaze shifted behind me. "And what of your friends? Have they become your followers?"

"We are not followers," Callan snapped.

Kodiak and Galen both elbowed him in his

ribs. Ivoria saw this and laughed. "Ah, still the same person, I see. Well, Earth candidate, I'm sure you'll find this negotiation very enticing."

"Get straight to the point," Galen demanded. "What do you need to speak to us about?"

Ivoria held a staring contest with Galen for a few seconds. Galen never blinked or backed down.

Ivoria leaned back. "It really does surprise me how much you children have matured in this past year. I'm expecting to be able to speak to you as adults. I really do despise speaking to children."

With that, she turned and walked away.

Galen immediately walked after her. I followed him, letting him lead for a while. I took this time to walk next to Callan.

"Hey," I said. "What did Kodiak say back there?"

Callan muttered, "Yeah, I know. Sorry."

I sighed, annoyed. "Kodiak. I don't need to tell you, right?"

Kodiak sighed in return. "Come on, Callan. I'm supposed to watch you again."

Callan stared angrily at the floor. "If I don't say anything else, I'll be fine, right?"

I looked at him. "That's all up to you. But

Kodiak will be right there."

Callan looked up at me in agony. "Why are you doing this to me? Why are you treating me like a kid?"

I sighed. "It's just.... This is important. It could cost us our lives. One wrong move and we're dead. Everyone at home would be gone. Do you understand?"

"Of course I do," he said. "That's why I'm here. But how do you know I don't have something to contribute? I might even be able to save our lives."

I stretched my neck. "We'll see."

Callan looked away, hurt.

"Hey. I'm sorry, but -"

Callan kept walking.

I glanced at Kodiak. "Did I say something wrong?"

Kodiak shrugged. "I mean, I didn't hear anything wrong. It was constructive criticism, I would say. Don't take this too hard. Callan's an only child, so he's not used to being disciplined."

I sighed. "I hope you're right. Callan's pretty good for an only child. I've seen some people who were so spoiled, they would sue you for passing by if they could."

Kodiak made a face. "Callan? Nah, he's pretty

bad."

I glared at Kodiak. "He's your best friend! How could you say that?"

Kodiak gave me a side glance. "You barely know him. Why are you defending him?"

"Because -" I made a noise of annoyance. "You know what? Why are we even talking about this?" I stomped up ahead to where Galen was walking.

I've never seen such a serious face on my friend before. Maybe he really did grow up a little.

Then I noticed that he was a few inches taller than me. My jaw dropped. "What?!"

Galen glanced at me. "What?"

"You're taller than me!"

Galen's gaze shifted to the top of my head. "Hey, you're right!"

Ivoria's voice suddenly sang, "You children really are getting comfortable in this place! That gives me one less job to do!"

We immediately clammed up and walked the rest of the way in silence. Ivoria spoke up mockingly, "Oh, now really, why the silence?"

I glared holes into the floor. ARGH!

I REALLY DON'T LIKE HER!!

"Will you please tell us where we're going?" I

said through gritted teeth.

Ivoria stopped when she reached a steel door. She spun around with a dangerous smile.

"The negotiation room, of course."

Chapter 25

We all entered the room silently. There was a humongous space with a single table in the center of the room with six chairs. I stared at it in disbelief.

That's it?

What was all this empty space for?

The walls were made of the same smooth marble as the floor. I squinted my eyes. The floor had decorative grooves etched in. I was very confused.

"Why did you choose this room?" I asked. "It has an unusual amount of space."

Ivoria grinned. "Why are you so suspicious? It is only a room for us to talk in."

"Talk". The way she said it. I narrowed my eyes and exchanged glances with Galen.

Yup. We're going to do a lot more than talk.

Ivoria ushered us out. "You children must be exhausted from your journey here. I'll show you to your rooms."

She led us down the hall until we came across five doors. Each door was labeled with a certain tribe name.

Wonderful. She doesn't know our names.

"Of course, I wasn't sure who Emily was going to send as her representatives, but I had a hunch that she would send one person from every tribe; it's the most logical thing to do. So I have prepared rooms to cater towards each tribe member."

"Cater". That suspicious tone again. I exchanged another glance with Galen as I opened the door to the room labeled "Fire".

"Ah, are you sure you're in the right room?" Ivoria laid a heavy hand on my shoulder. "Shouldn't you be in the water dorm?"

I didn't move. "Then what would Kodiak be here for?"

Ivoria gave me a chilling smile. "Very well."

Her hand lifted from my shoulder and I stepped into the room.

The bedroom was every inch comfortable. A huge king-sized bed with silk sheets and an overstuffed couch; if this wasn't Ivoria's place, I'd live here!

Everything was colored red. I guess Ivoria wanted to match the theme of fire....

I walked out and looked to the right and left. My room was in the center with Cosmos and Earth on my right, and Wind and Water on my left. Ivoria had already left; I'm assuming we're starting to talk tomorrow.

I knocked on the "Cosmos" door. Sirocca answered and let me in. "How's your room?" she asked.

I shrugged. "If you're used to the color red, it's not that bad. What about you? Does it feel weird being in a Cosmos room?"

Sirocca shrugged. "The color isn't too far off from my usual color. I don't think it's too bad."

I nodded. "That's good."

HEY RINA!

I gave a sudden jump. *Yeah?*

Don't say anything!!! If you're with Sirocca, DON'T TALK!

I immediately lifted a finger to my lips, signaling Sirocca to be quiet for a second. She understood and sat down on the bed.

What's wrong?

I think I found a bug in my room.... Galen said.

I nodded. *I thought so. Is it voice or video?*

I think it may be just voice. I think it heard me burp just now....

Ew. I didn't need to hear that. But that's typical of Ivoria, I said. *Extra precautions in case we're planning something.*

Yeah. Check all of your rooms thoroughly. I found mine underneath the bed.

What were you doing underneath the bed?!

Part of it was to inspect the room. The main reason was to find a place to keep my dirty laundry.

I sighed, and shook my head. *Of course you were.*

What?! I want to see how well Ivoria can keep our rooms clean!

Sirocca waved her hands and asked if she could speak now. I nodded and turned to her.

"You should do something next time you and Galen -"

"Sirocca, do you think we should rest?" I cut in suddenly. I searched through her desk drawers for pen and paper. "I mean, for you, flying for almost three days straight is exhausting, isn't it?"

I found some and scribbled: Galen said he found a bug in his room.

At first, it didn't seem like Sirocca saw. "Yeah, you're right. I've never flown that far before. I'll just sleep now. Are you staying in my room for a

236

bit or are you leaving?"

"I'll stay here for a bit. I want to see how different your room is from mine."

I sat on the bed next to her and handed her the pen and paper. Sirocca wrote: *Next time you speak with Galen, don't just randomly freeze. There might be cameras in here.*

I felt sick. So we can't talk at all?

I wrote: *Galen told us to inspect our rooms. He found his under his bed.*

Sirocca gave me a strange look and I shrugged. It's Galen. What can you do?

I had a thought just then. Wait. If there are cameras, then how is this not suspicious?!

I quickly stood up and stretched, dropping the pencil. "I thought we were going to rest, Sirocca. I wrote down one word problem that's been bothering me this whole day and now it's a math lesson?!"

Sirocca laughed. "Sorry, math is one of my favorite things, you know?"

I sighed. "I'm going back to my room now, then. I'll keep thinking about the problem," I gave her a look, "Hope you get used to the room. You're one of those people who can't sleep on new beds, right?"

Sirocca made a face. "Yeah, new beds are too stiff. I don't understand how people can sleep anywhere! I've seen people sleep under a desk once."

I laughed. "Maybe it's the material?"

Sirocca made a thoughtful face. Did this girl take acting lessons or something? "You have a point," she said. "I'll see if I there's a tag on this bed later tonight that lists the material. Thanks!"

Now she gave me a subtle look. I nodded. "Anytime!"

I walked back to my room. *Alright, Galen. Find anything new?*

No.

Sirocca suspects cameras. See anything?

Nothing! He sounded frustrated.

I opened my door and stepped in. *I'm in the room next door to you. Cameras would most likely be more concealed. At least that's what I've read in books. Or was it about the bugs...?*

Well, whatever it is, I've only found a bug. Maybe speaking in the garden outside sometimes?

Yeah, that might work, except there are probably security cameras everywhere.

ARGH! We can't do anything!

Well, to be fair, if I was Ivoria, I'd do the same.

YOU'RE NOT SUPPOSED TO BE ON HER SIDE!

I sighed and sat down on my bed. *Come on. You know me the best here. I'm going to check for bugs.*

First, I looked under the bed. I kinda suspected it wouldn't be there, since it wouldn't be too smart to place all the bugs in the same place. Then I checked under the dresser. Nope.

I eventually got too lazy to search. I figured if there really was a bug somewhere, I'd find it sooner or later. I flopped down on the bed and told Galen my predicament.

YOU CAN'T BE LAZY AT A TIME LIKE THIS! He screamed furiously at me. I got a headache. *COME ON!!*

Yeah, but I'm tired. And searching the entire room will take too long.

I heard Galen sigh. *Sleep, then. You never know when Ivoria is going to call us.*

I made a face. *Exactly why I shouldn't sleep. Who knows what she's doing?*

Want to go with me and sneak around? His voice was mischievous and eager. *Let's prank her or something!*

Are you crazy? We'll die here if you did that! I didn't say anything for a while. Maybe the day after tomorrow if we're still here.

ALRIGHT!, he cheered.

Knock on my door if anything happens. I rolled over and tried to sleep. Unfortunately, I was too restless, so I opened my dresser to see what kind of stuff Ivoria had for us inside.

Clothes.

Of course. It's a drawer.   But they were girl clothes. I narrowed my eyes.

Did Ivoria know who the representatives were going to be?

I closed the top drawer and opened the next one. The first drawer had been casual clothes. The second drawer was filled with dresses. I pulled one out then made a face. It showed too much skin and looked really uncomfortable to wear. I shuddered. I will never wear these.

I looked around. So. Just a desk, a drawer, and a huge bed. Oh, and a nice little bedside table too. There was also a huge window right above the desk.

It was then I realized there was no bathroom. I groaned, then stepped outside the room. I looked both ways, trying to decide which hallway looked more promising, then headed left.

I can't believe I'm looking for a bathroom.

Luckily for me, I didn't have to look far. It was just down the hall.

Whew!

Chapter 26

"Order!" Elece shouted. "Get into position!"

"Yes, sir!" All the higher level students at the Academy froze in orderly rows in front of the school campus. Near the front, two boys were nudging each other. Two girls to the right were giggling and gossipping.

Elece pressed her fingers to her forehead. "It's only been an hour and you can't even stand still?"

Why did Emily command this…?

After Emily's drop-in yesterday, she sent a notice out, telling the people about the need to prepare for war. She assigned Elece and Derrik with the task of training the students at the Academy. The other four trainers were assigned to train the adults. Elders and younger children were exempt from the training.

"Everyone needs to be prepared should Ivoria come and attack us," Emily had said. "We need everyone to fight against her if we want to win. Who knows how many people Ivoria has enhanced with your blood? We want to heighten our chances of winning against those soldiers, correct?"

Derrik snapped his fingers and eight lions prowled out of the surrounding forests, snapping Elece back to the present. The students stiffened immediately, but no one screamed.

"Your commander gave you an order, and you're expected to obey," Derrik growled. His glowing eyes glared threateningly across the crowd from behind his half-face. The lions surrounded the students, prepared to pounce. "If you decide to not answer, you will answer to the queen herself. Is that clear?"

The students shuffled and stared at the ground, mumbling, "Yes, sir." One defiant boy glared at Derrik. "You're younger than all of us. Why are you commanding with Elece?"

Elece flashed forward until she was standing face to face with the boy. He was her age, she could tell. "What's your name?" she asked lowly.

He glared at her through his brown hair. "Bryan Roots."

"Well, Roots. If you're so confident in your ability to command an army, be my guest." Using her speed, Elece stepped forward and pushed Bryan behind her, switching place with him in a nanosecond. Bryan stumbled and looked startled to be in the front of the school. Elece stood there nonchalantly, watching him attentively. "Your orders, Commander?"

Bryan sneered at Elece, and in one smooth snap and swing of his arm, all the trees around him stretched and bent towards Elece, their roots reaching for her. Elece touched each root and they each turned char black, letting out a zap.

Bryan paled. His eyes, which had flared a bright green seconds ago, died until they returned to their normal gray.

Elece dusted off her hands. "Yeah, even after knowing I have the Lightning Talent… not the smartest move." She glanced up at him. "What's next?"

With a grumble, Bryan shuffled up to her and took his place. Elece stepped back up to the front, returning Derrik's grin with the slightest smirk.

"Let's try this again," Elece said smoothly. "The Islands may be thrown in war very soon. Everyone needs to be prepared to fight."

"But what if we don't want to?" a girl peeped.

Elece stared at her for a second. "You will still need to contribute to the war effort. However, you still need to learn the basic self defense moves should you be suddenly attacked by an enemy soldier."

The girl trembled and nodded.

Elece bit her lip for a quick second before resuming her attitude. "GET MOVING, SLOWPOKES!"

As the students started running a few laps around campus, Derrik sidled up to Elece and murmured, "This is going to take a while."

Elece rubbed her eyes. "No kidding. I told Emily that it would be better if each tribe was trained separately, but she said we didn't have enough people to train them like that. It doesn't make sense to me either way. There are professional commanders and officers in each tribe. They can train them."

Derrik shrugged. "We would have had enough people if...." He left the sentence unfinished.

Elece sighed. "Yeah." She gazed off into the distance, taking a moment to remember an airheaded dark-haired boy and a clueless brown-haired girl.

The clouds ahead rolled dark and spooky.

Elece glared at them with narrowed eyes. "Derrik?"

Derrik nodded. It had been cloudy all day. "ALL RIGHT! BRING IT BACK! TRAINING IS OVER FOR TODAY! MEET BACK HERE TOMORROW!"

The crowd of students stopped once to give a short salute before dispersing into the Tunnels.

Chapter 27

Ivoria summoned us to start the negotiation the same day. It appeared as a yellow scroll resting on our beds. We found them after we decided to take a walk in her garden at the back of the mansion. Staying in our rooms was too confining, and despite the hatred Islanders felt towards Mainlanders, they were still able to create impressive gardens out of dry dirt and polluted air.

We also tried to talk about some sort of plan, but that ended up with half of the garden destroyed by boulders and half of the trees windblown and upturned.

AHEM!!

Anyways, the scroll's message was pretty simple:

Your presence is requested in the Negotiation Room.

Formal attire is instructed.

Yeah, I don't know why she could've just said, "Meet me in this room and wear a dress."

I upturned the second drawer trying to find something suitable. I threw seventy-five percent of the dresses out the window, finally picking a dress that looked decent.

I slipped it on, tied back half of my hair into something called princess hair then stepped outside.

Sirocca, and Galen had finished already. Galen bounced on the heels of his feet nervously. He was wearing a suit, but his hair was as unruly as always. Sirocca kept twisting her fingers, a small crease in between her eyebrows. She wore a floor-length bright yellow gown, her hair curled in light waves.

Did she bring her own curling iron?

They both looked up when I walked out, and they both tried to give me relaxed smiles.

"You look nice," Sirocca said, nodding at my dress. "Red is a new color on you."

I made a face. "Well, everything in the drawer was red, so what choice did I have?"

"You know what I'm wondering?" Galen

asked, tugging at his collar. He wore no tie, but he seemed just as uncomfortable. "How did Ivoria know what genders we were going to be? I walked in and everything was arranged for a boy."

I nodded. "Yeah, I wondered that too."

Sirocca scratched her head. "You know when Enzo walked us in? He was probably stalling while Ivoria took a quick look at the cameras and told whoever took care of this place to prepare for two girls and three guys. I mean, she recognizes all of us from our last encounter, right? So she'd know which tribe we were coming from."

I gazed at Sirocca in awe. "Amazing."

Galen sniffed. "What about you? There are two Wind Islanders here."

Sirocca shrugged. "You seem more Wind than me. I'm usually dressed in something yellow, the signature color of Cosmos, so I think she made the connection."

How did she figure stuff out like this?!

Callan came out next. Unlike Galen, he had tried to do something about his hair, so it was flatter and kept his face clear. I was not used to this image. I haven't even gotten used to his dyed hair yet!

"Is Kodiak done yet?" Galen asked impatiently. "I'm pretty sure Ivoria's not going to be happy if we're late."

"Since when were you so concerned with keeping her pleased?" Callan asked.

Galen's eyes glittered dangerously. "Do you really want to know?"

I groaned. "You know what? I'm too tired to resolve this."

I walked over to Kodiak's door and knocked on it. "Kodiak! You almost done?"

Something thumped softly onto the ground, like a phone dropping. A second afterwards, Kodiak opened the door, tucking something in his back pocket. "Yeah, sorry. Had to make a quick call home."

I nodded slowly. He's been making calls home quite often….

"Everything good?" I asked.

He gave a start and nodded rapidly. "Of course."

I frowned. This was starting to bug me….

Kodiak sighed. "I'll tell you soon."

I smiled. "Great! That's all I needed to hear."

I turned back and Callan seemed to glare at Kodiak. Suspicious….

What was going on here?

Whatever. We needed to get to the Negotiation Room. "Uh, does anybody remember the way there?"

Galen snorted and shook his head. "Rina, you are hopeless with directions."

He marched down the hallway on the right. After a few seconds, he said, "It's right here."

"Oh. Okay. Thanks!"

We stood in front of the door, not saying anything. "So. You guys ready?"

"No."

We walked inside anyways.

Ivoria sat at the head of the table, drinking from a mug. The scent of coffee drifted over to us.

"You children enjoy taking your sweet time, don't you?" Ivoria asked, eyes closed.

We filed inside silently. Each seat had been marked with a specific tribe, so we sat in our respective spots. Kodiak was to the right of Ivoria. Galen was next to him. Across from Kodiak was Sirocca and Callan sat next to her, facing Galen. I sat at the foot of the table, directly facing Ivoria.

Drinks had also been prepared for us. I stared at the strange liquid. Did she really expect us to drink a whole cup of tea at this age?

I mean, we've all drank tea before, but it

wasn't the wisest thing.

And it was probably poisoned or drugged, anyways.

I stared at Ivoria, waiting for her to finish thinking. When she finally set her cup down, we had been in the room for ten minutes already.

"So. Let us begin." Ivoria smoothed down her skirt. She always wore the same business suit.... "I assume you children have already been aware of my... decisions and rules of negotiation?"

I glared at her. "We're very familiar with them."

Ivoria gave us a chilling smile. "Splendid. That'll make today a lot easier.

"I'll also continue to assume that Emily has informed you of our agreement?"

I kept my gaze level. "Which one would that be?"

"My decision to wipe out the Terrenian Islands, of course."

I struggled to keep my calm. "You won't wipe us out if we agreed to come negotiate with you."

Ivoria laughed. "Dear child. Your assumptions have taken you too far. I never promised that my attacks would be restrained if you simply come and talk with me."

"What about your assumptions?" I snapped.

"You didn't expect children to come negotiate with you, did you? A "Boss" who sends a servant to greet her "guests" as a phony act of diplomacy."

Ivoria displayed a fake smile. "'Phony'? Why, I was busy at the moment -"

I snorted. "Yeah. Busy spying on us, then sending your other servants to prepare rooms accordingly to make it seem as if you knew exactly who was coming."

"Child, I would warn you to -"

"Oh, you would, would you?" I snarled. "Please. You're not fooling anyone by speaking so formally. We all know that you hate us. We're not convinced by your false act of 'kindness'."

Ivoria massaged her temples. "This is exactly why I do not like dealing with children," she spat. "Honestly, I had thought you'd matured, Fierina Flameton. Maybe your sister really would have been a better leader for this mission."

Being addressed by my full name took me by surprised. It caught me off guard.

"Well. Nothing to say, have you?" Ivoria smirked. "You see, young one, we are negotiating at my base. I don't think it would be very wise for you to provoke me here. Not when I have all the resources, and you have all the disadvantages here."

"Oh, really, now?" I leaned forward.

Galen kicked my feet from under the table. *ARE YOU CRAZY?! Stop provoking her before you stamp our death certificates!!*

"All the resources, you say?" I said, ignoring Galen completely. "Well. There you go. The last time I checked, you lived on an island with no mines, no crops, and barely any connections with your 'Provincia'."

Ivoria snickered. "Oh, the things you have yet to know -"

"You know, I realized you say that all the time." Now I leaned back in my seat, crossing my arms. "'Oh, the things you have yet to know, young one.' You quoting someone there? Maybe your favorite villain or something?"

In a split second, a thunderous roar, like the wave of a tsunami rose up behind me. I didn't see it, but I sensed it.

But I didn't move.

The wave dove down closer and closer. Ivoria chuckled. "There are always more than one way to solve a problem, you know."

I got my answer. I jumped up and reacted a split second before the water drenched me. My body moved on its own. I stood up and snapped my head back, directly facing the water. I could feel my eyes glow a bright blue as I swung my arm forward in a strong throwing motion. I threw my whole body into the swing, making me almost parallel with the table. The wave curved down a little bit before speeding straight for Ivoria, faster than I have ever redirected water before.

I didn't realize just how much water was about to drown me until the whole room was about a foot in water. Ivoria just smiled, unfazed and untouched, then clapped her hands. Drains slid up from the floor, and within seconds, the room was dry, except for everyone's pant cuffs. The fact that Ivoria was completely dry didn't bother me as much as the fact that the wave was there in the first place.

"I see what you did there," I said promptly, casually, as if being attacked by water happened to me everyday. "Very clever."

The grooves in the floor that I had thought were creative designs were actually pumps or vents. The flooring slid back to push whatever was underneath upward with a great force. In my case, water.

I glanced at my nameplate, which said FIRE, and scoffed. "Playing dirty, I see."

Ivoria didn't look the least bit remorseful. "It's not playing dirty, child. I'm merely evening out the odds. You have Talents and I don't. And, it wouldn't be so nice, say, if you walked in by accident and there was a wall of fire right in front of the door. I planned this out to be as harmless as possible."

I raised an eyebrow. "Really. Then would you be so kind as to give us a tour of this place? Personally?"

When Ivoria stiffened, I placed a hand on the table and gave her a sweet smile. "It's evening out the odds. You know this place and we don't."

Whoa! Nice!

Galen and Callan tried to swallow a smile. Sirocca and Kodiak tried to keep their mouths from falling open.

Ivoria's face remained emotionless. She stared at me unblinkingly, so I stared at her right back.

"Nicely done, Fierina, nicely done," Ivoria said slowly. "I see that you are a clever little child. Very well. I will grant your request. You must, however, in turn, refrain from using Talents as long as you are on this island. The second I see your Talents being used, you'll -"

"We'll never see our beloved Islands again." I finished for her. "Understood."

Ivoria smirked. "And, as a side note, should you interrupt me further in the future, you will not be having pleasant experiences. Have I made myself clear?"

"Crystal," I said, our gazes equally intense.

"Splendid. As of right now, our meeting is adjourned." Ivoria stood up to leave. "Your guide will call you later in the day. Until then, I expect you to stay in your rooms."

"That's not what we agreed," I said coolly. "You agreed to a tour personally led by you. And I just don't trust your servants, who don't know this place as well as you."

A vein in Ivoria's neck twitched for a second, revealing her true feelings behind that smile. "Of course," she said through gritted teeth.

"Then in that case, we won't mind staying in our rooms," I said. "How long before the tour?"

Ivoria cleared her throat. "You seem to have forgotten who was in charge. I will call you when I call you."

I narrowed my eyes. "Fair enough."

Ivoria suddenly shot me a sly smile. "Until then…."

She walked out of the room, heels clicking.

Chapter 28

We didn't speak for a long time. The instant the clicking sound faded, everyone was upon me.

"WHAT WERE YOU THINKING?!" they roared.

I scooted back a few paces. "Sorry," I mumbled. "What'd I do?"

"You almost killed us!" Callan and Galen said in unison. Immediately, they shot each other dirty glares.

"The way you challenged her is beyond me," Sirocca said. "My heart nearly stopped when I saw that wave!"

Kodiak grinned. "But, if I was being honest, that was amazing!! She was like, 'It's called evening out the odds', but then you totally threw her words right back at her!"

I ducked my head. "It wasn't much," I

mumbled again.

"OH YEAH!" Galen hollered. "I'd like to take this time to talk about how amazing that redirection technique was.... *But what were you thinking?!*" Galen looked at me furiously. "Were you planning to gain something after all those challenges and being haughty? Besides the risk of never making it back home?!"

I frowned. "Let's go outside. I'll tell you there."

"We're supposed to go back to our rooms, aren't we?" Callan checked.

Galen scoffed. "But do you really expect her to give us an honest tour?"

Callan paused. "Fair point. Let's go."

We headed outside to the garden. Like last time, Galen led the way. I was still trying to memorize the path throughout the mansion.

Amazingly, the garden had already been restored. The rocks had been cleared and new trees had been planted in place of the fallen ones. These servants of Ivoria were very efficient! Probably from the fact that if they don't work fast enough, Ivoria would kill them. Something along those lines.

"Let's hope that you two don't destroy this garden again," I said with a pointed look at

Galen and Callan.

They both glared at each other, then looked away.

I sighed. "Okay. First off, Galen, are there any cameras?"

Galen flew into the air and did a quick flight around the garden. "None that I can see."

I nodded. "Callan?"

The walls of the mansion trembled slightly. Callan kept his gaze, glowing bright green, fixed on the roof.

"There used to be one up there," he pointed to the space right under the roof, "but it's gone now."

"So. No cameras?" I asked.

"Nope."

I nodded once. "Good."

"Alright! Explanation time!" Galen plopped himself up high on a tree branch and leaned in close to listen.

"Okay. I don't know where I was going with those challenges -"

"WHAT?!" they yelled.

"But I figured if I poked her enough, she would slip and give us a nugget of information about this place," I finished. I cast them all a dry look.

"So you did have a goal," Sirocca checked.

I shrugged. "Something like that. I just didn't know what kind of information I was aiming for.

"But towards the end of the negotiation, she activated that huge wave of water right behind me. That changed things up a bit. It revealed how little we know about this place, so I bargained for a tour."

"Which was a pretty smart thing to do," Galen said. "Like I said before, Ivoria's not going to be completely honest about where everything is, but at least it gives us an idea."

I nodded. "Exactly. And I have to say, getting on Ivoria's nerves was fun! I mean, catching her off guard. Making her angry is a totally different story. I'm pretty sure everything she was planning to 'negotiate' with us wasn't even brought up!"

"Because of you," Kodiak said.

I grinned. "Yup!"

"Okay, now that you've explained everything, what are you planning next?" Galen asked.

I shrugged. "I don't know about you, but it's been a long day. Ivoria called a negotiation the day we get here, and I woke up early today, so I'm going to go take a nap. Goodnight."

I walked back into the mansion.

Unfortunately, I got lost as soon as I got inside. Everyone was still outside.

I made it my temporary life goal to memorize this mansion until I knew this place like the back of my hand.

The next day, I asked to go exploring with Galen. Ivoria didn't show up at our door yesterday (no surprise), so we decided to make the most of our time. "So, is there a reason you want to see the beach?"

I walked down the sandy path. "It looked really nice when I saw it last time. Plus, I wanted to see if there was a dock. But if it's just a really nice beach and nothing else, I'd still be satisfied." Galen nodded. "Ah, okay."

"What were you planning to do today?" I asked him.

Galen shrugged. "Fly around, swing from a few trees, nothing special, really. At least with you, you're actually doing something."

I smiled. "Okay."

We squeezed through the bushes and bounced down the rocks. I jumped and landed on the sand. "Made it!"

"Wow, you kinda have to get through a lot before actually reaching the beach," Galen said, grunting as he squeezed between two closely-grown spiky bushes and hopped from rock to rock. Right when he reached the sand, he groaned, "Oh wait! I could've just flown over these! ARGH!"

I laughed. "We all have those days, don't worry."

We walked up and down the beach, not finding a dock anywhere, which led me to the conclusion that the only way to get off this island was somewhere in the front, since the beach circled around the back.

"Well, we didn't find anything, so do you want to go take a look inside?" I asked, taking one more sweep of the beach before turning to Galen.

Galen thought about it. "Yeah. We should probably investigate the front of the island later, too. Remember those men you told me about when we were back at the first or second Stone?"

Oh yeah. I forgot about them. I nodded. "Yup. Thanks for reminding me."

We walked back inside since the air was getting colder. And because the gray skies were starting to make me sleepy again. But no one needed to know that.

Galen and I walked around for some time. I opened every door we passed by, curious to see what was inside. Galen kept questioning if I was getting lost. Gee, thanks, Galen. Your trust in me really touches my heart.

So far, all of the rooms we've seen were offices, storage rooms, and a bunch of really boring stuff. I frowned, wanting to pick up the pace. "Hey, there's an open door just up ahead! Do you want to take a look?"

Galen shrugged. "Sure. I mean, I'm just following you, so go ahead."

I walked quickly until I reached the right door.
I peeked my head inside, confused on why the door had been left ajar. The wall parallel to me was covered with huge windows, overlooking the garden. The left wall was empty.

Galen entered the room after me. "What's this room for?"

I looked around. "Looks like a tinkering room," I said, pointing at the littered floor. Nuts and bolts were scattered everywhere. I wondered why this door was left open. There was a dusty imprint of something along the empty left wall. "Wait a minute…."

Galen walked over to the empty space and crouched down. "Something was here, but there's no trace of it now. I wonder what it was...."

I shook my head. "Seems like a large machine of some sorts. Based on the imprint it left.... Maybe it's a weapon?", I murmured to myself. The imprint was large and had strange, sharp angles. It could've been a base for something.... I really hoped I was wrong.

Galen whistled. "That's pretty big, then."

I sighed. "Well, I was too late, I guess. I'm assuming it really was one of Ivoria's 'projects'."

I walked over to the drawers lining the right wall. It had an enormous chalkboard covered with equations and drawings, but I was more interested in what was inside the drawers. I pulled each one out and emptied the contents. The room was already hopelessly unorganized; who cared if it became even more messy?

"You're right," I said, after a while. "They're all tools." I looked up at the board, squinting. "Do you know what this is?"

Galen came over. The drawing looked half-wagon, vaguely half-weapon, but it was hard to tell what it was exactly. "Nope. And can I borrow your charger?"

I didn't know what he was talking about for a second. "What?"

"I was going to take pictures, but my phone is

out of battery."

I nodded slowly. "Uh, sure…. I'll give it to you when we get back to our rooms."

Galen smiled. "Thanks! But for now, I guess we're using your phone."

His hand slipped my phone right out of my back pocket. He quickly snapped a photo, then handed it back to me.

I shook my head, annoyed.

"Come on," Galen said. "Let's get out of here. Before Ivoria catches us."

We darted out of the room. I checked the map again, then we headed back to our rooms. "We should show this to the others. They might be able to tell what it is."

Callan and Sirocca didn't know, and Kodiak wouldn't answer the door. I decided to assume that he was asleep.

Since it was still day, Galen wanted to check the front of the island. And since I didn't want to admit I was sleepy, I agreed to go with him, even though I was starting to feel a bit cranky.

We walked out the front door, down the pebble path. I glanced at the bird trees.

Galen led us back to the place where we first arrived on the island. It was the same as last time, rocky beach and all. I dubbed it "Rocky Beach" in my mind and "Sandy Beach" on the other side.

"Nothing here," Galen murmured to himself. "Maybe on that side...?"

He wandered over to the right with me trailing after him. "Hey," I said, stifling a yawn. "What are you expecting to find?"

"A dock," Galen said simply. "Like you were doing back at the other beach."

"Oh."

Galen kept walking until he reached what looked like the end of the beach. When he didn't see anything out-of-the-ordinary, he made a sharp one-eighty turn and marched back the other way.

"What if nothing's there?" I asked. "I'm getting bored."

"Then we'll know that we don't have to search here anymore," Galen said.

"You seem very determined," I said crossly.

"You were too," Galen replied. "Remember when we were in the scrap room? I want to be thorough."

I growled. "But that was different."

Galen gave me a backward glance. "You're tired, aren't you?"

"NO!"

Galen nodded. "Sure."

I growled again, slowly growing angry. "I'M NOT!!"

Galen turned around and kept walking. "Okay."

I glared at his back. Why was he making such a big deal out of this?! I wasn't tired! DON'T ARGUE WITH ME! I KNOW I SAID IT EARLIER!

Galen muttered something under his breath. Even though I didn't know what he said, I hollered, "I HEARD THAT!"

Galen sighed. "Do you want to go back inside?"

"I'LL GO BACK WHEN I FEEL LIKE IT!" I hollered.

Galen kept walking. "Okay, then." He glanced backward at me one more time before turning around.

I stormed silently behind him. Deep down, in a place I didn't want to admit it existed, I knew I was being unreasonably angry because I was tired. I've always detested that place because it clouded judgment and decided based solely on feelings, usually anger. So I felt bad for yelling, but I didn't feel like apologizing or stopping, you know?

Galen suddenly stopped short. I almost

crashed into his back. "Why'd you stop?" I snapped.

Galen's eyes sparkled and a huge grin spread across his face. I blinked in surprise. I hadn't been expecting this.

"Look!" he said excitedly. He started to run. "I found it!"

I chased after him, all feelings of anger gone when I saw what he had seen. It wasn't a dock, like we'd been expecting.

It was a portal.

Chapter 29

My jaw dropped when I caught up with Galen. It was only the second day, and we were already discovering secrets! "How'd she create another one? Didn't Callan, Kodiak, and the others say they only created one?"

Galen furrowed his brow, thinking. "I honestly don't remember what they said about the portal before, but I don't think they created this one. Sirocca, Kodiak, and the other guy didn't seem to recognize this Stone when we arrived."

I gasped, realization dawning. "What if…" I whispered.

"What?"

I grabbed Galen's shoulder in horror. "What if their brains were wiped?!"

Galen stared at me flatly. "You really need to

sleep, Rina."

The ridiculousness of that theory hit me. I dropped my hands and rubbed my eyes. "Ugh. I do."

Callan had even said they were transported instantly to the Mainland from the Islands after they created the tunnel. There were no stops in between.

Galen approached the glowing portal. It swirled with bright colors just like last time, but this portal seemed to have more purple-ish pink in the mix than any other color. "Where does this go to?"

"Are you going in?" I asked, dubiously.

Galen glanced at me. "You think we should?"

I shrugged. "I mean, if you're going, then I'm going."

Galen turned back to the glowing hole. "Let's go, then."

Grabbing his hand, I took a breath, and we stepped through.

When I opened my eyes, I sighed in relief. I had been expecting something to jump out at us, or arrows whizzing straight at our hearts, or more of those "guns" that Ivoria had used on me last time, or chains to magically wrap around us, choking us to death, or -

Yeah, I was severely sleep-deprived….

"Okay, that wasn't as bad as I'd thought," Galen said, obviously relieved too. "And it wasn't as exciting, either. Let's go back."

He was starting to turn around when I grabbed him again. "Look! Does anything look familiar?"

Galen scanned the surroundings, eyes widening. "We're at another Stone!"

To us, all the Stones looked the same with some sort of beach forming the perimeter, then came the ring of trees, with the cluster of buildings in the center. This portal had placed us right on the border between a beach and the trees. I could see the gray buildings in the distance to our right.

"Why this Stone, though?" I asked. "What makes this one important or special?"

I exchanged glances with Galen. "We gotta take a look at those buildings," we said at the same time.

We dashed toward the buildings. I faintly thought about stealth, but I was feeling too rushed for that.

Which led to me almost getting caught if instinct hadn't taken over.

We had reached the largest building when

two men came out of the doors. I froze, invisible, and watched. They were the same men Kodiak and I almost ran into at the first Stone!

"I can't believe counting cannons takes days," Connery grumbled. "How many cannons does she need? We've been here, what? Two weeks?"

"About a week, actually," Brian said. "So what do we do now?"

Connery sighed. "We go home. See whatever task Boss wants us to do next. I don't know."

They headed toward the beach, where I could see a boat was docked. Galen and I glanced at each other.

We were at the first Stone. Connery and Brian didn't know about the portal. I bit my lip. This was SO important.

"What about the second Stone?" Galen whispered into my ear.

I shrugged. "We might have to find another portal," I whispered back.

We ran back to the forest and jumped through the portal. When we landed, we didn't see a huge mansion.

"Where are we?" I asked in horror.

The scene in front of me was the mirror image of the place we just left.

Galen looked panicked as well. "No way. Is

273

this…?"

"An alternate reality?" I finished, terrified. "We're lost, aren't we?"

Galen stopped being afraid long enough to give me another "Really?" look. "I was going to say: 'Is this another Stone?' and it obviously is."

"Oh." I blushed, then shook it off. "Okay."

Galen laughed. "Well, then. Let's see exactly which Stone this is."

We headed toward the buildings on our left. We tried to be as cautious as possible, but both of us were pressing for time, so we didn't do a good job of being quiet. And since it's been a long time since I've tested my evaporation, I didn't know how long I would be able to stay invisible.

We reached the largest building and Galen flung open the door. Now that I knew what might be inside, I didn't mind the darkness as much. We turned the corner and…

Rows and rows of vials and lab equipment filled a hallway.

Galen nodded as he surveyed the room. "We're at the second Stone."

I frowned. "How did that work?"

Galen turned around and ran back toward the door. "Hurry!"

I did my best to catch up. "Are you heading

back to the portal?"

Galen nodded as he ran, his eyes fixed on the path in front of him. "I have a theory about how it works."

When we reached the portal, I was out of breath. Galen didn't look winded at all. Figures. He was a Wind Islander.

He studied the portal. "So..." I puffed, hands on my knees. "Are you gonna explain?"

Galen leaned back. "You see these pink-purplish colors?"

I nodded, finally catching my breath. "There are a lot more of those than any other color," I said.

Galen nodded. "I think that might have something to do with where the portal goes."

I looked at him doubtfully. "A change of color? Are you sure?"

Galen bit his lip. "Okay, my science is terrible - I'm failing it, by the way - but you know how light comes in different wavelengths?"

"Yeah."

"That might affect where the portal goes."

I was still skeptical. "Okay...." I mean, there really wasn't any other explanation. The other portal wasn't like this. But then again, we only went through it once.

"But!" Galen held up a finger like he was making an important point in a speech. Which he probably was. "We were talking about the second Stone when we came through, right? So we were thinking about it. Which might've, I guess, 'told' the portal where we wanted to go."

I nodded, understanding what he was saying. "But how did you connect that with the colors?"

Galen shrugged. "That was just a guess. The colors might've been more of one element that allows this portal to do this. But, again, everything is a theory until we try it."

He moved to step through but I grabbed him and pulled him backward. "Don't you dare leave me here," I demanded.

Galen blinked. "I was going to try it."

"What if your theory doesn't work and you end up who-knows-where? I'd have to make it back to the third Stone by myself! And I'd have no idea where you are!"

Galen's face froze, then slowly spread into a grin. "I get it. Thanks."

I sighed, then released his arm. Then what he said hit me. "Thanks for what?"

Galen looked up with a wolfish grin. "For worrying about me."

I rolled my eyes. "We're friends, aren't we?" I

grouched.

Galen laughed. Whenever he laughed, his cheeks shrank his eyes a little, his mouth open wide. He always looked so happy whenever he smiled. It was the kind of laugh that made the people around him want to smile and laugh with him, to share whatever joy he was feeling.

"What're you laughing about?"

"Nothing," he said with a mischievous grin. I narrowed my eyes at him, but he looked away, still smiling. ARGH! Too bad Bond telepathy didn't exactly let you read the other person's mind. "You're just a funny person, that's all."

I frowned at him. "Funny how?"

Galen pushed my head, almost making me tip over. "That's for me to know, and you to find out."

I glared at him and kicked his shin. "AH!" He doubled over in pain. "What was that for?!"

"You know what it's for," I snapped.

Galen sighed. "I marvel the miracle of friendship."

"Yeah. So do I. Now, where do you want to go to test your theory?"

Galen slowly straightened, one hand still rubbing his leg. "We should probably try to get back to the mansion. Who knows what Ivoria might be doing."

I nodded.

"Don't think about anything else as we're going through," he warned. "We might be separated."

"What about you?" I shot back. "You seemed pretty distracted just now."

Galen looked like he was at the brink of laughter again. "No, I'm not."

"You're not fooling anyone, you know?"

Galen snorted. "Whatever. But just for a precaution…." He took my hand. "I doubt this is necessary," he said, "but if you do start thinking about a different place, hopefully, I drag you to the right place."

I rolled my eyes. "What if I'm the one dragging you?"

Galen shrugged. "Then make sure I arrive in one piece."

I shoved him away, then jumped through the portal. "Hey, wait!" He managed to grab my hair before I disappeared.

OW!!

I did my best to think through the pain. Ivoria's house. Ivoria's house. Ivoria's house.

We landed on a rocky beach with an enormous mansion off to our right.

YES!

The second I landed, I started screaming. "LETGOLETGOLETGOLETGOOOO!!"

"Oh. Sorry."

Using all my strength, I encased him in a bubble and pushed him far out to sea. Galen looked terrified. "Wait! Rina -"

He splashed into the ocean.

I took this time to laugh for a few seconds before fishing him out again.

Galen stood in front of me, his thick hair plastered to his forehead and shivering. "Y-you're s-so mean...."

I sniffed and rubbed my nose. "I know. Sorry about that. But, you know, you kind of deserved it."

Galen's eyes darkened. "Why did I ever agree to be friends with you?" he moaned.

"We had this conversation before," I told him. "I have no idea why you did, either."

Galen looked at me for a long moment, then sighed. "Can you at least dry me off? I'm freezing."

I drew out the extra water and flung it back into the ocean. "Still feel cold?"

Galen rubbed his arms. "I don't know if I'm really cold, or if it's just an illusion." He looked up at me. "I blame you if I get sick."

I made a face.

"Then I'll make sure you catch the cold so you'll suffer. And make me happy."

I made another face. "Ew. Just don't sneeze on me."

Galen's eyes lit up. "I was going to make you throw away all my dirty tissues, but thanks for the idea! That's even better! Why waste a bunch of tissues when I have a reusable one right here!"

I shuddered, revolted. I imagined Galen wiping his snot all over me, froze, then bolted toward the house. I'm taking a shower the second I get back into my room. Then I'd wash all my clothes three times. And after the threat of throwing up passes. THAT KID IS DISGUSTING! I hope he's kidding....

Galen ran behind me. "Well, anyways, the good news is, we found out how the portal works! See, aren't you glad you came with me instead of being holed up in your room?"

I darted through the door, pausing briefly to glance at the halls. Before I could answer, Galen said, "You still don't know the way?!"

I didn't bother answering anymore. I was starting to get the hang of it, and we arrived back at our rooms quickly.

Enzo was waiting right in front of our doors.

Chapter 30

Her hands were shaking. Her eye twitched in anger. Her fingers were curling tightly around the parchment, crinkling the edges.

Thora slid closer behind her sister, trying to hide her fear of the queen.

Emily's face was twisted in anger and horror. Her fingers looked ready to shred the letter, but instead, she flung it onto her desk and whirled around to face the window behind it.

Thora stepped forward slowly and picked up the paper.

Dearest Em,

I hope your duty as queen is proving as fruitful as you'd initially expected of yourself.

You've agreed to my terms, I see. I have to say, I

am delighted with your choice in representatives. Two children from the first "mission".... Wise decision. I hope they will be the leaders you expected them to be.

Do not worry. They are in good hands. This matter will be resolved fairly quickly, I can tell.

Sincere wishes,

Aura Ivoria

Thora passed the letter to her older sister and bit her lip. "Emily?"

Emily was physically shaking in rage. "This woman," she spat. Her fingers were curled into fists, slowly shining with a bright light. "Get Andy!"

Elece sped out and back in with Andy in the same second, holding the older boy by the ear. He was hollering his lungs out, spewing words at Elece that made Thora want to stick her fingers into her ears.

"Stop whining," Elece barked. Thora watched her eye glint, the way her eyes darkened, the way her left eyebrow twitched. "Your sister told me to get you."

She must've had a rough day....

Andy must've sensed it too. He immediately

stopped talking and glanced at her. "You doing okay?"

Elece's fierce glare silenced him, but Andy still looked skeptical and slightly worried before he turned to Emily. "What's up, sis?"

Emily whirled around, eyes ablaze and shoved her hand toward the letter in Elece's hand. A bright beacon shone right on the parchment. "Read it."

Andy read it in ten seconds, and his eyes widened. "She's going to kill them off?"

Emily gritted her teeth and didn't respond.

"Well, she didn't explicitly say she was going to kill them," Thora said quietly.

Elece finished reading the letter as well and immediately, her body flared up until she was a lightning beast. "The nerve of this lady," she stormed. "If she lays one hand on them...."

Emily slammed a hand down on her desk. "I've already given her what she asked for, and this is what I get?" she boiled. "A consolation letter?"

Thora slid behind her sister again, suppressing a whimper. Derrik rushed into the room just then, barely out of breath. "Sorry," he puffed softly. "Glenn kept me back a bit longer to-"

Elece shoved the letter in his face. Derrik's eyes quickly scanned the content and he frowned, confused. "Um, huh?"

Thora felt relieved she wasn't the only one who didn't understand.

Elece rolled her eyes. "She makes it look like we're playing right into her grand plan. 'This matter will be resolved quickly'. Think about it. Rina and Galen are there. She has a special hatred toward us four since we destroyed her initial plans. She's going to kill them while she has the chance!"

Emily grabbed a sheet of paper, a fancy queenly fountain pen, and started to scribble messily:

Ivoria:

You've made your point. I'm glad you feel so satisfied with my decisions. After all, I am a queen.

All I have in response to your letter is this: my team is clever. Should they ever ask for privacy, I request that you grant it to them. Any demands they have, grant those also. I understand that it may seem as an offense to you, but diplomacy is key here, correct? While that stands, I will expect no interference with their personal business.

And lastly, if any one member on my team is missing when they return home, I cannot guarantee you a quick and easy victory.

-Queen Aurora

Emily hastily rolled up the parchment into a scroll and shoved it at her brother. "Send this to her immediately," she instructed. "I will not have my friends harmed while in her custody."

Andy nodded. "There might be consequences when you send this letter," he told her. "Ivoria won't react to this very well. How do you know you're not driving the team to their deaths?"

Emily trembled, but shook her head. "We both know Ivoria values professionalism above all else. Diplomacy is our biggest advantage here. As long as everything is in a 'professional' manner, Ivoria will agree, even if the request is against her."

Andy nodded again. "Let's hope you're right." Then he rushed away from the room.

Thora sidled closer to Derrik. "Do you think Rina and Galen will be killed?"

Derrik hesitated, then shook his head. "They're smart," he reassured her. "Remember, Rina was shot, but she still fought. Galen might be airheaded, but he is smart. They'll figure out a way. Besides, they have Callan, Kodiak, and Sirocca with them. They'll be safe." He turned away, murmuring, "They'll be safe...."

Thora wanted reach out and take his hand comfortingly. But right when her hand started to move, Emily sank into her chair and buried her face into her hands. Thora hesitated for a moment before shuffling over. She crouched down beside the young queen and started to sing.

A beautiful song filled the room. The faint sound of bubbling streams, quiet forests, spring and summer, midnight stars, and chimes on the wind echoed on the walls and touched the hearts of anyone who listened. Thora's fingers flicked and tapped to the beat she'd created.

Emily's hands slowly dropped from her face. She looked at Thora in surprise, then smiled. "Thanks, Thora," she murmured.

Thora grinned shyly, then stepped back. Derrik's eyes shone in admiration. "I'm sure they'll be fine," she said quietly. "Rina was smart enough to free us on her own once before. She'll succeed this time too."

No one wanted to repeat the traitorous words. Once...

Just once before...

Chapter 31

I skidded to a stop. Galen froze next to me, too.

"What do you want?" I asked harshly.

Enzo rolled his eyes. "Ah. It's you. Good thing you had your friend there or else I would've have been able to tell you apart."

Great. Now he's not even making sense.

"I'm here to escort you to the Negotiation Room," Enzo said. "It's about time you came, too. You're an hour late."

My eyes widened. "Ivoria called for another negotiation session?" So much for sleep.

Enzo snorted. "Yeah, they've been in there for about three hours."

About an hour after we left, I'd guess, Galen said. But I honestly don't know how long we were gone.

I held my head high. "We'll go by ourselves." I whirled around and began to walk away.

"Uh, Rina...."

Enzo suddenly barked out a laugh. "Silly girl. You're going the wrong way."

I clenched my jaw. "Then what're you waiting for? Lead the way."

Enzo walked especially slow, taunting me the whole time. I think he was walking slow on purpose to buy him more time to torture me. "You have the brain of a seal!" he said. "You can't even find your way out of a paper bag if you tried!"

My face burned with anger.

"HEY!"

The shout was so sudden and so loud, I jumped. I glanced at Galen, but he wasn't looking at me. A gust of wind blew suddenly, out of nowhere, but I didn't feel it. I could only see it as it swirled around my friend. "Watch what you're saying, old man," Galen said, eyes blazing.

Enzo looked surprised, but then he snorted. "Ah, lovesick young'uns...."

I suddenly had a coughing fit. WHAT?! AGAIN?!

Galen's wind swirled faster. It became more dangerous. "And for your information, I happen to believe that seals are pretty smart. Haven't you seen those animals at the circus and stuff?"

Wait, so was he saying I belonged in a circus?

Enzo rolled his eyes. He didn't bother answering and kept walking. At least he was walking normally now.

"Uh, thanks," I mumbled, taking extra care to keep the extra space between us.

Galen shrugged, but I could see he was still annoyed. "Only I could say that, you know?"

So he's bragging about himself now? "Say what?" I asked, to clarify.

"Only I'm allowed to make fun of your lack of direction," he said with an evil smile.

I stewed inside, then shoved him. Hard. He hit the other wall with a thump, eyes wide. He gasped for breath.

"Hey. When'd you get so strong?" he wheezed.

"Since now," I snapped.

Galen coughed once, then burst out laughing. He immediately shut his mouth with a cautious glance at Enzo. "Let's go," he said, suddenly serious.

I wanted to tear my hair out in frustration. Why is this guy my best friend? Sometimes, I really wonder what I was thinking back when I

290

was in first grade.

When we entered the Negotiation Room, everyone looked up. Ivoria looked irritated. Kodiak and Callan glared at Galen when we came in, and Sirocca looked at me, slightly annoyed.

Uh-oh.

Sirocca never gets mad. Which means she was REALLY mad right now.

"Ah, it's about time you showed up," Ivoria said smoothly. Kodiak and Callan kept their death stares on Galen, even though he didn't seem bothered. Or maybe he didn't see. I'd have to keep an eye on the boys later. Who knew what was going to happen?

"Excuse us," I said curtly. "My friend and I had to check on something important."

"And what would that be?"

"None of your business, that's what," Galen snapped. "Please spend your time filling us in on what we missed. I understand that we were absent for quite a long time, but we had to fix a problem."

Ivoria had a big stare-down with us. I didn't care.

"Very well," she said shortly. "Your friends have been doing a decent job of upholding the discussion without their leaders -"

"Leader," Callan emphasized. "He's not my leader."

Galen's eyes flashed, but he didn't say anything.

"Oh, really?" Ivoria said slyly. "Interesting."

"So?" I prompted, taking my seat and doing my best to ignore the pining stare Ivoria was giving me. "What have you discussed so far?"

Ivoria filled me in. It really wasn't anything interesting: threats, deals, blackmailing, et cetera. They were trying to come up with an agreement on Ivoria's threat. It was a terrible thing to do, but I got bored quickly and barely listened.

The second Ivoria finished talking, I sighed and rubbed my temples. I really needed to sleep, and after everything that just happened, I'm not sure I could stay awake much longer.

I opened my eyes slowly and looked straight at Ivoria. She looked at me with a small smirk on her face, as if testing me and my abilities in negotiation. Well then, I'll bluff my way out of this test! I've never been in a negotiation before until now. Because I never needed to! What am I talking about...?

"I see an easy solution for this negotiation session," I said.

Ivoria raised an eyebrow, her smirk not leaving her face. "Oh?"

"We need a contract," I said. "To confirm each other's honesty. Let's create a contract. You promise not to bomb our Islands as long as we promise follow your rules here and not cause trouble. Barring all the requests we made, of course."

"And how will this make sure you'll actually follow through what you say?" Ivoria asked.

"Don't forget to include yourself in this," I told her. "We can write that if one person does not hold up their part of the contract, the other party is given the right to do whatever they wish. In your case, bomb our home. In our case, destroy your Stones and wreak havoc here."

Ivoria narrowed her eyes at me. I could see her mind's gears turning slowly. I took this time to glance at my team. Sirocca was nodding at me with approval. Callan was staring at me intently. Well, that was a bit uncomfortable, so I looked at Kodiak... who was also staring at me with equal intensity. What's up with them? Galen was on the same team as Sirocca.

You're doing everything, you know?, he joked. *There's pretty much no use for the rest of us.*

That's not true! I protested.

Think about it. What have been the rest of us been doing to contribute to this? It's all you.

He had a point.

Moral support?, I supplied weakly.

Galen looked like he was going to burst out in laughter.

"I'm impressed," Ivoria spoke. "I agree to these terms."

"What?!" Callan exclaimed. "That's it? That only took three minutes! Do you have a special liking to whatever Rina says or something?"

I watched in horror as humongous roots exploded out of the vent from behind Callan. He tried to fight it with his rocks, but he was in a room covered with tiles and cement, so it didn't work. He was lifted out of his chair and squeezed in a matter of seconds.

In a flash, Galen stood up and swept the plants away with a powerful gust of wind. Sirocca made sure he reached his chair safely. Callan gave them grateful glances, especially to Galen. Galen brushed himself off and sat down with a single nod at Callan.

"I do not appreciate your interruption, Earth candidate," Ivoria rumbled. "I assure you, I detest Fierina Flameton and I will for as long as I live. But her skills in negotiation exceeds yours, which is why this matter was solved quickly as soon as she arrived."

Oh. Well. Okay. I wasn't sure whether to take that as a compliment or not. On one hand, it was a compliment. On the other hand, it was coming from the person who just said she hated me in the sentence before.

Ivoria stood up. "This negotiation session is adjourned. I will bring a drafted contract next time."

She walked toward the door. When she passed by me, I said, "And when will the next meeting be?"

Ivoria glanced at me, a smile playing on her lips. "Whenever you aren't ready," she said. And then she left.

Chapter 32

Immediately, the other three pounced on us. "WHERE HAVE YOU BEEN?!"

Sirocca dragged me away. "You have NO idea how hard it was without you!"

I ducked my head. I felt like I was being reprimanded by my mother. *My* mother. "Sorry," I mumbled. "I'll tell you when we get to the garden."

"YES! You better!" Callan immediately started to drag Galen out the door by his ear.

Galen screeched in pain. "LET ME GO YOU BLOCKHEAD! I SAVED YOUR LIFE!"

"Yeah. I already thanked you for that."

Callan suddenly tipped sideways, his head colliding with the wall. He let go of Galen to clutch his head with a groan.

Galen had one hand on his ear. "That's what

you get!" he crowed.

Kodiak immediately encased Galen in a thick bubble of ice and rolled him out the door. "Come on!" I could hear him whine.

Sirocca picked me up with her wind and carried me out. Unlike Galen, I knew it was fruitless to struggle.

Once we reached the garden, Kodiak froze us to trees. He froze us in a way where the trunk dug into our backs, so it was both freezing and uncomfortable. Unfortunately, this was really smart because both Galen and my Talents couldn't break ice. And my back was starting to itch.

"Alright, talk," Callan commanded. "Where were you guys?"

It hit me suddenly while we were surrounded by Sirocca, Kodiak, and Callan.

Galen and I were the youngest out of the whole team. Which means I was literally the youngest since Galen was about a month or so older than me.

NO!

While I was being silent, mourning over this revelation, Galen said, "We were taking a look around the beach, okay?"

Sirocca suddenly smiled. "Were you guys…?"

"NO!" I hollered, using all my lung power. It actually hurt afterwards. "WHY DOES EVERYONE KEEP SAYING THAT?"

"Because you guys -"

"BEEEEE QUIEEEET!" I screamed, panicking. "WHY ARE YOU DOING THIS TO ME?"

"Sheesh, you make it sound like we're torturing you," Callan grumbled.

"You are torturing me!" I said.

"No, I'm just asking you a few questions," Callan said, looking intently at me. "So answer."

"WE WERE LOOKING FOR A DOCK, OKAY?!" I screamed. I quickly snapped my mouth shut. Maybe I shouldn't have said it that loud....

Sirocca's eyes gleamed teasingly. "So you two could escape the island by yourselves? Elope?"

I wanted to cry. Or sink to the bottom of the ocean and never resurface. Whatever to save myself from this. I settled for banging my head against the tree. Hard.

"Heyheyheyhey!" Callan quickly freed me and I almost landed on my face. "Don't hurt yourself!"

Galen had been silent this whole time, letting me vent. Now, he exploded, "WHAT?! What about me?!"

"I didn't hear you complaining," Callan said. Galen turned a scary shade of red. "Let. Me. Go," he said murderously through gritted teeth.

I paled. He really was going to explode; I could tell right away. "Uh. You better do what he says."

Callan glanced at me. "What -"

"JUST DO IT!" I yelled, quickly trying to find a place to hide.

There were none.

Callan gulped, nervous at my panicking voice, and broke the ice with a rock. Everyone was immediately blown backward by a hurricane-like wind. I tried to find a good place to grab onto until the storm died, but I was sent crashing back into a tree, knocking the wind out of my lungs. I could barely breathe - there was too much air - and I was stuck in the branches.

"Galen…" I gasped.

Immediately, the wind died and Galen appeared next to me. "Sorry," he muttered shamefully.

I gulped in deep breaths of fresh air. I held up a hand. "Hold on," I wheezed.

Galen sat there, staring at the bark until I was able to breathe normally and free myself. "Okay."

"You okay?" he mumbled, picking at the bark.

I smiled at him. "Yeah, I'm fine. Don't worry about it." I glanced up at the garden and felt sick. "Uh, you might want to worry about the garden, though...."

We - or rather, I - promised Ivoria that we wouldn't wreak havoc and destroy the garden. We're going to get in trouble. "Can you fix everything really quick?"

Galen bit his lip. With a few waves of his hands, everything was righted, except for a few trees. "I don't think I can put those back now," he mumbled.

I made a face. "Can you at least try? I don't care if it looks terrible."

Galen sighed. After a few minutes, the bigger trees stood lopsided, but their roots were in the ground. Most of it, anyways. Now the garden didn't look that bad....

Callan staggered over, favoring his left arm. "What was that?!"

Galen didn't say anything. Want me to say anything? I asked.

Might as well, he said miserably.

"I've only seen this happen once before," I began.

Callan exhaled in disbelief as Kodiak and Sirocca walked over, having a few cuts and bruises. "Wow. I can't image what your house would look like."

Galen glared at Callan, and the older boy took a step back. "Sorry."

"Anyways," I continued, "it happened when we were in fifth grade. Remember the time before the grades were turned into levels?"

When the other three nodded, I continued, "Galen's older brother Skye had been enlisted in the Wind Army two years before. That day, I was at his house, and his mom came in crying, saying Skye had been injured severely during the trainings. He exploded back then too. But we hadn't activated Talents back then, so he basically overturned the whole house. I had to hide under the couch, and even then, it was scary."

Callan didn't say anything for a minute. "I, uh, I have to say this, but I really don't mean any offense. I just want to ask: what does this have to do with why he just exploded now? And how many siblings do you have?"

Galen spoke up this time. "I have three brothers and four sisters. I honestly don't know why I exploded, either. But the only connection I can make is that when I get really angry, that happens. I can barely think during that time. I really don't like it when it happens." He kicked the trunk of the tree with a swing of his leg. "Rina was the only one outside my family who knew. And since it happened only once, both of us forgot about it, I guess."

"So. When you get mad, you turn into a ferocious fighter kind of thing?" Kodiak asked, entranced.

Galen winced. "Can we just change the subject and say I overreacted?"

I shrugged. "Sure."

"But before we do that...." Callan waved an arm and rocks steadied the roots of the trees, balancing them in the earth. Now it looked like nothing had ever happened, save for the bare trees and littered leaves. I gave him a grateful smile.

"So. Tell me more about what you found," Sirocca said, trying to smooth the awkward transition. "On the beach, I mean. I'm assuming you found something since you guys were gone for so long."

Galen nodded, obviously relieved he wasn't the main topic anymore. "I found a portal -"

"WHAT?!" Everyone shrieked.

"Hey. Listen!" Galen said. "So Rina and I went into the portal -"

"WITHOUT US?!"

Galen frowned. "And then, we appeared at the first Stone -"

"WHAT?!"

Even I was getting annoyed. "Okay. Save all the exclamations until we finish talking, okay? It's already almost dark, so we need to hurry."

Everybody glanced at the sky, then nodded. Galen quickly said, "So basically, we went back through the portal, expecting to come back here, but we ended up at the second Stone instead. So I figured how to make the portals work, and by the time we returned, you guys were already in the Negotiation Room."

"We need to see this portal," Sirocca said immediately. "But I can't believe you two went without us. We're a team."

"Yeah. That's not fair to us, you know?" Kodiak said, looking a bit hurt. "It was really difficult in the Negotiation Room because we didn't plan anything ahead of time."

"Sorry," I mumbled.

"We weren't thinking straight," Galen said quietly. I glanced at him in surprise.

We're the youngest, aren't we?, he said gruffly. *And it really wasn't fair to them. Remember what I said about the rest of us not doing anything to contribute?*

303

Hey, I already feel bad.

Okay. Just wanted to clarify.

Oh, so he realized we were both the youngest, too! *Did you pluck that out of my head?*

Maybe.

I sighed. "Okay, then."

"What?" Sirocca said.

I hadn't realized I'd said it out loud. "Sorry."

"Show us the portal tomorrow since we don't have time today," Sirocca said decisively. "We need to agree on what to do and Galen needs to teach us how to use it."

"Well, I still have to test it one more time to be sure -"

"Shh!" Sirocca said. "Then teach us whatever you know."

"Okay."

"Now, let's get some sleep, today was a big day." Sirocca turned around to lead the way back.

The rest of us followed her. Sirocca really did seem like the leader of this team. Pretty mother-like.

I walked next to Galen. "You okay?"

Galen nodded. "Thanks for being so normal about it," he said softly. "Like it's a totally normal and everyday thing to explode and destroy a garden."

I shrugged. "I try not to make a big deal. Besides, I've already seen it once before, you know?"

Galen grinned, truly grateful. I was taken aback. "Whoa."

"What?"

"Nothing."

"Okay."

"But why did you explode?" I asked.

Galen's eyes furrowed. "I don't know. I think it might've just been the built up frustration I have against Callan."

I glanced at him quizzically. "You haven't told me why you guys argue so much."

Galen stiffened, then gave me an easy smile. "I'll tell you eventually," he said.

I frowned. "Why?" I whined. "You told me that last time! Consider it as a contribution to the team!"

Galen laughed. "Nice try."

I growled. "Fine. If you won't tell me, then I'll find out myself."

I stomped faster until I was walking with Callan. "Hey. Why do you and Galen fight all the time?"

Callan looked startled by my question. "Why

do you ask?" he said carefully.

"Because Galen won't tell me. Consider it as a contribution to the team," I said again.

Callan laughed. "Sorry. If Galen won't tell you, then I won't tell you."

I almost burst. "WHAT?! You guys finally agree on something and it had to be this?!"

Callan shrugged. "I honestly can't tell you if Galen won't."

"You can't or you won't?" I challenged.

"I won't," he said.

I groaned, tugging at my hair. "FINE!"

I stomped into my room, slamming the door behind me.

It's only been three days, and our team was already breaking apart. Sirocca seemed like the one in charge. Callan and Galen were always arguing, despite my threats and constant annoyance. Galen blew up for the first time in four years.

What was I supposed to do?

I pulled out my phone, staring at it for a few more minutes before trying to dial Elece's number again.

She didn't pick up.

I sighed sadly, then hung up. Don't get me wrong... I loved that Elece was one of Emily's top guards, but I really hoped she would call back sometime.

I wondered what they were doing....

Derrik and Elece were training, of course. Emily was busy leading. But what kind of queenly stuff was she doing? Has she found her motivation for leading our nation yet?

I felt very, very homesick. That led me to think of Zin, and I almost cried.

Was she recovering well? How was she doing? A small tear trailed down the corner of my eye and got lost in my hair.

So many people at home.... Why am I here?

I fell into a restless sleep.

Chapter 33

Derrik grit his teeth. So many wires....

A pretty twelve year old girl crouched beside him, her adorable tongue sticking out of the corner of her mouth as she tried to see the problem.

Derrik saw the loose wire before she did and twisted it with another one. He pressed the button on the side and a faint, telltale beep brought a smile to his face. "It works!" he cried.

Thora let out a happy cry, clapping her hands. Her short hair swished as she bounced gleefully. "Let's test it!"

They ran to the training room and into the control center. Thora set the intercom down and Derrik plugged a cord into the metal box and started to type furiously. "I feel really bad we've put this off until now," he told her. "Emily wanted this about a week ago, right?"

Thora shrugged. "The beginning of this week, actually, but close enough."

Derrik paused to frown at the calendar. "Wow. Time goes by very slowly."

Thora shrugged again. "Yeah, I guess."

There was an awkward silence except for the clacking of Derrik's fingers on the keyboard. "And... done." He tapped the microphone next to his computer and spoke, "Testing, testing."

What came out of the intercom was a sound like gloopy soup.

Derrik's face fell and Thora stifled a giggle. Derrik frowned. "I don't get it."

Thora smirked, and Derrik saw her pinky twitch. His eyes widened. "Hey! You sabotaged me!"

Thora started to howl with laughter after that. "Try again," she gasped. "I promise I won't do anything."

Derrik grumbled to himself as he stretched for the microphone again. "Testing."

His voice came out crystal clear.

Derrik grinned. "Yes! If this works, I think I can connect it to the system we created." He unplugged the microphone from the box and walked over to the main computer. He found the port for the cord, plugged it in, and tapped the microphone again. "Test -"

His voiced boomed from the walls, nearly shaking the computers off their places on the desks. Derrik screamed and yanked the cord out.

Thora sat off to the side, a thin, blurry bubble around her. "Wow. You need to fix the volume."

Derrik rubbed his ears. "Yeah, I got that."

After a few more tries, Derrik and Thora were able to change the sound calibrations until Derrik was able to scream into the mic comfortably. Thora smiled proudly when everything worked perfectly.

"Great!" Derrik cried gleefully. "Now, all I have to do is to set the coordinates of the school, then the walls will be connected to this system." He glanced at Thora. "You soundified the walls, right?"

Thora wrinkled her nose at him, amused. "Soundified? Um, yes, I did."

Derrik had asked Thora to run her hands over every wall in the Academy and to figure out a way to be able to make the announcements be broadcasted through the walls instead of speakers. They never found a good word for that process until Derrik's came up with the perfect word for it.

"Okay, now let's test it in three…."

He typed in the coordinates.

"Two…."

His finger hovered over the button.

"One."

He slammed his eyes shut and drove his finger downwards.

Thora walked over and spoke into the mic. "Hello!" Immediately, she received a call from her sister.

"It works!" Elece cried. "And! You managed to scare Roots in the process. I think he peed his pants."

Derrik snickered as Thora hung up. He couldn't believe it! An entire sound system for the Academy, designed by him!

"We did it, Thora!" he cried excitedly. "Thanks for your help!"

He flung his arms out to give her a quick hug, but his hand smashed against the keyboard and there was an ear splitting screech.

Then silence.

No…. no no no no no!

"What…?" he stared in horror at the computer. It would take forever to redo everything again.

"… test the machine," came a strange voice. It

was crisp and had a foreign accent, but strangely familiar. "I want it to be in prime condition in three days."

"Yes, Boss," a man's voice said humbly before footsteps rushed off.

Derrik's eyes widened and he exchanged horrified, yet joyful glances with Thora.

"We need to tell Emily!"

Chapter 34

The next morning, I threw back the covers and ran out of the room after I finished getting ready. Who knew what was going to happen today?

The others walked out of their rooms at the same time. "Ivoria's probably not going to call us out this early. You have something planned?" Galen asked as we walked out to the garden.

I scowled at Galen. "You know me best, Galen. I'm not much of a planning person. Besides, we're still waiting for that tour she promised us."

Galen shrugged. "Okay, then. I'll take over."

"Oh, no…." Callan muttered. "This isn't going to go well."

"YOU'RE LUCKY I DON'T FEEL LIKE SWEEPING YOU OFF THE ISLAND RIGHT

313

NOW!" Galen hollered. "Anyways, after Ivoria gives us the tour, we explore the whole mansion by ourselves." He climbed up the Discussion Tree and sat in its branches.

"She's not going to let us do that," Sirocca warned as we all came to a stop below the tree. "The dangerous thing about Ivoria is that she's clever."

Galen nodded. "I know. But not as a whole group, obviously. Just one at a time. See what we find."

I frowned. "Won't that make us more vulnerable? You know, pick us off one by one?"

Galen shrugged again. "It's just a suggestion."

I snapped my fingers. "Oh! That's right! I didn't tell you guys this!"

"What?" They all leaned in.

"Okay, so long story short, Galen and I were wandering the halls and stumbled across this room. The floor was littered with nuts, bolts, and those kinds of tools. There was a huge imprint on the floor, and there were plans to create this giant machine kind of thing. The door to that room was open; that's how I found it."

"What was the machine like?" Kodiak asked eagerly.

I looked down sullenly. "I don't know, but

Galen took pictures."

"It's not another weapon, is it?" Callan said.

Galen snorted. "How are we supposed to know? We've never seen it before, and this is Mainland tech we're dealing with."

We all sat there, frowning and thinking, until Galen brightened. "Hey!"

"Man, you're just full of ideas today," Callan said sarcastically.

Galen ignored him. "Rina! Toss me your phone!"

I looked at him suspiciously. "Don't you have yours?"

Galen made a face. "I forgot to charge it. And you haven't given me your charger yet."

I shook my head, clicking my tongue, then tossed him my phone. "What do you need it for?"

Galen grinned, eyes sparkling. "You'll see."

He dialed someone's number, then held it to his ear. The rest of us waited curiously with bated breath. Who was he calling?

After what seemed like forever, Galen blinked, then smiled. "Hey! How're you doing?"

I almost dragged him out of the tree. WHO IS IT?!

Galen waved me off, then laughed. "I'm putting you on speaker now. Rina is about to rip my head off."

He pushed a button on my phone, and a voice rang out.

"Hi, Rina!" Elece said. "How's it going over there?"

"ELECE!!" I shrieked. I flew up the tree and grabbed my phone. Galen laughed and scooted over to make space. "You're not training?! I've been trying to call you for days!"

She laughed. "We're on a break right now. I have to say, this is probably the best job in the whole Terrene Islands! I'm sort of acing everything right now! Yesterday, Melody had be command the Cosmos Army for a while. It was amazing and terrible at the same time! The kids are so annoying!"

I grinned. My heart warmed at Elece's ecstatic tone. I've never seen her this enthusiastic about anything before. "How about Derrik?"

There was a pause, then another familiar voice cried, "RINA?! Is that really you?!"

"DERRIK?!" Galen and I leaned toward the phone. "No way!"

His voice was still high-pitched, but he sounded older. More experienced. Wow, what were Galen and I missing out on?!

"Hey! How's your training?" Galen asked.

Derrik laughed. "It's intense, but it's really fun! I made the intercom Emily wanted me to build, and Glenn had me plan strategies as a test. I passed!"

"Congratulations!" we said.

Elece chuckled. "You guys should see Derrik now! He's way taller, just past my shoulder, and a lot more muscular!"

"I'm not buff!" Derrik protested.

"What, you want to stay short and skinny? You need to get a deeper voice, too. You still sound like a ten-year-old."

While they bickered, I shot Galen a huge smile, eyes wet with joyful tears. "I can't believe you finally managed to call her!"

Galen laughed. "Why are you surprised? I caught them on my first try! And it took you, what, ten tries?" He stuck his tongue out at me, and when I lunged for his throat, he tipped backwards, hanging upside down from the branch by his legs.

"So, uh, you guys going to fill us in?" Kodiak spoke, eyes twinkling teasingly. "Or are you going to leave us here guessing and watching you guys have a reunion?"

Galen grinned, still hanging. "I'll fill you guys in later. Rina and I need to ask her something."

317

"Who's 'her'? And why do you both need to ask?" Callan said.

Galen's face froze over, and he flipped back onto the branch, totally disregarding Callan's question. Callan held his hands up, a gesture of disbelief, then shook his head, annoyed.

"Anyways, Elece, we have to ask you something important," Galen said. "And if Rina's phone dies on me right now, I'll blame you if I don't make it back to the Terrene Islands."

Elece laughed. "Wow, Rina. You seem to be a lot more like me now!"

I frowned. "Thank you?"

"It's okay. On my terms, it's a good thing. Anyways, what's your question?"

"Alright. Long story short, Rina bargained with Ivoria, and now we get to have a tour of this place personally led by Ivoria herself. But, we're kind of debating what to do next."

"We found a strange room, but didn't really understand what it was for and what the drawings on the board were," I added. "Any ideas?"

"I do!" Derrik said. "It's pretty simple, actually. I'm surprised you guys didn't think of this."

"What?"

"While you're touring, take note of what Ivoria labels that room you saw. Then split off into teams to explore different areas of the mansion. If she catches one team, just ask Ivoria to give another tour since you guys are still 'lost'."

"Wow, pretty impressive, Jayson," Elece said. "My idea was a bit more complex."

"OW! Okay! Let go! I get it!!" There was a hiss of pain from Derrik, and a small sound of satisfaction from Elece. "Rina, when you get back, I hope you're not like her."

Immediately, Derrik's footsteps pounded away. I could imagine Elece rolling her eyes. "Yeah, running away now was wise. I'll catch him later."

I laughed. "Okay. Do you think his plan would work?"

There was a pause. "Yeah. I mean, between the both of us, Derrik is the better strategist, so there's a high chance it would work. But I'll just add something. To reinforce your lie, draw a map of the mansion. Don't fill out everything. If Ivoria catches you, claim that you were trying to figure out the rest yourselves, then ask for the second tour. That way, it's not as suspicious if she sees you looking inside the rooms."

"What if she asks why we're making a map?" Galen asked.

"Uh, Galen? I don't think she's going to ask that," I said. "I mean, if you're making your map, it's pretty self-explanatory. You make a map so you can use it. I mean, why else would you need a map?"

"Because we're not going to be here for long," Galen said. "If we're making a map and we're only going to be here, say, about a week, a map would be useless."

"So? We still would need the map to get around," I told him.

"Yeah, but the only rooms we'll really need is the Negotiation Room, and our dorms." He gave me a quick glance, then added cheekily, "And we already know where all those rooms are. Right?"

I glared at him. "Elece?"

"I agree with you, Rina, but Galen has a point. But that was just a suggestion. You also need to consider the unexpected."

I groaned. "So what do we do?"

There was a muffled holler, then Elece said, "Derrik says to just go with what we just suggested. If anything comes up, just wing it."

I frowned. "That doesn't sound too safe."

"Where you're at right now isn't safe."

Galen nodded. "Good point. Thanks, Elece!"

Derrik's voice came back on. "I also wanted to tell you two that Elece is now head of security at the Academy and I have been in charge of the sound at the school. Ivoria doesn't stand a chance!"

There was a strange force to his words, like he was trying to convey a deeper meaning. I stared at the phone, confused. "Um. Congratulations!"

"What he means to say is, Ivoria can't spy on us, right? She has no idea what we have in store for her," Elece said in a prompting tone.

"Of course, don't act like it's a big deal," Derrik added. "We want it to be a surprise. Don't underestimate your enemy, right?"

Galen frowned at his phone. "You guys are making no sense. What is going on?"

"Never mind, then. Oh! Hey! I wanted to tell you guys something hilarious!" Her voice sounded mischievous.

Galen and I exchanged curious glances. That was a sudden change of topic. "Yeah?"

Derrik popped back up. "Ooh! Ooh! Are you telling them about -"

"Ha! Yeah!"

"Ooh! Can I tell them?"

We waited patiently until Derrik said, "So

Elece and I spent one of our breaks a few days ago in the library. We had to study our own things, but anyways, I got really bored, so I started to look up books about Bonds."

Galen leaned in. "And then?!"

"I found this book about all the stories of past Bonds. And the thing was, they all got married when they grew up!"

Silence, then disgusted yells from the both of us. "EW! GROSS!"

We scooted away from each other, shuddering. Elece and Derrik were hooting with laughter.

"Isn't it so funny?! I mean, one day, you and Galen -"

"NO! BE QUIET! NONONO!" I hollered, scrambling to mute the phone. "DON'T SAY ANYTHING!"

Unfortunately, in my haste, I knocked my phone off the branch. It plummeted to the ground, right in front of the other three.

"- might get married!" Derrik's gleeful voice continued. "It seems strange and awkward now, but it'll lead to affection in the future; I just know it!"

My heart sank. *NOOO!!*

Kodiak and Callan looked up, both quirking

an eyebrow. Sirocca held a fist to her mouth, struggling not to laugh.

I slumped on the branch. Galen was nowhere to be seen.

"Oh! We need to go now! You guys should call at this time! It's when we usually have breaks! Bye!" Derrik and Elece hung up.

There's no way I'm getting off this tree now.

Chapter 35

"Come on! You guys have been up there for ten whole minutes! What if we missed the tour already?" Callan called.

"GO AWAY!" Galen yelled at him from somewhere above me, hidden in leaves. "We need time to get over this awkwardness!"

"Well, can't you guys get over it in your rooms?" Kodiak asked. "We're on a mission, remember?"

Kodiak was right. Galen was my best friend. I mean, I'm pretty sure not ALL of those Bonds ended up together, right?

AH! Why was I worrying about this? I'm only fourteen!

I climbed down the tree and retrieved my phone from Kodiak's hand. "Hey, Galen! Come on!"

"You're over it already?" His head popped out from behind some leaves. "That was a lot faster than I expected."

I narrowed my eyes at him. "You don't seem to be very embarrassed…. What are you doing up there?"

Galen made a face at me, then climbed down. "I got over it seven minutes ago. I thought to myself, 'Hey, I'm only fourteen! The future is so far away! I'll get to it when I get to it.' I was keeping track of how long it would take you to get over it."

I sighed. "You know, I'm just not going to answer you."

We walked back inside the mansion. I spoke up, saying, "So. Anyone know the way back?"

"Yeah," all four of them answered. "You don't?"

"Of course I do!" I bluffed. "I was just checking. Let's go!"

I walked a few steps behind Sirocca, pretending like I knew these halls like the back of my hand. I was slowly starting to get it. "How long did it take you guys to remember this?" I asked casually.

"After the second or third try, I got it down," Kodiak said. "We visit the garden pretty often."

"Yeah, same," Galen said, throwing me a significant look. I returned it with a dark glare. He just grinned widely and turned back around.

By the time we returned, Ivoria was waiting in front of our doors. "Are you children done playing?" she asked with a dripping smile.

Everyone froze in surprise, then I walked up to her. "Let us get some things first."

Ivoria kept her gaze level. "You have ten seconds."

Sirocca rushed into her room and grabbed the notepad and pen. After she came outside, Ivoria immediately turned and started to walk quickly. "Let's go."

The tour took an hour to complete. Sirocca had amazing mapping skills and kept up with Ivoria's rapid talking. I think Ivoria was trying to discourage her by talking so fast, but Sirocca wasn't bothered.

I figured, since we had the map, I'll memorize all the paths later. Instead, I kept my eyes and ears open. The room Galen and I had discovered was open again. I only knew this because of the tile floor and the pile of bolts right by the doorway.

"This is my scrap room," Ivoria was saying. "Whatever I do not need but can still be used for other projects, I leave in here. Please excuse the mess."

"What project are you working on now?" I asked.

"That is for me to know and for you to find out," Ivoria said, smug. "Two can play this game, Flameton."

I shrugged. "Okay. I wasn't playing any games, you know. I was genuinely curious.

Ivoria narrowed her eyes at me, then turned away. I smiled to myself.

I didn't really pay attention to the rest of the tour. All the other rooms were boring. What made me start listening, however, were the ones that were "off limits".

"Why?" I asked.

Ivoria kept walking past three doors, all which were "off limits". "If I am to respect your privacy, you are to respect mine," she said.

"Oh, privacy, eh?" I said. "Then I would like to make one more request."

I knew she would probably grant it. If she wanted to be diplomatic (and she obviously does, except for those underlying threats), she'd grant the request as an act of hospitality.

Ivoria didn't turn around, but I saw her fingers twitch and her jaw clench. "Children are so needy. Very well," she said stiffly. "What is your request?"

I exchanged a grin with Galen. "Give us the garden. We need a place to talk and plan our decisions. To regather our thoughts, you could say. Let us use your garden free of any cameras, microphones, or any other means of privacy invasion or security."

Now Ivoria turned to look at me. "You children already use the garden to meet and converse."

I scoffed at her. "However, we are always meeting under the impression that you might be listening in. I don't think we would be able to have successful negotiations if you do not let me speak with my team in between."

"You strike hefty bargains, Fierina," Ivoria said slowly, eyes narrowing. "A large request must only be met with another large request. The garden is yours if you agree to meet my request."

Making a big request always came at a risk. But I had expected this, so I gave her a sweet smile. "What kind of request?"

Ivoria's lips stretched into a thin smile. "Well, for a request that large, it is going to take some time for me to think of one worthy of countering it. So? What's your choice?"

I glanced at Galen. Galen glanced at the others. They all nodded.

"Deal," I said confidently.

Ivoria's eyes lowered, turning her smile into a crafty smirk. "Wise choice."

Oh, no. Don't get me wrong - Ivoria didn't scare me as much anymore. But it's never a good thing when a villain tells you that you've made the "wise choice". It made me feel nervous. Were we playing right into a trap?

"I take your word that you'll keep your end of this bargain," Ivoria said before turning around. "I'm sure you're aware of the consequences if you choose to back out."

We continued with the tour. Again, I tuned out. Well, only until she led us outside. That's when I started paying attention.

The only place I've been to outside was the garden, which was also the right side view of the house. The bird-shaped trees were around the corner, in the front of the house.

Behind the house was a sandy path. It led through a band of bushes, a ring of trees, and down to a small beach bordered by rocks. It was beautiful! Even with the sun's light being heavily dimmed by thick gray clouds, it seemed to fit the scenery of the ocean just right. Or was that just me getting used to the pollution in the sky? I squinted at the beach and smiled to myself. It was Sandy Beach.

Anyways, as soon as I remembered the way to the garden, I'm going to visit this beach again. I'd named it Sandy Beach in my mind because of how clean the sand look. I'm weird; I know.

Ivoria led us back inside. It took another hour to tour the upper levels. Apparently, there were three more stories that I have never noticed.

The higher stories were more... homey... than I expected. The floors were carpeted and everything seemed warmer. But these floors were smaller, about half the size of the facility-like first floor.

I frowned. That didn't add up. From the outside, the house looked like one huge cube-ish shape. If the upper floors were smaller, it was supposed look more like someone forgot to make the layers of a cake gradually smaller and made only two layers instead.

Which means....

Do you see any secret rooms? Galen asked, without looking directly at me to throw off suspicion.

Just what I was thinking, I told him. *I haven't begun looking yet.*

Where do you think they are? What do they hold?

I don't know. We need to thoroughly examine each room downstairs, too.

ARGH! Why do mansions need to have so many rooms?!

Because it's a mansion, dude! They're supposed to have this many rooms!

ARGH!

Nothing about the higher floors interested me other than the possibility of secret rooms. When Ivoria took us back down to the first floor, she turn to us, a ghost of a smile playing on her lips.

"I hope that tour was enough to satisfy and hold up my end of the bargain. Now I trust that you'll keep your part?"

I kept my face dead serious when I nodded. "Of course…."

"Good." Ivoria turned and walked off. Probably to her office, if she had one. "Naturally", I didn't know where it was.

After she left, I grinned and muttered under my breath, "Of course my end of the bargain will be held just as truthfully as you held yours."

Which means, UNLEASH THOSE TALENTS!

Okay, I think I've been using my brain too much today. Too bad I'll be using it a lot more before sleeping tonight. Unlike the last mission, this one required a lot of mental energy.

Sirocca consulted the map before leading us back to the garden. "Alright. Let's talk. Rina, I'm going to assume you weren't listening this whole time, so here." She handed me the map.

"Wow! How'd you know?" I asked, taking the notepad.

Sirocca snickered. "You looked bored the whole time!"

"Well, she was!" Galen said, plopping down beside me and leaning in to look. "We all know that Rina can't find her way out of a paper bag, even if she tried!"

I smacked Galen. Before he could retaliate, Ivoria popped back up from around the corner. "Oh, and just a heads up, you children might want to check up on your family and friends from home before tomorrow's meeting. And do not worry about whether or not your phone call signals will be tracked."

Before we could ask what she meant, she ducked out of sight.

We stood there in silence, pondering what she meant. Then a sudden dread cloaked the atmosphere between us. "Is she...?"

Everyone dashed into their rooms and whipped out their phones. I quickly dialed my mom's phone number, biting my lip as I anxiously waited for the ringing to stop.

Was Ivoria planning to attack the Islands tomorrow?!

Chapter 36

SHE CAN'T ATTACK THEM TOMORROW! What would we do here?! We want to be back at home fighting, even though we probably wouldn't be much use at home either.

My mom took forever to pick up. At least, it felt like forever. After what must've been the thirteen-billionth ring, she finally picked up!! "Rina?!"

A rush of sudden relief came over me. "Mom? You're alright?"

"Of course I am! What about you? Is something wrong? Where are you? I still can't believe the queen sent you!"

I was taken aback by the sudden bombardment of questions. "Everything's fine. I'm just glad you're safe," I added after a pause of hesitation. "Uh, can I talk to Dad...?"

"Of course!"

While I waited, I took this moment to think. Wow, my parents changed so much! Or was it just me? Did I start to see where they showed their love? Or had it always been there? Or did they really change?

"Rina!" my dad's voice traveled through my phone. "How are you?"

"H-Hey, Dad!" I stammered. I haven't talked to my dad in a long time. "I'm good, thanks."

"I bet you're busy saving the world from a crazy lunatic, but I'll tell you a secret to get rid of whoever they are, Rina," my dad whispered. I leaned in, even though I wasn't at home. "When she annoys you, or makes ridiculous bargains, you drown her. Got it?"

I was speechless. "Uh... okay."

"That's the spirit!"

I felt a warm feeling in my chest. What was it? Before I could stop myself, before I realized what I was doing, I blurted, "I love you, Mom and Dad."

Immediately, I realized what I had said and hung up in haste. I sat crouched on my bed, not saying anything for a long time.

My phone rang. Mom.

I slowly picked up, not sure what kind of

reaction to expect. "H-Hello?"

"Rina! How could you hang up on us like that?"

I swallowed hard. "Uh..."

"Especially after you finally told us the very thing we've been wishing to hear ever since you were born!"

"I-uh..." What?

"We love you too, Rina!" Mom's voice called.

"Really?" I managed, my voice thick.

"Of course!" Dad said. "You never knew?"

I cleared my throat. "Well, uh, I got kicked out of the house last year...."

They were silent for a moment. "We're sorry, Rina. We were dealing with a lot last year. There was a huge increase of responsibilities on the Council suddenly, and we were stressed. And after the shock of your Talent, we went overboard."

I bit my lip and gripped the edges of my blanket. WHAT WAS HAPPENING?!

"But that doesn't excuse the way we handled ourselves last year. We're sorry," Dad said.

My head spun. WHAT?!

"Uh, I...." I licked my lips, unsure what to say. I wanted to ask them why they favored Mira so much, but my tongue wouldn't form the words. "...Thanks," I mumbled, which didn't really fit into the conversation. But at this point, I was desperate to return to territory I was more comfortable with. "So, you guys are okay right now? Even Mira?"

"Yeah, we're all fine," Mom said.

"And Mira?" I pressed.

There was a short pause. "I think she's fine," Mom said slowly.

My pulse thundered in my brain. "What do you mean?" I demanded.

Dad took the phone. "It's nothing you need to worry about," he said hastily.

"Tell me!" I nearly screamed. "WHAT HAPPENED?!"

"Nothing happened!" Dad hurried to say. "What we mean to say is, she's probably doing fine, but she has been struggling to keep up with projects lately."

Oh. Whew. Just school. But alarm bells rang in my head, so I started to ask a lot of questions. "Really? What kind of projects? Which class? How many?"

"Rina!" Mom said suddenly, sounding impressed and surprised. "I didn't know you were so worried about your sister! If I knew earlier, I would've told you some time ago!"

"Told me what?" I asked, my blood suddenly growing cold.

"Well, Mira hasn't been home for the past few weeks," Mom started.

"WHAT?!" I shrieked. "Then where has she been?"

"Be patient," Dad scolded suddenly. "You need to hear the whole story first!"

"Okay," I frowned. "But that's not normal."

"Yes, it isn't," Mom agreed. "So we called her to check up on her after she was repeatedly leaving the house for four days in a row. She said she had a humongous project to work on with a friend, so she wouldn't be able to be at home as much. Then she asked if she could just stay over at her friend's house from then on, to max out their efficiency. After some discussion with your father, we agreed. We figured if she could finish her projects faster, she'll be able to come home faster."

"That makes sense," I said slowly. "But a few weeks?!"

"Every week, Mira called to say her projects got a lot more complicated," Dad said. "Then her other teachers started to give her projects too."

"And you didn't call the school about this?"

"Why do we need to?" Mom asked. "It's near

338

the middle of the school year, close to finals for the first semester. We thought this would be a part of the testing grade, so we agreed."

"Why would a project be a part of the finals?" I argued. "Aren't they usually tests?"

"That's how it was when we were attending the Academy," Dad agreed. "But this is a whole generation later. Maybe they changed things up."

"You can still call the school and ask for their testing curriculum, right?"

"Why are you so riled up?" Mom asked curiously. "I mean, it's not bad or anything, but you seem a lot more upset than I thought you would've been."

I went with the excuse they told me earlier. "I was curious," I said. "Mira usually isn't like this. Even when she has a homework overload, she usually stays home. If she goes to a friend's house, she's always back by dinner unless she's having a sleepover."

I could imagine Mom and Dad nodding to what I said. "Yes. That's why we always called. But Mira is always responsible, so we decided to trust her on this one."

I pursed my lips, thinking. "Okay. I see. Did she ever tell you which friend?"

Mom sighed. "No. We didn't ask. I'm

assuming she's at Alina's."

Alina was Mira's best friend, as far as I knew. "But that's enough about Mira for now. What about you?" they asked.

I quickly gave them a vague response. I wanted to sit on Mira's case for a little longer.

After I promised my parents to call soon (whenever that may be, considering my circumstances), I bounced backward onto my bed and stared at the ceiling.

What was Mira up to?

If she hadn't been at home for the past few weeks, where had she been? Well, if I wanted to be obvious, the answer would be "at her friend's house". But Mom didn't specify which friend aside from Alina, and she isn't even sure if it's really Alina. Which means that on my terms, Mira is missing.

Again.

I groaned. "AGAIN?!"

It was ironic how much our roles had changed. Before, it seemed like I was the one who always caused Mira trouble. But that was nothing compared to disappearing for weeks on end, even if your parents believed that she really was "at her friend's house".

I wasn't buying it for one second.

I quickly ran outside and banged on my friends' doors. "HEY GUYS! Can we talk in the garden for a second?"

It took five minutes before everyone was assembled in the garden. As usual, Kodiak was the last one, looking even more agitated than before. "What is it?" he asked harshly. "I need to check on something really important."

Well. That stung. "I was just going to ask how your families were, first of all," I said. "Then I was going to tell you what I learned about my sister."

Kodiak's gaze remained hard for a bit before he sighed. "I'm sorry. I'm feeling really stressed right now."

I stared at him intently. "Oh, really? I didn't notice."

Kodiak held my gaze shamefully. "I promise I'll -"

I sighed. "I don't want to pressure you into telling me. But I really hope you'll tell me what's going on very soon. You've been acting really strangely, and if it's affecting you this much, I want to know why and how I can help."

Kodiak gave me a strained smile. "Thanks, but I don't know if you can do anything."

I was about to ask why, when he continued,

"So how were your families?"

Callan shrugged, but he was obviously relieved. "Nothing bad happened to mine. When Ivoria told us to check on them, I'd thought...."

I nodded. "Me too. My family was surprisingly... friendly."

Galen's eyes widened. "Seriously?!" he yelled. I nodded again, leaning away from his voice. "They told me they, uh, loved me. For real," I whispered awkwardly.

Galen's eyes glittered. "That's great!"

I squirmed. "This is awkward. So what about you?"

Galen made a loud sound of disgust. "Well! Wendy picked up the phone, since Mom was in the shower, and she shattered my eardrums!"

Callan nodded. "Ah, that's why you're yelling. I'd thought it was just because you're naturally loud."

Galen scowled at him. "BE GLAD I BARELY HEARD THAT OR ELSE YOU'D BE FLOUNDERING ABOUT IN THE MIDDLE OF AN OCEAN RIGHT NOW!"

Callan rolled his eyes. "Sure."

I grabbed Galen's arm before he could blow up a storm. "Don't you think Ivoria might use your weird rivalry with Callan against us? You

342

don't want that, do you?"

Galen kept his dark glare on the older boy. "I think I can deal with that if it comes to it."

"The feeling is mutual," Callan retorted.

I sighed, once again tired by this exchange. "Fine, then. Do whatever you want."

I turned to Sirocca. "Yours?"

She gave me a smile. "My grandparents are fine. Nothing happened, either."

I smiled back. "That's good." I turned to Kodiak. "You?"

Kodiak suddenly took on a strange expression. "I already went."

I frowned, thinking. "Did you?"

"No you didn't!" Callan nudged Kodiak with a shoulder. "Come on! Is your memory that bad?"

Kodiak stood stiffly. It wasn't what anyone expected from the kind, easy going person we all knew him to be. "My family's... the same as usual," he said carefully. "Nothing's changed...."

Everyone stared at him skeptically. "Really?"

Kodiak looked panicked. "Really."

I decided to spare him. "Okay, then! So, moving on to what I wanted to say, my parents told me that Mira has been staying at her friend's house for the past few weeks due to school

343

projects. Naturally, I don't believe this one bit, even if my parents do. Which means that to me, Mira is missing, using school and friends to cover up her absence. Do you think I'm overreacting, or is this really something to worry about?"

Galen spoke up first. "I agree with you. Out of all of us - besides you - I think I know Mira the best, and I can testify to say that it really isn't normal Mira behavior. And based on the last time she was missing, it can't be anything good."

Callan made a face. "You know, I have to say that your sister isn't the most... pleasant person to be around."

I frowned, but didn't say anything.

"So you want us to keep an eye out for her, is that right?" Sirocca asked.

I sniffed and rubbed my nose. "Well, obviously, we can't look for her because we're over here, but can you guys do me a big favor and ask your relatives to keep their eyes open?"

"Of course!" everyone chimed.

I ducked my head. "Thanks. Sorry for always asking you guys to help me with stuff."

Galen nudged me with his shoulder. "Yeah. You owe me, you know? Why don't you keep Wendy for a while? Out of all my brothers and sisters, she's the one I have problems with the most."

I laughed. "Uh, sure! Anything you guys need from your side?"

Everyone looked around, so I assumed it was a no. "I have a question though," Callan spoke up. "Is it just me, or is Ivoria really going to track our phone signals? She'll find the Terrenian Islands, right?"

Galen rolled his eyes. "I can't believe you forgot."

Callan turned a rock-hard gaze at him. "Care to explain, then?"

"Ivoria already knows where the Terrenian Islands are. Remember?" Galen shook his head disbelievingly. "She grew up there, then left."

"Oh yeah!" I exclaimed. "I forgot!"

Galen shook his head again. "You too?! I'd thought you out of all people would remember this."

"Hey, I have a lot to think about," I defended.

Galen shrugged. "Fine. I'll give you that. You made a good point. But that old man over there -" he jerked his head in Callan's direction, "- needs to get his mind refreshed."

Callan's eyes would have shot a million holes into Galen if it could.

I rubbed my eyes. "Okay, that's all I wanted

to say. Do you guys want to go back inside now?"

Kodiak, Sirocca, and Callan nodded. "I'm going to ask my parents to look out for your sister," Callan said, motioning toward the house.

I smiled. "Thanks. What about you, Galen?"

Galen shrugged. "Nah. I've been inside for too long. I want to stay outside and explore a bit."

I grinned at him. "Cool! Let's go!"

We walked a few laps around the outside before I decided to head inside. "Keep walking around and exploring," I called behind my shoulder before I headed inside. "I need to use the bathroom."

Galen laughed and stuck his tongue out at me. "Go ahead!"

I didn't want to walk all the way to the other side of the dorms and back. It would take too long; I've been holding it in all morning.

Maybe there was another bathroom closer to the garden.

I walked inside the mansion and started my search.

Chapter 37

Andy watched with arms crossed as his sister sat stone still, every cell in her body inclined to listening.

"The measurements are correct?" Ivoria's voice floated out of the speaker. Derrik had connected a more powerful speaker to the computer to make it easier to listen to. Everyone was crowded around, listening intently.

"Oh, yes, Boss," a man's voice said. His voice was oily and made Andy think of greasy hair. "My team has double checked everything."

Ivoria nodded. "Well done."

There was a pause and then a chuckle. "I see our little swan has gotten a bit lost," she said, amused.

Andy frowned. *Swan?*

Bad Hair Maintenance chuckled. "She's

swimming downwards," he murmured softly.

There was the clicking of heels. Andy noticed Emily stiffen. She was nervous.

"Let's guide our little swan back to shore," Ivoria said, her voice smiling. "Everything is in place?"

"In a moment, Boss. I will have twenty men stationed in a split second."

There was a slight pause. Maybe Ivoria was nodding? "You are a much better scientist than Elias ever was," she said with a hint of pride. "You will be very well rewarded, Nicholas."

Nicholas? Andy's eyes widened and exchanged horrified glances with Emily. "Nicholas?" he mouthed at her.

"It is my pleasure to serve you, Boss," Nicholas said with that slippery tone again.

The clicking of heels faded and there was the sound of fingers on a computer keyboard. "Terrin, station your group in the art room in the left wing. Boss's orders. The entry code has recently been changed. It is…"

Emily scrambled to grab a pen and started to jot the number down on her arm. Andy leaned in closer to listen.

"7456. Left wing, Art. Bring the gun with you." There was a click, then continued tapping of the keyboard.

Emily paled, and Andy was pretty sure he looked ghost-like too. "Call Rina," he commanded Elece. "Now."

Elece immediately whipped out her phone, which surprised Andy. She wasn't usually so eager to listen to his instructions.

"What's wrong?" Derrik demanded. "Who's Nicholas? Why did he trigger such a reaction from you two?"

"Nicholas Fri is my dad's second-in-command," Andy explained. "He is very clever, especially when it comes to assassination."

The room immediately silenced. Thora took a step closer to Derrik. "What about the swan?" she asked, voice trembling.

Andy paced. "That's got to mean one of the members of the team," he muttered. "They're the only ones who aren't usually there. Swan...." He froze and the world spun. "Oh no...."

"She's not picking up," Elece said, eyes frantic, but voice strong. "Galen isn't picking up either."

Andy cursed under his breath, immediately regretting it when Thora flinched. "Find a way to get to Galen, then," he demanded. "Tell him Rina is in danger. Left wing, art room, 7456. ASAP."

Elece nodded absentmindedly, dialing Galen's number.

There was another click from the speakers, drawing everyone's attention to the computer again.

"What do you mean, you don't know where the art room is!" Nicholas barked. He let out a frustrated groan. "Why Aura wanted to appoint this blockhead as a head, I have no idea.... KEYPAD BESIDE THE GARDEN DOOR! Do you want me to broadcast it?"

Emily furiously scribbled on her arm. Elece's foot tapped a hundred times a second.

"Come on...." Andy growled.

There was a sudden shift in Elece's expression. "GALEN! WAKE UP! IT'S RINA!"

Chapter 38

It felt like I had been walking for hours....

I was lost.

I pulled out my phone to text Galen. Turns out, he had left me a message:

GALEN: DUDE, WHERE ARE YOU??
RINA: I'M LOST.
GALEN: OF COURSE YOU ARE.
RINA: WHAT'S THAT SUPPOSED TO MEAN?
GALEN: NEVER MIND. I'LL COME FIND YOU.
WHERE ARE YOU?

I glanced up at the wall. *In a hall with a million doors.*

Gee, thanks. That really doesn't describe all the hallways in this mansion.

Well, what else do you want me to say?

Which way did you go after leaving the garden?

I rolled my eyes. *Do you think I'd remember? I'll just call Callan... maybe he's nearby....*

NO! DON'T CALL HIM!

I paused, startled. "Why not?"

Just DON'T. Okay? Call... Kodiak. If I take too long.

I sighed. *Your arguments with Callan needs to stop. At least tell me the reasons.*

I already told you before. I won't. But that's not important right now. WHERE ARE YOU?

Before I could respond, I received another text:

CALLAN: MEET ME BACK AT THE GARDEN IN AN HOUR.

I stared at it.

RINA: WHY SHOULD I?

CALLAN: I NEED TO TELL YOU SOMETHING IMPORTANT.

RINA: WHAT IS IT?

CALLAN: JUST MAKE SURE YOU COME BY YOURSELF. ONLY YOU CAN KNOW THIS AS OF RIGHT NOW.

I frowned. Fine. If I could find my way back to the garden, at least.... Maybe he would tell me the conflict between him and Galen, I thought, immediately brightening. Besides, I had left Galen in the garden, so it'd be killing two birds with one stone.

I really needed to go though....

Fifty-five minutes later, when the walls were starting to look more familiar, I got another text.

KODIAK: HEY, RINA. CAN I TELL YOU SOMETHING?

Him too? I bit my lip, trying to think of a response. I couldn't talk to two people at once.

I decided to write: SURE! BUT NOW IS REALLY NOT A GOOD TIME, SO CAN YOU CAN WRITE IT HERE? I'LL READ IT LATER. I'M KIND OF BUSY RIGHT NOW...

I managed to find my way back to the garden in time. The bathroom would have to wait....

Callan was waiting under the same tree we were talking at earlier. I must've been wandering around longer than I'd expected. It was already night.

How was that possible? It had just been the morning a few hours ago!

Callan smiled. "I need to tell you something, Rina. You might want to brace yourself."

I opened my mouth. "Why -?"

"Rina...?"

I spun around, squinting at the plants. Did I just hear Kodiak? I frowned. Nah, couldn't be. I couldn't imagine why he'd be out at this time, so I started to turn back toward Callan when I caught a glimpse of two blue eyes shining from behind another tree.

No way.

"Kodiak?" I called, horror slowly creeping into my veins as I thought of the text I had sent him. "What are you doing here?"

Kodiak stepped out of the shadows. Dark rings hung around his eyes. How'd he get those in an hour? He looked haunted.

"What are you doing here?" he asked in return.

"We're conducting a test for a school project," Callan said. "I just remembered that earlier, so I called Rina out to help me. It's really big, and it's due the second we return. But dude, what happened to you? You're never out this late."

"Liar," Kodiak whispered. He looked at me. "You lied to me."

My head spun. What's wrong with Kodiak? "What?" I said. My brain was working too slowly.

"That was the most ridiculous lie I've ever heard," Kodiak spat. "There is no school project. We're in the same level, Callan. I would know if we were doing a collab assignment with Rina's level."

Callan and I looked away and shuffled our feet. I didn't really want to hide what Callan wanted to tell me, but I wanted to be sure exactly what it was before I shared with the rest of the team.

"Why?" Kodiak asked. His eyes revealed so much pain.

It hurt me to see him this way. He'd been just fine an hour earlier. What'd happened after we returned to our rooms? Then it hit me: did it have to do with all those phone calls?

"Look, I can explain," I tried.

I really was going to explain. I didn't want any of my friends looking this hurt. But Kodiak shook his head. "No. You told me you couldn't listen. I assumed you were asleep." He glared at Callan. "Since you guys just got here and seemed to have a good time, that explains everything. You promised me, Rina." Kodiak looked directly into my eyes. "You promised me," he whispered brokenly before running off.

"Kodiak!" I yelled after him. I was so, so

worried.

"What was that all about?" Callan asked. "What's up with him? I've never seen him like that before. He's so melodramatic!"

"This is all your fault!" It was strange to feel so unreasonably angry at Callan. "What did you call me out here for?"

Callan stared at me in shock. "What'd I do? I was just going to tell you that I found out something important about your sister. You agreed to meet me here."

I let out a frustrated growl and ran off in the direction Kodiak left. Why did he look so hurt? Why was he out here so late? How long had he been out here?

I found him by Sandy Beach. He was sitting on one of the rocks, staring out to sea.

"Kodiak?"

"You didn't have to come after me, you know?" he said, his eyes glued to the black waters. "Pretend you didn't hear what I said earlier. I'm fine."

I stepped forward tentatively. "Are you sure?"

There was no reply for a few seconds. "Of course. Why wouldn't I be?" he said coldly.

I sat down a few paces behind him. "What are

356

you doing here so late?"

"I ask the same about you," he said rigidly.

"Callan had something he needed to tell me. It's about my sister," I explained.

"So. You really weren't busy."

I bit my lip. "I was. I got lost in the mansion, but Callan said it was important, so I was planning to meet him for a few minutes and find out what he had to tell me. I managed to find my way back to the garden."

Kodiak was silent. "I see."

I waited for him to say more. When he didn't, I said, "So…. What did you want to tell me?"

Kodiak mumbled, "Nothing. You can go finish talking to Callan." He stared so intently at the horizon, I was expecting the sun to rise in the middle of the night. Or for his eyes to fall off. Or lasers to slice the sea in two.

I sat back. I really hated the feeling of knowing that someone you cared about was suffering, but you didn't know why. You were then forced to wait. But this time, it was my fault.

"Well," I said slowly, repeating the lines I've told him millions of time, "I won't ask if you don't want to tell me." It was hard getting those words out. Half of me was overwhelmed with curiosity, and the other half hurt for him. "I'm

357

going to see if Callan is still there. Call if you need me."

I stood up and made my way back through those bushes. I was actually going to ask Callan to talk to Kodiak. After all, they were best friends, right?

"My sister is gone."

I was squeezed in between two especially thorny bushes when he spoke. I stopped in my tracks and looked backwards to where Kodiak was sitting. "What do you mean?"

I couldn't see his face - only his back. But he shuddered every time he spoke. "Alaska. My sister. She's..." Kodiak's voice cracked. He didn't speak for a few seconds. He rested his head between his knees and whispered, "Gone."

Everything became a blur. I barely realized I was still standing.

Gone?

The girl he was speaking with before? Who seemed so carefree and joyful? Sure, I didn't know her, but she seemed so bright and beautiful. She's gone?

The world became a dream of confusion. "Gone?" I whispered. "You mean -"

"We don't know if she's dead," Kodiak interrupted, voice shaking. "But... she's been missing for over a month now."

Over a month...?

"But... that girl I saw that other day at school...."

"That wasn't her," Kodiak said. His voice caught regretfully when he continued, "I thought it was her. But it wasn't. She only looked like Alaska from far away."

So that's why he'd look so confused when he walked back. "B-but, where are the signs, the-the posters?" I stammered. "If she's been missing for so long, why hasn't anything changed? There's nothing on Jetstream, and -"

"Because I don't want to make this public!" Kodiak spat. He looked up at me. "I know that isn't a wise decision. But Alaska went missing after school. She was supposed to walk home with me, as usual, but I went to Callan's house that day instead. He wanted to show me his new video game. We've been waiting for it to come out for a whole year."

Kodiak dropped his head onto his knees and smacked the rock with his hand. I waited for him to continue.

"When I got home, Alaska wasn't there. Mom and Dad thought she'd been with me." Kodiak drew in a shaky breath. I made my way back down the rocks, not caring how the thorns made little rips in my clothes. I sat down beside Kodiak, laying a hand on his shoulder. He barely noticed.

"We looked for days. I wasn't too worried then since everybody knew Alaska. I figured someone was bound to spot her somewhere, or that she ran off somewhere to explore, like she usually does. But no one called."

"That's why you're always rushing home or on the phone. You always look agitated afterwards," I said, finally understanding.

"I don't like failing my family," he whispered. "This is the worst thing that could ever happen. Every time I call, it's either a false alarm or my parents slowly starting to believe she's really...." He couldn't continue.

"Put up posters!" I said urgently. "If no one knows she's missing, then no one would look carefully. If they saw her, they might have assumed their own stories and didn't bother reporting because they didn't know she was supposed to be home."

"No, I can't," he said despairingly. "If I do, people will think our family is -"

"KODIAK!" I grabbed his shoulders and forcefully turned his body so he was facing me.

"Which is more valuable to you: your pride or your seven-year-old sister?"

Kodiak's eyes ignited in a furious blaze for a minute before drowning into a deep ocean of shame and sorrow. He leaned away from my hands and turned back to the ocean.

"I'm a terrible brother," he said, voice dry. "You can go now. That's all I wanted to tell you."

I knew what was probably going to come next. I stood up and walked away. But before I crossed the line of bushes, I turned back to say, "Hey, if you need anything, you can always come to me. I know I haven't exactly been keeping my promise to you…. I'm sorry. I'll start doing a better job. I hope you believe me."

Kodiak just nodded blankly in response. I turned away. The last thing I heard before I was out of earshot were muffled, heartbroken sobs.

Chapter 39

I walked back to the tree where I had left Callan. He wasn't there anymore, and I mentally smacked myself.

Why did these things have to happen?

I walked back inside the mansion. Luckily, the way back to the dorms was easier for me to remember, so I didn't get lost on the way back. I stood in front of our dorms, taking a deep breath before walking up to Callan's door. I hesitated, then knocked.

Callan opened the door before I even finished knocking.

"What?" he asked coldly.

I winced. "I, uh…."

He kept staring at me so darkly, I had to stare at the floor. "I'm sorry about earlier," I mumbled. "I had been frustrated for a long time, and it kind of... unleashed back there."

Callan snorted. "That was an understatement."

I bit back a retort. "Sure."

Callan sighed. "So. You still want to hear what I wanted to tell you?"

I nodded silently.

Callan suddenly snickered. "Are you afraid of me?"

I gave a start. I didn't expect this. But then again, I really wasn't expecting anything. "Uh...."

Callan rolled his eyes. Or, I imagined he was. My eyes were still glued to the ground. The most I could see of him were his shoes.

"Hey." He gently knocked a fist against my head. I flinched instinctively, even though it didn't hurt, and finally looked up. Callan grinned. "Finally. Why were you so scared?"

"I wasn't scared!" I protested. "I was... You were kind of...."

"Scary," Callan finished promptly. "Right?"

I made a face. "Well, you were kind of... intimidating...."

Callan snickered. "I wasn't!"

"Well, how would you know?" I mumbled. "It's your face; you can't see it. You looked ready to lock me outside in pouring rain or something."

Callan shook his head disbelievingly. "You don't know me very well, then. I would never lock you out."

I scowled. "So. You were saying...?"

Callan walked out of the room, closing the door behind him. "Let's go to the garden," he said.

My mind quickly flashed to Kodiak. "Uh, how about the other side of the garden?" I asked hastily. "You said this wasn't for everyone's ears, right? It might be more secure there, since we always meet at the same place."

Callan had looked at me suspiciously when I first suggested the change, but after I explained, he relaxed. "Very true. Okay, let's go."

I led him out into the garden, then as far away from Sandy Beach as possible. I'll check to see if Kodiak was still there later.

Callan started talking as soon as I stopped walking. We were almost at the Rocky Beach.

"Alright, so I told my parents what happened with your sister, so they told me they'd keep an eye out. They reached out to all my relatives, and it turned out my second cousin is friends with Mira."

My eyebrows shot up. "Really?"

Callan nodded. "Yeah. I mean, I think she used to be though, so not currently. But anyways, my cousin started to ask all the people she knew that hung around your sister. Guess what? None of them said that Mira was staying at their house for a project."

I frowned. "Could they be hiding it? Did she ask everyone?"

Callan shrugged, but he didn't look convinced. "My cousin has a knack for sniffing out lies. Believe me; I know. At a family reunion once, I stole her shoes and hid them in a tree. She knew it was me immediately when I came up with a pretty good lie."

"So she's also a mind reader?!" I yelped. "Is she half-Cosmos?"

Callan gave me a strange look, reminding me that I was still sleep-deprived.

"Uh, no. Anyways, I think this confirms your theory that Mira is missing."

I nodded gravely. "Anything else?"

Callan nodded seriously. "Yes. My cousin also hacked into the Academy's attendance files -"

"How talented is your cousin?" I marveled. "She's so cool!"

Callan laughed. "Yeah. That's the other one. This one's a guy. I'll take you to meet them later.

They're twins, you know? The girl twin is the lie-detector. This one's a hacker. Okay, enough tangents. My cousin found out that Mira's attendance markings have been faked."

I furrowed my eyebrows. "That's possible?"

Callan shrugged. "I don't know. But he said when he sorted out the marks, it says that Mira hasn't been in school for the last three weeks."

I stopped. "Three weeks."

Callan nodded. "But to everyone else, she has. It's just no one has seen her."

I closed my eyes. "But what about her classmates?" I asked. "That doesn't make sense. How can people not question that she's 'here', when she doesn't even show up to class?"

Callan shrugged. "Weird things happen sometimes. Students probably thought she was occupied during that particular class or something. People like to assume stories that make out-of-the-ordinary activities seem ordinary."

I thought back to what I had told Kodiak. Callan has no idea….

"So what are you going to do?" Callan asked, looking at me with concern.

I sighed. "I don't know. I mean, what can I do? I'm all the way over here. There's nothing I can really do to look for her." I sighed again. "Why does she have to disappear all the time?"

Callan shrugged. "You can ask her when you find her."

I glared at him. "Not funny."

Callan grinned.

"But thanks for telling me," I told him. "I'll share this with the rest of the team, just so they're updated."

Callan nodded. "I decided to just tell you first, since it regards your sister, and because it hasn't really been fully determined yet. My second cousins are smart, but what they find might not be what it seems, you know?"

I nodded, then we headed back inside. I collapsed onto my bed as soon as I entered my room, falling asleep before my head even hit the pillow.

I didn't realize until I woke up the next day that I had forgotten to reply to Galen and check up on Kodiak.

Chapter 40

Thora was shaking by the time Ivoria's voice returned to the speaker. "Next time," she said calmly, anger lying just beneath. "She found her way to the garden. Emily requested their privacy."

Thora wanted to collapse and sob with cool relief. Instead, she flashed a huge smile at Emily, who looked just as relieved as Thora did.

"Do you want me to call off the men?" Nicholas asked.

"Keep them on duty," Ivoria said. "She tends to get lost often. Keep watching. Watch for the falcon as well. He is irritable and hotheaded. He might come in use."

Falcon?.... "He"?

There were three guys on this trip. Unlike swan, falcon could be anybody.

Andy's face was scrunched up in concentration. "Falcon..." he muttered. "The only one who's remotely related to birds is...."

Thora came to the same conclusion as Andy did, but Andy was quicker to voice it out. "Contact Galen. Tell him to watch his back."

Thora nodded. "Shouldn't we warn all of them?"

Andy frowned, thinking. "Best not to scare everyone. Galen already has both warnings. If he thinks it's important to tell the rest of the team, he will."

Emily shushed everyone. "I'm trying to listen," she snapped.

Elece lowered her phone from her ear. "These kids are never picking up," she grumbled.

"Um, quick question," Emily said suddenly. "We can hear Ivoria so clearly. Nicholas is obviously the head of her control center. Which means they can probably hear us, too, right? Or, at least know that we've hacked their sound system?"

Derrik shook his head hesitantly. "I don't think they can," he responded. "Thora and I created this system to link with the walls. We're hearing these voices as they're being absorbed by the walls, and since this room is filled with electricity, we're able to pick up on the sounds from this room, even though the walls haven't been soundified."

Emily nodded slowly. "Okay…. I see."

Elece snarled, her fists tightening around her phone, eyes glowing dangerously. "I am so tempted to fling this phone across the room," she muttered. Little bolts of lightning flashed around her dark hair.

Thora bit her lip and prayed silently for the team to be safe.

Chapter 41

Galen immediately exploded in my face the next day, after he dragged me out to the garden by my ear. "WHAT WERE YOU THINKING?!"

I squirmed, grabbing for my ear. "What? I already said I was sorry millions of times already."

"HOW COULD YOU JUST STAND HERE AND TALK TO ME LIKE THIS?! DO YOU KNOW HOW LATE I STAYED UP LAST NIGHT?"

I made a face. "Do you think I wanted to? I really was going to tell you, okay? I forgot."

Galen laughed dryly. "Ah. 'You forgot'. You know, you really scared me, okay? I thought you disappeared."

I stared at him. "You were scared? Why?"

Galen glared at me. "Don't you dare say

anything."

I blinked and looked away. "No, don't worry, I won't. I'm just surprised, that's all." I glanced at him from the side of my eyes. "You took a long time, you know"

Galen snorted. "Come on. You were LOST and didn't know where you were! I could feel you close, but you kept moving. You really believed that Bonds wouldn't be able to find each other? What use would a Bond be, then?"

I smiled. "Thanks!"

Galen rolled his eyes angrily. "YOU-!! ARGH!!" He stormed back into the building.

Oops.

I followed him tentatively. "Hey. Sorry. I was lost, then I found my way back to the garden, then made my way back to our dorms from there."

He sighed. "What am I going to do with you...? You're our leader. You can't just disappear like that."

I frowned. He had a good point. Galen had as much experience as I did, even though he wasn't very mature about it sometimes.... "Fine. We'll both be co-leaders of this mission. I need you to help me make decisions and oversee everything."

Galen's eyes widened. "REALLY?"

"Don't start jumping around like a happy puppy at a buffet," I grumbled. "And don't you dare annoy me about needing your help."

I could hear Galen laughing behind me. He ran up to me again. "Come on, what's so embarrassing about that? Huh? Huh?" He kept poking my side. "Admit it."

I twitched and sidestepped. "STOP! I already did!"

"But I need to hear it again!"

"No, you don't!" I walked faster. "I'm still not familiar with these halls. Are you going to help me find the way back or not?"

Galen cackled one more time before flying up above me. "Fine, fine. Whatever you say."

I kept walking, but I could still hear him snickering and shaking his head in disbelief. What was so amazing about me asking him for help anyways?!

Galen tilted his head to the left. "This way."

I ran to keep up. "How do you know?"

"Someone's blasting the AC in their room," Galen said. "It might be...."

Galen led me down a few more hallways. Honestly, I really don't get how people can maneuver through here so easily!

I almost ran past the five doors if Galen didn't

drop down right in front of me. I plowed into his back. "HEY!"

Galen glanced backward with a smirk. "Sorry. Thought you'd read the signs, genius."

I glared at him. I couldn't say anything.

"Oh. Haha! Turned out it was my room that had the AC on!" He looked at me, eyes laughing. "Who knew?"

I smacked him then stormed into my room. "GOOD JOB."

"Thanks!"

I was about to close the door when five fingers and a strong hand blocked the doorway. I glanced up at Galen's face. He had suddenly become very serious.

"Seriously, though," he said. "Don't go running off to wherever next time. What am I - what are we supposed to do without you? Who's going to make all the decisions?"

I blinked. "Uh, you?"

Galen stared at me. "Me. Really? Who believes that?"

Good point.

"But you're the next choice," I said. "I mean, we were on the first mission together. Both of us are the most experienced ones here - even though we've only done one mission...."

"Just stop." Galen pulled the door open wider. "Do you really think anyone would listen to me? Do you really think that I am able to be a leader of this mission? Sirocca's the one that seems a lot more experienced than me!"

"But you're the one that knows what to do in situations that Sirocca can only visualize because you've been through it."

Galen glared at me. "Stop changing the subject. My point is, don't just disappear like that. You can't just say 'goodbye' and ignore every question I asked afterwards!"

I grinned sheepishly. "I was - uh, preoccupied, so I didn't hear you ask questions."

"EXACTLY!" A brief gust of wind made the curtains of my window dance, but it died down seconds after it had started. "Just.... Yeah."

He left.

I stared at the space where he had been. "Okay."

That was an excellent clincher.

I understood Galen's concern. What I didn't understand was why he wanted to drill it into me. I got lost trying to find a bathroom - what was there to be angry about? I tipped my head, confused.

Galen and Callan were too much alike.

When we returned to our rooms, there was a note on my nightstand. I didn't bother trying to find out where it came from.

You have been granted a day of rest.

"Uh, okay...." I said aloud. I didn't really get the purpose of this note, but it was nice to know that we had the whole day off. Maybe I'll walk around Sandy Beach for a while....

As if everyone had the same mind, everyone was assembled under the "Discussion Tree" (that's what I decided to call the tree we were talking at yesterday) by the time I got there. They all looked up when I walked by.

"What're you all doing here?" I asked them.

Everyone shrugged. I noticed that Kodiak's eye bags weren't as visible. He seemed normal to everyone else, but I saw the way he held himself and the way his lips were pressed in a tight line. I bit my lip, worried.

"We saw the note, and decided to come here," Sirocca said. "We honestly don't know what else to do."

I frowned, rubbing my forehead. Suddenly, it just dawned on me.

376

"Y'know, it's not like Ivoria to do this, right?" I asked. "So this can go two ways. One, she's really telling the truth, which is possible. Two, she's observing us to see what we'd do with an opportunity like this. Oh wait, that goes into number one...."

Galen chuckled. "Two, she's really not telling the truth, and she's hoping we'd take this opportunity to do something reckless so she can bust us off the island for it and use it as an excuse to destroy our home."

"Ah, there it is," I said, grinning.

Sirocca nodded. "So which way should we take?"

I thought hard about it, subconsciously glancing sideways at Galen. He shrugged, and I made the decision. "Let's give her the benefit of the doubt," I said. "Let's go with number one."

"WHAT? ARE YOU CRAZY?" Callan exploded. "That's a dangerous thing to assume with Ivoria!"

I had already expected this kind of reaction, so I stood there calmly. "But," I said, "it gives us time to finally figure out some sort of plan to stop her. Since she claims we have a whole day, let's not waste it."

Callan growled. "I still don't like this."

377

I stared at him for a few seconds. He was biting his lip, his eyes flickering toward the ground. His right eyebrow twitched.

"But you have a plan," I prompted.

He stared at the ground. "How'd you know?"

I grinned. "I can see it on your face. Spill it! 'Cause I don't have one."

Callan mulled over his thoughts slowly. "Okay. Divide and conquer. We'll split the job. Some of us explore the first floor, and the others search outside."

"Didn't we do something like that already?" Sirocca countered. "We already had a tour."

Callan nodded. "We did, but we weren't being as thorough. Now that we have some idea of what we're looking for -"

"We do?" Galen interrupted. "Be more detailed, please. This is a plan, you know?"

Callan scowled. "The thing Rina saw on the board has to be important somehow if something that looks like a weapon was moved away from the room it had been in originally."

I blinked, confused. "I told you that?"

Sirocca looked at me sheepishly. "Um, I swiped your phones when Kodiak and Callan bound you to the tree...."

My jaw dropped. "You... you guys really

went all out, didn't you?"

Callan shook his head roughly. "That's beside the point. Sirocca looked through yours, since Galen's was dead, and told us what she found. We don't know exactly what the blueprints are -"

"But I didn't take a picture of the empty site," I interrupted.

Galen snorted. "You were too busy looking at the blueprints. I did."

I rubbed my eyes. I really needed to start paying attention.

"Anyways, can I get back to my plan now?" Callan spoke.

I nodded. "Yeah, go ahead. Sorry."

"Okay, so I was planning to have Galen, Sirocca, and Kodiak search outside -"

"I DISAGREE!" Galen roared, making me jump backward in surprise.

"So do I," Kodiak spoke for the first time.

Callan rolled his eyes. "Can I finish -"

"No!" they shouted.

Sirocca suddenly burst out laughing. "This has an easy solution. Rina and I will search inside. Anyone who argues with me will risk some confessions that will definitely be *very* interesting to watch. Any complaints?"

The boys glared at her, then glared at each

other, but nobody said anything.

Meanwhile, I was still sitting there, confused, like I usually was. "Uh…. Confessions…?"

Sirocca smiled at me. "Don't worry," she whispered to me playfully. "It's a strategy."

I nodded slowly. "O… kay." I pretended I knew what she was talking about.

"Alright, now that we have that solved, continue with your plan, Callan," she said with an innocent smile.

Callan glared at her. "You and Rina will be searching the entire first floor. Now that we've been here for about a week and a half now, we should know the place pretty well. Find something interesting. Anything.

"The rest of us," he continued with a disgusted look in Galen's direction, "will be looking around outside investigating that portal that Rina and Galen obviously thought was too unimportant to tell us, but important enough for them to go through by themselves to have some quality time."

I winced. His voice was not only dripping with sarcasm, it was drenched and it basically soaked the path beneath our feet.

Galen shrugged, but there was a small glint in his eyes. "What can I say? It was a great

380

experience. I learned a lot -"

Galen suddenly disappeared. I jumped up, panicking. "GALEN?!"

Callan laughed. "Don't worry. He has enough air."

The ground beneath me suddenly exploded, and I flew backwards. Galen shot straight up. "Nice try, rockhead!"

Callan rolled his eyes. "Immature."

"ANYWAYS!" Sirocca hollered. "CAN WE GET A MOVE ON?! WE DON'T HAVE ALL DAY!"

"Technically, we do -" I started.

"DON'T EVEN START OR YOU'RE JOINING THE BOYS!"

I shrank back. "Okay," I peeped. I didn't want to find out what a "confession" meant.

"Alright. Let's review. Boys will search outside and inspect the portal. Probably go through. Girls will search inside for the mystery weapon-thing. We'll meet here afterwards. Am I missing anything?"

"How're we going to contact each other?" I asked.

Galen grinned. "Through us!"

"Oh yeah…!"

"We have phones, you know?" Callan spoke

up irritably.

"I know, but where's the fun in that?" Galen asked cheekily.

"OKAY!" Sirocca said before another argument could break out. "Let's go."

Sirocca and I headed back into the building while the boys shuffled off towards the beach.

"What happened back there?" I asked. "You know, the boys are so rowdy. It's good you can do something to contain them. Whenever I say something, it never works."

"Oh, really?" Sirocca said with a glint in her eye. "I think it works well."

I grumbled. "No, it doesn't."

Sirocca laughed. "Don't worry. Just let the boys resolve it on their own. It'll work out in the end."

"What's 'it'? What will work out?"

Sirocca smiled mysteriously. "You'll find out."

"Does it have to do with why Callan and Galen are always fighting?" I asked. "Because if it is, I want to know."

Sirocca laughed. "Yes, it does, and no, I can't tell you unless you figure it out yourself. But by then, I won't have to tell you!"

I growled. "So now everyone knows why they

fight except me?!"

"Yeah, that's pretty much it. Don't worry, Rina," she said, when I sighed. "You might wish you never knew."

I looked at her curiously. "Why?"

Sirocca shook her head. "So where do you think the object might be? Any speculations on what it actually is?"

I decided to go with it. "It's probably some sort of machine." I pulled out my phone to study the plans. "Yeah, see?"

There were many different parts to it, all of which I don't understand. But as I looked closer, it it seemed to be was some sort of strange cannon.

Was she going for an upgrade?

A chill crawled up my spine. Where would she hide a finished, upgraded cannon?

I whirled back to Sirocca. "We gotta get to the first Stone!"

Chapter 42

I raced back out the garden door and ran towards Rocky Beach. I hoped that Galen's theory was correct.

I grabbed Sirocca's hand, envisioned the first Stone, then flew through without stopping. When I opened my eyes, I sighed with relief.

"Wow! That was the portal?" Sirocca stood up and dusted herself off. "How'd that work?"

"Galen figured it out. He said if you think about where you're going to go before you pass through, it'll take you there."

"So could it take us back home if we wanted?" Sirocca asked, her voice laced with sadness.

I opened my mouth to answer. "I… actually, I don't know…."

The older girl shook herself off. "That's okay," she said briskly. "What matters right now is this

Stone. What did you figure out that brought us here?"

"Well, the machine in the tinkering room seemed to be some sort of cannon," I began. "Kind of like the cannons here, but different. I figured, if Ivoria finished making another cannon, where would she store it? With the other cannons!"

Sirocca nodded. "I see. Let's go!"

We flew towards the buildings in record time. Sirocca blasted the doors open and we flew inside.

Good thing no one was there when we forgot to check and be cautious.

I scanned the rows of cannons. Everything looked the same. "Where...."

Sirocca looked around. She bent down and studied one of the weapons. "You know, these are interesting.... Hey, Rina! Can I have your phone?"

I absentmindedly threw it to her, not really caring if she caught it or if it crashed to the floor. Where would it be...?

I walked to the other end of the room and poked my head through the doorway. More cannons. It would take forever to search here.

I tried to remember the shape of the imprint.

It had been relatively wide, with distinct curves and angles. It shouldn't be too hard to find, considering that it seemed to be twice as large as one of these cannons. But since nothing seemed to be out of the ordinary here, did I assume incorrectly?

I walked back toward Sirocca after one last look. She was still crouched by the cannons.

"Did you find something interesting?" I asked, peering at the space where she'd been staring intently at. I didn't see anything.

"Yeah, but I needed Derrik to help me with something." She handed me back my phone. "Thanks."

"Uh-huh," I said. "What is it?"

Sirocca narrowed her eyes. "I think I - oh, wait. Just kidding. Never mind. I'm wrong." She stood up. "Let's go. I think we got the wrong place."

I looked at her, confused. "What?"

"Let's check back at the mansion," Sirocca said, her eyes subtly signalling urgency. "There's nothing here."

"Oh, okay." I stood up and followed her.

As soon as we were out of the building, I waited twenty steps until I said, "Okay, spill."

"I think I might've found a flaw in the

designing of the cannons," Sirocca said without hesitation.

"Really?" I said, surprised. "You know this stuff?"

Sirocca shrugged. "I know random stuff. I was reading something in history about wars, and it led to cannons." She grinned sheepishly. "But I need Derrik's confirmation to be sure."

"Wow! I wish I brought you along with Kodiak when we first found this," I exclaimed.

Sirocca laughed. "Nah, I'm pretty sure Kodiak didn't want me there."

My jaw dropped. "Are you two having a fight too? Come on! First Galen and Callan, now you and Kodiak?" I narrowed my eyes at her. "Now that I think about it, I've never seen you two talk much…."

Sirocca laughed again. "Stop imagining things! There's nothing wrong. Just one of my suspicions." Her eyes looked at me with a strange gleam. It made me feel awkward and wiggly inside, so I shrank back.

"O…kay…."

We passed through the portal, and the mansion came into view. I sighed, not sure where to look next. "We've pretty much seen the whole first floor already, right? So there really isn't a need to..."

Sirocca was gone.

I blinked, looking around, afraid. "Sirocca?"

My heart skipped a beat. "Where'd you go?!"

Sirocca popped out of the portal behind me so suddenly, I screamed. She yelped and tumbled back into the portal.

"SIROCCA!" I hollered.

She reappeared. "Hehe... sorry. I guess I should've mentioned that I wanted to check if this went home."

"Well, did it?" I asked eagerly.

She shook her head mournfully. "No. I guess we'll have to manually fly home again."

"Or we could create another portal home," I suggested. "Like you guys did last time."

Sirocca frantically shook her head. "No. Last time, that took up so much energy, we all slept for two days straight. And after that, they did more tests while we were still exhausted. Creating portals take too much work."

I took a step back. "Oh. Sorry."

She shrugged. "It's fine. But we should check out the second Stone. You went with Galen that time, so I want to have a turn."

I nodded. "That's a good plan." A thought hit me just then. "Wait, where're the boys?"

Sirocca frowned, then disappeared. When she came back a few moments later, she stepped out of the portal and stood next to me. "They're at the second Stone. Galen told me to tell you to check the first floor."

"But we did that already!" I complained. "And the first floor is huge! I'm going to get lost. Again."

"We didn't see the whole floor," Sirocca said. "We only checked out that 'scrap' room."

"Yeah, but the whole floor is still humongous! It's going to take forever!"

"Not if we plan," Sirocca said. "Look. We see about half of the first floor every day when we walk from our rooms to the garden. Let's save that area for last. What we need to do is to inspect the other side of the first floor."

I nodded. "Okay. That makes sense. But I'm following you. I don't want to crash into Ivoria again."

We walked around the halls and looked through all the doors. Most of them were locked, but we tried our best to guess which room was for what. All the open doors had been storage rooms or closets. And an occasional bathroom.

Sirocca marched us back to our dorms. "Well, that wasn't too fruitful," she said. "Let's check all the doors on the path that leads to the garden."

I sighed. Here we go again.

We opened every single door past our dorms. About half of them were locked. The other half led to empty rooms. I was starting to get bored when I came across a room with a bed and dresser.

Another dorm.

It was about five doors down from ours. I stuck my head inside to take a closer look.

It was identical to ours, except for the color change. Everything was red, orange, or yellow. In fact, it was the mirror image of my room. I frowned. Did Ivoria have another guest…?

Nah. That wouldn't make sense. We were bound to run into each other if there was another person living here. Our rooms were so close!

Yet, I sensed that there was someone still staying here….

Shivering, I scrambled backwards and slammed the door shut. That room was creeping me out.

The next door was locked, but the door after that wasn't. I shuddered when a strange scent hit me. It was kind of like perfume, but it made me feel sick. It took me a while to register that it was another dorm. The color theme was white with thin lines of red and blue running through. Not wanting to investigate any further, I shut the door and ran back to Sirocca.

"Did you find anything?" I panted.

Sirocca shook her head. "But I'm going to assume that you did. You look like you saw a ghost!"

I gulped. "I might've. I found two dorms that were empty, but it looked like someone was still living there!"

Sirocca's eyes widened. "Let me see!"

I groaned, but turned around. I led Sirocca a few more steps, then gestured weakly at the doors. "I think it was these two...."

Sirocca barged right in. I remained outside. Whatever Sirocca found would've been something I didn't find.

Sirocca came back outside and immediately rushed to the next room. When she emerged, she was still empty-handed.

"Didn't find anything?" I asked.

"Nope," she said, disappointed. She looked like she wanted to kick the door. "This place was cleaned out. I can't find any trace of a person living here. Except for the clothes, but they haven't been worn. ARGH!" She tore at her hair. "We got so far, but we're still getting nowhere at the same time!"

I shrugged. "Want to see if they boys have found anything?"

Sirocca nodded. "They better. Or this day would've been wasted."

HEY, GUESS WHAT WE FOUND!!

"Oh, just in time," I said aloud. What? We didn't find anything. Well, we kind of did, but you go first.

Okay, so we were visiting the first and second Stones. The first Stone didn't reveal anything, but the second Stone!

I waited for him to continue. When he didn't, I said, And then?

I'm pausing for effect.

Your pause is way too long.

Hey, stop ruining it. Anyways, so the second Stone was supposed to be filled with weird blood and potions, right?

Yeah...? I think it's supposed to be 'weird potions and blood', but keep going.

ANYWAYS! Well, when we got there, we were, uh, messing around and inspecting VERY CAREFULLY and we discovered what the potions are!

Didn't we find out last time? Weren't they the liquefied elements?

Yeah, that's what we think! But we found out that instead of combining the blood and the elements, like we thought, I think she's separating them.

That made me pause. Really?

Yeah.

How do you know?

Well, for one thing, the liquids were flowing out of the main red stuff, separating into a lighter red, but still dark, and an element color thing. I think that was pretty self - explanatory.

That's it? It could still be anything!

I know! But we did, uh, some other stuff, and discovered more info!

Like what?

We need Derrik to confirm this, though, before I share it. I sent him what we found.

So everything rests with Derrik now. I bit my lip, thinking a secret wish.

Derrik, it's all up to you now….

Chapter 43

Derrik's phone pinged, drawing his attention away from the speaker. Nothing interesting was going on, anyways. Ivoria was gone, and all they were listening to were Nicholas' attempts at finding a girlfriend. Good luck with that.

Derrik pulled the phone out of his pocket, startled when he saw two messages. The first one was from Rina, and had an image attachment:

RINA: HEY, DERRIK. THIS IS SIROCCA. WE WERE INSPECTING THESE, AND I FOUND THIS. IS THIS WHAT I THINK IT IS? THANKS!

Derrik tapped on the photo and zoomed in. It was an image of a golden sphere. Derrik narrowed his eyes. Was that…?

His eyes widened and he quickly typed a

response.

DERRIK: SIROCCA, IT'S EXACTLY WHAT YOU THINK IT IS. I'M ASSUMING YOU HAVE SOME BACKGROUND KNOWLEDGE ON THIS ALREADY. GOOD LUCK.

Derrik sighed and rubbed his eyes. *Well, now we know Ivoria has cannons....*

Hopefully, Sirocca knew that destroying the power spheres would disable the entire cannon.

Hopefully, Ivoria didn't realize her cannons have a giant flaw in their design.

Hopefully, she also didn't realize that Sirocca discovered the flaw and knew how to destroy the cannons.

This is a lot to take in, Derrik thought. *On to the next message.*

The second message was from Galen, also with another image attached. *What's up with this all of a sudden?*

GALEN: DERRIK! WHAT ARE THESE USED FOR?

Short and sweet. Just like Galen.

Derrik tapped on the image and zoomed in. "What're you doing, Derrik?" Thora asked as she walked up to him.

Derrik looked up at her and smiled. "Galen and Sirocca sent me images. They want me to clarify something for them."

Elece immediately pounced on him, pinning him to the floor. Derrik yelled in surprise, then his legs flew up, throwing Elece off balance. Derrik rolled over, then sat on top of Elece. *I did it! Training paid off!*

"Galen contacted you?" Elece asked with masked patience. "Did he say anything?"

Derrik shrugged, still squashing Elece. "He sent me a picture of…." he squinted at the image. "Chains?"

He typed back a message:

DERRIK: UM, THOSE ARE CHAINS…. MOST LIKELY FOR KEEPING SOMETHING TIED DOWN?

That should've been obvious to even Galen.

Elece growled. "I meant about danger."

Derrik shook his head. "Nope."

Elece sighed, looking defeated. Derrik quickly scrambled off of her, worried. *Elece never gave up.*

The older girl slowly sat up, rubbing her head. "Well, there's nothing else we can do from here," she said. She looked at him sadly. "I guess we'll have to wait it out and see."

Derrik was about to nod when something caught on the corner of his eye. He frowned at his phone, staring at the small space beneath his reply message. It should have sent already.... I guess they have bad reception.

Or....

Derrik smashed his phone on the floor, startling everyone in the room. The screen shattered, but Derrik stomped on the phone for good measure.

Everyone stared at him when he was done.

"Wow...." Elece said, taking a step back. "I know I said I wanted to destroy my phone, but I didn't think you'd actually smash yours like that."

Derrik shook his head, running his fingers through his hair. His breath was heavy, and it took some time for his heartbeat to return to normal. "Ivoria is probably checking their messages," he said. "The message didn't send all the way."

"That could mean anything," Thora pointed out.

Derrik nodded, making a face. "I think it's best not to interact with the team anymore," he said softly. "We might be putting them in unnecessary danger."

All of them were quiet for some time. Derrik knew none of them wanted to leave the team on their own like that, especially now, after they were able to listen in on Ivoria's plans. But it seemed like that was the best way to help the team now.

Everyone turned to look at Emily, who looked at Andy. "What do you think?"

Andy pursed his lips, thinking. "I agree with Derrik," he said finally. "It would be the best if we refrain from contact with the team again. All phone calls could be intercepted, all messages could be read."

Emily sighed, then put on a brave face. Derrik admired her strength in these times. "Very well," she said, then made a face. "We'll just spend our time listening and taking notes."

Jordan spoke up, "Yeah, I think that's a great idea, but I think Elece and Derrik need to resume their training. They need to be prepared for anything. I trust that if there's something important, you'll let us know?"

Emily nodded, then waved them away. "Keep training," she told Derrik. "I'll call you if I need your help with anything."

Derrik gave a single nod then walked out the door toward the stairs.

Now, to replace his phone....

Chapter 44

We all met up back under the Discussion Tree. I immediately marched up to Galen and said, "Spill. What did you find?"

He looked at me, puzzled. "Didn't I just tell you?"

"What was the 'new info' you found?" I clarified.

Galen grinned. "You'll see."

I didn't have the patience for this today. "Galen. We are so close. Spill right now, or I'm going to sink you underwater."

Galen looked at me for a long time before he said, "The labs have another purpose. Another smaller lab was in the back. There were chains and a gurney. Based on what it seemed, someone had been operated on recently. The chains were also cast aside carelessly, like someone had thrown them away."

I paled. "So. She's still experimenting on people…"

Galen hastily added, "We don't know for sure. I sent a lot of pictures to Derrik to see if he would be able to tell if the chains were used for a specific purpose. These chains looked a little different. They were smoother and thinner, instead of the rough metal chains are usually made of. They actually looked pretty cool."

I gave him a sharp look and he darted backwards. "I'm sorry! I know it's terrible, but they were this awesome silver and sleek. They didn't look like they were used for holding someone down. More like decoration."

"How thin were they?" Sirocca asked.

Galen closed one eye to estimate the distance between his fingers. "Um, maybe about this thick…?"

His fingers were almost two inches apart. I frowned, trying to visualize the chains in my mind.

"How long were the chains?" I asked him.

Galen's frown deepened. "How do you want me to describe it? My arms can't stretch that long, you know."

Sirocca bit her lip. "Describe what they looked

like on the ground. Like, trace images on the sand."

Callan stepped up. "I can do that. I remember almost exactly what the chains looked like."

He bent down and dragged his fingers along the sand, drawing coiling, winding lines all around. "Uh, can you move your foot - thanks."

By the time he was done, the ground all around us was scarred with lines.

That was one long chain.

"Alright, so it could be used to hold someone if it was this long," Sirocca concluded.

"Yeah. That's why we can't tell for sure. We're still waiting for Derrik to get back," Kodiak said softly.

We all turned in surprise. Kodiak never talked anymore. Kodiak shrugged, looking away.

"Okay, anyways, did you guys find anything?" Galen asked.

I glanced at Sirocca and she nodded. "We were with the cannons -"

"What?" Callan interrupted. "We were there too. Weren't you guys supposed to be checking the first floor?"

Sirocca glared at him. "Wait 'til I finish. There's more to the story.

"We were at the cannons because Rina formed

402

a theory about what the mystery object in the tinkering room was."

I nodded. "Based on the drawings, it looked like some sort of upgraded cannon, so that's what I assumed it was. Then I thought, 'Where would she put an upgraded cannon?' Most likely with the other cannons, so I took Sirocca to the first Stone through the portal."

Sirocca nodded. "All the cannons there looked the same, though. So I bent down to look at one. I noticed that all the cannons had some sort of glass bubble covered with gold under the actual cannon part. I think it might've been a glass orb covered with gold paint. But anyways, you don't usually see that on a cannon. Since Derrik is an expert with weapons, I snapped a picture and sent it to him."

Galen nodded slowly. "So everything is up to Derrik now...."

I nodded in agreement. "In the meantime, why not investigate something else?"

Callan and Kodiak both looked up at me sharply. Say nothing, they seemed to say, but for different reasons.

I ignored both of them. "There are too many secrets going on here. We need to sit down and talk."

Both glares turned murderous. I looked away. "This is essential if we want to work together better as a team," I said quietly. "How will we know what to do when someone isn't looking like they're feeling well? If one of us pulled another one of us out to talk, but didn't tell the others, wouldn't the rest of the group be dying to know what they're saying?"

Galen and Sirocca nodded vigorously. "You only realized that now?"

I bit my lip. Was I making a foolish decision? "Well -"

Callan abruptly spoke, "I'm going to my room first. I want to - uh - check on something." In a flash, he was gone. Kodiak looked like he was going to be sick, so he ran off too.

"O… kay…." I said. "Do you guys need to go too?"

Sirocca shook her head. "There's no way I'm missing this."

Galen had climbed a tree and was resting in its branches. "Me too. I'm staying here until everything is uncovered."

I frowned to myself as I waited.

Why did Callan run off? Didn't he say it would be fine if I shared it with everyone? Kodiak, I understand. But Callan?

It would be fine if Kodiak didn't show up for this. I'd expect him not to, but ten minutes later, Kodiak stumbled over, a little green.

"You okay?" I asked, worried.

He nodded stiffly. "Fine."

Suddenly, Callan burst out of the doors to the house and stomped over angrily. He left cracks in the earth wherever he stepped.

Wow. He must be furious.

His hand gripped his phone so tightly, his knuckles were white. We all watched him cautiously. What was he going to do?

Callan went straight to Kodiak and shoved his phone in his face. "What is this?" he asked through clenched teeth.

Kodiak took one look....

And vomited.

Chapter 45

It splattered all over the base of the tree. Galen leaped up, even though he was well out of reach.

I wasn't so lucky.

But I didn't care. I barely registered that the base of my jeans were soiled. I snatched the phone away from Callan with one hand and patted Kodiak's back with the other.

MISSING: ALASKA TORRENT

There was a picture of a seven year old girl too beautiful for her age. Her smile was so bright, it immediately gave someone the feeling that everything was right in the world. I realized the family resemblance a few seconds afterwards.

The eyes. A clear, bright blue.

There was a "LAST SEEN" date and a phone number.

The world spun. "Where'd you get this?"

Callan looked at me with shock and disbelief. "So. You know already."

I swallowed. "Well. I was going to tell you guys..."

"So. You were going to betray Kodiak?"

I was confused. Was he mad at me for letting him know, or at Kodiak for not telling?

"You guys look like you just witnessed war." Galen dropped down from his branch, taking extra care to avoid the spill. "What is it?"

I slid the phone into my pocket, vaguely remembering that it wasn't mine. "I'll tell you as soon as Kodiak feels better."

Kodiak was now slumped against another tree, his head between his legs, taking deep, shuddering breaths. I walked over and felt his forehead.

Honestly, I'm not sure why I did that. He wasn't sick, exactly.... But I wrapped him in a warm cocoon of water anyways to help the shock.

"Can I tell them?" I whispered to Kodiak.

"You're asking for permission now?" he mumbled.

I bit my lip. "I'm sorry," I mumbled back. "I was annoyed that we couldn't do anything else."

"So you want to tell."

It wasn't a question, more like a statement. I sighed. "I won't tell."

Kodiak slowly lifted his head. "So you're backing out now. Just stick with a decision and go with it!"

His voice was so harsh, I scooted backwards. Even though I understood where he was coming from, it hurt.

I stood up and walked back to the group, who were looking more than irritated. I walked over to the fountain and sat down with a loud sigh.

"What's going on?" Galen demanded. "How much have you been hiding for other people?"

"We're a team," Sirocca added. I've never seen her frown before. "If you can't respect that, then this whole thing is useless."

"I understand why'd you do it, but revealing someone else's secret to the rest of the team isn't okay," Callan said.

I glared fiercely at him. "So what, you guys are all ganging up on me now?" I glanced angrily at Callan. "You told me I could tell what you told me to the rest of the team. So why were you so upset when I was about to? That's on you."

Callan's eyes opened wide. "I said that, but that didn't mean you could do the same thing to

Kodiak!"

"WE AREN'T TALKING ABOUT KODIAK!"
I hollered.

"IT'S THE SAME THING!"

"NO IT'S NOT!"

"HEY!" Galen roared. "You guys are leaving
us out again. WHAT did Callan tell you? WHAT
is Kodiak hiding? WHAT is going ON?!"

I hadn't realized I'd stood up and stood face
to face with Callan. I stayed standing for a
moment longer before turning away.

"Kodiak's sister is missing. She's been missing
for over a month, and Kodiak is blaming himself
for what happened. Actually, he blames Callan,
but he feels responsible for what happened."

"What?! Why's he blaming me?" Callan
exclaimed.

"Go ask him yourself," I said curtly. I turned
my back on him and quickly filled Galen and
Sirocca in on what they'd missed and what I'd
been keeping from them.

"WHAT?!" they shouted simultaneously.

As expected.

"Something this colossal happened and you
didn't tell me?" Galen spat. "Why? Did you think
I wouldn't take it seriously and laugh it off? What
was the point in 'making me co-leader' of this

mission if I don't even know half of what's going on?"

Sirocca's response was much more calm. She sat down on the sand path and rubbed her forehead. "This is a lot to take in at once."

Galen snorted. "Yeah. It would have been so much easier if we'd known right from the start, don't you think?" he asked sarcastically.

I winced. "Fine. I get it. I'll be sure to tell you next time, but can you please put all this aside and focus on the big problem here? You guys can yell at me all you want later, but the Islands know that Alaska's missing now. My sister has disappeared. Again. Is there some sort of connection between the two?"

Galen was silent for a bit, then he reluctantly replied, "I wouldn't be surprised if there was. Want to take another sweep of this area?"

"That took a long time," Callan said. "We've already used up half of the day."

"Then we use up the other half," Galen said stubbornly. "Emily sent us here to figure out what's going on. That's what we're going to do."

I nodded. "We have to."

Callan rolled his eyes. "I mean, that part was very obvious, but how are we going to do it?"

I shrugged and stood up. "Now we have a

vague idea of what we're looking for. If our guesses are correct, we should find some kind of hint on where Alaska and Mira are. You guys already found a room where someone would have been kept as a captive. Now, we're finding more solid evidence and the captives themselves."

Sirocca nodded. "Let's all search the interior of the mansion this time. We need more people on this task."

"What about the equipment on the other Stones?" Callan spoke.

With difficulty, I said, "We'll investigate those later. I think we can all say that sooner or later, we're going to destroy those."

After they all nodded, we turned to Kodiak. He had stood up and was walking toward us calmly. "Then what are we waiting for? We don't want to waste anymore time, do we?"

We all marched back inside the house. Sirocca and I decided to lead them to the extra bedrooms. I tried the handle on the blue and white room, and it was unlocked. I slowly inched the door open, feeling antsy.

Everything looked the same it had been earlier, untouched. Although I had pulled the door wide open, none of us stepped inside.

Kodiak surveyed the room with narrowed eyes. He worked his jaw slowly, calculatingly….

"So, uh, yeah. This is one of the rooms we found," I said. "The other one is over there, five doors away."

We walked them closer to our dorms. Galen sucked in a sharp breath. "They are five and ten doors away from us, and we never knew?"

I shrugged. "It's not like we should. I thought they were storage rooms or something."

"Same," Callan said, glancing around. "Are these all more dorms, then?"

Sirocca shook her head. "Don't know. These were locked."

Callan tried the handles as we passed by. "Still are."

I opened the door to the mirror-image room. "Here."

"Hey, this is your room?" Callan stuck his head inside. "Wow. It's clean."

I snorted. "Gee, thanks. And this isn't my room."

Callan immediately stiffened and backed out slowly. "Well. That's pretty creepy."

I nodded. "Exactly. Any thoughts?"

"Show us everything first," Galen said. "I want to see everything you found before we -"

A loud thud and scrape resounded through the halls, making everyone jump in surprise.

I opened my mouth to say something, when another sound made us all freeze in place.

The sound of chains being dragged.

Chapter 46

Immediately, I rushed in the direction of the chains. I didn't know where I was going, but I followed the sound of the chains. There were soft thumps coming from that direction now, and I quickly pivoted and ran in another direction.

RINA! Where are you going?

There's no time! I told him. *That can't mean anything good. Just go and destroy the other Stones. Meet me back in the dorms when you're done.*

But -

GO! I'll be back. I want to see what it is. Don't worry. I'll try not to get involved.

I kept running forwards. I reached a fork, looked right and left, then turned right. I kept walking, then reached another split, and turned left.

The halls were starting to look familiar; I was

heading towards the garden.

I heard a sound up ahead and froze. I listened attentively. There were thumps. Scrapes. Clatters.

I narrowed my eyes and took a cautious step forward. I walked carefully until I reached the bend right. I cautiously peeked my head around the corner.

I pursed my lip when it was clear and frowned. Where was the sound...?

I turned around and ran straight into Ivoria. I screamed instinctively and jumped back, crashing into the corner and falling onto my back.

Ow.

I scrambled up. This was it. This was where I would lose my life.

Ivoria loomed over me, smiling. "There you are. I was just going to go call you."

I gulped. "Y-Yeah?"

Ivoria arched an eyebrow. "What's wrong, Rina? You don't seem to be too articulate right now."

I cleared my throat. "Do you need something?"

Ivoria's eyes gleamed suspiciously at me for a moment before melting into a warm smile. I shuddered. How deceiving.

"What were you doing, wandering these

halls?" Her voice concealed the blade of a knife.

I didn't let myself be intimidated. "I was trying to find a bathroom since my room didn't have one. You should really label these doors." I rolled my eyes to reinforce my bluff.

Ivoria chuckled. "Well, this doesn't look like a bathroom to me. What are you doing here?"

I growled in annoyance. "In case you didn't notice, you startled me and I FELL!"

Ivoria shook her head slowly then started slowly walking towards me threateningly. "Come with me."

I stood up, brushed myself off, and looked at her casually. "Why?"

Two humongous guards appeared next to Ivoria. One of them was Enzo. She gave me a small smirk. "You want to find out where your Talent came from, do you not?"

My... Talent?

And she said she had been coming to get me anyways?

I stared at her suspiciously as I mulled over this decision. This information was coming from Ivoria. Who would trust her? But then again, the person who mastered and gave the ancient Islanders our Talents was a Mainlander... I might be able to escape this....

416

Ivoria led me down the hall. I followed solemnly. There would most likely be little chance of me escaping. All the walls looked the same as well as the doors. Ivoria would trap me like a mouse in record time.

I tried my best to remember the path out anyways.

I counted the clicking of heels on tile floors to entertain me and to take my mind off of my doom. One, two, three, four….

I lost track somewhere after thirty. This was making me extremely nervous.

Ivoria led me to a separate wall. We were about to walk out into the garden until Ivoria spoke coldly, "Take her."

My brain barely had time to register what was going to happen before a sharp chop to the neck knocked me out.

Chapter 47

Everyone was scrambling all over the place. Derrik was bouncing from monitor to monitor. Thora was helping to take down notes and distinguish the commands being given through the speakers. Elece was frantically dialing Galen, despite the agreed decision not to have any sort of contact with the team. Andy sat next to Emily, helping where he could.

Emily? She was the one orchestrating this chaos.

Nicholas had sent a message to Ivoria through her in-ear: "The swan is roaming again," he told her.

A faint crackle, then Ivoria had responded, "We will catch her this time."

"Make sure the info gets through to Galen," she commanded Elece. "Art room, keypad by the garden door, 7456."

"I KNOW!" Elece snapped. Emily didn't feel the strike, though. Everyone's temper was short.

"Thora! Don't miss a command Nicholas is saying," Emily said.

"Yes, ma'am," Thora said absentmindedly, her usually perfect penmanship being reduced to illegible scribbles.

"Anything going on, Derrik?"

Derrik looked frustrated. "The only way to see what's going on is if we hack into their actual security system, which would be detected. My skills aren't that advanced yet."

"Do it," Emily said without hesitation. "I want my whole team to return in one piece."

"But you'd endanger provoking her anger if you do," Andy pointed out. "You know what she'd do then."

Emily twisted her hands. "Put that aside for now, then," she told Derrik. "Can you set up another speaker to listen to the other walls of the facility?"

Derrik immediately headed to a new computer and started to copy the building's information down. He tweaked a few numbers, and....

"... Take her."

Emily's blood froze. The voices were faint, but the effect was the same.

No....

There was a thump, then a deep voice. "Done, Boss."

"As expected, Enzo," Ivoria said.

Andy cursed. This time, Thora started to shake.

"Let's go," Ivoria commanded. "It will not be long before one of her friends comes in search of her. Most likely, it will be the falcon."

"I can take down a li'l birdie easy!" Enzo crowed. There was a cracking sound and Emily shuddered.

Ivoria snorted. "Maybe. He is an impulsive one, so we may be able to kill two birds with one stone today."

Andy gagged at the pun.

There was a slight grunt and then footsteps. Derrik's fingers twitched slightly as he switched numbers to follow the sound of the footsteps. They faded until a heavy silence was all that was left.

"The swan has been captured," Ivoria's voice came from the other speaker. It was very smug.

Derrik muttered to himself as he slapped his hands across the screen of the computer. "Those walls aren't soundified," he grumbled. "I can't follow them anymore. The other walls had at least the basic wiring for a PA system, but this room is completely empty of anything."

Emily sighed and rubbed her eyes. "Our only hope is Galen."

Elece's eyes widened, her phone pressing into her ear so hard, Emily was sure it was going to leave a mark. "Galen! GO TO THE ART ROOM! NOW!"

There was a slight pause as everyone stared at her in anticipation.

"Next to the door by the garden! Enzo's there with Ivoria and another soldier. GO!"

"WAIT!" Thora cried before Elece hung up. "Nicholas stationed twenty men there before, remember?"

Elece's eyes burned at the speaker. "Just kidding, G. Bring the whole team. There are at least twenty men with Ivoria in the art room. 7456. Go!"

Elece hung up, and they all sat in silence, expressions grim.

Chapter 48

I woke up to a raw, biting feeling in my arms and legs. I slowly opened my eyes and gasped. My arms had been wrenched above my head, chained to the wall. My feet were crossed, also chained to the wall. Thick chains wrapped around my entire body, making me unable to move.

Not again....

"LET ME GO!" I roared. I struggled against the chains but it was useless. I was just peeling off my own skin.

"So. Fierina Flameton..." Ice crept through my veins, freezing my blood when I heard my name.

The tell-tale clicking of heels on tile floor. Ivoria appeared from the other side of the room. Everything except my wall was dark. There was a spotlight on the ceiling right above me, reminding me of some art museums I'd visited at home. "So gullible... so trusting... and yet..." Ivoria gestured to where I was. "You're here."

I glared at her. I struggled and struggled, not caring if I was going to bleed or not. I tried to reach my friends. "GALEN! SIROCCA!"

Ivoria chuckled. "Your friends will never find you here. The entrance to this room is hidden."

No!

I was in a secret room. The one Galen and I were going to find together...

"What do you want?" I asked harshly. I glanced down at the chains, trying to find a weak link when I recognized the designs, even though I've never seen these chains before.

These were the chains Galen and Callan described....

I could've laughed right then and there. None of us knew it was made to keep me on the wall like some trophy.

"Oh, you already know what I want," Ivoria purred.

"Then why am I here?" I spat.

Ivoria walked closer, one hand reaching up towards my face. I jerked away, but she grabbed my face anyways.

Now I know what Andy meant.

Pain. Sharp nails digging into my flesh, a strong grip nearly crushing my jaw.

"You had some nerve during the negotiations," she murmured dangerously. "Challenging me like that... it was a first."

"That's because your people are too afraid to challenge you face to face! Do you have any idea of what they say behind your back?" I snarled. I worked my jaw, gathering a generous amount of saliva in my mouth, then spat in her face.

Ivoria screamed, disgusted, and shoved my head away from her. It slammed into the wall with a crack, and stars swam before my eyes. Despite the pain, I laughed.

That had to be the best thing I'd ever done in my entire life.

Ivoria shouted a command and the two guards marched up towards me. My laughter died and I watched them walk closer.

What were they going to do?

One of the guards pulled back his fist and socked me in the stomach.

I gasped in pain, all breath knocked out of my lungs. I tried to bend over against the pain, but I couldn't. The other guard pulled back his fist and punched my face.

I cried out over and over again as they used me like a punching bag. "STOP!" I gasped, tears rolling down my face. Fire blossomed angrily inside whenever their fists hit their mark. "PLEASE!"

Ivoria stood up, laughing slowly and wiping her face. "Learned your lesson? Well... you still need to face the consequences."

I glared at her murderously. My body was already in total pain, numb to any kind of sensation except attacks.

How fortunate.

Ivoria smirked and waved a hand at the guards. They took a step back and I was able to breathe. Or try to. There were sharp pains in my sides, like knives, making breathing very difficult.

The tears kept coming. How was I going to survive this?

Ivoria walked closer. The two guards stepped back. One of the guards looked at me full in the face and smirked. My jaw dropped.

Enzo.

Rage overpowered me. When Ivoria was close enough, I lurched forward against the chains and tried to bite her face.

She jerked backwards, and immediately

425

afterwards, something cold and razor sharp was pressed against my face. I kept shaking from pain, anger, hopelessness, and terror, but didn't move my head anymore.

"Good girl," she chuckled.

I gulped, heart pounding, the tears flowing numbly now. "So.... What are you... going to - do to me now?" I forced the words out. My sentences were broken, my breathing heavy and irregular.

Ivoria smiled cruelly, then snatched back the knife in one quick motion. The blade slashed quickly, drawing a deep gash in my face. I cried out and thrashed my face to the side, blood dripping down the side of my cheek.

I was never going to survive now.

"Are you...." I gasped, tasting the saltiness of my own tears. "Why not just kill me right now?"

Ivoria ran a finger lightly against the edge of the blade, wiping the blood off the shining metal. "What fun would that be?" she asked cheerfully. "Revenge is a dish best served cold, as you might know. It is a dish meant to be enjoyed and savored with every bite."

I closed my eyes. The skin beside my left eye to the corner of my lip felt swollen.

Ivoria smirked at me and backed off. I hung

there, breathing hard, dripping blood and sweat, body aching. I closed my eyes tiredly, the adrenaline replaced with defeat.

"There's another thing you should know," Ivoria said, walking closer. "Two things, actually."

I didn't open my eyes, didn't move.

"Alaska Torrent…."

My head snapped up and I looked deep into Ivoria's dark eyes. "What… what did you do to her?"

Ivoria smirked. "She is no longer your concern."

The way she said that, the way her eyes glinted, the way her lips twitched….

"NO!"

I had no reason to believe that Alaska was dead. Ivoria was a criminal. Why should I believe her words?

She is no longer your concern….

Kodiak was going to be devastated. I started to sob, crying for my friend who would never see his sister again.

Why?

Why was my life like this?

Everything was leaving scars across my heart:

The two hundred abducted kids.

Zinnia's capture.

The bullet I took that almost killed Callan.

The brokenness of the team Emily sent to negotiate with Ivoria.

My unworthiness and lack of ability to be a leader.

Even Galen's rivalry with Callan. How could I lead my team to success? I couldn't even prevent two of my friends from fighting, and now, I was the one captured and tortured.

And now... Alaska.

What part of me would be left after all this was over? The wound on my cheek burned as my tears slid over it.

"And the second thing...." Ivoria said coolly, paying no attention to my tears.

I didn't care what it was anymore. It couldn't be worse than Alaska's death.

"There's someone that would like to see you."

I glanced up, daring to hope. Rescue?

A girl stepped out of the shadows. My jaw dropped and my eyes widened. My heart jumped and plummeted at the same time. She was wearing skinny jeans, an orange t-shirt, her arms were crossed, and her long brown hair was tied back into a ponytail. I shook my head slowly.

No....

A face identical to mine smirked at me as she walked up to me. "Hello, sister."

In a flash of fire and pain, the world turned black.

Chapter 49

I didn't fully wake up. My mind did, but my body stayed painfully asleep. I heard voices…

"Your hunger for revenge has been fulfilled," someone said. Ivoria. "How does it feel?"

"It's the best feeling in the world!" I could have recognized my sister's voice anywhere. My stomach churned.

"You know, you do not have a reason to turn against your sister."

Mira snorted. My left cheek burned. So did my stomach. Everything smelled like smoke. "Look at her. She's so pathetic. She's hardly recognizable now. She stole everything that was mine. I'm just taking it back."

I still didn't move. I refused to. I couldn't.

What did I ever steal?

I could hear the smirk in Ivoria's voice.

"Interesting answer."

I imagined Mira standing taller.

Why was my stomach burning? Why did everything smell like smoke?

"Well, well, well…." Mira sneered. "She's awake."

Huh?

"Open your eyes, sister."

I slowly cracked open an eyelid. I was still bound to the wall, the chains were still digging into my skin, everything was still hurting. My face felt so swollen, I was pretty sure it was nonexistent at this point.

"All the way."

With much difficulty, I forced my eyes to adjust to the light as I opened them. I barely had time to glance down at myself before a flaming fist connected with my jaw.

I screamed as my flesh burned and my jaw cracked.

There came a round of punches: to my stomach, my chest, my sides, more to my face…. I nearly passed out again.

"Don't you dare pass out on me," Mira warned.

What? How…?

"Dummy. We connected a wire to your brain.

431

We can hear everything you're thinking, in case you decide to get rebellious."

Why would you…?

Mira leaned back. "You know what? You're not even worth wasting my breath. You'll rot away here, and we'll gladly watch you die."

No. I can't call her my sister. She disowned me. She won't feel anything for me.

Of course….

Mira snorted. "I'm NOT your sister."

"That is enough, Mira. Continue your training. I need some space for private interrogation."

"Aw, can't I stay?"

"Leave."

Mira grumbled as she walked away. I was starting to feel a bit of cool relief until Ivoria grabbed my face again and leaned in close. I flinched from her touch. Her fingers dug into sensitive, damaged parts of my face.

"Surprised?"

You really don't know anything about my Talent, do you?

Ivoria started to laugh. "If I say yes, what would happen?"

I focused on breathing. "Do you?"

Ivoria smirked, then released my face. I

sagged in pain and relief. "So you really want to know?"

My tongue was parched, and it stuck to the roof of my mouth. My throat felt raw. What's the cost? I wouldn't be surprised if there was a price I had to pay.

Ivoria let out a cackle. "Why, there is no price. The information comes free. I just need a sample of your blood."

She whipped a syringe out of nowhere and stabbed the wickedly long needle into my right thigh where a patch of my jeans had been ripped to shreds. I screamed in pain as she slowly watched the dark liquid fill the empty space.

"Thrashing does not help you."

I knew that. At this point, I didn't have the strength to lift my head. I could have been considered 'near-death'.

Again.

No, I thought firmly to myself. I'd survived death before, I could survive it again.

Ivoria laughed. She yanked the syringe out of my leg, issuing another cry of pain from me. She shook her head and looked at me pityingly. "You still believe you have a chance to live."

"Isn't... that... better... than willingly... agreeing... to die?" I choked out.

Ivoria shrugged. "Consider me benevolent. I will grant you a few pieces of information as a last wish to you before you pass.

"I will return in a few minutes with a full report on your Talent origins. I have complete faith that you will not try to escape."

She cast one last undermining glance at my chains, scoffed to herself, then walked away with my blood in her hands.

I exhaled slowly, my skin burning. With great effort, I craned my neck downwards and nearly threw up at the sight of my own body.

The fabric was burned wherever Mira had struck me. Blackened, burned skin lay underneath, raw in some places. There was a huge hole over my stomach and patches of missing denim in my jeans, my clothes still smoldering from the attacks.

Dark lines of red traced rivers down what was left of my clothes and bruised skin. It dripped down, staining my shoelaces and leaving a small puddle below where I hang.

This was horrific. I felt like part of a scene in a horror movie.

I sighed, flicking my finger. A thin, weak stream of water started to coil itself around me, doing its best to cool the burns and wash away the blood. I groaned with the pain.

Burns.

My mind started to wander. How was the rest of the team doing? Did they successfully destroy the Stones? I regretted coming here alone. How did I think that I would be able to do this alone?

There was a rustle in the darkness. I looked up, squinting, daring to hope again.

Galen?

There was a snort and a voice said, "I'm not Galen, you dummy."

I rolled my eyes, closed them, then sagged down again. "What do you want?" I murmured.

Mira walked up close to me. She fingered the chains that were binding me to the wall. "I wonder what would happen if I kept my hand here…."

She grabbed at the chains, hands red hot. I watched her, confused, until my clothes started smoking again, and the chains burned right through them. My eyes widened, and I struggled, squirmed, and tried to get away from the searing metal.

"What are you doing?" I cried, fresh tears rolling down my face. "Do you really want to kill me?"

"Yes," she said through gritted teeth. "I do."

"BUT I'M YOUR SISTER!" I wailed, using the last of my lung power to try one last time.

Mira smirked. "You were. But not anymore. I won't deny I want you to be out of my life. But I decided to not deny the fact that we are, in fact, related. I won't kill you."

I sobbed, pain taking over my body, fire destroying my skin, relief flooding my soul.

"But watching you physically suffer in the same way I had to suffer emotionally," Mira snickered. "It's giving me so much joy."

"YOU HEARTLESS -!"

A new voice exploded out of the darkness, screaming words that burned my ears in a different way than fire did. I was terrified for a second, confused.

Who was this?

A huge gust of wind was born out of the darkness, blowing Mira away from me, shattering everything that might've been in its path.

Strangely, I was unaffected.

I let myself sob once with relief.

GALEN!

Chapter 50

Andy watched the control room go crazy. Derrik had five more speakers set up, listening to different Stones. Galen had informed them that he'd sent Sirocca and Callan to destroy the equipment at the first and second Stones. Although everyone knew rescuing Rina was more important, Emily had asked Derrik to watch the pair.

Andy listened to Sirocca's speaker. There was a shattering noise as Derrik smiled proudly. "She's destroying the power spheres!" he said happily.

"Power spheres?" Andy asked.

Derrik curved his fingers into a ball. "Sirocca sent me a pic with these spheres on the base of the cannons. Their purpose is to hold munition to fire the cannons."

Andy scrunched up his face. "I've never heard of that."

Derrik shrugged. "It's a Terrenian thing," he said. "Those were used hundreds of years ago, back when the tribes started to - you know what? Never mind."

Andy nodded, grateful he had been saved from a long history lecture. "So destroying those spheres would disable the cannons?"

Derrik nodded. "Basically, yeah."

Andy nodded. "Not many girls know their weapons," he said, impressed. "Just her and Elece, I guess."

Derrik gave him a suspicious sideway glance. Andy pretended not to notice.

There came a shattering sound and everyone snapped their attention to the second speaker. Glass shattered and there was the faint lap of spilled liquid as Callan destroyed all the vials.

"What if they're poisonous?" Thora asked.

"Even more reason to destroy them," Emily said. "Besides, Callan knows what he's doing. He won't touch them."

There was a satisfied grunt, then footsteps as Callan and Sirocca simultaneously rushed off. Andy bit his lip. Hopefully, they were heading to the third Stone to assist Galen.

Everyone sat, tensed. "I hope someone brings Rina bandages, just in case," Thora whispered shakily. "She... She might need them."

Nobody was brave enough to agree with her. Andy had a feeling everyone was wondering if she was even still alive.

Chapter 51

Hair flowing wildly, eyes blazing angrily, fist and jaw tightly clenched, Galen stepped into the light. He glared angrily at Mira, who was struggling to hold her own against the wind.

"You disgust me," he spat. "Words can't even begin to describe what I feel towards you right now."

Mira managed to scoff. "The feeling is mutual." Stretching out an arm, she fired long flames towards the boy of the winds.

Galen remained untouched. His power was too strong.

I wanted to scream, cheer, and cry at the same time. But at that moment, a loud screeching noise, like claws on a chalkboard, stopped everyone in its tracks.

The darkness of the room slowly began to

lighten until I could make out distinct shapes.

Ivoria.

Twenty men.

One huge cannon.

My throat closed.

"Well, well, well." Ivoria walked over slowly, face expressionless. "I have to say, I am surprised on a few different matters."

Mira scrambled to her feet, wiping her face, brushing her hair back, and smirking at Galen. "You're doomed," her face seemed to say.

Galen, run!

"Ah, ah, ah," Ivoria clucked. "There's no running now." She ran her fingers down the length of the cannon's barrel, smiling to herself. "I would like to show you something."

"This is hardly the time for show and tell," Galen snarled. The winds began to pick up again.

Ivoria clicked her fingers. The cannon fired something bright and blue, smashing against the wall next to me, leaving a giant burned hole in the plaster. It narrowly missed me by a few feet. The winds died.

"Thank you," she said, smiling. "Now that I have your attention, I would like to introduce my ray gun. It is based off of the inverse formulas of Egghead's -"

441

"Get to the point," Galen said harshly.

Ivoria smiled slowly, hand on the controls, fingers twitching. "It has the ability to extract the Talent from the person it hits - forever."

I froze. "And I assume I'm going to be the sacrificial lamb?"

Ivoria laughed. "Oh, no. Your dear Alaska Torrent was. Little did I know, she had not activated her Talent yet, so the ray took her life instead of her Talent." She scoffed. "Humans are so weak."

I rolled my eyes. She was human too.

"Ah, ah, ah," Ivoria tittered. "There's a difference between weak humans and strong beings. I happen to be part of the latter."

Sure.

Galen suddenly took a quick step towards me and ripped the chains off the wall with a strong gust of wind. I fell to the floor, stumbling before landing on my knees. Everything ached and burned, but I forced myself to stand up.

Ivoria's sweet smile had turned infinitely sour. "Take them," she commanded coldly.

Immediately, Galen's tornado whipped up and he took out half of the men rushing towards us. The other ten snarled and erupted with many different Talents.

I groaned. Not again.

At that moment, Five of the men froze over or were trapped in a deep mountain of ice. Kodiak stepped out, rushing towards us. "Are you two okay?"

"Yes, we're fine," Galen said hurriedly. "Get Rina out of here and make sure she's safe!"

"I'm fine!" I protested, despite the sudden dizziness. "Just fight!"

Kodiak snatched me up in his arms. "Not on my watch, you're not. You're pretty much dead!" He started running towards the nearest exit, which I hadn't noticed before.

"NO! PUT ME DOWN!" I screeched, trying to struggle, but failing. My body and voice were too weak. Everything burned. "You can't leave Galen here on his own!"

"Galen will be fine," Kodiak soothed. "I'll come back to help him. For now, just -"

I cried out suddenly. A flame had flown by, close to my face, narrowly catching Kodiak in the chest. He skidded to a stop and his jaw dropped. "Mira?"

Mira blinked at him once, then immediately switched to flirting mode. "Kodiak? What are you doing here?" she asked sweetly with a huge, excited smile on her face. In my opinion, though, my sister could be pretty irresistible sometimes, "Where are you going? Can I come with you? *Pwease?*"

Ugh.

Kodiak looked revolted as well. "Watch what you're saying," he said. "What are you doing here?" He took a step back, holding me tighter against him.

Mira took a step closer and touched my arm. I froze, afraid of what she was going to do. "I was about to free my sister, of course," she said. "I surprised you, didn't I? Looks like you beat me to it."

Kodiak glanced at her warily, then down at me. Since Ivoria had turned on the lights, and we weren't moving anymore, Kodiak took this time to examine my body. He noticed the burns and his eyes widened in shock. "You...."

Mira's smile wavered, but she managed to hold it. "What's the matter?"

"YOU BURNED HER?" His eyes hardened and shone a bright, light blue; Mira was immediately encased to her neck in ice. Sharp shards protruded out of the top, pricking her neck. "How dare you.... How could you?"

Mira dropped the crushing-girl act and sneered at me. "See? You've won him over too.

What was I supposed to do?"

"Wait, wait, wait," I said. I slid down from Kodiak's arms and held onto his arm for support instead. "So you're telling me that you tortured me and nearly killed me because of a guy?!"

Mira rolled her eyes. "Among other things, yes." She closed her eyes and it started to glow under the ice.

Uh, oh.

She exploded out of the cube, the chunks immediately melting in her heat. I actually thought it was pretty cool until she threw a fireball the size of a basketball at my head.

Instinctively, I protected myself with a thick shield of water that could only hold for a few seconds.

Mira kept picking things up, setting them on fire, and shooting them at me. I barely had enough strength to deflect them.

Kodiak tried to step forward but I stopped him. "NO! Go help Galen! I'll be fine on my own."

"But -"

"GO! Don't leave Galen by himself like that!"

Kodiak hesitated for a second before running off.

Mira kept attacking and I kept defending.

Every stream of water was weaker than the last, and every step I took made me stumble more than before.

"So. We're in another battle, sister."

"Yeah, I guess we are," I muttered.

"The exact same roles," she fired ten at the same time, "and the exact same problem. You."

I narrowly danced out of reach, a fireball almost blowing off my arm. That was way too close.

"Weak," she taunted as she jumped to another place in the room. She launched a flaming chair in my direction. "You puny, disgusting disgrace!"

That hurt a lot. It punched a hole so big in my heart, it didn't leave much space for anything other than emptiness.

That's it.

I'm not going to let her pick on me like this. I didn't do anything to deserve this, and I can't keep defending myself anymore.

I need to protect myself.

A sudden, strange strength emerged from my core, flowing through my veins, numbing all sort of pain I had. I stopped putting up water shields and just stood there, eyes closed, relishing the warmth and power.

"Wow, giving up so soon?" Mira sneered. She jumped down from where she had perched on a tall wooden crate. "Oh well. Makes my job easier."

She pulled back a fist and a flaming ball formed.

This power... it was deep. It was strong. It had taken hundreds of years to grow. It was generations old.

It was the same power our ancestors had learned to control and use.

The ball flew towards me.

My eyes flashed open and a powerful force rushed out of my body. The wind blew Mira backwards, throwing her against the crates that had raised her so high before.

Wind....

I flicked a finger and the wind shifted, curved. The current traveled behind me, crushing everything in its path.

I could suddenly see through another's eyes.

No room to breathe, twenty men surrounding, about to attack at once. A sudden hurricane plowed through the men, leaving me on the floor, gasping for breath, running my hands through my short, dark hair, relieved.

Hair....

Galen!

He froze, and suddenly, water exploded out of the ground, an enormous geyser stopping my sister in her tracks. I came back to my senses and whipped around, staring in shock and awe at the pillar of white water going up, up, up.

What kind of power is this?

Galen dusted his hands and stepped on the chest of one of Ivoria's soldiers on his way to the other side of the room. My heart stopped when I saw his glowing eyes.

One pale gray, the color of a cloudy sky.

The other bright blue, the color of the ocean.

My jaw dropped, and I stepped back in fright. What was going on?

"So, Mira," Galen said, voice powerful and threatening. "You done?"

Mira sidestepped the thirty-feet long geyser, which had blown the walls and ceiling off this room. I recognized my surroundings and realized we were fighting in the open now. The garden was right behind me.

"You two are pathetic," she spat, but her eyes flickered with fear as she glanced from Galen, to me, then Galen again. "Wait until I tell Mom and Dad you've been doing some fishy things with a Wind Islander."

I thrust my arm forward and Mira shot upward, fifty feet in the air. I jumped up and flew alongside her casually, halting her when I thought she was high enough. I looked down, and I could see all the Stones, but I couldn't see home or the Mainland.

Home....

"What were you saying?" I asked, leaning an ear towards her. "I couldn't hear you over the roar of the waters."

Mira growled and swiped her flaming hand towards me. The winds immediately blew it out. In the skies, her fire was as weak as a birthday candle.

I started to laugh. "Even you have your own limitations, Mira."

Mira glanced down, shivered, and turned back towards me. "Two Talents, huh? Where'd the Wind come from? You stole Ivoria's lab equipment?" She crinkled her nose in disgust at me. "That's really low."

I forced her backwards, earning a frightened squeak. "I'll wait until you figure that out for yourself," I said sweetly. "You've pushed me around long enough. It's not my obligation to answer to you."

Mira's arms suddenly swung up. I recognized

this move....

After I had returned to the Academy, I had studied more about the ancient ways of Talent control. Ways so ancient, nobody knew how to use them.

Until now.

This particular move would be able to summon all the fire in the world and answer to her beck and call. It had been considered the most dangerous of all the stances.... The Talent Call. In Mira's case, the Fire Call.

HOW WAS I SUPPOSED TO FIGHT SOMETHING LIKE THAT?

She swung her arms, eyes closed, then glared at me. The last move.

I glanced down as the earth started to heat up. Thousands of wildfires started to make their way to us, destroying everything in its path.

Chapter 52

Elece ground her teeth. "Train, they said," she muttered to herself. "Train, while we wait."

She punched the bag to smithereens then whirled around and grabbed a sword from the weapon wall.

"Rina is captured, but they say 'train'!"

She left deep gouges in the wall and flung the sword as hard as she could. The blade buried itself into the plaster. She twirled her fan-dagger from her back pocket and zoomed toward the dummies, ripping them to shreds in a matter of seconds.

"All the action is over there, but they say 'train'!"

Out of things to do, Elece ran laps around the training room, running fifteen laps a second. Normally, it would've exhausted her, but her agitation sped her forward.

"Little do they know training doesn't help anyone at all," she snarled. "'It makes you faster,' Melody says. 'It makes you stronger, a better warrior'. Well, a warrior goes where the action is!"

She stopped, lungs burning, sweat dripping off her brow. Her long hair brushed her legs right under her knees as she bent over, catching her breath.

Rina is captured.

Galen might be too late.

Elece closed her eyes, silently feeling angry at Galen. "Dude, why'd you take so long to pick up?" she muttered.

Why didn't she go?

Why didn't she take Emily's offer?

Derrik appeared just then, yanking the sword from the wall as he passed by. His crossbow was best used for long distances; Glenn had wanted him to train with close-combat weapons. "Fight me," he said.

Elece wasted no time and had her fan pressed against his neck in a split second. "Ha, too sl-"

Derrik's sword was pressed against her neck too. Derrik grinned. "I did it!"

Elece rolled his eyes. "You just raised your

452

sword."

Derrik shrugged. "It was faster than the first time."

"You still would've died."

Derrik looked at her evenly. "That's why I train, right? I know you're perfectly capable fighting on your own. But I need to fight. It bugs me that the trainers tell me to do close-combat when what I'm really skilled at is on the computer." He peered at her. "Don't you agree?"

Elece stared at him, working her jaw. Her fingers twitched, then she lowered her fan. "Let's go again."

This time, Derrik moved faster than Elece expected. She instinctively swiped at the space he'd been, but he was already moving and had Elece pinned and in a chokehold before she could get a grasp of what was happening.

Elece let out a cough of surprise. "Well. Nicely done. But if you can let me breathe a little bit more, that'd be even better."

Derrik grinned.

Chapter 53

Wildfire....

Wildfire.....

Galen flew up next to me at that moment. "What's going on?" he demanded, his eyes still different colors. "Why was it so hot down there?"

I merely pointed and Galen gasped. "Wow...."

"Galen...." I murmured. "Help the others get out. I'll be back."

"NO WAY! Last time you said that, you nearly got killed!"

I glanced down at the blood still flowing from some burns. It didn't hurt... not at all. "I'll be fine. Besides, I have you, right?"

Galen stared at me in surprise, then his face broke out into a gentle smile. "Always."

Then he flew back down, towards the first

Stone.

I focused on the ocean, raising it up little by little. I couldn't raise it more than an inch.

How do I do this?

The fires were coming faster. Mira sneered in triumph.

Wildfire....

Wildfire....

Tsunami.

A strong connection with my title. Tsunami.

I am Tsunami.

Water destroys fire.

The ocean became light as a feather and I raised it up. Mira's eyes flickered for a second and the fires stopped their race before starting up again, burning faster than ever before.

Too bad that the earth was seventy-percent water.

I quenched the fires in two seconds, mentally apologizing to all the residents who might've been living in its path.

This was the reason I had been born to activate Water.

Mira's eyes blazed with anger. The fires rekindled and leaped into the sky, merging with my sister's body until she became one blazing, almost inhuman being.

Another ancient tactic.

I called up the water, forming it into a huge wall behind me. Of course, it wasn't the whole ocean. Just enough to make sure I would be safe. Imagine what the earth would look like without the oceans!

Mira came at me with everything she had. All I did was lean backwards into the wall and out the other side. As soon as I emerged, the wall curved inwards and trapped Mira inside the giant bubble. I curled my fingers into a fist and the bubble slowly started to shrink.

"I thought you would've learned your lesson by now, Mira," I said softly. "Water destroys fire."

I couldn't see Mira from inside the bubble; there was too much water. But I stuck my thumb out of my fist, and a small portion of the bubble caved in near the top. Water started to pour in, the bubble slowly collapsing in itself.

There was a horrendous scream. I waved my arms and the top half of the bubble became transparent, allowing me to see my drenched sister.

The second I allowed myself this tiny bit of mercy, my sister exploded out of the bubble, her heat a hundred times stronger than before. I gasped in surprise, lost control, and fell down towards earth, barely managing to catch myself in time. When I glanced up again, Mira was rocketing towards me, so I used Galen's wind to carry me down faster than she could fall.

I landed on the ground with both feet, my knees bending to absorb the impact. Behind me, Mira basically punched the ground with her feet. When I turned to look, she was crouched on the ground, one hand on the floor, staring at me defiantly in the classic comic book pose.

I was immediately surrounded in a huge dome of fire. My sweat rolled down my face, stinging my wound.

"You've lost, sister," Mira cackled. "You're too easy to beat."

I wasn't worried. I still had the ancient-old power on my side, something Mira didn't have. "You forgot already, Mira," I said playfully.

I swept my arms quickly around me, wrapping myself in a hug. I closed my eyes. I could feel the wind and waters rushing towards me.

The fire dome was extinguished in seconds. The water flowed beneath my feet, carrying me up in its waves. The wind spun around me, playing with my hair and protecting me in a vortex.

Mira gaped at me, slack-jawed.

"The skies and oceans are on my side," I said with a smile. I uncurled my arms and the two elements combined, creating one powerful hurricane. I was the eye. It sucked Mira in and spat me out. I landed softly on the ground, watching in satisfaction as the bursts of fire within the spinning disaster were no match for the wind and waters of the earth.

I think she would be safe in there for some time.

Chapter 54

I ran back to what had been the torture chamber and gasped.

The rest of the team had returned from the Stones and were battling Ivoria's empowered soldiers. And judging from Kodiak's crumpled figure, sobbing and shaking, she'd revealed the truth about Alaska.

"Kodiak! Get up!" I shouted. "Come on!"

Kodiak's tear-stained face looked up wearily and stood. "Give me a moment..."

I glanced over at Callan, who was barely holding his own against another Earth-powered soldier with the Plant Talent. The boulders he flung were easy obstacles for his bulky opponent. "Rina! You're alive!"

"Of course I am," I snapped. I swept the man aside, sending him crashing into the wall.

As soon as he was free, Callan rushed over and scooped me in his arms. I froze, not sure what to do .

"Do you know how worried I was?" he murmured. "I thought you died."

He pulled me back to inspect my face. He ran a finger gently alongside the wound, not touching it, but acknowledging it. One arm was still wrapped around my waist. "Your face…"

I pulled away. "I'm fine."

"You look terrible."

Gentle Callan made me feel a tiny bit uneasy. He stepped back and ran a hand through his dark brown hair. "Sorry about that…."

"No, it's fine. Thank you for worrying about me," I said with a small smile. "I'm fine."

He watched me worriedly. "You sure? You look…."

I laughed. "I'm fine. If Galen didn't show up when he did -"

Something happened then. Callan had his arms around me again, pulling me close. This was a tiny bit awkward….

"I guess I have to thank Galen, then," he said softly. "I'm sorry I wasn't the one who showed up."

I blinked. "Uh… w-well, it's fine. I would've

460

been grateful to you the same way. But, um...."

"Yeah?" he asked, hugging me tighter.

"GET YOUR HANDS OFF OF HER!"

Callan suddenly lurched to the left, almost dragging me down with him. He landed on the floor with a thud.

Galen stood there, eyes blazing. "In case you haven't noticed, pebble brain, we're in the middle of battle. There's no time for indecency."

"INDECENCY?" Callan spat, rubbing his head. "I'm just happy to see Rina alive. Is that a crime? And did you really have to kick me?"

The tension and energy in Galen's eyes could have burned Callan into cinders.

"H-Hey, um, thanks," I mumbled. Then I bolted and threw myself into the heaviest part of battle that I could find.

Sirocca materialized beside me, helping to fight off more of the soldiers. "I saw what happened, by the way," she said teasingly. "Tell me all about it later. But for now," she continued, cutting off my protests. "What's the plan? I think we all can notice that huge spinning cyclone outside. Mira's inside, isn't she?"

I nodded. "She is. For now...."

"For now, we need to escape this island and get to the portal," Galen commanded. He took out another soldier and added, "Bring Mira too. I'll try to get to Ivoria."

"Wait!" I shouted, but he was already gone.

Flames, that kid was going to get himself killed if he went after Ivoria!

I needed to get to her first.

I did a quick scan of the room and started racing towards the evil woman the second I spotted her. She had a few more soldiers in a protective circle around her while she was crouched behind the controls of the gun.

I got there first.

I took out guard after guard until Ivoria was left vulnerable. Galen came then and pushed me out of the way. "What are you doing? You're going to kill yourself!"

"Same thing goes for you," I shot back.

Ivoria stood there, chuckling. "You guys were very close, but also far from success." She flashed a foot at us, kicking us away from her a few feet then held us down with the barrel of the cannon. "I have raised the power of this gun to the maximum. Who knows what it would do once I trigger it?"

I slowly backed up on my arms, trying hard not to stare at the hole the size of my head. The one where it was going to shoot a ray that would potentially kill me.

Galen…

I kicked Galen in the stomach, and he rolled away from the gun, moaning in pain. "WHAT DO YOU THINK YOU'RE DOING?" he shouted.

"Help Sirocca!" I shouted back, eyes still on the cannon, arms still pulling the rest of my body backwards slowly.

"There's no way I'm going to let you give up your Talent just like that," he demanded. He started to rush at me.

Ivoria cackled. "Brilliant! Two-in-one package deal. One…."

I kicked his shin when he got close. He fell almost on top of me, but started to pull me away.

"Two…."

My pant leg was pinned under the two-hundred-pound barrel of the cannon. There's no way I would be escaping now. "Galen…."

"Three."

I saw blue light flash in front of my face, and everything went dark.

Chapter 55

Thora grumbled softly to herself as she scuffed and dragged her feet down the tiled floors of the hallways in the Royal Palace. "Why can't we be there?" she whined. "We were the ones who helped them find the room, weren't we?"

Beside her, Derrik sighed, slumping as he walked. After Thora discovered that there were more men marching towards the hidden art room, Andy had told her and Derrik to go and make themselves useful elsewhere.

"We'll handle it," he had said. "Don't worry about it for now. Can you two go to the palace library and see if you can find any extra information on weapons? Maybe Talent use, too. We'll need that later on."

"They always say we're too young," he

explained monotonously. "You remember Skit? The spider I introduced you to? Yeah, I rant to him all the time."

Thora wrinkled her nose as she recalled the black widow she'd met. She's spent the whole time stiff and pale, her face drained of blood.

Derrik stomped his foot. "You were right, Thora."

Thora jumped at this sudden outburst. "Wh-what?" she squeaked.

Derrik walked up to her, so close that she had to take a step back. "We need to show them that we're mature enough to handle this."

Thora felt a spark of rebellion in her core. "So what are we going to do?" she asked eagerly.

Derrik frowned. "Well, I was going to suggest storming back in there and demanding we have a say. After all, you're the one who soundified the walls and made all that possible in the first place! And you were the one listening and keeping track of what happens in Ivoria's control room. You have every right to be in there!"

Thora blushed. "You're giving me way too much credit. You were the one who built the speakers, remember? And you were the one who found Ivoria's facility. You're the one who started all this. I just helped a bit."

Derrik snorted, forcing Thora to bite back a giggle. "I would argue against this, but we'd waste time. Storming back in there wouldn't prove anything to them. The best we can do now is...." He paused for a dramatic effect. "Do the best library search in the history of the Terrenian Islands!"

Thora groaned, but inside, she didn't mind. If she had to be stuck in a boring library with anyone, it'd be Derrik.

They marched to the library and as soon as Thora passed through the doors, Derrik wilted. She looked at him, confused, before gazing at the palace library and slumped along with him.

The library had millions of shelves, some holding books, and others holding thousands of ancient scrolls. The shelves stretched like a maze in front of them.... Thora doubted they would be able to do anything productive for a very long time.

"Why did Andy send us here?" Derrik muttered. "Did he have something against us or something?"

Thora sighed, then dragged her feet towards the closest shelf. She brushed dust off the label and it read: PLANTS. She made a face and kept walking. Plants were boring. She moved onto the next section. WEAPONS.

"Hey, this is perfect!" Thora squeaked. "We're in the right place! Come on, Derrik!"

Derrik was too busy ranting to another spider. Thora rolled her eyes. "DERRIK!"

He jumped, then sheepishly grinned at her. "Coming! You found the weapons section?"

Thora nodded. "Yeah. What are we supposed to search for?"

Derrik shrugged. "Anything useful, I guess?" He stood on his tiptoes and rummaged through the scrolls in the topmost shelf. "These are all so old. Can we find the more - hey...." Thora saw him grab something and dust it off. She coughed when a huge billow of dust flew in her face.

"Sorry," Derrik said. "But look."

There were letters written across the roll of the scroll in the old Terrenian language. She squinted and struggled to remember the alphabet she'd learned in school. "T... h..."

"Wait." Derrik grabbed her hand and raced to the nearest reading corner. He then plopped down on a beanbag chair, displayed the scroll on the smooth wooden table, and shoved the pen and paper already provided at Thora. "Here. Try again."

About ten minutes later, Thora had decoded

467

the ancient language. "The Tale of Titans," she said. Thora scratched her head. "This doesn't belong in the weapons section."

Derrik nodded. "Look at the design around the edges of the scroll. The design doesn't match the rest of the designs in the weapons section. It's pretty close, but not the same."

Thora squinted at the faded curlicues. Something smudged and hazy was kind of covering the design. "What does the design have to do with anything?" She gently tried to rub the mess off.

Derrik smiled. "You haven't visited the ancient sections of the Academy library, huh? That's my favorite place. The librarians organize the ancient scrolls by the design on the paper. Luckily for them, the older generations have been categorizing their writings using those designs. We should put this back, but I'd thought you'd like to know more about the ancient stories. They're pretty interesting!" He leaned in and ran his fingers gently around the edges. "Watch for these curls next time. Those - wait." He frowned at the smudges too.

Thora blinked. "What?"

Derrik took the scroll from her and brought the paper even closer to his face. Thora was afraid he was nearly going blind when he said, "Someone's been trying to hide this scroll!"

The heavy silence that followed afterwards was so eerie, Thora shivered, shrank into the beanbag, and tried not to think about the dark creatures that might leap out of the ancient scrolls. "What?"

Derrik quickly unrolled the scroll again. "Quick. Try to -" He stopped again.

Thora's eyes were flicking back and forth in fear now. "What? Keep talking, Derrik. You're scaring me!"

Derrik looked at her, and his face softened. "Sorry. These smudges were in the design of the scrolls about weaponry. Someone tried to change the design of this scroll to hide it." He laid the scroll back onto the circular table and pointed it out to her. "But you see, when I unrolled it, someone else has already translated everything for us!"

Thora squinted and recognized the faint marks of the modern-day pencil in between each line of the story. Thora gasped, and Derrik nodded. "It could be nothing, but it could also be something."

"It probably really is nothing," Thora said softly.

Derrik shrugged. "Maybe. But I like to think that we found this secret all on our own. Maybe it's an ancient secret told in the form of a folktale? Maybe it will help us save the islands!" Derrik gasped. "What if it makes us king and queen?"

Thora giggled. "Those are highly unlike-" She paused, then blushed when she processed Derrik's last sentence. "Um...."

Derrik realized it at the same time and cleared his throat. "I mean, um...." He snatched the scroll and stood up. "Let's put this away in my room for now. We can show it to Galen and Rina when they're back. They won't think we're too young."

Then he raced out of the room.

Thora squeaked, and ran after him. "W-Wait for me! We haven't found what Andy wanted us to find yet...!"

Chapter 56

I kept thinking, *Nonononononono…..*

Until I realized I was still able to think in the first place.

I dared to open my eyes, but I still couldn't see anything. Something was covering my face. Something solid, but soft, with cloth over it.

Whatever was on top of me shifted and groaned.

KODIAK!

I squirmed and tugged hard on my leg. My pant leg ripped and the metal scraped my skin, but it was small in comparison to what happened to Kodiak.

I wiggled my way out and Kodiak rolled down my body until I had him on my lap. His eyes were closed tight against the pain, and there was a gaping hole in the front of his shirt.

Strangely enough, there didn't seem to be a wound I could see.

That scared me even more.

"KODIAK!" I shouted, shaking his shoulder. "Wake up!"

Kodiak didn't move.

Galen let out a cough. "Can you please move his head? All his weight is here, and I can't breathe...."

I slid my arm underneath Kodiak's head and gently raised it the tiniest bit so Galen could move. He squirmed away, and I was about to rest Kodiak's head back down on his lap, when he said, "We're still sitting in front of a cannon."

Right.

We dragged Kodiak away and laid him behind some crates so he'd be safe. I glanced up, feeling a strong sense of fury and protection.

Not a good combination.

"GALEN!"

"Right here," he said immediately. We made twin tornadoes and crashed into the cannon, hopefully destroying it. Galen kept going and trapped Ivoria in his spin cycle.

It couldn't have been that easy.

"LET'S GO!" Galen commanded.

We all flew out. I picked up Mira along the

472

way, and everyone headed for the hidden portal. Most of Ivoria's men had already been knocked out; the ones still conscious didn't bother to run after us.

This was way too easy.

We kept running with Galen in the lead, managing to reach Sandy Beach in record time. Unfortunately, something else held us back.

My best friend skidded to a stop, the rest of us nearly crashing into him.

Rows and rows of enhanced soldiers guarded the brightly shining portal, seconds away from collapsing it.

There was a creepy cackle from inside Galen's tornado. Mira heard and started laughing along right after her.

Have they lost their minds?

"Fools," Ivoria sneered. "Children are so gullible."

Galen flew up and his foot slammed down onto her head. She was silenced for a long time afterwards. Maybe I should do that with Mira too….

One of the soldiers stepped forward. My eyes flashed when I recognized his thin frame, his blond hair.

"You're too late," Connery said harshly. His

blue eyes flashed and he waved a hand, urging the soldiers to work faster. "The portal is being destroyed. Boss orders us to capture you immediately."

I didn't have time for this. "Ivoria is in our hands. Make way or else we'll have to use force."

Connery snorted. "I don't care who's in your hands. Your friend will live. Boss's orders are law. Don't think I'd let you pass this easily."

The portal began to crack.

Sirocca leaned in suddenly. "They're collapsing the portal the long way. We have about five minutes before it's completely destroyed."

I gave her a subtle nod and I turned to the soldier. "You haven't been enhanced yet, have you, Connery?"

His jaw dropped and he took a step back, but hastily tried to cover it up. "Stop speaking nonsense," he snarled. "I am a loyal soldier of Boss's army -"

"Yet, you didn't even recognize her name when I told you," I said sympathetically. "Your leader is Aura Ivoria. She is currently unconscious in that tornado over there." I pointed to the left behind me. "Now. Will you let us pass?"

474

Connery looked at me suspiciously, so I kept going. "Where's Brian?"

His eyes widened in fear.

"You two must feel a lot of bitterness towards 'Boss', am I right?" I sighed. "I mean, I wouldn't like her very much if she gave everyone else Talents except for me. After everything I've done for her.... I've followed her orders without question for so long already, yet here I am, still Talentless, still oblivious to whatever grand plan she's swirling up in that brilliant mind of hers..."

I was suddenly knocked back, pinned to the floor. Connery's hands were wrapped tightly around my throat, blocking my windpipe. I struggled to breathe.

"Who are you? What do you want?" he asked lowly. "It should be in your best interest to answer while you can. HURRY UP! WHAT'S TAKING SO LONG!" He hollered the last words behind me.

But while Connery had been distracted with me, Sirocca had dove into the thick crowd of soldiers, blowing them all aside and directed a strong current of wind into the portal. Everything the soldiers had been trying to do was undone.

Sirocca had managed to save the portal and buy us time.

I kicked my foot upwards as hard as I could, my leg colliding with Connery's sensitive area. He froze for a split second before letting out a howl, almost crushing me as he fell. I rolled away as he crumpled to the ground, groaning in pain, curled up in the fetal position. I could see miniscule tears at the corners of his eyes.

"Just listen!" I snarled. "I was there when you went with Brian to count the cannons at the First Stone. My friend and I heard everything. I think we can be allies. You help us escape, and we'll take you back to our home with full honors."

Connery managed to look at me suspiciously. "What's the catch?"

I rolled my eyes and drew my foot back again, this time, aiming for his head. He quickly stumbled to his feet and pushed my shoulders. "Why should I believe you? You four are just children."

Four...?

I CAN'T BELIEVE I FORGOT ABOUT KODIAK!

Got him, Galen said suddenly. Picked him up on the way out. He's in the same tornado as Ivoria. He should be fine.

GOOD!

"We're in the same position," I said finally.

"We want to escape from this place and go home. So do you. Are you going to help us, or not?"

Connery was still hunched over, even though he was standing. He looked off into the trees, thinking.

"WE DON'T HAVE ALL DAY, CANNARY!" Galen hollered over the throng of soldiers.

"IT'S CONNERY!" Connery snapped back. He rolled his eyes. "Fine."

"Great. That's all I needed to hear. Call off your men, and let's go," I commanded.

Connery glared at me. "I want to add to the deal."

Well. That was unexpected.

"What is it?" I asked impatiently.

"Give me Talents as well as honors when you return to your Islands," he said firmly. "Then I'll call off my men."

I paused. "That's not possible."

Connery sneered. "Liars. The evidence is in a swirling whirlwind right behind you!"

"No, I mean we were born with it," I said sharply, glaring at him. "To be injected will kill you just like it killed our ancestors."

Connery stared at me flatly then gestured at the enhanced soldiers. "Any more excuses?"

I sighed. "Fine. I'll bring this up to our queen.

477

Whether or not she'd agree to it is a different story. That is not my responsibility."

Connery seemed to be satisfied. He stuck two fingers in his mouth and let out a shrill whistle. "Return to base," he commanded. "Let them pass."

"But sir -" One soldier objected.

"Are you questioning my orders?" Connery spoke coldly. "Let. Them. Pass. If you choose to refuse, I wouldn't want to be there when you face Boss's consequences for you."

The man dipped his head and stepped aside.

Immediately, my friends and I rushed into the portal. Galen and I dragged the twin spinning whirlwinds....

And we landed on soft green grass with a looming tower in the distance.

We were home.

Chapter 57

Galen tumbled through after me and collapsed onto the green grass. "Did we make it?" he mumbled. "Did we make it to the right place?"

I leaned down, nodding. "We're home. The soldiers must have fixed the portal!"

He breathed a sigh of relief. "YES!"

Everyone else came through afterwards. Callan fell back a step when he saw the castle. "We really made it."

As soon as Sirocca passed through, she collapsed the portal. A loud BOOM resounded through the land, just like I had remembered last time. We wasted no more time and made a break for the castle.

"Whoa…." Connery mumbled. "You guys live here?"

We all ignored him; there was time to answer questions later. I threw myself at the doors, miscalculating the distance and crashed into them instead. I had meant to try to knock, but the collision was loud enough to startle anyone who might've been working inside the palace. Maybe I scared a few kitchen workers and shattered some plates....

The door immediately opened to us by the doorman-butler-guy as I scrambled to my feet. His eyes widened when he saw us. I couldn't tell if it was from fear, joy, or horror at the sight of our dirty clothes. "In," he commanded.

I left Mira and Ivoria outside, and we all barged in through the doors and down the halls. By this time, I knew the path back to the guest wing Emily had built for us. I demanded an audience with the queen along the way.

"I am afraid I cannot do that, miss," Mr. Butler said hesitantly. "You have brought a stranger. It is not wise to -"

"People's lives are on the line," I demanded as we ran. "He is with us, and is a Mainlander. I'm sure we can handle him. Just get the queen!"

We collapsed through the arch to the guest wing, and we all sighed with relief and comfort as we sank to the ground. My leg started bouncing quickly against the hardwood in anticipation.

Emily rushed into the room with Andy and Tawny just then. She stopped dead in her tracks and took us all in with her big eyes. I saw her mouth quickly moving inaudibly, and her head nod along with it, then she screamed.

We all scrambled in alarm, trying to find the enemy when she suddenly enveloped us in an enormous, bone-crushing hug.

How long were her arms?! They reached around all of us!

Barely.

"YOU GUYS ARE ALIVE!" Emily nearly shouted. She quickly pulled away to inspect us carefully. "Is anyone hurt? And who's that?"

I brushed her off. "No, no one's hurt, but we brought two people you might like to see. I'll tell you about this man later. Hurry!"

We all rushed outside again, Connery following a little bit slowly in confusion, and as soon as we burst through the main doors, Andy and Emily's eyes widened until I was afraid they wouldn't be able to keep their eyeballs inside their heads anymore. Galen condensed the tornadoes into tight spheres, presenting our two prisoners to the queen and her royal advisor. A larger, less violent sphere of wind was floating behind them, containing Kodiak.

"Where's the doctor?" I suddenly demanded, mortified at myself for forgetting again. "Kodiak's hurt. He's been unconscious for a long time because of the ray blast-thingy that he took for me. I can't believe I forgot!"

Immediately, Mr. Leafstern was rushing out of the palace. Only until then could I start breathing. I trusted Mr. L.

The family friend quickly picked Kodiak up in his arms and swept him away out the door. Sirocca start to tell our story a bit shakily.

Andy's jaw dropped and squinted at the sphere on the right. "You caught Ivoria?!"

Emily laughed. "Among all the things I was expecting out of this mission... this was not one of them."

I shrugged. "We were sent to figure out what she was going to do, remember? Then we were commanded to put a stop to it. So we did. We captured the person behind it as well."

"And a traitor," Galen added.

Emily turned a cold eye on Mira. "Traitor, you say?"

Through the sphere, Mira seemed to be even more fidgety now that she was in front of the

482

ruler of the Islands and unable to move or escape in any way.

"So. What makes her a traitor, exactly?"

Sirocca told her the story, exactly as she had heard it from us. Connery started to nod in agreement as he listened. "She's your twin, right? She looks exactly like you."

After she was finished, Emily's face was void of any expression. I think that was more frightening than if she had exploded with anger.

She walked in a slow circle around my sister, hands clasped in front of her, tapping her right fingers against the back of her left hand. "What shall we do with you?" she murmured.

Mira was visibly shaking, but she didn't say anything.

"You thought you'd get away with this, didn't you?" Emily continued, her eyes never leaving the girl in the bubble. "Let me give you some advice."

She reached out with a finger and tapped the sphere once, the wind immediately dissipating. Mira tumbled to the floor, limbs getting tangled in their haste to right themselves. Before she could fully stand up, Emily leaned in towards her suddenly, forcing Mira down lower without physically touching her. "Don't hide things from your queen. Especially not since your assault on your sister. Secrets are meant to be kept hidden, but nothing stays in the dark for long. The longer you hide, the greater the consequence."

Mira's eyes were as wide as moons by now. She licked her lips, swallowed, and said, "S-So.... What does this mean for me, Y-Your Highness?"

Connery's jaw dropped. "Wait, wait, wait! She's the queen?! She's so young!"

I gave him a hard elbow to the ribs, and that silenced him.

Emily leaned back, glaring at Mira. "Supposedly, you were going to be thrown into the dungeon along with Ivoria to serve a temporary sentence before your final punishment."

Mira's mouth dropped in horror when she heard this. I didn't blame her. My mouth was wide open too. "Dungeon?!"

"But!" Emily continued, demanding silence. "Since you are not above eighteen years old, I will postpone your punishment and shift to a lighter consequence that doesn't involve your neck on a chopping board or through a noose."

Mira fainted right there and then.

I nearly did too.

Connery paled. "All hail the queen...."

Emily glanced disdainfully down at my twin sister then looked up at me. "How can your faces be so similar, but personalities so different?" She shuddered. "It's... strange."

"You really were going to kill her just like that?" I rasped. "That... That doesn't sound like something you'd do, Emily."

Emily blinked hard. "I don't want to. Not ever. But I'm a queen now. I need to do things that will ensure the peace among my people and within my nation. I can't let one individual disturb that."

"But she's one person -" I began to protest.

"One person who could easily influence many others," Emily interrupted. She gave me a sad smile. "I'm sorry, Rina. I really am. I've been wishing for the longest time that Mira wouldn't do anything else, especially not something this big. She's your sister. Your twin, at that."

I sat down on the floor; my legs couldn't support my body anymore.

If Mira died, that'll be the end of many things.

The end of being a twin.

The end of having a complete family.

The end of a possibility to get along.

The end of a greatness only Mira could've achieved.

"Hey." Callan leaned down next to me. "Stop worrying. Mira's not going to die."

"She was about to...." I said faintly.

"But she isn't," Emily said firmly. "She better be grateful she didn't do this five years later. Things would've gotten messy if she had been nineteen." She rubbed her eyes. "Being a queen is stressful."

Galen laughed, but it didn't fit the situation. "You think? You're in charge of an entire nation!"

"HOLD ON!" Connery hollered suddenly, making everyone jump. "With all due respect, erm, queen... but can someone please explain to me what is going on?"

I sighed, stood up, and started to explain from the beginning.

Back when I first activated Water.

Back when two hundred kids were abducted.

The others filled in details I forgot. Connery leaned back when we finished. "Wow... That's not the version I heard...."

He sat down against a tree. "What did you hear from Ivoria?" I asked.

He rubbed his eyes. "There are seven islands just to the west of us. The technology they've fashioned is unlike anything the world has ever seen. That part was right," he chuckled. "But

Boss visited these islands, asking for a part of the technology so she would be able to modernize it, to share it with the rest of the world. She was rudely turned down and banished from the islands. She had even proposed a deal, where these islands would receive a hundred percent of whatever she earned, but they gave her threats against her life instead.

"The thing was, Provincia was losing in a war against the rest of the world. The last to grow, the first to be attacked. Boss knew the islands' technology was going to help establish power, so she decided to make a plan to sneak some of the technology out of the islands, study it, and create it herself. If those islands weren't going to share, she would make it herself. She wasn't going to let millions of lives be lost because of some other nation's selfishness." Connery glanced up when he was finished. "So which story is accurate?"

Chapter 58

The silence that hit the atmosphere just then made us freeze and could have shattered us into ice bits if Mr. Leafstern didn't come running up to us saying, "Kodiak is awake!"

That pushed the play button and everyone started moving again, trying to act natural. Mr. Leafstern sensed the awkwardness and took a step back. "Okay. I'll just be leaving now. As soon as Kodiak regains his strength, he can go home."

With that, he walked off toward the tunnels and stepped through the one that led to Earth Island.

"Meet me in the conference room after you have finished visiting Kodiak," Emily said in her queen voice. "I want a report on his condition and his story afterwards." She turned to leave, remembered something, then turned back. "And when you come, bring your sister. We'll discuss her punishment while she is safely held somewhere else for the time being. Mister.... Connery, was it? Please follow me."

With that, she disappeared back into her palace.

I scooped Mira up into a bubble then we all headed in slowly. Connery gave me a small salute then walked after Emily. The the realization that Kodiak was alive hit the rest of us and we were speeding through the halls.

I burst through the door to the room that I had been in last year when Ivoria shot my arm.

Kodiak was lying in bed, very, very still.

"KODIAK!" we all shouted with joy. "You're alive!"

Kodiak slowly turned his head when he saw us and smiled weakly. "Of course I'm alive," he said softly.

"We thought you'd die," I said, tears coming to my eyes. "WHAT ARE YOU DOING HERE IN BED YOU SHOULD BE AWAKE AND UP AND HEALTHY! WHY DID YOU DO THAT?!"

Kodiak looked overwhelmed, suddenly, and tried to sink deeper into the bed, but relaxed when I stopped yelling. "I did what I couldn't do for Alaska," he said quietly. Everyone was silent at the mention of his sister. "There's something I need to tell you," he continued. "Privately."

He cast everyone else a significant look. Callan and Galen looked at him suspiciously before leaving the room after Sirocca, who complained, "I'm always being left out, did you realize that?"

Kodiak didn't speak until after the door closed. He didn't speak for a few minutes afterwards either.

The first thing he said was, "You know, I bet they're eavesdropping on the other side of the door right now."

I laughed, imagining Callan, Galen, and Sirocca pressing their ears to the wood, trying to stay out of sight from the window on the door. "They probably are."

Kodiak looked away. "Well, it doesn't matter. They'll all find out later anyways, so they might as well just find out now."

"What?" I said, all the crushing events in the past few weeks crowding my mind. "Tell me."

Kodiak took a deep breath, exhaled, and looked at me with eyes full of melancholy. "Watch."

He turned his head to the glass of water by his

bed. Lifting a hand, he moved his fingers in a certain gesture.

Nothing happened.

He tried again and again and again.

Still nothing happened.

It hit me right then, what Ivoria had said. It has the ability to extract the Talent from the person it hits - forever.

"You...." I said shakily, tearfully. "You mean...."

Kodiak looked at me with tears of his own and nodded.

I couldn't do this. Why?

Why did he have to jump in front of the gun?

He wanted to make atonement for what had been done to his sister, but he couldn't have given up his Talent.

I should've been faster.

I should've been smarter.

I should've been stronger.

I wanted to scream and cry to my heart's content, but Kodiak was still recovering, and I the last thing I wanted was for that process to slow down. I settled for sinking to the floor and burying my head between my knees and arms.

"Hey. Look up."

I refused.

"Hey. Come on. Please?"

"Why?"

"Because. It makes me sad to see you like that."

I wanted to resist and act spoiled because I wanted to stay in my little ball. But I forced myself to straighten and look at him. "Why?"

Kodiak slowly pushed himself up into a sitting position. The light from the window struck his face and I was so startled, I nearly toppled backwards.

He'd changed.

He was so much paler, his hair so much lighter. Even his eyes had lost some of the blueness.

What had happened?

"What?" he said tiredly. "What's wrong with me?"

I opened and closed my mouth. "Nothing."

"Tell me."

"You're... you look different."

Kodiak held out his hands and studied them. "I'm paler, aren't I?"

I nodded, which was saying a lot. His skin had been very fair to begin with, and his hair had been so dark. The vast contrast gave him a very dramatic look. But now he seemed faded, like something in him had been erased.

Something had been.

It had been stolen.

Because of me.

Kodiak ran his fingers through his hair, getting glimpses of the tips. "Does it look bad?"

".... No."

He glared at me, and I ducked my head. "I'm just not used to it."

He sighed, then glanced out the window. "After I woke up, I did some thinking."

"About what?"

He was quiet for a second. "About Alaska."

This was dangerous.

"Okay…. And then?"

A pained expression crossed his face for a few seconds before disappearing behind a cool mask. "I can't do this anymore, Rina. Being stuck here like this, useless, it's…."

"You're not useless," I told him. "You've helped me out a bunch of times."

Kodiak snorted. "Like when?"

"You were there when I was terrified in the facility before we found the light switch," I offered with a small, embarrassed laugh. "And you always keep Callan in check."

Kodiak scoffed. "Anyone could've done that,

honestly. Callan only listens to gentle voices of someone close."

"You."

"No. Not only me."

"You. He doesn't listen to me. I don't even know if we're considered 'close friends', but he doesn't listen to anyone else. Which is good, in a way, I guess. You can help me prevent him from fighting with Galen."

Kodiak shrugged half-heartedly. "What use is a Terrenian without his Talent?" he asked me miserably. "I can't go to school. My future is ruined."

I stood up and sat down on the other side of his bed. He looked up at me, and I stared right back. "Your future isn't ruined," I told him. "Not if you choose to do something about it."

Kodiak's lips set in a firm line when he understood what I was talking about. "You know what happened back then when the original islanders were injected with the elements," he said.

"Yes. But that was back then," I told him. "They didn't have the technology we have now."

"But -"

"No buts, Kodiak. Do you want your Talent back or not?"

He looked at me, eyes wild. "Of course I want it back. I'm just worried about what it'll do to me if I try."

I gave him a small smile. "I'll ask Elias. Although we'd prefer if it was soon, I'll tell him there's no rush in figuring out how to do it. But I'll tell him to put it as number one on his priority list."

Kodiak's lips twitched. "There you go, contradicting yourself again."

I shrugged. "It's not contradiction if it makes perfect sense to me."

He laughed, the first I've heard in a long time. It made me smile, and it released the grip of fears and worries on my heart.

He sent me a smile. "Thank you, Rina," he said.

I waved a hand. "For what? It's nothing."

"No," he said, an intense look in his eyes. "It's been everything."

I looked at him, not sure what to say.

At that moment, Callan burst through the doors. "OKAY! That's been enough alone time for you two!"

Kodiak glared at his friend. "I can't believe you nearly forgot about me, guys. Don't think I didn't notice when it took you ten minutes to come after Mr. Leafstern left."

"Hey, that's not fair!" I protested. "How do you know Mr. Leafstern wasn't walking slowly?"

Kodiak snorted. "Please, do you think I'm that unimportant? I'm hurt."

Callan pushed a fist against Kodiak's head, accidentally making it hit the wall. "HEY! OW!"

"Dude, do you know how bad you looked?" he demanded. "You nearly died!"

Kodiak rolled his eyes while he rubbed the side of his head. "Well, I'm sorry for saving Rina's life."

Callan started laughing. "It's nothing. We've all done it before. Well, three of us have, anyways."

I glared at both of them. "You guys are terrible. I'm leaving."

I stomped out of the room, crashing into Galen on the way. "Hey! What're you doing?" he exclaimed.

"They're talking about how I always get into near-death experiences," I grumbled. "Go visit Kodiak. I'll be back."

Galen shook his head. "Nah. I'd rather go with you. They're going to pick on me if I go in there."

I laughed, knowing it was true. "Okay, then."

Sirocca shook her head at both of us. "You guys are hopeless," she said before walking into the room. She was gone before either of us could ask her to explain what she meant.

"O... kay...." Galen said slowly. "That was strange."

I nodded. "Yeah." Then I turned and started walking away.

"Hey, where're you going?" Galen rushed to catch up.

I smiled to myself. "To visit some old friends before we have to go meet Emily."

Chapter 59

We walked down the halls, slowly finding our way to the training room. I had forgotten where it was, since I'd only been there once.

When we found it, we were immediately attacked by two people, a girl and a guy in black suits and masks that marked them as guards. "RINA! YOU'RE ALIVE!" one of them shouted before we took another step.

They moved so fast, I didn't see them.
They moved so quietly, I didn't expect it.
They held us in choke holds so strong, I couldn't breathe.

"State your business," a gruff voice said.

"Hey...." I gasped. "Can you...?" I frantically gestured at their hands.

"Oh."

The guy released my neck just the tiniest bit,

just enough to let me breathe. "Whew. Thanks," I coughed.

These two were good!

"So?" the girl asked coldly. "We give you three seconds. We're not the most patient people."

Galen laughed. "We know that fact so well, don't we?" He shot me a knowing smile.

I laughed too. "How've you been, guys? You two are so cool now!"

Immediately, they peeled off their half-faces and their eyes glowed. "You still remember us!".

"Of course we do! What do you think we are?" Galen scoffed. "Whoa. Derrik. You really did grow!"

"NO!" I wailed. I scampered over to Derrik's side and my jaw dropped in horror. "YOU'RE TALLER THAN I AM! WHY AM I SO SHORT?!"

Derrik laughed, his voice lower than I had remembered. "Well, you know, training. Glenn made me train so much, it's painful."

"Of course. That's the point of training," Elece said, her eyes glinting when she gave him a look. She was still taller than all of us, even though Derrik was catching up. The small boy I had remembered was now half a head taller than I was.

I whimpered. "How much did you eat?!"
Derrik squinted his eyes and moved his hands to about the size of a Thanksgiving turkey. "Maybe about.... This much?"

"A day?"

"A meal."

I looked away, sighing. "Of course."

"Welcome to the tall life, Derrik," Galen said, slinging an arm around his shoulder. "Here, everyone is taller than Rina and we get to mess with her!"

"HEY!"

Derrik laughed. "That sounds fun, but I don't think she'd like that. I'm sticking with her on this one." He sidled over to my side.

"THANK YOU!"

His child-like gentleness was still there. Except when he was choking someone. He couldn't have eased it up even just a little bit?

I glanced at him. "You did get more muscular, though. Elece was right." I poked at him teasingly. "Is there a reason behind it? Hm?"

He blushed. "Hey."

Elece rolled her eyes. "Galen, you took forever to answer your phone."

Galen's eyes scrunched up. "Sorry. I had to take naps."

Elece rolled her eyes again, glancing at him with disappointment. "You're lucky you didn't arrive any later."

Galen nodded. "Yeah." He took a small step closer to me.

I blinked. "What's going on?"

Galen explained it in a rush. "I received a phone call from Elece when you were captured. She led me to the room, then I found you, and you know the rest. By the way, how'd you guys know that Rina was there?"

Elece gestured at Derrik and Derrik lowered his eyes. "I accidentally found a way to eavesdrop on the facility you and Ivoria were negotiating in."

My eyes widened. "WHOA! That's so cool!"

Derrik frowned. "I tried to tell you over the phone call, but I guess I didn't do a good job. I might've been able to do more, but some people, ahem, didn't let me in because I was 'too young'." He shot a glare at Elece. "But by then, it was too late, anyways."

I laughed, remembering the random nonsense Derrik had been saying during the phone call. "Oh, so that's what that was."

Elece shook her head. "Well, anyways, good to see you guys again. You going to start training

501

again soon?"

I laughed. "I hope so. If you guys keep going, you're going to smite us in ten seconds!"

"We're aiming for five."

I glared at Elece. "Hey. That's not fair."

She shot me an innocent smile. "Deal with it. Wanna have a showdown later? I think that'd be fun."

A feeling of dread washed over me, but the competitive side of me was insistent. "Fine."

"WHOO!" Galen and Derrik whooped. "Let's see who will be victorious!"

I laughed. It was great to be back with the original team again.

Even if our first encounter after a few weeks involved a blocked windpipe.

"We need to go," I told them. "Emily wants to tell us something."

"What is it?" Elece asked.

I sighed, then gestured to Galen. "Complications after the mission. We'll fill you in later. Bye!"

We burst into the conference room under the impression we were late.

And we were.

Very late.

Emily was not pleased. "I had asked you to

come straight here after your visit. Where have you two been?"

We looked at the floor and scuffed our feet against the tiles. "We went to check up on Elece and Derrik," I mumbled. "We haven't seen them in a long time, and -"

"I understand. Besides. It doesn't matter now. We need to start this discussion. Connery told me about his contribution to the team and has informed me more about Provincia."

"Shouldn't you already know these things?" Connery spoke suddenly. He was leaned way back in his chair, arms behind his head, feet propped up. "We're both from the same place."

Emily bristled. "That doesn't mean I know the same things you do. I spent so much energy trying to divulge a tiny secret from my father. You're a soldier receiving commands."

"But a soldier doesn't know everything either," Connery pointed out. "We're only given the basics."

"Which is more than I've ever received," Emily retorted. "Now stop arguing with me. We need to figure out what to do. You may have contributed to this team, but you still worked with Ivoria and if I'm being frank, your help is very reluctantly received. "

Connery sighed, sitting up properly. "Fine."

"So what's up?" I asked, interrupting.

Emily glanced up at me. "We are going to orchestrate an interrogation. We need to find out what Ivoria had planned as well as why your sister switched sides. But Ivoria is of top priority right now. We have no time to lose."

Chapter 60

We left the conference room right then. Without saying anything, all of us walked toward the dungeons with Emily in the lead.

We walked down a flight of hidden stone steps. It was dank, it smelled, and it was cold. Moss grew rank between the cracks in the stone.

It was perfect to house a criminal. Or two.

There were no torches, which meant no light. That wasn't a problem for Emily. She rubbed her hands together and created an orb of bright yellow light. She gently raised it into the air and it started to float ahead of us.

"Whoa!" I said, awed. "That's cool!"

Emily just smiled. "It comes in handy."

The dungeon looked very similar to the cells I had seen back at the Mainland. There was a lot of space with rows of cells on either side. The walkway in the middle was wide, and the cells were relatively small and compact. The iron gates and ragged stone walls made it look very intimidating.

"There are only two prisoners here," Emily said. "It should be easy to spot them."

Mira's face suddenly appeared from behind one of the bars. "You guys are here," she said. "What is it now? My execution?"

"We're not here for you," I said coldly. "What do you think we have in mind for your punishment?"

Mira looked at me pleadingly. "Please, Rina. We've been together since before birth! You're my sister. My twin."

"Yet, there wasn't one day where you treated me like one," I told her. "You had fourteen years."

We continued walking. I didn't care if Mira would hold this against me. She already hated me. What difference would it make?

As long as she wasn't dead, I'd be happy.

We stopped in front of Ivoria's cell. She was sitting, tied to a chair with heavy, heavy ropes and chains. Her legs were cuffed to the chair leg and a giant weight sat off to the side, its chain leading up to the cuff on her neck.

She wasn't going anywhere.

Satisfied, Emily opened the gate with a key she had in her back pocket. Galen and I shuffled inside while everyone else stood and watched.

Ivoria glanced up, her eyes deeply shadowed. "What do you want?" She snapped.

After everything that had happened back at the third Stone, Ivoria's clothes remained wrinkle-free and whole. In fact, she looked exactly the same, except that her hair was unkempt and there were parts of her business suit that were still wet. Her dark eyes were dangerous orbs that swirled with hate and bitterness.

How are you going to question her without giving anything away? Galen asked.

I don't know, I replied. Any ideas?

"Well, are you going to say anything?" Ivoria sneered. "Or are you going to stand there and stare at me all day?"

I narrowed my eyes at her. "I'm sure you know why we're here."

Ivoria sniffed. "You children are never going to be able to obtain any sort of information from me."

I frowned. How were we supposed to drag the information out of her? I didn't even know what kind of information we were looking for.

Emily stepped forward. Ivoria's eyes twinkled. "Ah, dearest Em."

"Stop calling me that!" she snapped. "You're not my mother."

Ivoria shrugged. "I would not want to be."

Emily's eyes narrowed dangerously but she didn't retaliate. "Do you know what intrigues me the most?" Ivoria continued, staring at Emily. "How did such a powerful young lady be abandoned by such a powerful woman?"

In a flash, Emily backhanded Ivoria across the face. "Are you finished?" she asked emotionlessly. Her hands were starting to glow as well as her eyes.

Ivoria chuckled, the left side of her face slowly starting to turn red. "You still have the same temper, dear Emily. It pleases me to see you have not changed in the slightest bit."

Emily's eyes were bright amber orbs. Her finger twitched, and in a flash, Elece was by her side. She gave Emily a short nod before striding forward and placing her hands gently on Ivoria's chains, her dark eyes glowing a bright yellow. She said softly, "I thought it would be good for the both of us if I showed you what would happen should you decide to not obey the orders of our queen." Her eyes flashed, lightning bolts crackled around the powerful teen for a split second before it disappeared and Ivoria was left giving a single jerk, causing her hair to stand up on end.

Ivoria's eyes showed real fear this time.

I stepped forward then. "Let's negotiate one final time," I told her. "You like that, don't you?"

"Do not toy with me, Fire Defect," Ivoria spat. "With your impaired Talent, who would want to negotiate you?"

"You," I said simply. "I vaguely recall a certain lady complimenting my negotiation skills and being willing to accommodate her in her mansion. Now, here are my conditions," I told her. "Tell us exactly what you're planning, and we'll give you the piece of information I believe you're dying to know."

Ivoria quirked an eyebrow. "And what will that be, exactly?"

I leaned forward. "That's for you to figure out for yourself. Maybe it is where the armies are weakest. Maybe it is the path to sneak into the Royal Castle."

Careful, Tsunami, Elece warned. *Don't get her too curious.*

I need to give her some incentive, I replied.

Ivoria narrowed her eyes. "Very tempting, but what exactly do you want to know from me?"

Emily glared at Ivoria. "What goes on through that dark mind of yours. What are you planning for the war?"

Ivoria's eyes glinted. "What are you going to do to stop it?"

Chapter 61

In the end, Ivoria still didn't tell us anything. She kept her mouth shut and didn't reveal a thing. We left the interrogation with Ivoria half-conscious from the constant shocks from Elece.

We all knew that Ivoria's information was the only thing keeping her alive. We needed to do our best to sniff it out, and she needed to do her best to hide it. It was a battle of the mind.

Emily had sent Galen and I to the training rooms after our trial interrogation was over. "You need to catch up to where Elece and Derrik are now," she had said.

So now, we were in the training room. Elece was hollering at me to keep up with running my laps, but I hardly had time to have a nap ever since I came back home.

I sighed after the tenth lap. "I'm tired, okay? It

was a long mission."

Elece rolled her eyes. "And we've been here stressing the whole time. Believe me, I think the team here is even more tired than you two."

Galen made a face at her. "You didn't have to live in the same space as a psychopath."

Derrik frowned, then looked at Elece. "True. We'll have to give them that."

I sighed. "So what do we do now?"

Derrik smiled. "We train." In a split second, he had his sword at my throat. The cool blade sent chills down my spine.

Whoa.

Derrik flipped his sword and returned it to his side. "We need to work on your reflexes." In an instant, he was at Galen's throat too. But instead of freezing like I had, my best friend ducked and swept his feet out in an attempt to knock Derrik off balance. Derrik leaped over his legs instead, smacking the top of Galen's head with the flat of his blade.

It occurred to me: it's training. I should orchestrate a surprise attack.

I brushed my thumb over my wristband, and in an instant, I was at Derrik's throat too. But I felt a sharp prick against the back of my neck. The staticky feeling that made my hair stand on end told me who it was.

Derrik had his foot on Galen's chest and the sudden clang of swords clashing brought my attention back to the front. Derrik twisted his wrist, spinning his sword and making me lose my grip on Snapdragon.

"You guys are way behind," Derrik laughed.

I glared at him. "It's only been a few weeks," I muttered.

Elece shrugged. "A few weeks is a lot of time to train."

Galen groaned. "What do we need to do?"

We spent the remainder of the day training hard with Elece and Derrik. They became Jordan and Skye's assistant in "getting us back into shape".

It seemed more like torture.

"See what we had to do while you were gone?" Derrik asked, triumphant after another victory against me. "I'm not really looking forward to that match between you and Elece anymore. She's going to mop the floor with you."

"HEY!" I complained. "We spent our time in the mansion doing our best to prevent the Islands from blowing up. Cut me some slack!"

Jordan walked over just then. "Alright, Jayson, let her up."

Derrik walked over to where his trainer was standing, allowing me to get on my feet.

"You've slowed down a lot," Jordan sniffed.

"Well, I did have only one training session with you prior to the mission," I countered.

Jordan narrowed her eyes. "Very true. Now, tell me what you did at the Mainland. Did you fight at all, or was it all just wits?"

"It was all just -" I paused then, remembering my battle with Mira. "Actually, I did fight."

Jordan's eyes glinted. Her eyes flicked briefly to the left side of my face before focusing on me again.

I had completely forgotten about the burns when I returned. Emily had thought the dark spots on my face were dirt, but after she told us to wash up, she screamed for the doctor to come and heal me right away. I had burns all over, and it should have taken weeks for me to completely heal, but by the time Mr. L rushed over, Galen had been by my side and the burns were already starting to fade.

The only thing left to remind me of the torture was the scar running down the left side of my face.

"Well?" Jordan prompted. "Tell me what happened."

I explained to her what happened in the torture room and the battle against my sister after that. When I talked about Mira summoning all the fires and my ability to raise the ocean, Jordan's eyes widened. "You used an Ancient Tactic?"

I blinked sheepishly. "It was on acci-"

Jordan rubbed her eyes. "You used a Tactic…."

I wasn't sure if that was a good sign or not. "Um. Jordan?"

Jordan looked up at me with a weary smile. "I am not sure how else I'm supposed to train you. Of course, I will teach you the basics, but when it comes to Tactics, there's nothing I can do."

"What do you mean?"

Jordan walked over to where the spears were resting on their rack against the wall. "You see, I'm a master of weaponry as well as battle. But this barely has an effect when Talents are involved." She turned to me with a bashful but defiant glint in her eye. "You see, I'm Talentless."

My jaw dropped. "What?"

Jordan shrugged as she picked up a spear. "I've always been. Therefore, I can't teach you the basics and advance techniques of Talent use, but I can teach you the fundamentals of wielding a sword or spear."

"Wait, wait, wait," I blundered, ignoring the fact that it was rude to interrupt my instructor. "You're Talentless?"

Jordan rolled her eyes, and in a split second, I was on the floor, wheezing for breath. "How come you never told me?"

"Would you have let me train you if you knew I wasn't Talented?" Jordan snarled. I flinched. "Nobody knows except Universa, Emily, and now you. Do you think the people would have agreed to me become a part of the Queen's Guard? No. But they don't question when they see me fight. I may not have a Talent like you, but I have skills that exceed yours. And that's what's led me to survive."

I coughed and struggled to sit up. My ribs felt crushed. "I don't doubt that...." I wheezed. "Teach me everything you know."

Jordan narrowed her eyes at me. "Any more comments before we continue?"

I frowned thinking for a short while, before saying, "You're awesome for proving your worth to the world like this."

I had expected Jordan to give me a small smile at least, but all I got was a snort in response. "I've always had worth," she said. "I never needed to prove it to others in order to prove it to myself. It just took everyone else a long time to see it in me."

Chapter 62

Emily released us from training the next day to spend some time with the pixies. I felt a bit guilty that I had forgotten about Zin in the days I've been back home. As I watched them tumble with a small smile, I thought about what Jordan had said. It made me reflect on many things about myself.

It also helped me take my mind off the fact that I remembered far too late that I had promised to get Zinnia a souvenir.

"You promised!" she screeched.

"Okay! I'm sorry! I'll go get one right now!"

"What's the point? I can just go and visit her now, anyways." Zinnia sulked. "So. No teeth?"

"Uh, no."

"No strand of hair? Piece of clothing? Nothing?"

"I'm sorry. No."

As she continued to list off possible things she could have gotten from me, I breathed a sigh of relief to see her completely healthy and alive. The dark streak in her hair was still there, but it gave her a cool, rebellious look. I was sure she didn't mind.

The other pixies were gathered around their Links. Callan and the others had already been here for some time before Galen and I joined them. "You guys are safe?"

"Yup! We're perfectly fine," they would answer.

"Thanks for watching over Zinnia while we were gone," Galen told his pixie, Stratus. "Hope you guys didn't get too bored."

Stratus laughed. "No! Of course not. Pranking Zin was the best!"

Zinnia sulked again. "Yeah. Stratus always pranks me. It's not fair."

Stratus stuck his tongue out at Zinnia. "It is too! You're just gullible."

"Am not!"

"Are too!"

"Am not!"

"Yes, you are!"

We spent the rest of the day in the garden

519

with our little friends, and fell asleep under the light of starlight through the glass ceiling.

The next day, we were startled awake by a zap that made us smell like smoke and made our hair stand straight up.

"Wake up!" Elece barked.

I groaned. "You couldn't have used some other method? Like shaking us awake or calling our names like a normal person?"

"What fun would that be? Come on. Don't you want to hear the consequence announcement?"

All of us jumped to our feet. "Let's go!"

We rushed out of the garden and out of the palace into large field where everyone usually gathered for an assembly. Emily had wanted us to help set up, but by the time we got there, everything was already in place. Sections of the field were roped off to organize the people and some chairs were laid out.

That meant this assembly was going to be very serious.

"Emily wants us to stand in a line behind her at these stairs," Elece said. "Right in front of the door, so we can give the whole stage to her while being present at the same time."

I nodded. "Okay. That works for us."

We sat at the stairs and chatted for a bit before people started to come. I realized then that we weren't dressed up at all. "Wait! Is this supposed to be formal?"

Elece snorted. "If it was, who cares? We're the guards! We don't have to be formal. Let's just stay in our training clothes."

"But I'm not in my training clothes!" I said. "Only you and Derrik are."

"Then change! Unless you want to change into a dress -"

I was into the palace and heading for the training room before she had a chance to finish that thought.

I do not like dresses.

Galen followed after me. Callan, Sirocca, and the rest of the group panicked for a second, then ended up being too lazy to try to dress up.

Maybe I should've done the same.

But we were already halfway to the training room, so might as well just keep going with it.

Both of us grabbed our training clothes and quickly went to change, then we raced each other back outside.

By now, many people had gathered. I didn't know if everyone in the Terrenian Islands was

521

going to be here, but there were quite a lot of people here already.

Emily hadn't made an appearance yet, and everyone else was still lounging around in a line near the palace doors. Galen and I took our places with the rest of our friends. Our trainers lined up by the palace doors, all with stoic and stern expressions. After about ten minutes, the whole field was crowded, murmuring to each other about their guesses on who the captured villain was.

Since it was daytime, the castle didn't glow to signal the start of the assembly. Instead, the walls began to turn from their usual gray to snow white. The crowd made noises of awe while we stood up and did our best to look professional.

Emily walked out in a stunning dress. It was different than the one she wore to her coronation, but it had the same effect. The people immediately quieted when they saw her standing regally on stage.

"Good morning," she said, her voice as loud as if she were using a really high-tech microphone. Her voice was pristine and clear. "Thank you all for coming so early in the morning. I don't want to waste time on formalities when we have an issue to deal with at hand." She turned to Elece and gestured.

Elece zoomed into the palace with her speed and brought out Mira. There were many strands of hair that hung loose from her usual ponytail. She glared at everyone she passed by.

She really did look like a criminal.

"Flamira Flameton of the Fire Tribe," Emily introduced.

"She's innocent!" a voice called from the crowd. A hand waved wildly and two people stood up.

Mom and Dad.

"She hasn't done anything wrong!" Mom cried. "She's been studying and preparing for finals the whole time! You've all seen her grades, her dedication to the country -"

"Dedication?" Emily shouted. "She was found when I sent my team to negotiate with Ivoria. She was assisting Ivoria in trying to capture my team. Is that dedication?"

Mira scowled at the floor.

Mom and Dad's eyes widened in confusion. "Why -?"

Emily rubbed her eyes with two fingers. "Ivoria contacted me a few weeks ago, asking to negotiate. I obliged and sent a team to talk and uncover what Ivoria has planned. She'd created a cannon that could extract the Talent out of the person that it hits."

"How?" someone yelled. "Our Talents are in our DNA!"

Kodiak stepped up then. "I speak from experience," he said, voice cracking. "I was hit by the ray gun. Flamira Flameton was the one operating it."

Many people cried out: Kodiak's parents in anguish and despair, Mom and Dad in anger, disbelief, and shock. I snuck a glance at Jordan and her eyebrows were raised in surprise.

"There's more…" he whispered, but his voice carried and silenced the crowd. "There's another person…."

I stepped up then. "As you all know, Alaska Torrent has been missing for some time."

Mr. and Mrs. Torrent paled right then. Mrs. Torrent stumbled and Mr. Torrent caught her and held her close as they listened intently. Kodiak stared at the ground and couldn't bear to look at his parents.

"When we searched Ivoria's mansion, we found a lab and chains. When we mentioned Alaska's name in Ivoria's presence, she revealed she knew something."

The Torrents let out a shrill cry of sorrow. It

was enough to make the people around them shed tears as well.

I was nearly close to breaking down too. "She had been the test run for Ivoria's new invention," I said. "Unfortunately, Ivoria didn't know that Alaska hadn't activated yet, so the blast took her life instead of her Talent."

A large portion of the crowd fainted, including both of Kodiak's parents. Kodiak toppled over on the stage too, and didn't get back up. "Where is she now?" a girl yelled. She looked about my age, had her brown hair tied up in a ponytail, and freckles scattered across her cheeks and the bridge of her nose. Her gray eyes were filled with grief.

"Can we bring Alaska home?" A boy with an identical face stood up too. "Where do we go to bring her home?" These must be Callan's second cousins.

I opened my mouth to speak but I didn't know what to say.

Mira laughed. "You guys don't know? You're missing some vital information."

There was a loud rustle of surprise and I turned to glare at Mira. She glared right back. "I'm sure the Torrent family would want to collect the body of their daughter, am I right?"

The Earth Tribe twins started to push forward against the crowd. "Where is she?"

Mira laughed again. "After I was with Ivoria for some time, she took me out on a boating ride. I assumed it was another lesson, but the men she brought were in charge of carrying one lone potato sack. As I watched them dump it into the ocean, I asked her what was inside. Ivoria responded, 'Nothing important. Something that is not of use any longer.' Up until now, I had assumed it was just trash. Now, I'm thinking it could be something else."

There was a heavy silence for a full minute before the girl twin let out a horrendous wail. Her brother looked at Mira, haunted, and Callan came running, tears in his eyes, and ushered them away as he did his best to comfort them.

I staggered over and grabbed Mira by the shoulders. "You knew all this and you didn't say anything?"

Mira just laughed. "You heard Ivoria say that Alaska was no longer your concern. What, you didn't believe her?" Mira shrugged. "It's hard to believe the words of a criminal, isn't it?"

I slapped my sister across the face, then recoiled afterwards at my own act of violence. It didn't compare with the words I had said to threaten people, but still. Actions speak louder than words.

"I had hoped we could repair things between us," I told her coldly. "I guess we can't."

Mira chuckled, her face red from where I had struck her. "No. I guess we can't."

"So what should the punishment for this criminal be?" Emily asked Elece loudly, her lip trembling slightly.

Elece stepped forward. "The appropriate punishment for this treason is death," she began. "However, she is a minor. Her age has pardoned her from any serious consequences. But a crime this big cannot go ignored. She will be forced to spend ten years in the palace's underground dungeon, and when she is released, she will spend an additional five years to make up whatever costs she needs to pay. That includes the Torrent family."

"Don't let that child anywhere near the Torrent family!" someone yelled. "She has caused enough hurt to their children already!"

Elece nodded. "That will be taken into consideration, then. After the ten years she spends in prison, the five years will be determined after a meeting between the queen and her family." Elece stepped back.

Emily nodded her approval. "Ivoria is still being held underground. She has valuable information we have yet to uncover, so her execution will be postponed. Take the criminal back down to the dungeons.

"I apologize that the message of this meeting was very dark, especially after a long period of peace and prosperity," Emily said as Elece disappeared with Mira. "To send a message of hope, I have splendid news."

We all glanced up at Emily in surprise. She hadn't told us this part.

"For generations, the queen of the Islands has preserved the last of the once flourishing species of pixies," Emily began. "However, we humans began to abuse the special connection between a pixie and a human, nearly wiping the little creatures off the planet entirely. Over the last few decades, the pixies have been living secretly and safely within the palace grounds. As a gift to you all, I am willing to release the pixies back to the public."

Chapter 63

There was a lot of chatter after the queen made her big announcement. To everyone else, pixies had only been a myth. The teams and I exchanged surprised glances. Was this safe?

"I will release the pixies only if you are willing to set a few ground rules," Emily continued. "First, there will only be natural Links being formed. Forcing a Link or stealing someone else's pixie for their own is against the law. Should someone break the law, Cinnabar Trials will be held within this palace, open to the public. Anyone who interferes will face dire consequences.

"I want to invite Rina to share her experiences in the Cinnabar Trials as a message and warning to you all should you abuse this privilege."

As Emily gestured for me to take the stage, I

asked, "Amaryllis is okay with this?"

Emily smiled. "I've been talking to her about this for some time already. She agrees with me. I would never do something to endanger the pixies without the pixie queen's consent."

I thought that last sentence sounded funny, but I nodded. "Okay."

I stepped forward and said, "Before the Cinnabar Trials, my sister captured my pixie and forced a Link with her. She turned the complete opposite of who she really was. She controlled the shadows and silence instead of music and plants. The only way to save her was to either kill her or let her kill me. Otherwise, she would remain as 'Midnight' for the rest of her life.

"We entered the Cinnabar Trials, which is basically a duel between the human and their pixie. I couldn't kill one of my best friends - someone I had promised to protect, but failed. That is what makes the Trial so difficult. But as she zoomed in for the final kill, I caught her between my hands and just held her there as she slowly sucked away my life force."

Everyone listened, enraptured.

"I was able to save her and turn her back into Zinnia," I said, "But she was very weak, and so was I. I had aged so much, almost to the point of death. It took me a long time to recover, and without the help of Mr. Leafstern and my Bond, Galen, I would probably be dead with the appearance of an old lady. I spoke with the pixie queen and she said both parties have never emerged from the Cinnabar Trials before, so I was very lucky.

"However, you should not take this lightly. If a Cinnabar Trial should happen, the chances of both people coming out alive is very, very slim. One of you will die if your Link with your pixie is not strong enough. Even to this day, Zinnia bears a scar. I am hoping that you will treasure and guard your Links wisely and passionately."

I stepped back, but a person shouted, "Can we see your pixie?"

I glanced at Emily for permission, and she just smiled. "They're already here."

I looked at her in confusion before something bounced against my leg. I glanced down in my training clothes and saw a lump in my pocket that I hadn't noticed before. Zin shot straight up and sat on my head. "Hi!"

There was a lot of clamor and surprise. "That's a real pixie! The myths are true!"

Zin looked so proud to be in the center of attention.

My smile was so wide, I couldn't stop. "You were here the whole time?"

Zin snorted. "Do you know me? Do you think I would miss something as big as this?" She waved her arms at the crowd. "Besides, after the people say yes, I can see sunlight again! Do you know how tight and dark your pockets are?"

I laughed and grabbed her between my fingers and hugged her as properly as I could, considering our vast size differences. "I missed you a lot, you know?" I told her. "I was so scared you were going to die."

Zin smiled. "That's easy for you to say. I was afraid Ivoria was going to do something to you and you weren't going to come back. Who would argue with me then?"

I laughed and released her. "So you're not bitter that I didn't bring you a souvenir anymore?"

Zin's smile immediately turned into a scowl. "You better make it up soon."

"Um. Okay. I will."

Blizzard was flitting around Kodiak's head nervously. "Hey. Kodiak. Wake up. It's me!"

Kodiak's eyes slowly opened. "Hey, Bliz."

"You okay?"

"Yeah. Just... not feeling too well," he

mumbled. "Sorry."

Blizzard shrugged. "That's okay. I'll just sit with you." He landed on Kodiak's forehead and just sat there.

Kodiak sighed and closed his eyes again. "Thanks." After some time, he said, "You know what? Alaska would've liked you."

Blizzard's eyes brightened. "Really? Your sister?"

"Yup."

"Tell me about her! What was she like?"

"Well…."

He began to share stories of Alaska with his pixie. I watched as the worries slowly left his face and a smile began to show as he recounted the happy memories he shared with his sister.

He was going to be okay.

While I was watching Kodiak and talking with Zin, Emily had gotten the people to agree to the ground rules. Queen Amaryllis had appeared as well, and signed a contract with Emily. After the contract was signed, thousands and thousands of pixies flew out from the palace doors.

I had no idea there were so many!

The colorful creatures began to mingle with the crowd and sounds of happiness filled the field.

The pixies brought a new hope. A new happiness.

We were going to rip that secret out of Ivoria and keep our nation safe. Things were turning out for the better!

Epilogue

Meanwhile…

Ivoria sat in the cell quietly. She listened intently at the sounds of laughter above.

Ignorant people, she scoffed. *They have no idea what is going to happen to their country. Young Alaska Torrent won't be the only one to fall at the end of this, oh no.*

The solution has been delivered. Despite everything that has happened to delay my plan, everything is still going as expected.

Ivoria glanced at the food leftovers the kitchen staff had thrown at her. She thought back to when a mysterious kitchen maid had snuck her a watch with a few precious instructions.

"This is what you asked for," she had said softly. "We figured it out. Slip this into your food and you'll be set." She had held out her watch and flipped the lid. Inside, there was a dark liquid the color of soy sauce.

Ivoria leaned back in thought. *It is time.*

Gritting her teeth in pain, she twisted her arm to grab the watch that she had hidden inside the back of her shirt. She squeezed her arms between the ropes, scratching and rubbing off some skin in the process.

It would not matter once I am free.

With great difficulty, she reached for a piece of bread. She ripped it open, flipped the watch, and spilled the contents inside, taking extra care to not spill any of the evidence on the cell floor.

That would not matter once I am free as well.

She flung the watch away and stuffed the bread into her mouth. She did her best to chew and swallow as fast as she could. Immediately, she could feel the power gripping her muscles and flowing through her veins.

Finally.

She flicked her pinky finger and the ground trembled. She flexed the fingers on one hand and everything began to shake. The stone walls started to crack and the iron doors fell out of place. The chains that once bound her shattered and the ropes fell away.

Ivoria tipped her head back and laughed.
Finally.

Acknowledgments

The second book is finished! I'd like to thank everyone for waiting this long for the sequel. I hope you enjoyed it and that you're looking forward to the last book of the Wildfire's Twin trilogy! Thank you to all the readers who questioned when the next book would be out! It was a lot of encouragement and urged me to hurry and finish. XD

First of all, thank you, God, for giving me the inspiration to continue the story from my last book and for giving me so many opportunities and experiences because of this. I've learned a lot and I can't wait to discover more about You on this journey! :) Hosanna!

Thank you to my mom and dad for continuously supporting me and encouraging me to write! Your idea to try digital art for the cover helped a lot and I enjoyed it! Thank you for always being the first to get a copy and read!

Thank you to my sisters again, for always being the first to finish my book, before anyone else! Your feedback and speculations on the story are fun to listen to and argue about. I hope this story met your expectations!

Thank you, Ashley C. and Katelyn W., for being two of my best friends! Your enthusiasm to help and support me always warms my heart and makes writing more fun!

Thank you, Jubilee K., for being the first to offer to be my editor! Your thoughts and feedback as you read were very helpful as I was writing. I hope you enjoyed this book, too! :)

Thank you, Keith D., for also being my editor for this book! It was just what I needed to make my grammar better! Thanks for waiting for weeks for me to continue, then to find out I only wrote one word due to writers' block. Thank you for all the time you've put into this book, and thank you for your ideas during that time to inspire me and to help me continue! Your support means a lot to me, and I look forward to working with you even more in the future! :)

Finally, I am very grateful to Ruskin Elementary, Sierramont Middle, and Summit

538

Rainier for providing and encouraging me to write throughout my years in school. I especially thank my teachers for continually supporting me and cheering me on, even after I graduated. You are my inspiration! :)

Made in the USA
San Bernardino, CA
13 January 2020

63145156R00334